ANNA'S TIME

A Novel

DONNA BERTLING

Year of the Book
135 Glen Avenue
Glen Rock, PA 17327

ISBN: 978-1-64649-173-5 (print)
ISBN: 978-1-64649-174-2 (ebook)

Library of Congress Control Number: 2021912193

Cover image: Courtesy of Martin Bergsma.
Licensed from AdobeStock images.

DEDICATION

For Norbert

For Mom and Dad

CHAPTER 1

Baltimore
Spring 1904

Anna used a tea towel to shoo thick black smoke out the window. She stood back and assessed the damage. Soot clung to kitchen walls and cabinets like black lacquer to a wooden box. It would be impossible to hide her carelessness from Mrs. Pendleton.

"Not again, Anna."

"I'm sorry. I was baking Chorley cakes for tea today and my mind wandered a bit. I'll clean up the mess right away."

"You certainly will. This is the second time in two weeks you've burned something in the oven, turning my home into shambles and fouling the air to the third floor. I've a mind to cast you out this minute, without your bags."

"Oh, please don't, Mrs. Pendleton. I promise to be more conscientious. I'm not the best of cooks."

"No, you aren't. Girls of privilege who can't find husbands should learn to fend for themselves. Mayhem will never do, not in my household."

"It won't happen again."

The proprietress dug her fingers into the upholstery of fat above her hips and tapped a swollen foot. She thought about the rent Anna was paying, never late, and the extra money Anna's father quietly sent each month for Mrs. Pendleton to pay special attention to "the weal" of his daughter, as he put it.

"Fine, I'll give you one more chance. But mind you, another incident like this and you'll be dining with beggars and thieves on the street, young lady. Do you understand?"

"Yes, ma'am."

Anna spent the remainder of Sunday afternoon scrubbing the kitchen until her fingernails were as ragged and raw as Mrs.

Pendleton's nerves. Anna had ruined the weekly tea for residents of the Boardinghouse for Young Women of Good Repute, where she lived on Pratt Street in East Baltimore. It was the custom for residents to take turns cooking to prepare for married life.

Later, as the sun reverently bowed to the horizon on this day of rest, the girls would have to sip their tea while nibbling stale ladyfingers from the pantry, instead of homemade sweets.

After following the recipe card, filling dough with sugared fruit and forming the round, flat confections, Anna had put the Chorley cakes in the oven. Then, her mind wandered to the disturbing news that Robert M. McLane, the Mayor of Baltimore, had died, possibly due to a self-inflicted gunshot wound. The headline bounded from the *Baltimore Herald*. Anna believed the story to be true. She trusted the printed word of this newspaper without reservation; it was her employer.

The death had occurred a few days before. Anna perused the story five times, hoping to grasp meaning. The city's youngest mayor had been doing a fine job of rebuilding after the Great Fire in February destroyed most of downtown. And he had just gotten married. Why would he do himself in now?

Anna couldn't wait until teatime. She wanted to piece this puzzle together with her housemates, even though she wasn't comfortable calling any one of them "friend." They merely happened to be all the companionship she had.

Most were as helpless as a cloud trying to hold back the rain, and as quick to release their own tears. They worked as office clerks, seamstresses or telegraph operators... jobs meant to support themselves until husband material showed up on the doorstep with a colorful nosegay and box of Whitman's Chocolates. Anna saw herself above these brides-in-waiting. She had embarked on what she hoped would be a long-term career as a photojournalist.

Anna knew the subject of death by gunshot, with all its imperative blood and gore, would not bear proper conversation over soothing Oolong and raised pinky fingers. But she needed to talk to someone.

"Heavens to Betsy, must you bring up such a hoydenish matter over tea?" said Adelaide. The tall, thin girl scowled, turning her plain face to gargoyle.

"Hoydenish? What does that mean?" asked Anna.

"Your vocabulary obviously lacks polish," Frances chimed in. "Were you not raised in a forming school? In New England or, perhaps, France? And you, a doctor's daughter."

As soon as she finished her admonishment, Frances retreated to the corner of the room and remained there, smiling like the fabled Cheshire cat. The other girls nodded in agreement amid snickers muted in their porcelain cups. They failed to take note of their ill-bred reflections in the gleaming tea.

"Hoydenish means 'rude, unbecoming a lady,' Anna," said Adelaide. "Only men would discuss such a sinful topic as suicide, and then behind doors closed to delicate feminine ears, like ours." She frowned and dropped the dry ladyfinger she had been eating on her plate. "And who provided these abominable pastries? Anna, wasn't it your turn to bake for tea?"

Anna ignored the pinprick and insisted her voice be heard. "Why would he shoot himself? Why, after laboring over the blueprint for building up our fair city grander than before?"

"I, for one, do not know, and don't care a whit," said Jane Catherine. She turned away from Anna and addressed the others. "There is a new pink dress with angelic ruffles in the window of O'Neill's. Did any of you see it?"

"I did," said Naomi. "It's lovely but beyond my paycheck, I'm afraid to say. And I've already spent my father's clothing allowance."

"We're close in size," continued Jane Catherine. "Maybe we could pool our money and share the dress. You wear it on Monday, I'll take Tuesday..."

"Don't forget me," said Rosemary.

"You haven't even seen the dress yet," said Jane Catherine.

"If it will snare a man, I'll wear it sight unseen."

"How about you, Josefina? Interested?" asked Frances, with a raised eyebrow.

"You know I only wear black."

"And why is that?" asked Frances.

3

"I care little for women's foolish fixations on appearance. It's the artistic mind that counts," replied Josefina.

"Oh yes, that," Jane Catherine said, yawning. "Maybe you and Anna can share a drab dress, if you pool your resources. She always wears black, too. I doubt O'Neill's has anything for either of you. You might want to try a nunnery."

Most of the girls laughed full-heartedly, glancing at one another.

"Now, what were you saying, Anna, about suicide?" asked Adelaide.

Anna rose and returned her teacup to the tray on the table. The drink and her enthusiasm had cooled. As she entered the hallway, she came upon Mrs. Pendleton, who held a fresh pot of tea. She had heard some of Anna's encounter with the others.

"Anna, you must learn the etiquette of conversation. Did your mother or governess never take you aside whenever you strayed from polite exchange?"

Anna snapped at the woman, as though she had thrust a lance through her heart. "Never speak ill of either of them. My mother died when I was two and my nanny was... and still is... a sainted woman, who treats me as her own. I know I'm a headstrong girl. But headstrong girls get things done."

"Yes, I know one thing they accomplish. They alienate friendship."

"I don't want to be friends with girls who only discuss fashion and fanciness. I want to talk about the world, what happens beyond the commonplace."

"Like what?"

"Like woman's suffrage, and Baltimore growing from the ashes of the Great Fire, and why the mayor would suddenly take his own life. I can't believe it; I just cannot. What his bride must feel."

"Did you know the man?"

"Not really, but our paths crossed during the fire, while I was taking pictures that I sold to the *Baltimore Herald*."

"I see. And that's what got you started in your job?"

"It is a career, Mrs. Pendleton. As sure as any man's calling in life. It's everything to me."

"Anna, you feel too deeply. You seem to be placing the world and all its troubles on your shoulders, like Atlas. And his burden was a punishment. Yours is self-imposed. You must free yourself from furrowing thoughts. You are a young girl. Go out and enjoy life once in a while. Buy a new dress, a colorful one. You always wear black, like Josefina. Black is for older ladies. Laugh a little. When you smile, which happens so rarely, you are pretty. Don't you want to be pretty?"

"You don't understand."

"Then help me understand."

"When I take a photograph, of anything... a flower, a building, a family playing in the park... I capture a moment in time, a speck of truth. Its meaning is not found in the overall composition, most times, but in small things. In the bug pollenating the bloom, in a crack in the cornerstone, in the tiny hint of regret on a mother's face. In real life, which is always moving, you might not notice such telling details, but the camera never lies. And, as the photographer, I feel powerful and truthful, like God is speaking through my pictures."

"You border on blasphemy. I won't hear anymore."

"I'm sorry if I offended you. Goodnight, Mrs. Pendleton."

"Goodnight? We haven't finished tea. What about our supper at seven?"

"I've lost all appetite for food or friendship today. I'm filled to my collar with disappointment."

Mrs. Pendleton didn't respond. She simply shook her head and watched Anna walk away.

As Anna climbed the stairs to her room, she remembered a day, not that long ago, when she wasn't so austere, when she allowed herself a grand time, enjoying the company of one special person, a man. His name was Adrian, and he would have laughed off the burnt Chorley cakes and eaten them anyway.

After a long night of unquiet sleep, Anna woke up in a taffy-twist of covers. Her pillow lay on the floor. Her braided hair looked as frayed as early sunlight straining through her eyelet curtains.

When she had first moved into the boardinghouse, she shared the room with another young woman she barely tolerated. After the roommate left to get married, Anna insisted she could pay double to keep the whole space to herself. She was able to afford the rent, despite earning less money as a photographer than her male counterparts. She created additional income by photographing portraits of families in outdoor settings with her Brownie box camera. Also, by cutting silhouettes of children in black paper, if their parents preferred old-fashioned renderings. The silhouettes were pressed on white backgrounds, then framed and hung in parlors, creating shadow children who would never grow up. In this endeavor, too, Anna felt she had an otherworldly power to freeze time.

Often, she worked six days a week, leaving few hours for leisure. But Anna didn't mind at all. She was fulfilling her newfound dream, all on her own, and she preferred this lifestyle to wishing for husband material to knock on the door, hoping for a pink frilly dress to answer.

CHAPTER 2

"You are late, Miss Bainbridge."

The *Baltimore Herald* City Editor, H.L. Mencken, stood in the doorway of his office, staring at Anna with hungover eyes.

"I realize that, Mr. Mencken. No use in scolding; it will only waste time. I'm ready for my next assignment. Perhaps something to do with the mayor's death?"

"No, Miss Bainbridge. I want you to go to the Jewish Settlement House in East Baltimore. Their members are holding a clothing drive for immigrants. You are to capture the generosity of spirit as Baltimore rebuilds."

Anna yawned, either a natural response to listless sleep the night before or commentary on her assignment. H.L. Mencken ignored her, entered his office and shut the door.

Anna hesitated for a moment, then knocked.

"Come in."

Seeing Anna, he rested his cigar on an ashtray and crossed his arms on the desk. "What do you want now? I believe I was clear in my instructions."

"Yes, you were. But I would rather..."

"No."

"No, what? You don't even know what I was about to ask."

"You were going to ask to be assigned to the McLane story. No."

"But..."

"Miss Bainbridge, you are a novice photographer. Yes, I have seen that you were given a professional camera to use rather than that Brownie you were carrying around when you photographed the fire. That does not make you an expert. You still have much to learn. For now, you will take the ordinary stories, the ones that appeal to women. The news making the front page will go to the more experienced photographers."

"You mean the men."

"Yes. Now, go."

"How can I become more experienced if you won't give me something important to do? How can I compete with men?"

"You cannot. They've been doing this longer than you and they can handle all emotions associated with the unpleasantries of their work."

"You mean blood and death and danger."

"Exactly."

"I have no problem with..."

"You are testing my patience after a long night of..." Mencken touched his temple, "... of commiserating with fellow newspapermen at a local establishment."

"Didn't I prove myself during the Great Fire? Didn't I handle danger then?"

H.L. pointed to the door without saying another word. Anna grabbed her camera and left.

Outside, she meandered around work crews and supplies, steel girders and wood beams. Especially difficult to maneuver were the fireproof granite pavers being put in walking paths. Anna had become used to the dust and noise and general disruption of downtown workdays. She tolerated getting her dresses and underskirts dirty. This was Baltimore under construction, just as she was building her own life as a single woman on her own.

Deciding there was time to get pictures for both stories, Anna headed to Mayor McLane's home, which he had shared with his bride of a few weeks. Anna had no idea what to expect once she got there. On the way, her thoughts rested on the widow in the throes of grief. She recalled the news story on the mayor's death, its ink still fresh in her mind.

The mayor's wife, the former Mary Van Bibber, had found her husband's body on the floor of his dressing room, framed in a halo of blood. She immediately summoned her neighbor and friend, Dr. A. Trego Shertzer, who rushed to 20 W. Preston Street, where the couple lived.

He found the mayor's head turned to the side and, when he moved it to face him, the doctor discovered a bullet wound in the right temple and an exit wound over the left ear. Both had been bleeding profusely, though a faint pulse offered hope.

Dr. Shertzer noted a Smith & Wesson revolver on the floor nearby.

Efforts to save the esteemed politician failed. Within two hours, Mayor Robert M. McLane was declared dead. He was thirty-six years old and had been in office, serving Baltimore, for one year, winning the election by a mere six hundred and twenty-four votes.

After pulling the city through the Great Fire just months before, McLane had been hard at work, building skyscrapers in the devasted area with so-called "fireproof" materials, seeing that the city's first modern sewage system was installed, putting electrical systems underground, forming committees to oversee construction of new roads, securing temporary school locations, improving docks at Baltimore's wharf area, and providing relief to business owners who had lost everything. He had declined offers of financial help outside the state, preferring self-reliance. That didn't help the 35,000 people currently unemployed. Nonetheless, Anna admired his ability to accomplish many projects on his own.

After the body was found, an interrogator questioned the mayor's widow, a beautiful socialite who had the ability to turn men's heads without trying, even under dire circumstances.

"I'm sorry to put you through this so soon after..." He cleared his throat. "Can you tell me what happened, step by step?"

"If I can. My husband had been in good spirits all morning. He promised to take me out for a stroll as soon as he put his dressing room in order. That's when I heard..."

"Heard what, Mrs. McLane?"

There was a long pause.

"I know this is difficult for you, but we need to know, and so do our citizens."

"That's when I heard a loud noise. I thought something had fallen or one of the window shutters had come loose and thrashed against the brick façade. Lizzie corrected me..."

"Who is Lizzie?"

"Lizzie Redchurch, our housemaid."

"We'll need to speak to her, too. Go on."

"Well, Lizzie said the noise had come from my husband's private suite. We rushed there and found... I can't say it."

"It must have been quite a shock."

"Yes, without Lizzie, I don't know how I would have handled it."

Mary Van Bibber had come from a prominent Baltimore family. Yet, Robert's family had disapproved of his courtship with her, which spanned ten years before the couple secretly wed in Washington, D.C. The McLane family was aristocratic, reserved, well-known and moneyed. Robert's father had served as President of the National Bank of Baltimore. The rumored bone of contention? Mary was a widow and several years Robert's senior. Too worldly wise. For that, the McLane family had refused to support the union.

Police and detectives had searched high and low for motives in the death. Enemies? Political feuds? An accident? They even questioned Cabell Bruce, the City Solicitor. He and the mayor had been friends, but recently suffered a falling-out.

After the fire, a large sum of money had been designated to fix the damaged dock area, called The Basin. Cabell and Robert argued terribly over how that money should be spent. In the end, they compromised and reconciled.

Police directed their interrogation toward suicide and returned to the McLane residence to question Mary, once again, about her husband's state of mind.

"I told you. He was in good spirits that day."

"Was anything weighing on his mind generally?"

"He was mayor. Of course."

"Can you be specific?"

"He regretted some of the decisions he had made concerning the fire in February. Like setting dynamite firebreaks, intending to halt the blaze, instead, making it spread. And not calling for help sooner from the National Guard or from other fire departments outside of Baltimore. He also didn't think the rebuilding was moving fast enough."

"Most Baltimoreans thought he was doing a magnificent job," said the interrogator.

"I agree. I praised his progress all the time. How could he possibly find himself at fault when the fire of that magnitude was unprecedented in Baltimore? He was an inexperienced politician, I know, but he learned quickly what to do. Was he hiding some inner struggle from me?"

"I'm afraid we'll never know, ma'am."

"Was I a poor wife?"

"No ma'am, I'm sure you were exemplary. Inner turmoil can do strange things to the best of men."

It looked as though there might never be conclusive evidence to prove accident, murder or suicide. Because of powder burns on the mayor and proximity to the gun, authorities quietly leaned toward suicide, without making any official statements. Baltimoreans had to come to their own conclusions about what happened on the afternoon of May 30th.

With this terrible story playing back in her head, Anna was surprised to see that she had arrived so quickly at the mayor's home.

Almost immediately, she spotted a genteel lady being escorted out of the house by a man in a chauffeur's uniform, who walked her to a carriage. He placed a traveling bag inside. Anna recognized the woman to be Mayor McLane's widow. As the man helped the woman into the carriage, Anna took a picture from a discreet distance. She went undetected by the subjects, who rode down the street without the least bit of fanfare.

She did not escape the watchful eye of the police officer guarding the home. "What are you doing, miss?"

"Just taking a picture, officer. There is no harm in that, is there? Wasn't that Mayor McLane's widow?"

"Why do you need to know?"

Anna feared word getting back to Mencken. He might not stand for her defiance, unless it yielded an exclusive report. She chose not to identify her mission or her employer.

"Merely a matter of curiosity, sir. Don't you think it odd that the mayor would take his own life when everything was looking up?"

"No one said it was definitely suicide. Could have been an accident while cleaning his gun. In any event, it is not right for you or anyone to invade Mrs. McLane's privacy. Now give me that thing."

"This is my camera and my film."

"I should take you to the precinct. The sergeant will pry it out of your hands. What's your name? Who is your family? Who sent you here?"

Not wanting to get in trouble with both Mencken and her father, an esteemed doctor, Anna walked rapidly down the street. She glanced over her shoulder and noticed the officer wasn't following. A block away, she hailed a handsome cab to take her to her real assignment.

When she arrived at the Jewish Settlement House, she found no activity taking place. The neighborhood clothing drive had obviously ended.

"You should have been here an hour ago," said the supervisor. "There were so many people lined up and down the block, carrying donations, their generosity overflowing in these collection bins. Just look at all these garments... and shoes. We really needed shoes."

"Oh, dear. I was instructed to get a good photograph of the event for the *Baltimore Herald*."

"I'm sorry, it's over. Now, we begin the sorting, though not until tomorrow."

Anna had no choice but to photograph the stagnant, full bins. The clothes looked like deflated people waiting for a bicycle pump to breathe new life into them. She felt the same way. Her picture would show the outcome of the clothing drive, absent of human interaction, absent of emotion. It would never make print. And she would have to tell H.L. Mencken why.

The City Editor was none too pleased. "Miss Bainbridge, you defied my order, missing an event important to all Baltimoreans. You are to return tomorrow and capture volunteers sorting the donations. In addition, you are to write a note to the Jewish Settlement House, stating that you are sorry for missing the people lined up with their offerings yesterday. That it was your own fault. I made the arrangements for you to be there. I don't want your negligence reflecting on my newspaper. Do you understand? You are treading on thin ice, Miss Bainbridge, in grave danger of falling through. And what possible use would the paper have for publishing a picture of Mayor McLane's widow simply stepping into a carriage?"

CHAPTER 3

Anna placed her umbrella in the stand with a thud and slumped her shoulders. A long sigh attempted to erase a workday overcast with conflict.

"Why are you so sullen, Anna? Is it the rain?"

"Oh, Mrs. Pendleton. Good evening. I trust your day is going better than mine."

"By the looks of you, there is no doubt. What happened?"

Anna sat on the bench by the door and unlaced her wet boots, one knot proving difficult. As she yanked at it without trying to puzzle its loop, she stared at a crooked picture on the wall.

"It's what didn't happen. Why is everything in disarray?" Anna stood and straightened the painting. "I missed my assignment. I never took the photograph I was supposed to get."

"You didn't lose your position, did you?" Mrs. Pendleton half-hoped she had. Anna had become too much to handle for one widowed landlady.

"No, I just got a good verbal thrashing and warning."

"Oh? How severe?"

"I have to adhere to all assignments from now on, no matter the circumstances, or I'll find myself plugging cords into a telephone switchboard in a cold basement office somewhere else until the day I die."

"You must learn to follow rules. Your willful ways could prove costly."

"I can't help it. I want to get things done. I feel as if I've lost too much time already."

"The greatest thing a young woman can accomplish is motherhood."

Anna removed her hat, stood up and looked her landlady square in the eyes.

"No, I want to give birth to photographs for the whole world to see."

"My word, you are direct. In that case, you must bide your time, learn your profession, practice it and, above all, listen."

"I want to see my pictures on the front page now. For decades, even centuries, women have been trained to wait... wait for a gentleman caller, wait to be courted, wait to be asked to marry, wait, wait, wait."

"Patience is a virtue. 'All things come to those who wait,' if I may quote the poet, Lady Mary Montgomerie Currie."

"I didn't wait during the Great Fire and look at the outcome. A picture I took of the fire chief was published."

"That was a stroke of good fortune. And you had to have risked your life to get that picture. Don't you realize what horror you might have faced?"

"I felt no fear. This is what I was meant to do."

"Then you must take the necessary steps, one at a time, to achieve true greatness."

"Never. Women today are changing things rapidly. They are going out and getting what they want. The right to vote, for example. It will happen someday soon. I just know it. Women are challenging the rules of courtship, dressing in shorter skirts, traveling without a chaperone, even conversing on serious subjects, like business and politics. They are called 'The New Woman.' I've read about them in books and magazines."

"This 'New Woman,' as you call her, is degrading her gender, marching in filthy streets, holding signs about equality, shouting slogans. It's disgraceful."

"You don't understand."

"No, I don't. And neither do you. There are repercussions tied to such behavior and they aren't good. Perhaps you should spend more time with real ladies. There are some in the parlor, right now, if you'd like to join them. Maybe you'll learn something."

"What kind of repercussions?"

"The kind that get a young girl in trouble, like courting without a chaperone."

"I've already done that, and nothing untoward happened."

"Anna, I'm shocked. Your father allowed this?"

"He didn't know; it was a secret."

"I'm appalled, and most uncomfortable continuing our conversation. This subject is something you should talk over with a woman close to you, perhaps your nanny. She will set you straight. We will discuss it no more. Now, won't you join the others?"

"No, thank you. I think I'd like to be alone for a while. Please give those 'ladies' in the parlor my sincere regrets. I'm sure they will find something unladylike to say about it."

Anna went to her room and didn't come down until after dinner. She ate her meal cold, alone in the kitchen.

∽∾

On her next day off, Anna visited the Green Mount Cemetery in North Baltimore. The ashlar wall surrounding the graveyard looked as formidable as a ghostly scene from a Charles Dickens novel. The gatehouse rose up in two stone turrets flanking the arched entry, like spectral sentries. Narrow lancet windows shut out light rather than letting it in.

Such notables as John Wilkes Booth and his co-conspirators in the assassination of President Lincoln were interred there. And Johns Hopkins, a prominent businessman, who bequeathed starter money for a hospital and university. But Anna wasn't looking for their resting places. She wanted to find Mayor Robert M. McLane. She expected to see an engraved monolith surrounded by flowers and well-manicured lawn. And Baltimoreans paying their respects.

She was surprised to come upon the McLane family burial site, understated, simple, no different from anyone else's. The grass around the markers was just beginning to green. There were no other signs of life, only death.

Anna should have known there would be nothing to see here. It was too soon. She stared at the ground.

Ashes to ashes, dust to dust. What are we really made of? Why are we here?

Anna thought she was here to do exactly what she was doing. But she wanted more. On the grave of Mayor Robert McLane, she vowed to rise from the ashes of the Great Baltimore Fire to march with those women in the streets, to raise her voice in the fight for women's rights, rather than hide her potential in parlor gossip with silly, vapid girls. Bide her time. What an insult to "The New Woman."

CHAPTER 4

On an auspicious morning in June, Anna attended a gathering of the Baltimore City Suffrage Club at Friends' Meeting House on Park Avenue. She did not need to hear speakers or shake hands. She already knew she wanted to join. She set her mind, instead, on taking pictures of the meeting. A woman came over to her and questioned her motive. Anna explained who she was.

"A pleasure to meet you, Miss Bainbridge. How do you intend to help Maryland women earn the right to vote?"

"I have many ideas, which I'd rather discuss with the president of the organization. Do you know where I might find her?"

The woman offered a knowing smile and politely cleared her throat. "The president of the Maryland Woman Suffrage Association is Pauline Holme. She was unable to attend today's meeting. I am Emma Maddox Funck, president of this chapter. Now that you know I'm worthy, will you share your thoughts with me?"

Anna had been duly put in her place. For just a second, she chastised herself for a lack of humility. Knowing she had a rare audience with an important woman, she recovered and spoke her mind with confidence but without apology.

"I am a professional photographer, working for the *Baltimore Herald*. I've been looking for more important stories to capture than the ones I'm assigned. And suffrage marches and meetings would be perfect."

"I know your city editor, H.L. Mencken. I've tried to convince him to focus on our struggle, but he's a bit rock-ribbed, if I may be frank with you."

"Of course, you may. I prefer direct communication myself. Yes, Mr. Mencken is a bit difficult to convince. However, I assure you, once he sees the pictures I take and the stories they tell, he will not be able to refuse them."

"Photography is an unusual occupation for a woman. How did you come to be hired?"

Anna sat down with Mrs. Funck and explained that she had fought her way into the profession. Over lemonade and cookies, she spoke about the Great Baltimore Fire back in February and how she used nothing more than her Brownie box camera to document the blaze by immersing herself in the center of it for two whole days. H.L. Mencken used one of her pictures on the front page of the fire edition, at a time when he had no other alternative.

"That was quite brave of you, Miss Bainbridge. We need women who are fearless and determined. Are you willing to risk getting hurt, arrested or seeing your reputation ruined for suffrage?"

Anna spoke without thinking. "Yes ma'am, I am."

The image of Anna's father in her head startled her like a scolding. He was a prominent doctor in Baltimore, a man of integrity, though he held outmoded ideas about the roles of women. What would he think of his daughter walking dirty roads with protesters, being handcuffed and jailed, and building a police record for the sake of getting the right to vote? She had already upset him when she photographed the fire, causing him worry for two whole days, causing him pain rather than joy when one of her pictures made print. He found it embarrassing that his daughter performed such unmannerly work for a woman. How would new infractions reflect on him? For the sake of their relationship, he had forgiven her after the fire, even though Anna felt she had done nothing wrong. And, as much as he was against it, he had allowed her to move out of his Saratoga Street townhouse to live in a young ladies' boardinghouse in East Baltimore at the age of nineteen. How far could she push him before irrevocable damage was done?

She also wondered if she could make good on her promise to get H.L. Mencken to use some of her pictures... pictures of a different kind of fire, the kind that burns in women's souls and can't be doused with backward thinking.

Anna and Mrs. Funck continued talking after most of the others had left.

"Do you know who was the first woman in the United States to raise the topic of suffrage with government officials?" Mrs. Funck asked.

"No, I'm afraid I don't."

"As a newspaper woman, you should be fully informed. Her name was Margaret Brent," Mrs. Funck said. "Back in the 1600s, she came to America from England, became a citizen and settled in St. Mary's City."

"Where is that?"

"Southern Maryland. Hard as it is to believe, she became an attorney and handled the estate of one of George Calvert's sons, Leonard, I believe."

"They were a family of politicians, weren't they?"

"Very important people. They essentially founded our state."

"And this woman, Margaret Brent, became an attorney? That's extraordinary for her day."

"She was quite an outspoken lady. In 1647, she went before the Maryland General Assembly and urged them to pass legislation that would give women in this state the right to vote."

"All by herself?"

"All by herself. As we know, nothing came of it. Most unfortunate."

"But she tried."

"Yes, that's the point I'm making. With each woman who joins our ranks, with each woman who tries, we chip away at that boulder in the road that keeps us from reaching our destination."

"Thank you, Mrs. Funck. I'm glad I came today."

"As am I. I hope to see you again soon."

Anna couldn't sleep that night. Her mind raced through every possibility that lay before her. She couldn't wait to get to work the next day. She felt on the brink of something big and stood wide-eyed and ready for it.

CHAPTER 5

Bright and early, Anna met up with H.L. Mencken on the doorstep of the *Baltimore Herald*.

"Good morning, Mr. Mencken. Isn't it a wonderful day?"

"You seem more chipper than usual, Miss Bainbridge. I have a feeling that I'm not going to like the reason why."

"Listen first, if you will, before refusing me. Yesterday, I joined the Baltimore City Suffrage Club and I'd like to publicize their..."

"Stop right there. Are you suggesting I print a story on a group with whom you have a personal relationship?"

"Yes, sir."

"Let me give you a lesson in journalism. It is one thing to come to me with a non-partisan story idea."

"But..."

"It is another to promote your own agenda."

"But..."

"A true journalist knows the difference."

"But suffrage is so important. It's bigger than just me."

"I doubt anything is bigger than just you, Miss Bainbridge, at least in your own mind. This subject is only important to me if something printable happens."

"Such as?"

"Such as a massive march in the street, holding up pedestrians and carriages... or violence, destruction of property... or coercing young ladies to join their ranks against their wills."

"I didn't join against my will. I knew I was aligned with their goals before I went to the meeting."

"Was it peaceful? Did they plan anything illegal? Did they twist your arm to get a news article or photograph published?"

"Of course not."

"Then, there is nothing to report, now is there? Do you see the distinction?"

"I guess so. But I promised Mrs. Funck…"

"You promised what? That the *Herald* would print a story?"

"I told her I would try."

"Well, you tried and failed. Now, let's discuss the business of today. I want you to go to…"

"I know, another clothing collection, another food collection, another…"

"Will you stop talking over me?"

"Well, you're always talking over me!"

Mencken took a deep breath and fixed his eyes on Anna. At that moment, he regretted ever hiring her, although something held him back from dismissing her. His voice softened. "Let's start over. The assignment I'm giving you is connected to the Great Baltimore Fire. Does that gain your attention?"

"Yes, sir," Anna said with a broad smile.

"Good. I want you to go to Armstrong, Cator & Co. They're milliners, selling hats and notions, ribbons and such."

"Didn't that company burn down in the fire?"

"You are thinking of their five-story building on West Baltimore Street. That did burn down. In fact, the city blasted it down with dynamite to create a firebreak, a strategy that backfired. No, I'm talking about their current location at Hopkins Place. Just two days after the fire, they replenished their stock and started selling it out of a large warehouse there."

"I had no idea. That's remarkable. I'd like to meet the owner. What is his name?"

"I thought you'd be interested. You're to see Franklin P. Cator. He has a real story to share. His company is one of the largest milliners in the country right now, fire or no fire. Many people are seeking jobs there because of the company's tenacity and good business sense. And they're growing, with a flower department, hosiery, and ladies', uh, doodads. You are to go with a reporter, who will write the piece."

"I'm on my way," Anna said, as she headed for the door.

"Don't you want to know what kind of pictures to take?"

"Oh yes, I'm sorry." Anna returned to her seat.

"I want you to show individual workers performing their craft. And wide views of long worktables in use. And, of course, get a photograph of Mr. Cator. Do you understand?"

"Yes, I do. Mr. Mencken, isn't this a partisan story? I'm sure there are many other businesses making a name for themselves after the fire. Do you have a personal interest in this company?"

"You learn quickly, I see. No, I do not. This story is but one in a series we will be doing on various Baltimore businesses emerging from the ashes. Each week, we will feature a different one."

"I volunteer to photograph all of them. This is just what I'm looking for."

"I thought you'd say that. Don't let me down. Or you won't get the other assignments. Do you hear me?"

"Yes, sir," Anna said with a parting salute.

"And one other thing, Miss Bainbridge. Don't ever challenge my integrity or judgment again."

Anna didn't reply, too afraid of the consequences she might face. She simply left, her salute hanging in the air like a malodor.

A few minutes later, Anna joined reporter David Jameson on the short walk to Hopkins Place. There, they called on the owner, who gladly showed them around the warehouse, which also served as a workroom. He allowed Anna free rein in taking pictures. The place didn't offer strong lighting, so she focused on the areas closest to the windows, where shafts of morning glow illuminated dusty activity. Then she questioned Mr. Cator. "Why didn't this building burn down during the fire? The blaze started right near this intersection, did it not?"

"Yes, miss, it did. But it moved north rapidly, sparing this building. We were quite lucky to take possession of it to keep our business going."

"Yes, you were. Sometimes, opportunities fall in one's lap and go unnoticed. We must always remain keenly alert, so we are not passed by. Otherwise, that opportunity will just move to the next person."

"I couldn't agree more, Miss... ah..."

"Bainbridge, Mr. Cator."

"Miss Bainbridge, you are an astute and well-spoken young woman. H.L. Mencken is lucky to have you on his staff."

"Why, thank you, sir."

"I look forward to reading this story and seeing your pictures."

"I hope they both please you."

"I think we have all that we need here, Miss Bainbridge," said David. "We must move on to our next assignment. Thank you for your time, Mr. Cator."

When they reached the curb, David stopped to admonish Anna.

"Miss Bainbridge, it is inappropriate to shower the subject of a story with honeyed words."

"I wasn't flirting with that man. I was just being friendly, merely applying good business sense."

David mimicked Anna. "'Sometimes, opportunities fall in one's lap. We must always remain keenly alert.' Is that how you normally speak?"

"If you had said those things to him, I wouldn't have thought it wrong. You are judging me as a woman, not as a representative of my employer."

"I doubt it. But perhaps." He paused a moment. "Forgive me. I'm not used to working with photographers in dresses. Mind you, just the same, I intend to keep my eye on you."

"Very well. Then I will keep my eye on you."

Anna realized that she would have to win over her coworkers if she wanted to succeed in the newspaper business. She felt the need to commiserate with someone who could advise her, perhaps Mrs. Funck. Or, maybe her former nanny, Elizabeth, but not her father, not ever.

CHAPTER 6

Blocks away, during dinner, Anna's father opened the newspaper to find one of Anna's photographs on the second page.

"Well, see here? At least she's earning her keep," he expressed to Elizabeth, his housekeeper and cook, who was placing a hot plate of food in front of him.

"Yes, Dr. Bainbridge."

"Do you think Anna will really make something of herself?"

"I assure you, she will."

"Why do you think that?"

"She's determined. And there is nothing more unstoppable than a young, strong-minded, fearless woman."

"That's what frightens me. She doesn't realize that deception and danger hide in every shadow."

"Anna has a good head on her shoulders. She knows how to work through trouble."

"Just the same, I wish we had more supervision over her. Why don't you invite her to tea? Find out how she's doing. She is more apt to confide in you than me."

"I'd be more than happy to spend a pleasant afternoon with Anna. However, I won't betray anything she might reveal to me, sir."

"I understand. Just assure me that she still behaves as the daughter of mine should."

"I will. Your dinner is getting cold, Dr. Bainbridge. Please eat."

ॐॐ

Anna arrived at 4:00 P.M. on Saturday afternoon.

"You have on your chatelaine," Elizabeth said.

"Yes, I wear it often. It gives me strength."

"Then I'm very glad I gave it to you. It was always more than a practical piece of jewelry to me. It connected me to your mother."

"And now to me."

"Exactly. Isn't this pleasant? Just the two of us," Elizabeth said. "It's been more than a month since I last saw you. Are you too busy to visit your nanny more often?"

"Yes, as a matter of fact, I am." Anna caught herself and immediately said, "I'm sorry, I don't mean to be rude. But I take pictures all week and cut silhouettes for families on the weekends."

"If you are not finding time for your father or me, are you at least finding time for the Lord? Are you attending Mass?"

Anna's sheepish look answered the question.

"I am disappointed."

"I have my reasons. I'm working seven days a week sometimes, to earn money for a bicycle, so I can get around more quickly. And I want to buy clothes appropriate to my job. Less restricting outfits that allow me freedom of movement when I'm composing a photograph or riding my bicycle. I might even purchase men's trousers."

"Bless my soul, you cannot be serious."

"Oh, but I am. I've even tried on a few pair at a men's haberdashery. At first, they wouldn't accommodate me. They only relented when I threatened an outburst. Though, none of the pants fit me. I'm too short and a little more, well, you know, rounded than a man. I think I'll need some custom-made. But I do plan to buy men's jodhpurs and riding boots, in any case."

"And what about your underpinnings? They keep you modest."

"I'll dispense with those and just wear a chemise and bloomers. I need flexibility when I take pictures."

"This is not how a young lady should dress. I completely disapprove. And what will Mr. Mencken say?"

"Oh, he won't mind, as long as I deliver the pictures he wants."

"I dare not even think how your father will react."

"What is more modest when climbing through rubble or bending low to take a photograph or getting caught in a windstorm? A skirt that could blow up and reveal my legs or pants tucked into boots?"

"Well, you have something there. Still, I doubt your father will find it appropriate. And failing to go to church because of materialism... the good doctor will be overwhelmed with dismay."

Elizabeth fiddled with a doily, hesitant to continue her criticism. "Threatening an outburst in a store... why it's graceless. Are you so fully committed to your career that you would act outside your upbringing? And riding a bicycle. Many people in the medical field think this activity will render women unable to have children. What if you cannot provide an heir for your husband, a grandchild for your father? To take such risks leads me to believe that you'll do just about anything to succeed."

"I am fully committed to my new life and all its uncertainties. Although, I miss you and Papa."

"He misses you, too. You should make time for him. He's looking weary lately."

"I'm here now. He knew I was coming today. Why isn't he home, enjoying these fine cheddar scones with us?"

"He had to work."

"Does he attend Mass each Sunday?"

"He is often needed at the hospital."

"Well, if he is allowed to use work as an excuse, so may I."

Elizabeth poured another cup of tea for each of them, eyeing Anna the whole time. Anna, in turn, thumbed through some of the out-of-town newspapers her father read and saved for her. Ever since she had been a child, he urged her to read and learn about the big world outside her own tiny one, that had encompassed only a few square miles.

"How are you getting along with the young women at your boardinghouse, Anna? Are you making friends?"

"They are not women. They are children. So infatuated with courtship, they can't understand why they have not ensnared a husband, as if he were an animal to be trapped for sustenance. All they want to discuss are new dresses and dinner engagements with handsome men. And when one of the girls isn't home, the others gossip behind her back. It's appalling. There is not a single serious bone in any of them. It's as if they were all made of gelatin. Except Josefina. She's much like me, earnest in her endeavors. And she wears black most of the time, as I do. She doesn't spend her earnings on the newest fashions that will be out of favor next year. I don't really know her fully, yet. But I envision us becoming friends."

"How does she support herself?"

"She has a most unusual career. She's a Tirewoman at Ford's Theater on West Fayette Street. I rarely see her because she works at night during the shows."

"And what is a Tirewoman?"

"It's the name given to the lady's maid in the theater. I think it's an abbreviation for 'attire woman.' I'm not sure. A Tirewoman helps the star change her clothes so she won't miss a cue to the stage. Josefina also takes care of the wardrobe, cleaning and altering. She is an excellent sewer. She's helped me with my own mending."

"Sounds fascinating. Isn't Ford's also an opera house? I imagine she meets interesting people. Great tenors and sopranos, perhaps."

"I guess. I know she's met many actresses... Sarah Bernhardt, Edna Goodrich – she's a *Floradora* girl."

"I'm afraid I don't know who these women are."

"Oh, Miss Bernhardt is a dramatic actress."

"And what is a Floradora girl?"

"That's the name for the women who perform behind the star of a show called *Floradora*."

"You mean a chorus girl? A dancer?"

"Yes, that's it."

"Anna, these are women with whom you must not consort."

"Why? What's wrong with them?"

"They are women of ill repute. They don't wear many, uh, clothes. And they dance with feathered fans."

"No, you misunderstand. They are fully dressed in gowns and dance with parasols. They are respected women of the theater."

"I assume you have seen their show."

"Of course. Josefina got a ticket for me. And I went backstage. Oh, and rumor has it that the great Maude Adams will be appearing in *Peter Pan* soon. I'd love to meet her."

"This is unlike you. To be enamored so. I must advise you to stay away from this Josefina. Her associations make her unsuitable company. I fear for her influence over you. You've already become too excited about these actresses."

"I'm not excited about their celebrity. I admire their freedom to express themselves artistically."

"I feel certain your father will agree with me."

"You must understand that I make my own choices in life now. Wasn't that our agreement when I moved out after the fire?"

"Yes, it was. Nonetheless, will you promise me to be careful? And to not speak to men you might meet backstage?"

Anna raised her teacup with a nod and said, "Yes, ma'am." As she sipped the last of her tea, the residue tasted bitter, causing Anna to pull out her handkerchief and clear her throat. Or, perhaps, it was the words, "I take production pictures for display in the lobby," that got caught in her throat.

CHAPTER 7

When Anna arrived home, she read her father's newspapers, rather than face the guilt she felt. She had not told her nanny the whole truth about her life and the people with whom she was consorting, as Elizabeth put it. But Anna saw nothing wrong with thespian life. Everyone she had met, from star to stagehand, had been polite and upstanding. Anna thought Elizabeth was being closed-minded; she simply didn't comprehend. Ford's was not some burlesque venue. It was considered "legitimate theater."

Anna also regretted withholding information about joining the suffrage movement. Sooner or later, it was bound to come out, once Anna joined their ranks in a public march or openly recruited members.

Anna idly examined the papers, thinking back to the time when her father had first encouraged her to read and understand current events. It was her ninth or tenth birthday. Papa had given her a copy of the *New York Times*. He asked her to read it aloud.

"You read well, Anna. And now, you are old enough to educate yourself on the ways of the world. Not for the purpose of entering into discourse in mixed company, mind you. That would be impolitic. You are already too forthcoming with your opinions. Rather, I want you to learn you are only a small part of a vast universe and not the center of it. Do you understand?"

"Yes, Papa," Anna said. But she didn't, at all.

As told, Anna perused the pages, looking for something her young mind might comprehend. It seemed the most important story of the day was about a place called Ellis Island that had just opened to great fanfare.

"What does this mean?" she asked, showing him the headline.

"You read the story yourself, quietly now, and see what you can make of it on your own. If you find yourself lost, I will help you."

Anna took in the entire article. It spoke of people with hard-to-pronounce names, who visited the island by ship from far away and wanted to live in America. Three big vessels had already landed at Ellis Island with over 700 passengers on board.

"What are im-mi-grants? Where do they come from?"

"They are people who don't want to live where they were born. Instead, they want to live here, in America, where they might find better opportunities."

"What was wrong with where they were born?"

"Many were poor there. Others couldn't practice their faith. And some were just looking for adventure and a different life, in general. So, they decided to make changes."

"This newspaper says that many of them don't speak English. How are they going to get by?"

"They'll find a way."

"But how? Where will they live? How will the fathers find work? How will the mothers be able to buy meat if they don't know how to ask the butcher in English?"

"Dear child, you ask too many questions."

Anna hated when her father called her that. She often didn't feel dear to him at all. More likely... dismissed, as an annoyance.

"Do you think women will ever get to vote for president, even the immigrants?"

"Where did you hear of that?"

"Yesterday, I read a story in the newspaper about ladies already voting in a faraway place called Wyoming. They have been since, I think, 1869. That must be a long, long time ago. Will I be able to pick a president when I grow up? Can I choose you?"

"Don't be ridiculous. That nonsense in Wyoming and elsewhere will fade away. Women should never have the right to vote. They must not think for themselves. Instead, support the opinions of their husbands."

"Why?"

"Because that's the way it's always been and should continue to be so. It guarantees peace in the home. Couples shouldn't argue over politics."

"But you just said people must change."

"I was speaking of immigrants in New York, Anna."

Her immature mind couldn't figure out why rules applied in certain circumstances and certain places but not others. However, in reading newspapers, both local and from other states, she eventually learned not only how big and exciting the world was, but what it looked like.

In the late 1800s, photographs appeared in newspapers with regularity. Pictures captured Anna's attention more than words. They were portals she would walk through, like Alice through the looking glass. She envisioned herself in the middle of a ship's christening, the arrest of a famous murderer, or a battle in a country whose name she couldn't pronounce. She lived through her imagination. Photographs brought Anna greater understanding than the long-winded stories that accompanied them.

Every day, she searched the parlor for the latest editions of newspapers. She couldn't wait for medical associates of her father to send papers from their hometown states. Anna enjoyed the vastness and where she might fit into it.

On a humid August day, she spotted a story from the state of Washington, so far from Baltimore, Anna had to look for it on her father's globe. There had been a fire in one of its cities on the same date, years earlier in 1889. It was called the Great Fire of Spokane. A forty-block radius of downtown had burned to embers. The story explained how the area was getting rebuilt from the ground up. With all the inventiveness Anna possessed, she couldn't fathom such a tragedy, and how anyone might survive it. A whole city, "wiped out," as the report read. Its tallest skyscraper, four stories, housing several businesses and their opera house, gone. Stores, restaurants, libraries, everything charred and flattened.

There had even been pictures of the fire, its aftermath and rebirth. One caught her attention like no other. It was a photograph of three men and a woman standing in front of an erected tent. A cloth sign, hand painted, hung down the front reading, "Chronicle Office." It seemed the local newspaper had set up business right in the middle of the chaos, without brick walls or lavatories. They had not given up and, instead, made do the best they could. And one of those pictured was a lady!

Anna put herself in the woman's clothes. She wore a simple light-colored dress with a plaid overlay that draped like 4th-of-July bunting. A thin stream of ruffles connected collar to waistband. A dark waistcoat added a touch of authority, while her hat sat on her head like a man's, not fashionably cocked to one side. Her facial expression read stern, serious. In her hand, she clenched a rolled-up piece of paper. Perhaps a story she had written. *Could women work in the newspaper business?* Anna wondered.

A chill shivered through Anna's core, a premonition that somehow, and not through imagination, this woman's life would one day connect to Anna's own.

Could Anna be a reporter like the woman in the picture? No, she wasn't much of a writer. She loved to read books but, when putting pen in hand, not much materialized. Perhaps because Papa eschewed, even suppressed her opinions, Anna felt stunted, disobedient in composition.

But photography was a different story. Maybe she was looking at the Spokane picture from the wrong angle. Maybe she could be the one taking the portrait of the foursome in front of the tent. Maybe she was meant to be a photographer.

ॐॐ

In 1903, when Anna was eighteen, Anna had asked her father how much a camera might cost. He'd questioned her motives, discredited her justification.

Despite her father's opposition, Anna wondered how she could get her hands on a camera and explore its mystery, its ability to freeze a single breath of life. She saw herself holding a camera, using it, marveling at the results. That thought became a picture itself, a cherished one that she carried in her mind for several years, until she received an advertisement for an easy-to-use camera. One that was being mass marketed by a company called Eastman Kodak. And it didn't cost much at all.

Anna immediately sent away for more information. She hadn't known at the time that, with this one simple act, she was casting a ballot that would give her full freedom... from boredom, from Papa's rule, and from the dictates of society.

But she knew it now, after photographing the Great Baltimore Fire of 1904. She continued glancing over the newspaper Elizabeth had just given her. One article caught her attention. She checked the masthead and discovered the story came from *The Focus*, a newspaper in St. Louis.

The report centered on a woman named Jessie Tarbox Beals, a female newspaper photographer, who had been working in the business for over two years. Anna couldn't believe her eyes.

The article touted Miss Beals as the first female news photographer in the entire country. She was cited for her work in documenting the 1904 Louisiana Purchase Exposition in St. Louis, which had recently opened. In fact, she had been named the event's "official photographer." Anna read further and learned that this woman had a penchant for ignoring orders and, through hard work and perseverance, delivered pictures to six newspapers outside of St. Louis and all newspapers within the city.

In other stories over the past two years, she had shot everyday life and had endangered herself taking pictures of people in slums and prisons. She traveled on her job and shot photographs from St. Louis, Missouri, to Greenwich Village in New York.

A photo portrait of Miss Beals accompanied the article. She wore a plain dress, what Elizabeth would call work clothes. No adornments. No figure-forming underpinnings. Just an apron, much like a cook or blacksmith would wear. Yet, she donned a rather fancy broad-brimmed hat, incongruous to the rest of her outfit, perhaps a slight effort to look professional. Maybe, just a semblance of femininity. Or, more likely, a practical matter... keeping out the sun. Her only jewelry... a camera hanging around her neck on a long tether. A fourth appendage, as Anna liked to call her own.

Not hired by any one newspaper, Miss Beals freelanced for several, including *The Buffalo Inquirer* and *The Courier*. Magazines had also sought her expertise.

Anna's eyes widened as she continued reading. It seemed to Anna that Miss Beals possessed much of the same determination and daring as Anna herself.

In 1903, Miss Beals had scooped all other photojournalists during a sensational murder trial that forced the judge to prohibit picture taking in court. Not to be denied, she climbed atop a bookcase she found outside the courtroom and shot pictures through the transom.

For another story, she flew in a hot air balloon.

In between assignments, Beals ran her own photography business, taking portraits. Anna squealed to no one, "That's what I'm doing, too!"

Anna felt her insides might burst with pride. Jessie Tarbox Beals had validated Anna's own drive to become a photojournalist. She wanted to open the window and shout, "Watch out, Baltimore, here I come!"

Anna knew this woman would be her guide, her mentor, if only from a distance. Given the same job, under the same circumstances, Anna would have climbed that bookcase; she would have flown in that balloon; she would have defied the rules.

ॐॐ

Anna jotted down the names of other noted female photographers mentioned in the article, women on the ground floor of the medium itself, like Frances Benjamin Johnston and Gertrude Käsebier.

Anna became determined to follow these women's careers and form her own around their models. She snipped one of Miss Beals's quotes and placed it behind the glass in a framed photograph of her father she had taken at Patterson Park. It stood on her nightstand. She read the cutout once more before retiring and vowed to read it every night thereafter:

Newspaper photography as a vocation for women is somewhat of an innovation, but is one that offers great inducements in the way of interest as well as profit. If one is the possessor of health and strength, a good news instinct... a fair photographic outfit, and the ability to hustle, which is the most necessary qualification, one can be a news photographer.

Jessie Tarbox Beals
The Focus, St. Louis, Missouri 1904

Anna slept like a hibernating bear that night. She was comforted by the feeling that she was not alone in her profession. She dreamed that one day an article or biography would be written about her career, noting her pioneering contribution to the news field and, more than that, to women's rights and Baltimore history.

Not explored in the article, however, were mentions of struggle, sacrifice, prejudice, low pay, and suppression. These stumbling blocks, unlike the granite pavers being mortared in the streets of Baltimore, were not fireproof. Anna would have to learn how to traverse them without getting scorched.

CHAPTER 8

Anna put her nose to the grindstone over the next few months. She took any assignment with compliance and dedication. Her life was filled with news stories, which she offset with theater life at Ford's. She continued to attend suffrage meetings but only created silhouettes occasionally now. Even as a young, energetic woman, she could stretch her activities only so far. And, with income from Ford's, she no longer needed to cut portraits of children with no faces.

She saw her father and Elizabeth less and less.

Anna's world grew like the expansion of Baltimore, wider, taller, stronger. She learned from people she met and reveled in the privilege of hearing their stories. One would soon teach her an unforgettable lesson in humility.

As the holiday season approached, a time of merriment and shopping, Anna was given an assignment that put her in touch with Baltimore's most downtrodden residents and the people trying to help them.

"Miss Bainbridge, I want you and David Jameson to meet with Miss Ida R. Cummings," H.L. Mencken said. "She is a member of the Executive Committee of the Colored Teachers' Association of Maryland. Miss Cummings is an accomplished woman, the first kindergarten teacher of her kind in Baltimore."

"Do you just want an interview and portrait or is there a special event happening?"

"You are learning to ask the right questions before charging out of here with your camera. I am pleased. Yes, there is an event. It's called the 'Colored Empty Stocking Festival.' As you know, Christmas is coming, and many underprivileged children will have no treats. A new organization called the 'Colored Empty Stocking and Fresh Air Circle' is holding a fundraiser to provide toys for colored children this holiday season."

"What is the 'fresh air' part about?"

"That's why I'm sending you... to report the whole story. You are to speak with Miss Cummings to get a full understanding. Her committee meetings take place on Druid Hill Avenue. That's a couple of miles from here. I'll provide transportation for you and Mr. Jameson."

When they arrived, they were greeted by a shapely, dark-skinned woman projecting a friendly smile and kind eyes.

After introductions and tea, which took off the chill in the air, Anna and the reporter got down to business. David asked about the name of the organization.

"Our goals are two-fold. We want to provide Christmas toys and candy to children who would otherwise feel neglected and unloved. This time of year often renders them hopeless."

"And the Fresh Air Circle?"

"That's for warmer months. In summer, city children need a place where they can be close to nature, interacting with animals, playing sports outside, learning about flowers and plants, hiking trails, and seeing what it's like to live off the land. The Fresh Air Circle will collect money to send these children to a designated farm in the country, where they can do all of these things."

"Like a vacation."

"Exactly, Mr. Jameson, but an educational one. Let me interject one thing here and now. I am not doing all of this on my own. There is a whole group of people from various faiths and churches in Baltimore who have come together to make all this possible. Please include that in your article."

"Certainly, Miss Cummings. What is your background?" David continued.

While the reporter jotted down the story, Anna took candid photographs of this fascinating woman. Anna had learned to not only shoot posed portraits, but to catch the subject mid-interview with hand gestures and facial expression. These photos put *Herald* readers in the middle of the interview.

Anna was taken by this woman, who must have been in her mid-thirties, and, no doubt, had suffered prejudice in her life. Yet, she presented a poised, gracious and self-assured attitude, exhibiting no bitterness. Anna would remember her. As they parted company, Anna sincerely expressed a desire to meet again. She slipped Miss Cummings a small donation. In exchange, Miss Cummings gave Anna her business card.

෯෯

On the opposite end of the social spectrum, stars of the stage filled Anna's life away from the *Herald*. The actress, Maude Adams, did come to Ford's Theater to star in *Peter Pan*. Anna shot a picture of her with Baltimore's new mayor, E. Clay Timanus, a man of robust stature, who towered over the fair beauty. It was blown up to poster size and hung outside the theater entrance for passersby to see. The house had been packed every night of the play's run. The mayor, himself, asked for a desk-size picture to frame for his office.

And something unexpected happened. A closeness with Josefina blossomed, Anna's first real friend, other than her nanny, Elizabeth.

"You are becoming quite the successful photographer," Josefina said, one morning after breakfast, as they helped clear the table.

"I love what I'm doing. I can't think of anything more that could fulfill me," Anna replied.

"Not even marriage and children?"

"No, not right now. How about you?"

"Oh, I've thought about it some. And I guess I would like to eventually marry and see where it goes from there, I mean concerning children."

"Would you still work? Your career is so exciting, I can't imagine ever giving it up."

"No... no, I would stop. Definitely. When would I have time for my husband? He'd be working during the day and I'd be working at night."

"Yes, I see." Anna scraped food waste into an old newspaper, then folded it over to put in the trashcan. "Are you being courted right now? I've noticed a blush on the apples of your cheeks lately."

"Well... there has been a regular patron at the theater. He waits to get autographs after performances but caught my attention one night when I left through the stage door. I think I caught his, too."

"Have you spoken?"

"No, not yet."

"Well, what are you waiting for? Introduce yourself."

"That would be too bold. We must be formally introduced and then..."

"... he would have to ask your father for permission to court... and then you could sit in the parlor with Miss Pendleton nearby... and it would be months before you even hold hands."

"Anna, there is such a thing as decorum."

"Decorum can take years to unfold. Before you know it, you'll be a grey-haired spinster. Introduce yourself or, at least, make eyes so he knows you are interested."

"What about you? You offer advice freely but I don't see gentleman callers ringing the doorbell for you."

"I almost... I mean, well, I did fall in love over a year ago."

"What? Tell me about him."

"Maybe later. I'm not much for girlish talk."

"Oh, but you must. You've piqued my interest. It's Saturday. You don't have to work today and I don't have to be at the theater for a little while."

"Well, all right. Early in the spring of '03, I was leaving my home on West Saratoga, when a mail carrier dropped off an advertisement for the new Brownie box camera. He was singing but stopped and asked my name to make sure it matched the address. I think he just wanted to strike up a conversation. I was rather rude to him. We didn't see each other again for several weeks. After I bought the camera, as I was taking pictures of all the activities at Patterson Park, who should I run into, but that very same man. He said he was about to ascend the pagoda there on the edge of the park to get a full view of the surroundings and asked if I'd like to join him. He used the excuse that I could take a great picture from that vantage point. Somehow, I felt comfortable enough to agree. Mind you, I'm not the type of girl who would allow just any man such entry into my life. But he was different. I knew it."

"What happened? Did he ask your father's permission to court you?"

"No, we met secretly for weeks after that. Papa never would have permitted a romance between his daughter and a mail deliverer."

"Oh, I see."

"Our meetings were cloak-and-dagger, which made our romance more intriguing. We had so much fun... dancing, listening to music, going to fairs... even Electric Park, where we got on all the rides and took in a movie. Once, after we talked of marriage, I went to his apartment to see how I might fit in there."

"I can't believe you ever did all those things. You seem so, so reserved and focused on work now. Did something bad happen?"

"Yes, the Great Baltimore Fire. We had planned to elope..."

"Elope! You were that secretive?"

"Yes... on the very day the fire broke out, no less. I left him at the altar, so to speak, and spent the next two days taking pictures of the fire. I even got one published in the *Baltimore Herald*. I was in heaven, barely thinking of him, or the anxiety I caused my father, and Elizabeth, my nanny."

"And what was your betrothed doing all that time?"

"Searching for me, worrying about me. He even got hurt after falling."

"Oh, no. Did he break the engagement?"

"Just the opposite. He forgave me and still wanted to get married. I'm the one who backed away, asking for time to think of my future. You see, he wanted a wife who would raise a large family. After tasting the newspaper life, I had my doubts that marriage and children would be right for me... or him."

"You did the prudent thing. And now, how do you feel?"

"I love working. I really do. And, by now, I'm sure he has moved on to another romance. We don't keep in touch. I hope he has found someone he deserves." As Anna said those words, she secretly hoped he hadn't found another love. There was a part of her still possessive of Adrian.

"I hope so, too. Well, I need to get ready to leave for the theater. I'll see you tomorrow." She touched Anna's wrist. "I'm glad you confided in me."

"I am, too. Josefina?"

"Yes?"

"Tonight, do me a favor... make eyes at the man outside the stage door."

Josefina blushed, hugged her friend and swiftly made her exit.

CHAPTER 9

Anna got the idea of buying men's jodhpurs after reading an article about the Maryland Hunt Cup, a big event held among Maryland's elite each May since 1894. A Timber Race, it proved demanding for participants representing two competing fox hunts... Green Spring and Elkridge. Male riders and their horses had to jump twenty-two solid wood fences, spread out over four miles of hills and leas, to catch a fox and determine the best hunting horse. Women served as mere spectators who packed picnic lunches and fanned themselves under willow trees.

Anna thought the riding attire men wore would give her an advantage in her own competition... jostling photographers and reporters at news events. The jodhpurs, by design, would not be too tight or overtly comely and, when paired with a riding jacket and boots, would present a modest, professional look.

It was worth the expense to travel nineteen miles to Worthington Valley Hunt Club, where riding attire could be purchased. Anna had saved her money and hoped the transaction would run as smoothly as Redmond C. Stewart's winning horse, "Landslide," had most recently.

Upon arrival, Anna was greeted by a salesman, speaking in a manner she knew wasn't his birthright. "Good morning, young lady. How may I be of service?"

"I'd like to purchase jodhpurs for myself."

"I'm sorry, miss. We do not fit men's clothing to women."

"But I have the means, Mister, ah..."

"J.W. Wilton. My dear, we simply cannot measure. There are no female tailors to size you, only male. And that would not be permitted."

"Don't you have any jodhpurs already made that I could try on?"

"Miss, you are quite diminutive. Only racing jockey's attire would fit you."

"Surely there are short men among your clientele, Mr. Wilton."

"Yes, but this is most improper. There are only male employees and patrons here. And to allow a woman in a dressing room, to... ah... remove her... and try on... well, it's most improper. And any alterations would be out of the question."

"There is a woman, a seamstress I know, who could do the alterations."

The back-and-forth between Mr. Wilton and Anna attracted unpleasant attention. Men with high-hat surnames stared and talked among themselves, looking down their noses as though Anna were nothing more than a begging street urchin.

J.W. Wilton took note and hastened to find a remedy. "Wait right here, miss... quietly. Stay calm. I will be right back."

"I am calm. You're the one who's flummoxed," Anna said under her breath.

Mr. Wilton disappeared for about ten minutes. Upon his return, he showed a flushed face and an inability to make eye contact. He carried an outfit on a hanger as though it were infested with firebrats.

"I just spoke with the manager and we found this jacket and pants that were ordered but never picked up because the client suddenly passed on. It's a bit big for you but it might serve your purpose. Mind you, I will not allow you to try this on here and now. It would be most..."

"I know... improper."

"Quite."

Anna held the pants up to her and started to put the jacket on over her clothes.

"Tsk. Tsk," Mr. Wilton said, while wagging his forefinger like the tail of a fox hound on the hunt.

"I think this will work just fine. There's plenty of fabric for taking in here and letting out there," Anna said, while pointing at parts of her anatomy.

"Please, miss." Sweat collected in the salesman's philtrum like rainwater in a birdbath.

"I'll take them both. I have blouses to wear underneath the jacket and I can buy boots anywhere."

"Very well."

"Now, as to the cost. I'm sure you are willing to discount the original price, since you have not been able to sell these clothes to any of your male patrons thus far."

Mr. Wilton did not put up a fight. He was as spent as "Landslide" at the finish. After the salesman rang up the purchase, wrapped the clothes and gave them to Anna, he reached into his pocket and pulled out a handkerchief, which he used to dab the embarrassment on his face.

Within a few days, with the help of Josefina, Anna sported a well-tailored riding ensemble. She had yet to wear it, for her outfit was incomplete. What she still needed was her trusty steed... a bicycle. She would have to learn how to ride it but felt she could pick up the skill quickly. She pictured Mr. Wilton trying to teach her and could just hear him say, "This is most improper."

Quite.

ॐॐ

While walking down Liberty Street a week later, Anna passed a poster that featured the picture of a stern woman dressed in a dark suit, her hair haphazardly piled on her head. What caught Anna's eye more than the subject was the quality of the photograph. Not only in capturing this woman, who looked directly into the lens with strong intent but, also, in the clear definition in the film.

Without reading the poster, Anna continued toward The Basin. She was preoccupied by her goal, to purchase a bicycle at a new store near the wharf.

A few blocks away, something needled Anna, something she could not identify. It was almost as if a powerful force were trying to turn her around to take another look at the poster. It was the same push that returned her to the Great Fire just at a moment of despair, when she was about to give up her dream of photographing it.

That night, there had been the scent of rose water in the air, just as there was this day. Anna attributed it to nothing more than the perfumed handkerchief of a passerby. She listened to this inner voice anyway and turned back.

Anna stopped at the poster and, when she read the headline, realized that her intuition, or whatever this unseen power was, had been correct.

Noted Photographer
Frances Benjamin Johnston to Speak

It took a few moments for the information to sink in. Anna couldn't comprehend what she had just read. One of her idols, a female pioneer in photography, was coming to Baltimore!

Anna grabbed the ubiquitous writing pad and pen in her purse and, with hurried handwriting, jotted down the information. In a matter of days, this extraordinary woman was scheduled to speak at her alma mater, Notre Dame of Maryland Preparatory & Collegiate Institute, far north of the city, in rural Baltimore. Anna had never even heard of the place. No wonder; it stood seven miles from her home.

How on earth would Anna get there? A hired carriage would cost a fortune. And she had just spent a large fare to get to Worthington Valley. She couldn't ask Papa for money; he would never allow it. And it would place Elizabeth in a financial bind. She refused to impose on Josefina or Mrs. Pendleton. And the other girls at her boardinghouse were out of the question. Might H.L. Mencken advance her salary? Even though Anna had been acting on her best behavior at work, she doubted he would be so inclined, but she had to try.

"This is a most unusual request, Miss Bainbridge."

"Unusual but not unprecedented. Correct?"

"Well, yes. However, in this instance, I see no reason to comply."

"Mr. Mencken, hearing Miss Johnston speak will teach me so much, and you, yourself, have repeatedly told me I have a lot to learn about photojournalism."

Mencken ignored Anna. He leaned forward at his desk to open a Schafer-Pfaff box and lift out an Iraba cigar. Making Anna wait, he stared at the roll of tobacco like a true connoisseur, entering a world of thought deigned only for men. He preferred Havana Rose but, since his father had been a Baltimore tobacconist, H.L. supported local brands. Iraba had been one of many varieties manufactured by Schafer-Pfaff, whose company was located just blocks away in Fells Point. Mencken liked to walk there and engage with workers on the merits of American products versus Cuban. In this private world, he seemed to have forgotten about Anna. The editor lit the end and inhaled several short puffs, then eased back in his chair to enjoy the tobacco's smoothness. He twisted the cigar between his fingers and stared at it as if it were his most-prized possession.

"Perhaps we can kill two birds with one stone. Here's what I am willing to do. I will turn this into an assignment for you. I understand that Miss Johnston is not only a famed photographer but, also, a writer. Since you are so taken with her, how would you like to deliver both?"

"You mean, shoot pictures *and* write the story?"

"Precisely."

"I've never written a story before."

"Well, surely, you've read enough of them to know how to do it. What do you say?"

Anna didn't like Mencken's demeanor. She felt he was setting a trap for her to become mired in failure. Any excuse to get rid of her once and for all. Not one to shy away from a challenge, Anna set fear aside. She wondered how Frances Benjamin Johnston would react under the same circumstance.

"I say 'yes,' Mr. Mencken. I look forward to bringing you both story and pictures."

"In that case, I will hire transportation to and from the event for you."

"Thank you, Mr. Mencken. I won't let you down." What Anna really meant was that she was not about to let herself down.

"See that you don't, Miss Bainbridge."

Anna hurried from the office before her boss could change his mind. H.L. Mencken smiled as he took a long draw from his Iraba, a Spanish word meaning "was going."

∾∾

Anna arrived at Gibbons Hall on the campus of Notre Dame an hour early. She knew nothing of the school and wanted to get background information. A nun was kind enough to hand her a pamphlet on the short history of the institute, which had only existed since 1873.

Anna also received a printed biography of the guest speaker, which made the question-and-answer part of her job much easier. Miss Johnston, who hailed from Grafton, West Virginia, had graduated from Notre Dame in 1883 and moved to Paris to continue her studies in art. The beginning of her career and Anna's could not have contrasted more.

Anna had called Notre Dame in advance, requesting a half hour of the speaker's time. She was told the school had no authority to arrange such a meeting. She would have to go through Miss Johnston's friend and fellow photographer, Miss Mattie Edwards Hewitt, who was known for her expertise in taking home-and-garden pictures for women's magazines. But there wasn't time to get off a post to her. Anna would have to take her chances in person.

She asked the same nun who had helped her earlier to direct her to Miss Hewitt. The sister told Anna to wait a moment while she checked her availability.

"I'm sorry, both Miss Hewitt and Miss Johnston are in conference, making last-minute refinements to the presentation."

"Don't they know I am just like them? I'm a photographer and writer, too. Only, I am new to the profession and trying to succeed, just as they once did. Could you tell them that, please?"

Ten minutes later, the nun escorted Anna into a small room that overlooked the campus.

"Well, I am happy to meet a fledgling newspaperwoman," Miss Johnston said. Miss Hewitt remained quiet, almost receding.

"The honor is mine. I'm Anna Bainbridge, representing my employer, *The Baltimore Herald*."

"A fine newspaper. My mother worked for a competing publication here in Baltimore. She wrote theater reviews for the *Baltimore Sun* under the pseudonym, 'Ione.' Did you know that?"

"I take pictures for Ford's Theater on the side. And I..."

"Miss Bainbridge. I only have a few minutes to offer you. What would you like to know about *me*?"

"Forgive me, I'm a little nervous. How did you get your start?"

"I was a writer, just like my mother."

"Then, what led you to photography?"

"I was given the gift of a camera by a family friend, George Eastman. Have you heard of him?"

"Have I heard of him! My first camera was a Brownie from the Eastman Kodak company. I used it to photograph the Great Baltimore Fire earlier this year. And one of my pictures..."

"Yes, ah, anything else you'd like to ask me about *my* career?"

"Oh, of course. Do you develop pictures yourself?"

"Sometimes. I was formally trained in the darkroom by the director of photography at the Smithsonian, Thomas Smillie." Miss Johnston spelled the man's last name and watched Anna jot it on her paper.

Anna realized she was out of her depth. She could never compete with this woman, who enjoyed one opportunity falling in her lap after another. Anna focused more acutely on her mission.

"Who are some of the notables you've photographed?"

"The list is long, my dear. Several years ago, I was appointed official White House Photographer during Benjamin Harrison's term, and have continued since. I've also shot portraits of Mark Twain and Susan B. Anthony and so forth. Oh, and Admiral Dewey."

Miss Hewitt finally spoke up. "Have you read the article about women photographers Miss Johnston wrote for *Ladies Home Journal*?"

"No, ma'am. I have not had the pleasure."

"If you like, I will mail it to you. It was written in 1897 but is just as relevant today. The article is called 'What a Woman Can Do with a Camera.'"

"I would love to read it, thank you."

A nun entered the room and nodded to the women, signaling that it was almost time for the speaker to take the stage.

"May I quickly shoot a couple of photographs?" Anna asked.

"Yes, of course." Miss Hewitt stepped aside, as Anna took pictures of Miss Johnston looking out a window and standing in front of a small sign identifying Notre Dame.

"Thank you for this audience," Anna said. "I will remember it for the rest of my life."

"I will be most happy if you send me a clipping of your report in the *Herald*. You may exchange addresses with Miss Hewitt. I will take my leave now."

The receding woman gently touched Miss Johnston's hand, and smiled at her friend endearingly as she left the room. Then, she turned to Anna and spoke softly. "I hope you realize, Miss Bainbridge, that you were just sitting in the presence of a great lady, not just a photographer and writer, but the one who will set the standard for all newspaperwomen coming after her. I suggest you add that to your story, without quoting me."

"Yes, ma'am," was all Anna could muster. For only the second time in her life, she was silenced by awe. The first occurred when she faced the magnitude of the Great Baltimore Fire from atop Federal Hill. She didn't know which was more powerful.

Anna sat through the speech, taking as many notes as possible. After a half hour, her hand hurt, and her mind grew fuzzy with the enormity of the moment, but she pushed through. Exact quotes were most difficult to master. Through her concentration to get the words right, she neglected to put down her pen to take pictures of the speaker engaging with the audience.

She learned that Miss Johnston was a great proponent of women in journalism, whether writer or photographer. She repeatedly used the phrase "New Woman" in describing any female who broke the Victorian mold, choosing instead to enter occupations usually inhabited by men. She spoke of wearing men's suits to blend in with her male counterparts on assignment and riding a bicycle for quick mobility. This was exactly what Anna wanted to hear. It confirmed that she was on the right track, despite what her nanny, her father, or the boardinghouse ladies said. And she would prove H.L. Mencken wrong, too, by writing the most comprehensive, exciting article she could conjure.

CHAPTER 10

When H.L. Mencken arrived for work the next day, there was Anna, waiting on the sidewalk at the entrance to the building.

"What are you doing in those ridiculous clothes, Miss Bainbridge? Have you gone aslant?"

"No, Mr. Mencken."

"Then why are you dressed for the running of the hounds?"

"I thought these clothes would give me ease of movement as I take pictures, while still looking refined. Do you disagree?"

"Well, ah, no."

"Good. I also purchased a bicycle, which I placed inside the door. I learned to ride it in an hour. Now I have my own means of transportation with riding clothes to match. I'm ready for my next assignment."

"What about the one I gave you? The interview with that photographer woman."

"The pictures are in development and the story, 500 words, sits on your desk, handwritten, of course. I don't know how to type."

"If you want more writing assignments, you'll have to learn. There are classes at secretarial night schools you can take."

Anna knew this would interfere with her work at Ford's and would also draw focus off her real passion, taking pictures. She thought she could master the typing skill on her own, as easily as riding a bicycle. It was a matter of time.

Anna followed Mencken to his office and stood next to his desk.

"Do you mind? I'd like to read this without your overbearing scrutiny."

Anna sauntered out to the writing pool, where typewriters were clicking like a chorus line of tap dancers. She sat and waited for what seemed like eons. When Mencken's door opened, a gust of air blew wisps of hair fallen from Anna's chignon.

H.L. walked past her and handed her work to a typist. All he said was, "Next edition, local interest section, byline Anna Bainbridge." He hurried to the elevator and was gone before Anna could even stand up.

She walked over to the typist's desk. "May I see it?"

At first glance, all Anna discerned were squiggles and arrows. Whole sentences crossed out. Others added.

"Oh, dear," Anna said.

"Don't feel bad. These are editors' markings. Catching spelling errors, creating paragraphs and so on. The good thing is he's still allowing it in the paper. I've seen worse," said the typist.

"You have?"

"Certainly. Sometimes I have to fish a story out of the trash can. Consider this a breakthrough."

"Why didn't he say anything to me? Congratulate me, offer encouragement? This was my first story."

"You don't know H.L. Mencken very well. The best advice I can give you is – don't expect high praise, or any praise, for that matter. Just keep at it. You'll get better. He'll let you know when you're not up to snuff."

Anna's high spirits deflated. She had a long way to go before pleasing the likes of the *Baltimore Herald's* City Editor.

David Jameson stepped behind Anna and tapped her on the shoulder. "Miss Bainbridge." She didn't flinch.

"Miss Bainbridge. We have an assignment. We have to go to Washington Place, where the Municipal Arts Society is making a presentation. We only have a few minutes to get there. And may I ask, why are you dressed like that?"

"This is my new work attire. I can go anywhere, climb up high, crawl on the ground, whatever is needed to get the picture. And I'll get where I'm going faster on my new bicycle, which is downstairs in the lobby. What do you think?"

"I think you are full of surprises and I think you are out of your head. But I brought my own bicycle today, too, which makes things more convenient for both of us. Let's get going."

Upon arrival, they discovered that the Municipal Arts Society was about to unveil a statue of John Eager Howard, a revolutionary war colonel, former governor of Maryland and state congressman, among other titles. Both Howard Street and Eager Street which crisscrossed downtown, were named for him. As was Howard County, southwest of the city. And now, here he was, frozen in time, sitting astride his horse, in military regalia.

"David, why are there so many statues and monuments in Baltimore?"

"I guess to make sure that people who live in the here and now will never forget the great contributions and sacrifices of those who came before us. Don't you like these memorials?"

"It's not that I don't like them. It's just that they always seem to be associated with war."

"It's in battle that men often rise above their supposed limitations and perform courageous acts."

"And what about women? I don't see many monuments around town dedicated to them. I know they don't fight in battle. That doesn't mean they don't do great things."

"Like whom?"

"Like Ida Cummings starting an organization that helps children grow and learn with few resources and plenty of hurdles. You met her. You wrote her story."

David shook his head. "There's no comparison. Excuse me, I need to hear what the speaker is saying. You should start looking through that viewfinder."

෨෦ඦ

When *The Herald* was handed to Anna later that day, she hesitated to open it. What had become of her story about Frances Benjamin Johnston? The headline to the article read, "Leading Woman Photographer Speaks at College." *So far so good*, Anna thought.

As she read the piece, she noticed much of it missing. She counted every word and saw that her 500 had been whittled down to 237. She wanted to ask Mencken why. What had she done wrong? She knew he would not give her the time. Once an edition was put to bed, it was past tense.

She read the article over and over to see if she could figure it out herself. She compared it to her original. Eventually, Anna realized that the more succinct version was sharper, more interesting. There were no unnecessary words.

Anna wondered how to apply this lesson to photography. Should she frame subjects tighter, so there would be no wasted space? Take pictures closer to the action? Put the reader in the midst of the riot, the holiday celebration, the speaker's audience? Anna looked forward to her next assignment to show her boss what she had learned.

"Miss Bainbridge," H.L. Mencken said, "tomorrow you are going to spend the day at O'Neill and Company on Charles and Lexington. In *The Herald's* ongoing effort to show Baltimoreans how local businesses are growing from the ashes of the Great Fire, I want you to portray a day in the life of the store. If you recall, O'Neill's was untouched by the fire. It is, however, located close to the burnt district. David Jameson will write the story. You provide the pictures."

"I was hoping for something more... exciting."

"I don't care what you were hoping for, Miss Bainbridge. But I do care about your attire. You are to wear a dress. Mr. O'Neill is the epitome of style and graciousness. As a representative of this newspaper, you must put your best foot forward and exhibit top-drawer manners. Am I getting through to you?"

"Yes, sir."

"Be there at 8:30 A.M. to a dot. That's when Mr. O'Neill holds his staff meetings. Once the store is open for business, he will be engaged with his customers. Do not interrupt him. You and David are to be flies on the wall all day." He looked at a piece of paper. "Let me see, a Miss Hughes will be your guide."

"I understand."

Anna went home unhappy. She didn't know that her experience at O'Neill's was about to teach her another important career lesson, not in photography, but in professionalism.

Thomas J. O'Neill lined up his staff of salesladies who were addressed as "Miss" followed by their first names. In their black dresses with white collars and cuffs, they looked like penguins about to receive a king. Miss Hughes told Anna and David that these women had been handpicked for their jobs servicing customers based on two criteria... taste and manners.

She said, "Mr. O'Neill feels that knowledge of product, salesmanship, and the ability to handle a transaction can be taught. Dignity cannot. Oh, let's be quiet. Mr. O'Neill is about to speak."

"Good morning, ladies. Miss Emily, an important wedding couple will be arriving today to pick their china pattern. I want you devoted to their needs for the duration."

"Yes, sir. I will be most astute."

"Miss Geraldine, don't forget to sprinkle talcum powder inside gloves before a customer tries them on. It's much more sanitary and comfortable for our guests. I know you are busy, but we must keep up our standards."

"Of course, our customers deserve it, Mr. O'Neill."

"Good. Miss Rosalie, the display of hats looked a little sloppy yesterday at closing. Due to colder temperatures, many people are shopping for head coverings these days. They are often careless in replacing the items after trying them on. Please see to straightening each one before a single customer reaches the millinery department."

"Certainly, sir."

"You may get a head start now. Miss Marion, the Layette department will be receiving a new shipment today. Please see that the merchandise is put on shelves immediately and make your customers aware that the bedding and blankets have just arrived from France."

"I'm looking forward to seeing the pieces myself."

"Very well. You may all take your posts. We are about to open."

"Thank you, Mr. O'Neill," they said in unison, with a short curtsy.

As Mr. O'Neill addressed the salesmen, the ladies moved to their assigned departments as slowly and gracefully as ballet dancers. When all employees reached their posts, the doors were unlocked.

Mr. O'Neill caught Miss Hughes's attention by giving her a slight nod.

"Excuse me a moment, please," she said to Anna and David, as she walked to Mr. O'Neill's side. Anna leaned in to hear what was said.

"Miss Lila's chignon is askew. Will you please tell her to groom it?"

"Right away, sir."

Miss Hughes didn't rush. She walked calmly to the Hosiery department and spoke to the unkempt salesclerk. The two women stepped behind a display for a moment to tidy Lila's hair.

"I'm sorry for the interruption," Miss Hughes said, upon her return. "Now, where were we?"

"Does this happen every morning, Miss Hughes?" David asked.

"What do you mean?"

"This attention to detail?" Anna chimed in.

"Why, yes, of course. How else can we keep our quality of service at its peak?"

Throughout the day, the threesome walked around the store. Anna noticed that few customers used cash. She asked Miss Hughes about this practice.

"Most of O'Neill's loyal customers charge their purchases, which we encourage," Miss Hughes said. "Mr. O'Neill feels that a cash customer is not as frequent a buyer as one who makes purchases on account. For as long as credit customers are loyal to him, he is loyal to them. By that, I mean the store sends bills only twice a year, knowing payment will be remitted in full immediately. Trust is the hallmark of success in business."

"By the looks of them, I'd say most shoppers come from Baltimore's better families. Is that true?" David asked.

"Yes, it is, Mr. Jameson. Primarily from the Mt. Vernon and Guilford sections of Baltimore. These are educated, traveled people who want the best of everything, especially fine linens Mr. O'Neill personally brings over from his homeland, Ireland, as well as from European cities, like Madrid, Paris and Zurich."

"I noticed the Irish lilt in his voice," said David.

"Yes, Mr. O'Neill hails from County Caven, Ireland. He comes from a long line of merchants there. He settled in Baltimore in 1866 and opened these doors in 1882."

As they perused the various floor levels and sections, Anna saw that the multi-story building offered variety, from everyday clothing, shoes and millinery… to housewares, ball gowns and baby needs. She offered her observation to Miss Hughes.

"O'Neill's has become known as 'The Store of Specialty Shops,' with personnel well-versed in the products we sell. Service, however, is just as important as variety, maybe more so."

Anna had never shopped at O'Neill's because Elizabeth had always chosen simple clothes for her from more demure shops or sewed dresses for Anna herself. Dr. Bainbridge didn't care for ostentation in his daughter's attire, even though his home was filled with gilded mirrors and valuable art, velvet upholstery and fringed curtains.

Anna watched as Mr. O'Neill greeted customers, many by name, welcoming them at the front door. Dressed to the nines, he showed everyone the same graciousness.

"Each customer must feel like royalty," Anna said.

"They most certainly do," Miss Hughes replied.

Anna was enamored by Mr. O'Neill. He was a man of imposing physical stature and flame-red hair, matched only by his exuberant mustache.

"Does he always dress so fine? Even in the office?" David asked.

"By all means. He wears an evening coat during the day, rarely taking his jacket off, even when sitting behind his desk to look over accounts. He leads by example. He wants to be presentable to his staff and customers always, and especially to the many religious orders that come to his store."

"What do they buy?" Anna asked.

"They purchase their habits here. Mr. O'Neill is a devout Catholic. He makes sure the nuns feel comfortable trying on their garments. O'Neill's offers complete privacy and discretion when they arrive."

"What an extraordinary man," Anna sighed.

"Yes, he is. Thomas O'Neill's thoughtfulness extends to his entire clientele. Facial powders and rouges are hand blended by staff to specification. Evening attire can be examined in a 'dark room,' to simulate nighttime. A drinking fountain is available on each level and not one, but two elevators transport customers from floor to floor, so no one need wait."

"It proves that nice, polite people can be successful," Anna said. She was thinking of H.L. Mencken and how antithetical his business demeanor was to Mr. O'Neill's.

"Mr. O'Neill is among the best in Baltimore. And deserves his success. Over the years, his store has grown with the demands of Baltimore's high society, who want fur coats made from the best pelts, tuxedos and cocktail dresses from French designers, and fine china and sterling silver from England."

"Yet he treats everyone the same," David said.

"Mr. O'Neill never forgets those who come from more humble beginnings, customers who just want to purchase dress patterns and inexpensive materials to sew for their families. They are treated with equal attention and courtesy. He has done his forebearers proud, creating a life for himself in Baltimore and a mainstay for shoppers who want the best they can afford."

Anna and David thanked Miss Hughes for her time. Anna inwardly thanked H.L. Mencken for this opportunity to learn that professionalism pays dividends in every sense of the word. Although, she wouldn't necessarily be tenacious in adopting it.

CHAPTER 11

Mrs. Pendleton, a bastion of cleanliness and order, had created mailboxes for her residents in the entrance hall of her boardinghouse. Anna rarely received correspondence, only reminders from Elizabeth to visit her and her father. She was, therefore, surprised to find a small package awaiting her.

Anna raced up the stairs to her room and ripped the seal open. "It's from Miss Johnston!" she exclaimed to no one in particular.

Inside, she found the article promised her... "What a Woman Can Do with a Camera." She put it aside on her bed and unfolded the accompanying note:

My Dear Miss Bainbridge,

I am sorry it has taken so long to respond. The bane of being busy is that time passes much too swiftly even for proper etiquette.

I received a copy of your article on my speech at Notre Dame. I was most pleased to see verbatim quotes and an overall accurate representation of my visit to my alma mater. You are to be congratulated.

However, the accompanying photograph represented me a bit too formally. I would have preferred a candid picture taken during my presentation or following it, as I met members of the audience and some of the nuns. Nonetheless, I am happy to have made your acquaintance.

Miss Hewitt sends her regards, along with a copy of the article she promised you as it appeared in Ladies Home Journal.

Sincerely, Miss Frances Benjamin Johnston

"What?" Anna said out loud. "She didn't like my picture?" Anna folded the letter, then unfolded and read it again. "I can't believe it."

Anna sat on the bed, crestfallen. At first, she was angry with Miss Johnston. "How dare she reprove my work?" Anna said even louder. Almost in response, Miss Hewitt's words rang in her ears. *"I hope you realize that you were just sitting in the presence of a great lady, not just a photographer and writer, but the one who will set the standard for all newspaperwomen coming after her."*

For the next half hour, Anna wore herself out with feelings of outrage, failure, and anger. She sulked for the better part of the day. Even Josefina could not pull her from morass. Anna didn't even care to read the article Miss Hewitt had sent her. What words could Frances Benjamin Johnston possibly say to cheer her spirit?

"This woman is evidently a pillar in her profession," Josefina said. "Shouldn't you put aside concern about yourself and read her article?"

Anna turned her back and folded her arms. "I've heard enough already. Her letter has discouraged me completely."

Josefina spun her friend around and stared her straight in the eyes. "Look at yourself, Anna," she said. "Look at you, pouting like a child. Don't you realize setbacks are part of life? Do you think Maude Adams was born a great actress? She had to learn phrasing and breathing and staging and taking direction, even when she disagreed with the director's interpretation of her role. Do you think the critics were always favorable? No. But what has made Miss Adams a great actress, what makes anyone great, is learning from their mistakes. You are too impatient, Anna. Slow down, walk before you run, think about what you are doing beforehand, in the moment, and after. The 'after' part is most important of all. That's when you really assess life and learn."

"But..."

"There are no 'buts' about it. You will have other challenges. There will be more times when you feel bad. But you must go on.

Don't let this one letter stop you. Where is that Anna Bainbridge spunk?" Josefina said, as she moved about the room. "Is it hidden in the closet, under the bed, or behind your ear, waiting for a magician to produce it?"

That brought a smile to Anna's face. "You're right. I am too impatient. Everyone tells me so, even Mrs. Pendleton. You run along, now. I'd like to be alone for a while, to read this article." As Josefina left the room, Anna said, "Thank you for setting me straight. I hope I can be as good a friend to you as you have been to me."

"You already are. I'll see you at supper."

Anna sat quietly and read "What a Woman Can Do with a Camera" slowly, savoring each word, underscoring certain quotes, like this one:

"The woman who makes photography profitable must have good common sense, unlimited patience to carry her through endless failure... good taste, a quick eye, and a talent for detail."

Anna felt these words had been written specifically for her. They certainly applied. She underscored another passage:

"The best general rule to follow is to accept cheerfully any work that comes, doing what there is to do, rather than waiting for the particular kind that one would prefer."

Anna's thoughts immediately ran to H.L. Mencken and the number of times she begged him for particular stories to photograph... the death of Mayor McLane, the reconstruction of Baltimore, murders and other crimes. He was just trying to help her take tiny steps to hone her skills, train her eye and make her a better photojournalist.

Anna had a good long talk with herself. After freshening her appearance, she joined Josefina and two of the others for supper.

"Good evening, ladies. How is everyone?" Anna said.

"Are you speaking to us?" said Frances.

"Yes, I am. Frances, how is your job with Alex Brown & Sons? You are a typist, is that right?"

"Why, yes. It's going very well."

"Naomi, did you ever buy that pretty pink dress at O'Neill's?"

"No, even with pooling our money, we couldn't afford it."

"That's a pity. It would have looked beautiful on any one of you."

As Anna focused on her meal, passing rolls and watching her manners, the ladies looked around the table in disbelief. They were more incredulous when Anna offered to clear the entire table. She even helped Mrs. Pendleton with the dishes.

"What's overtaken her?" Rosemary asked Josefina.

"It's simple. Anna is learning to walk."

Chapter 12

With walking comes stumbling, even falls, sometimes painful. There were days when Anna stuck to her best behavior and days when angst and greediness to succeed ruled her actions. As she learned about the world, she understood how a solitary person could change it. She had seen it in Mayor McLane, and recognized it in Frances Benjamin Johnston, and Emma Maddox Funck, and even in H.L. Mencken, whose editorials helped mold the way Baltimoreans thought. These lessons sometimes came unexpectedly, not from the theater spotlight or City Hall or the pages of the *Baltimore Herald*... rather from the deep recesses of the city, at the end of the day, when one felt most weary and vulnerable.

Anna had finished shooting the last portraits of over twenty city officials. The *Herald* wanted these pictures on file to accompany news stories in which important people might be featured.

It was dark and all she wanted to do was get home and enjoy a good supper. She hoped Mrs. Pendleton had just taken a bubbling-hot Shepherd's Pie out of the oven, one of her favorites. Anna didn't notice a person standing in the shadows right outside the *Herald's* door.

"Please, miss, can you spare a nickel or a few pennies?"

"Who said that? Show your face."

A girl slowly stepped out of the penumbra. It was obvious that she was not much younger than Anna. But thinner, a lot thinner.

"Have you no work?" Anna said.

"No, miss."

"No family you can rely on?"

Before the girl could answer, Anna produced a quarter.

"I'm much obliged."

"Do you have a place to stay tonight?"

The young woman barely shook her head side to side.

Anna really didn't want to be bothered right now. But there was something raw and real about this person. Anna knew there was a vacancy at her boardinghouse. She wondered if Mrs. Pendleton would have mercy on this sorrowful soul and, at least, let her stay the night. Being that Anna had to work the next day, she would have little time to provide additional help. But she knew how it felt to be on the streets of Baltimore, alone.

"Come with me. I'll see if I can get you lodging tonight. Looks like it's going to rain." If worse came to worse, Anna would let the woman stay with her. There should be no problem; Anna occupied and paid for a double room with twin beds.

"If it won't be much trouble."

"None at all. What is your name?"

"Emmaline."

"I'm Anna. I work for the *Baltimore Herald*, taking pictures. What do you do?"

"Not much, really. I was going to school, but those years are behind me now."

"Just stepping out into the world, are you?"

"You could say that."

"What would you like to do? Are you trained for anything? I wasn't, but I made my own way."

"Well, I liked school very much. I'd love to be a teacher but that is not possible. I also enjoy cooking. Perhaps I could work in a restaurant."

"You don't look like a cook to me. You're too skinny. What's keeping you from getting a job, Emmaline?"

"Isn't it obvious?"

"Not to me. Can you do anything else?"

"Well, in school I was good with numbers. I can add and take away in my head without having to write anything down."

"That's what people call 'natural talent.'" I can't do numbers in my head. I envy you." That brought a demure smile to Emmaline's face.

The pair continued walking, sometimes chatting as they went, sometimes silent. They were almost to the boardinghouse when Anna noticed something unusual. "Where are your things, Emmaline? Don't you have a suitcase?"

"I have everything I need in this bag."

"But that's nothing more than a satchel. Where are your clothes and boots and..."

"Just this, I'm afraid."

Anna wondered what brought Emmaline to this juncture in her life. At that moment, Anna knew she had to help the young woman. Two blocks from home, Anna told Emmaline what to expect when they arrived at the boardinghouse.

"I really don't think this is going to work out," Emmaline said.

"Why not? Don't worry. Everything will be just fine. And tomorrow, you can get a fresh start."

The pair climbed the steps to the boardinghouse and walked in. It was suppertime, and the other residents were enjoying their meal in the dining room... fish stew and brown bread with pear tarts for dessert. Mrs. Pendleton, wiping her hands on her apron, reached the entry hall in a flurry.

"Anna, we waited dinner as long as possible. Please hurry before it gets... what have we here?"

"Mrs. Pendleton, this is Emmaline. She needs a place to stay tonight. If you don't have the vacant room ready, she can stay with me."

"We are not a hotel. We are a boardinghouse, with standards. Wouldn't she be more comfortable elsewhere?"

"If money is a problem, I will pay for her stay. It's only for one night."

"But, she's..." Mrs. Pendleton took Anna's arm and pulled her aside.

"She's what? A stranger? We were all strangers when we came here."

"She's colored," Mrs. Pendleton whispered.

"What does that matter?"

"We don't mix under one roof. Not at the dinner table and certainly not sharing bathrooms and beds."

"I don't mind."

"But the others will."

"Do you, Mrs. Pendleton?"

"Well, I... I... I can't do anything to cause my paying residents to suddenly up and leave."

"I'm a paying resident."

"And a handful at that. Always stirring the pot."

Mrs. Pendleton looked from Anna to Emmaline to the direction of the dining room.

"I see," Anna said.

Emmaline couldn't help but overhear the conversation.

"That's okay, ma'am. I'll go. Thank you, anyway."

"I'll hear none of it," Anna said.

Mrs. Pendleton asked Anna to keep her voice down. She didn't want the others leaving their dinners to see what the fuss was at the door.

"Here is what I will do, just for tonight. She can sleep in the maid's quarters downstairs. Since I sleep upstairs and do all the cleaning myself, I use the maid's room for sewing. But there's still a bed there and a washbasin. If she uses the chamber pot, she'll have to empty it and clean it herself... with bleach. I'll take her some supper. Anna, you join the ladies and don't say a word about this or I'll put you both out into the night."

"Agreed." Anna turned to Emmaline and said, "I told you everything would turn out just fine. I'll see you in the morning."

Emmaline said nothing. She followed Mrs. Pendleton to the back stairs. Anna sat down to a bowl of lukewarm stew, which she ate without acknowledging the other residents. Only Adelaide and Jane Catherine remained at the table. They had not experienced Anna's polite table banter a few nights before. And they would not this night. Anna was in no mood for reformation. She was upset that these women would have seen themselves above Emmaline.

"What are you looking so dour about?" Adelaide asked.

"Oh, she always looks dour," said Jane Catherine.

"You wouldn't understand," said Anna.

"Do you think us dolts?"

"I see you as unsympathetic, unable to put yourself in someone else's shoes."

"Well, if the shoes look like yours, always scuffed..." Adelaide's voice trailed off.

"It's a wonder H.L. Mencken keeps you on staff," said Jane Catherine.

"And what do you two do? Jane Catherine, aren't you a telegraph operator? Sitting in one place, sounding out code all day."

"I was hired for my graceful and fast fingers."

"And you, Adelaide, selling sheet music. Have you mastered the cash register yet?"

"I just engage the customer. Someone else rings up the sale."

"While I'm out in public all day, recording history. My pictures will be seen by generations to come. I will be immortal. Neither of you can say that."

"Oh yes, but you do a man's job. Will you be forever known as Andrew Bainbridge?"

Anna left the table before finishing her meal and removed herself from the room. It was too airless to think clearly.

"Look at that. It's a wonder she deems us worthy of a crumb of her brown bread," said Jane Catherine.

"And she didn't even take her dishes to the kitchen. Well, I'm not going to do it," said Adelaide.

"Neither am I. I have to save my delicate fingers for work," said Jane Catherine. Both women laughed as they leaned back in their chairs.

Later, as she prepared for bed, Anna regretted that she had told Emmaline everything would be okay. She meant it only in reference to having a place to sleep, out of the rain; she had failed to look at the larger picture. She wondered about this young woman, who must be down in the dark basement, feeling like a bowl of mixed emotions right now, ranging from fear to gratitude to worthlessness. She wanted to have a serious talk with this young woman.

When Anna awoke the next morning, Emmaline was gone.

"Well, at least she cleaned up after herself," Mrs. Pendleton said. "The room is spotless. And she left a cordial note of thanks on an old piece of paper. She'll get along."

"I'm not so sure. After what I experienced here last night, I fear for her well-being. Mrs. Pendleton, emancipation occurred decades ago. Why have things not changed?"

"Because change takes time."

"Time. What an ugly word. It takes time for women to be properly courted. It takes time for women to earn the right to vote. It takes time for people to accept that we are all equal human beings. Why does everything take so much time, when time is the one thing we have in short supply?"

"I don't know, Anna. I guess because time must brew like tea. It is worth the wait. And, just like a good Earl Gray, it has a soothing effect. It gives us the opportunity to reflect and grow. It heals when we are hurting. It makes us wiser. It hones our rough edges."

"Or makes them sharper."

"Yes, that too. People are imperfect. We need help to improve. Time is one source of help."

"That doesn't bode well for Emmaline."

"No, it doesn't. It doesn't bode well for a lot of people. Now, I must tend to breakfast. Will you set the table?"

Anna placed plates and bowls, glasses and teacups, silverware and napkins atop the lace tablecloth in the dining room. This morning the ladies would feast on cream toast and baked apples. Anna wondered how long Emmaline could eat on the quarter Anna had given her and who would serve her.

That day, wherever work took her, Anna kept a keen eye. She looked for Emmaline on the streets and in the shadows. Anna hoped she had found a place to stay among her own people and means to pay for it. It would be safer, for now. As night approached, she worried about this thin young woman and what might happen to her if she had no place to sleep. Now Anna understood how her father, Elizabeth, and Adrian had felt about her, alone on the streets for two days and one night, during the Great Baltimore Fire a few months earlier.

Anna had learned that time can be a valuable teacher, a lesson that can't be rushed.

Chapter 13

Anna participated in more and more suffrage marches. Somehow, she managed to keep her picture out of the newspaper. If she saw a photographer poised to click the shutter, she held a sign in front of her face or tilted her head down, allowing her hat to hide her identity. She was not ashamed of her allegiance to suffrage. She was concerned about repercussions.

Anna knew anonymity would prevent Papa from seeing his daughter "debase the family name," as he put it when displeased with her behavior. She also knew H.L. Mencken would not see her participating in anything political. He had often stressed to his staff that journalists must be impartial and should not reveal their affiliations.

Even with these restraints, Anna felt pleased with life. She was living on her own, thinking for herself, taking part in the community of women while working in a so-called "man's" job. At the most recent suffrage meeting, she received a "Votes for Women" pin, which she wore proudly when not working but never on her visits with Papa and Elizabeth. However, she could not elude criticism; it awaited her at the boardinghouse.

"This is not the way to find a husband, Anna," Adelaide said.

"What do you mean?"

"Wearing a pin like that. You are practically saying to men, 'I'm more important than you.'"

"No, I'm not. I'm saying women are *just* as important as men."

"And you expect a man to marry a woman who thinks such nonsense?"

"I'm not looking for a husband," Anna replied. "And I'll have you know, there are plenty of men supporting suffrage."

"Every young lady is looking for a husband, to take care of her and make decisions and leave her to womanly things. Then, again... maybe you are not a lady. After all, you wear men's clothing. Perhaps, you are another kind of woman."

"What kind is that?"

"Don't be coy. You know what I'm talking about. They are called inverts... lesbians."

"I've never heard those terms before."

"They are women who like women. Do you understand what I am trying to say?"

"No. I like women. I just don't like women who talk of things that don't matter to me, like fashion and being subordinate to a man."

"No, Anna. I mean women liking women the way a man and a woman like, or should I say, love each other?"

"I've never heard of such a thing. Next, you'll tell me there are men who like men that way, too."

"There are."

"And how would you know?"

"I am a woman of the world," Adelaide said. "I was educated in Europe and traveled extensively, exploring art and learning about people who created it. Even now, I continue to expand my horizons. I go to Ford's Theater, where all kinds of characters are portrayed. I'm well-read on a variety of subjects. I am what might be referred to as 'enlightened' in the ways of the world."

"Then what are you doing in this boardinghouse? It's nice but it's not The Belvedere."

"My parents separated while I was away. They live far apart now. I didn't want to choose one over the other, so I struck out on my own. Neither of them supports me. Still, I am quite experienced for a woman of my age."

"Well, I am not. Though, it might come as a surprise to you, Adelaide... that I was once engaged to be married. Can you say that about yourself?"

"What, you? To whom?"

"That is no concern of yours. But I chose to focus on a career in photography. And that didn't fit in with my fiancé's designs for marriage. He wanted children, a large family."

"Well, I'll be. I never would have thought you'd get swept up in romance."

"Now you know. Why you always seem to focus your attentions on me, I cannot fathom. Are you that kind of woman?"

Adelaide's face turned red. "Of course not."

"In the future, please keep your opinion of me to yourself. And I will do the same concerning you. Except to tell you here and now, all of your education and so-called 'enlightenment' have not provided the 'finishing' necessary of every young lady, no matter whom she loves."

"And what would that be?"

"Manners and dignity. You have neither."

"Look in the mirror, Anna."

"At least I recognize my faults and try to work on them. Goodnight."

Anna went to bed completely confused. She didn't sleep well at all. The next day, she went to the grave of Mayor McLane in Green Mount Cemetery. For a reason unclear to her, she was drawn to his resting place. Perhaps it was the quiet or the finality of death that lured her. She felt she could find solace and answers there. A simple headstone now marked the spot where the mayor found his own peace in death. Anna stood above the grave and mused, as if Mayor McLane could provide the advice she craved. She wondered...

When a person dies, the earth opens up to receive their body. Does it also reveal its truth to their soul? Does everything become crystalline? After all, it's in dirt that life begins... the flowers and trees and the harvest. Does Mayor McLane, in death, find life?

And then there were the thoughts Adelaide had put in her head. Anna wished her mother were still alive to help her through life's challenges and difficulties. Would she have been able to discuss matters with her? Anna would never know. Her mother died when she was two.

Women who like women. What does that mean? Anna thought. Anna liked Josefina but only as a friend. Not the way she had loved Adrian.

Then Anna pondered the obvious affection between Frances Benjamin Johnston and Miss Hewitt. She thought maybe they were more than friends. Did they kiss? How did they express their love? They couldn't marry or have children. What was the point?

Anna stayed at the gravesite a long time, thinking about life's complications and how isolated from worldly ways she had been growing up. What else didn't she know?

Her mind meandered to Adrian. Yes, she had loved him. Yes, she had wanted to marry him once upon a time. But she also wanted a career in photojournalism. And, yes, she felt there might be a man somewhere, maybe not in Baltimore, who would accept Anna as she was, with all her quirks and impatience, and time-consuming career. They could marry and maybe not have any children or only one. That wouldn't be so bad.

Anna looked at the grave of Mayor McLane and wished he had taken time to think things through. Perhaps, he wouldn't have ended his life.

Anna pledged to be open to all of life's possibilities. At the moment, she didn't feel that she liked women in that way, or that she should be thought of in that way just because she wore men's clothes at work. She saw her suit as a uniform, not a declaration.

She had no opinion, one way or the other, about people who did love their own gender. That was their business. It did not belong to her and certainly not to Adelaide.

CHAPTER 14

On a cool January morning, a month later, Anna raced down Pratt Street on her bicycle. A man stepped off the sidewalk into her path. Anna was traveling too fast to safely avoid him or come to an abrupt stop. Just as she was about to hit the man, he saw her and jumped back on the curb. Anna stepped on the brakes about a half block away and turned around to reproach the man.

"What's wrong with..." Anna began.

"Pardon me, sir," the man interrupted. "I was distracted and I..."

"Sam? Is that you?"

"That's my name. Have we met? I don't seem to remember."

"It's me, Anna, Anna Bainbridge. Adrian's, ah, fiancée, several months back."

"Anna? Yes, it is you. Why are you dressed in a man's suit and vest?"

"I'm a newspaper photographer now, working for the *Baltimore Herald*. I figure, if I have to compete with men for the best pictures, I need to dress as one to blend in. I want no special favors or disapproval because of my gender."

"I see. Well..."

"How is Adrian? Do you still work together at the Post Office?"

"... if you will excuse me..."

"You don't seem happy to see me. Have I said or done something wrong?"

"No. I just need to get home to my wife and daughter. Lillian is with child again, our second."

"That's wonderful. Congratulations."

"Thank you. I'm very proud of my wife. She has embraced marriage and motherhood completely and selflessly."

"Oh, that's it. You're upset because I broke my engagement with Adrian to pursue a career."

"He pines for you still. Do you ever think of him?"

"I wish him all the best that life can bring."

"That's not enough. I must say, as his friend, I find it painful to watch him suffer. Oh, he sees other young ladies from time to time but they are not you."

"Would it have been better if we had gone through with marriage, only to discover it a mistake for both of us?"

"In marriage, one must always make concessions. There is no room for selfish goals."

"I couldn't agree more. But why must it always be the woman who yields?"

"It doesn't have to be that way. Marriage is a daily exercise in give and take."

"And you think Adrian did all the giving and I, all the taking."

"I really must go. This is no concern of mine. Again, I apologize for stepping out in front..."

Another person caught Anna's eye.

"Emmaline! Emmaline! Wait! Sam, I have to go."

Anna whisked her bike past Sam, almost knocking him down in her haste. She wasn't about to let the very girl she had been searching for slip away.

"Emmaline, it's me, Anna."

Sam's eyes followed Anna. He scowled, then looked both ways before crossing the street. Meanwhile, Anna caught up with Emmaline, who was standing on the sidewalk, looking quizzical.

"Oh, I didn't recognize you, dressed as you are."

"I'm so glad I found you. Whew! I'm out of breath. Can we sit down a moment? There's a bench over there. Where have you been? What have you been doing? You left the boardinghouse so quickly, without a word. I've been worried about you."

Anna gave no thought to the rudeness of her brusque departure from Sam just moments earlier or her insinuation into Emmaline's life now.

"I haven't much to say. I take odd jobs here and there, cooking and cleaning. There is a board at the main Post Office that lists available day work."

"Does that mean that each day you never know if you are going to have an income?"

"Yes, some weeks are good, others are not."

"Where do you sleep at night?"

"Wherever I can, mostly churches. I've learned they are usually left unlocked."

"Well, we can do better than that. Let me give this some thought. Can you meet me here tomorrow at 10:00 A.M.?"

"I have to work."

"When are you free?"

"Uhm, well, Saturday. You know, you really don't have to..."

"Saturday at 10:00, it is."

Anna went back to her room at the boardinghouse. She didn't stay long. She had an idea. After rummaging through her bedside table, she found the key to Emmaline's future, a business card, the one Ida R. Cummings had given her a month before.

Mrs. Pendleton's boardinghouse had a telephone. Her home was one of the earliest to be fitted with electricity. Residents could only use the phone with permission. Each call was recorded on a ledger and, at the end of the month, the cost was tallied and attached to the rent bill.

Anna told the operator the number of the "Colored Empty Stocking and Fresh Air Circle" on Druid Hill Avenue in north Baltimore.

"May I speak to Miss Cummings? This is Anna Bainbridge. She might remember me from a *Baltimore Herald* article I worked on."

After a moment, a familiar voice came over the line. "How nice to hear from you again, Miss Bainbridge. We received an overwhelming number of donations after the *Herald's* story. Are you working on another?"

"No, not at this time. Miss Cummings, I'm calling as a private citizen today. Are you hiring?"

"Why? Have you left the newspaper?"

"No, ma'am. It's not about me. I have a friend. She's in need of work. She's very good with numbers and could possibly help you with your accounts."

"As it turns out, with all the donations we've been receiving, I could use a competent bookkeeper."

"Wonderful. There's one other thing."

"What is it?"

"She has no work experience in accounting and no home. But she's good with numbers, I assure you."

"Oh, I see. Well, I really don't..."

"Will you at least talk to her? I'll pay her fare to get there. I'll even come with her."

"You sound earnest. I like that. Very well, how about Monday at 9:00 A.M.?"

"I have a work assignment then. Can we make it at 4:30?"

"That's fine. I look forward to seeing you both."

On Saturday at 10:00 A.M., Emmaline waited on the bench for Anna, who arrived in a flurry of excitement.

"Good news. I have secured an interview for you, a real position, working with numbers. You said you were good at counting, right?"

"Well, yes. Where is this position?"

"Now don't get discouraged. It's northwest of the city about two miles from here. You could walk in good weather or the trolley can take you partway there. The tracks on the west side were not damaged by the fire. You should have no problem. Maybe you could find lodging nearby and wouldn't have to worry about travel."

Anna was surprised to see Emmaline looking forlorn rather than happy.

"What's the matter?"

"It seems so far away. I'm just now starting to find steadier work downtown."

"I'm helping you and you are turning me down?"

"No, no, that's not it. Give me time to think about this. I'm concerned about where I might find closer lodging."

"Well, if you don't want my..."

"No, I really do appreciate your thoughtfulness. I'm sorry. It's just that I'm not used to people doing for me. This is happening so quickly."

"I do things quickly. And I'm not going to leave you high and dry. I'll take you there myself. Does that make you feel better?"

On Monday at 4:30 P.M., Anna and Emmaline met with Miss Cummings. She excused Anna so that she could give Emmaline an arithmetic test. About a half hour later, the two women joined Anna with smiles on their faces.

"Well? What happened? I'm dying from anticipation," Anna said.

"I'm happy to announce that I have just hired Emmaline as a bookkeeper, three days a week."

"Oh, I'm so happy for you both."

"And she will reside with my secretary a few blocks away, for the time being."

"Emmaline, see? I told you everything would turn out just fine."

On the ride home, Anna said, "Now you have a real career and the rest of the week, you can take day jobs. You'll have an income you can depend on, and a place to stay. I think we should celebrate. Let's dine in a fine restaurant tonight. I will pay for us both."

"Oh, no. That cannot happen."

"Why not?"

Emmaline gazed out the handsome cab's window for a while before speaking. She seemed to be holding back tears. "Miss Anna, have you ever heard of the Kerbin 'Jim Crow' Law?"

"The what?"

"It's a law here in Maryland, named for William G. Kerbin. He's a politician from the eastern side of Maryland, a place called Worcester County. He got a law passed that says my people cannot mix with your people on boats and railroads, not in seating, not in dining, not in bedding for the night."

"What does that have to do with us eating together in a restaurant on land?"

"It's an unwritten law, an extension of the Kerbin Law. There are certain implied behaviors."

"You mean you and I can't have supper together because I'm white and you're colored? But there are colored cooks and busboys at restaurants."

"That's different. They are workers, not customers. We also cannot live in the same boardinghouse."

"What about sharing this handsome cab?"

"The driver probably thinks I am your maid."

"No wonder Mrs. Pendleton was upset when I asked if you could stay that night."

"I tried to tell you."

"I can't believe it. Emmaline, I am so sorry."

"That's water under the bridge. I know you meant well."

The two rode in silence for a while. Then Anna spoke. "See this pin on my lapel?"

"Yes."

"It says 'Votes for Women.' I've been supporting suffrage for several months now. Do you think colored women will get the vote, too, someday?"

"I don't know. I doubt it."

"Why do you say that? It could become law that all women can vote."

"What the law says and what really happens are often two separate things, Miss Anna. Many colored men still can't vote. White folks find reasons to stop them."

"There's no need to be formal with me. We are two young ladies out in the world, becoming friends, I hope. Just call me Anna."

"As you wish. Have you really looked at suffrage, at the ladies who march in the streets and attend meetings?"

"Of course. I join them as often as I can. I even bought a white dress. White symbolizes suffrage."

"Yes, I know. Have you noticed that there are no coloreds among them?"

Anna thought a minute, then looked aside. "No," she said quietly.

"That's because there are two separate groups of women fighting for suffrage, colored and white. The white suffragists are striving for one goal... to earn women the right to vote."

"Isn't that what you want, too?"

"Yes, but colored suffragists want something more... to fight racism and these 'Jim Crow' laws. White groups don't want us in their ranks because they think we will water down their singular message and even shame it."

"Just because of the color of your skin?"

"Yes, and the suffragists up north here don't want to rile the southern white suffragists, who wouldn't want us to get the vote under any circumstance."

"I can't believe it. I've lived such a sheltered life all these years. Forgive me. My eyes are just opening for the first time." Anna looked distraught.

"If you still want to share supper, I know a place where we will not be bothered," Emmaline said.

Anna gave the driver the address Emmaline whispered to her. The driver looked aghast and said, "Are you sure? It's quite a distance in the opposite direction. There's also a toll to pay."

"I'll give you the money. Now drive," Anna said.

The carriage turned east for a couple of miles, then north on the Falls Turnpike, a dirt road that ran through wooded areas, rolling hills, and small villages. The driver slowed to a stop at one of these hamlets, nothing more than a clump of houses on one side of the road and a schoolhouse on the other. A church sat nearby.

"Is this where you want to be, ma'am?" the driver said.

Emmaline nodded to Anna.

"Yes, it is," Anna said.

"Will you be long?"

"Probably an hour."

"I'm not waiting. Not here. You're on your own."

As soon as Anna and Emmaline disembarked, the driver turned around and headed back down the turnpike. He didn't even ask for toll fare.

"Well, where are we, Emmaline?"

"This is my home. This is where my family lives."

"I thought you didn't have a home or family."

"Yes, I do. You never allowed me time to tell you. This is the village of Bare Hills. It was founded by a colored man a long time ago. He called it Scott's Settlement. It's where many colored families have lived peacefully among white neighbors for generations. We look out for each other."

"Why don't you still live here?"

"There are not many opportunities for good-paying jobs here. My father is getting up in years and cannot move around well. He only works part of the time. My mother takes in laundry and raises the younger kids. I'm the oldest. I moved to the city for my finishing education at my parents' insistence. They want a better life for all their children. I was most grateful. A former neighbor, who moved downtown, took me in, gave me elocution lessons, and saw that I went to The Colored High and Training School."

"Where is that?"

"On the corner of Pennsylvania Avenue and Dolphin Street. After graduation, I decided to stay in the city in hopes of finding work that offered decent wages I could send home. Please, let's walk as we talk. Our house is only a short distance from here."

"Why aren't you still living with that woman?"

"She went blind from diabetes and moved in with her sister in Virginia."

They walked past houses where people sat on porches and chatted, offering pleasantries to passersby. A little boy took one look, however, and ran away.

"Do you mean to tell me that you send home all of your money and keep none for yourself?"

"I've survived, with help from others, like you. My family is poor. They need every penny. I am young and strong and able."

"Emmaline!" a woman's voice rang out.

"Mama!"

A woman as thin as Emmaline moved as if trying to run, but only managed a fast, unsteady walk.

"Cornelius come runnin' up on the porch, all outta breath, and told me you was here. I can't believe m'eyes. It's been a month a Sundays."

Anna and Emmaline became the center of attention at dinner, ham bits cooked with poke the kids pulled from the hill, and corn pone. Anna had never tasted this kind of food, so simple, earthy, salty.

After dinner, resting on the front porch, the group eased into a quiet feeling of self-satisfaction. Anna softly said, "Tell me about your village."

Emmaline's mother, Emma, spoke. "It all goes back to one brave man, a slave, named Tobias Scott. He was taken in Africa and put on a slave ship bound for St. Mary's County. And, 'long the way, there was what you'd call a mut'ny on that ship. The slaves done tried to overtake the white mastas. They meant to kill the captain. But Tobias, he stepped in and saved that man."

"Why? The captain was taking them all into slavery."

"I guess he understood that life means somethin', anybody's life. And that man paid him back kindly. He made a pledge that Tobias was to be a free man onest they reached land. And all his begotten was to be free. And he kept that promise, even though he was a white man."

"How did Tobias get here to Bare Hills?"

"It wasn't Tobias, but his son, Aquila, who moved here for work. Ya' see, the government, they was clearin' the way for the Falls Turnpike and needed hired hands. Reverend Aquila was a blacksmith and a wheelwright, when he wasn't preachin'. He he'ped take care of the wagons and horses that got the workers and their supplies here. The road was needed on account'a all the chromite minin' goin' on. That's why they changed the name to Bare Hills. Aquila had money from his pa and bought land here, two whole acres. That man was also a mighty fine preacher and did some serious whoopin' of the gospel. Eve'body loved him. I can show ya' his house up there on the hill. He done built it with his big, strong hands. And then he'ped other folks do the same. He died at the pulpit, right in the middle of a sermon. Can you believe that? I guess he wouldn't a had it any other way."

"I noticed some white families playing in yards with their children," Anna said.

"Yes, ma'am. Bare Hills has always been both colored and white. And we git along jest fine. That's the way Reverend Aquila wanted it. That's the way Tobias woulda' wanted it. That's respectin' his memory. The rest of the world should pay heed. It can be done."

"And your children go to the same school as white children, the one on the other side of the turnpike?"

"Well, I can't say as that's true. There's still some crossin' over that needs be done. That school you seen there on Falls Turnpike is white. We send our youngins to the public school over the city line about a mile up the road. Look at my Emmaline, goin' on ta git a high school education on top of it. Now she's livin' the city life on her own. Doin' us proud."

Anna wasn't about to reveal that Emmaline was living on the streets and keeping no money for herself. She was proud of her, too, in a different sense.

"Emmaline has some good news for you. Why are you waiting? Go ahead, tell them."

A moment's hesitation discomfited Anna. It was obvious Emmaline had wanted to tell her family in her own way and in her own time, but Anna had already tipped her hat. So, she spoke of her new job humbly and revealed what it could mean to the family's purse. There was much kissing and hugging.

When the hoopla died down, Anna spoke. "How have women made a living staying here?" Anna regretted asking the question as soon as the words left her mouth.

"Cleanin' rich folks' homes, mostly. They's a lot of big houses hidden amongst them trees. And washin' and ironin' rich folks' laundry. The men work the road still. The turnpike's movin' north."

After pleasant goodbyes and a promise to return, Anna stepped into a horse-drawn cart and was driven by Emma's cousin to the northernmost end of the trolley line. There, she took the long ride back downtown. Emmaline had decided to stay with her family for the weekend. Her cousin had offered to see her to her new job on Monday. As Emmaline looked forward to her future, Anna looked back at her life of privilege, shelter and ignorance.

She wondered if white people ever married coloreds. They lived in the same neighborhood. Why wouldn't they? What would their children look like? How would they be received by society? How would God judge them? How would God judge women who liked women and men who liked men?

Anna's mind became a hodgepodge of notions and reflections and religious rumination as she journeyed back to the boardinghouse. She stared out the trolley window. The night was dark and cloudless and, in the heavens, stars glistened with knowledge of the entire universe. Raw diamond nuggets burst with righteousness. And that was something Anna could not capture on film or even figure out in her own head.

Chapter 15

Anna invited herself to dinner with Elizabeth. She was greeted at the door by a wide smile and open arms. "Anna, I'm so happy to see you."

When Anna entered the dining room, she froze. "Papa, I didn't expect to find you here. What a pleasant surprise."

With no more affection than a gentle touch on the shoulder, Anna's father said, "I've already supped. I will be leaving soon for the hospital."

"Oh, I see. Do you have a few moments to talk?"

"Of course. How have you been faring?"

"Wonderfully. I'm learning so much about living on my own and working as a photographer and about life and the many interesting people who have experienced things I never knew existed."

"I hope you are not becoming too worldly."

"No, sir. You still don't trust me, do you?"

"I do, Anna. I don't trust other people. You must understand, at the hospital, I see patients who have made imprudent choices, resulting in injury and disease that can ruin their lives."

"I have done nothing of the kind, I assure you."

"Then, tell me what has been so captivating."

"Well, I've made a friend in one of the young ladies living at the boardinghouse. She is a seamstress." Anna intentionally omitted Josefina's affiliation with the theater. "And I've made another friend. She is an accountant for a benevolent organization that helps so many needy people." Again, Anna left out one thing, the color of Emmaline's skin.

"Well, that's sounds promising. I approve. And now, I must be off."

Anna pushed herself into an embrace, which her father reciprocated awkwardly. He offered her a cursory smile. After he left, Anna turned to Elizabeth in the kitchen. "Why is Papa so cold-eyed?"

"Your father is exposed to life's most tragic circumstances. They tear at the very fabric that holds families together, that rips husbands from wives and parents from children."

"You mean death?"

"Yes, and he still, after all these years, mourns the loss of your mother."

"Poor Papa."

"I'm glad you feel compassion for him. He is a great man, helping to save as many lives as possible and returning patients to their loved ones whenever he can. It isn't easy when someone under his care dies. He fears losing you, not to death but to the world."

"Why doesn't he show affection for me?"

"It's difficult for him. As a doctor, he must remain somewhat distant from his patients. Too much personal involvement can make loss even greater. I guess that carries over to his home life."

"I wish he could love me the way a father should."

"I know. I know, dear. Are you hungry? I've made Shepherd's Pie."

"You've read my mind."

During dinner, Anna confessed that she had left out important information about one of her friendships. Elizabeth already knew that Josefina worked in the theater. Thankfully, she had said nothing to Papa. But Elizabeth knew nothing of Emmaline. She wasn't taken aback by the news, at all. "Why didn't you tell your father the whole truth?"

"I was afraid he'd make me move back home."

"You must understand that he treats all his patients equally, regardless of the color of their skin. He would never turn anyone away due to their race. The same is true in his private life."

"I didn't think of that."

"I'm surprised you were so timid with your father. Part of maturing is standing up for your convictions. And being unafraid to proclaim them. Do you see?"

"I think so."

"You're usually outspoken. Why be silent now? I, for one, am proud of your friendship with... what is her name?"

"Emmaline, and she works so hard to help her family. Do you think I could invite her here for dinner or supper?"

"I would agree in a moment. But I cannot without informing your father. It would not be proper to welcome any of your friends here without his knowledge. Loyalty comes in many forms, you know."

"Would you talk to him for me?"

"I think, as a grownup young lady, you should ask him yourself. Perhaps, place a note on his desk before you leave."

"I'll do it. Thank you, Elizabeth."

Through Shepherd's Pie and a delicious Scottish cranachan, Anna talked nonstop about Emmaline.

"May I ask you one question?" Elizabeth said. "Why are you inviting your friend here? Don't you think the ostentation in the art alone, much less the fine furniture, will make her own surroundings seem more austere? Are you trying to put on airs?"

"I didn't think of that possibility. It's just that her family was so kind and gracious to me, I want to return the favor."

"Let's invite Emmaline to tea and sit in the garden. It will be more relaxing and comfortable. We can enjoy the early spring flowers."

"Will Papa still need to know?"

"Yes. I'm sure he won't mind at all."

A few days later, Elizabeth sent a note to Anna informing her of Papa's approval. Anna couldn't wait to invite Emmaline, who quickly accepted. On a soft, sunny afternoon, Anna, Emmaline and Elizabeth enjoyed pots of tea, warm asparagus soup, Melba toast with butter, egg salad finger sandwiches, and an assortment of bonbons.

They talked of freshness in the air and the pleasure of dining outside. And they admired the roses and daffodils, with their pleasing combination of pink and yellow. Anna wondered what nature was trying to express. So many contrasts in color, swaying harmoniously in the breeze, looking all the more beautiful combined.

After Emmaline left, Anna helped Elizabeth clear the table. "What do you think of my new friend?"

"I was quite impressed. She is poised, ladylike and seems eager to improve her station. In some ways, she reminds me of me, although, as a white woman, I never had to face prejudice."

"What do you mean?"

"Well, it's a long story."

"You have to tell me now, I'm intrigued."

"Very well. When I was not much older than you, I was on my own in the world and needed work and a place to live. I had been serving as a housekeeper for an elderly woman. When she realized she was dying, she wrote a letter of recommendation for me so I could find another situation. And that's how I came to live here. I remember it as if it were yesterday. When I arrived at this house, I met your father first."

"Was he stern and unfriendly then?"

"A little. Your mother was still alive. She kept his spirits somewhat high. Your mother was delicate in nature, I was soon to learn. My hands shook as I gave your father my letter of recommendation. He did nothing to ease my tension. He noted, 'It says here you were never ill or ill-tempered. You look rather frail and dour to me.'"

"I can just hear him now," Anna said.

"I assured him I was capable. He said, 'It also states here that you are trustworthy; you can read, write and put numbers on a ledger, and cook, among other things. That you spent time reading to your mistress, discussing important topics, and nursed her when she was dying. How is it that a servant girl of few means found her way to such elevation?' I told him that, even though I came from humble beginnings, my parents pushed me toward a better life."

"That's just like Emmaline."

"Exactly. To please my parents, I worked hard as a young student and always had my head in a book late at night. I read until the candlelight burned my eyes. And being the eldest of eight, I learned from my mother how to care for my brothers and sisters when they were sick. My mother taught me the importance of competence and compassion."

"Why, then, were you so strict with me?"

"I raised you in accordance with your father's demands. I softened things whenever I could. Don't you remember?"

"Yes, I do." Anna took a sip of tea. "Why didn't you become a writer or a banker?"

"In my time, those positions were not easily attainable by most women. The suffrage movement was just getting started."

"How did you find out that Papa needed help?"

"I answered an advertisement for a housekeeper who would live in. What I really wanted to be was a teacher and I told your father so."

"And he still hired you?"

"Yes, he expanded my duties to include taking care of you, seeing to your studies and upbringing. So, I guess, I got my wish after all. I remember his words... 'A high moral standard is exactly what we need these days. How would you like to be more than housekeeper here? Would you also serve as nanny to my daughter?' I accepted the offer right away."

"Without meeting me, without even knowing my name?"

"Yes, I moved in immediately. You were so tiny, not yet two years old. I fell in love with you at first sight. But your father often impressed one important mandate—that education in a girl came secondary to instilling humility and grace and dignity. Your mother was assigned to your religious training. She'd read the Bible to you just before bed. Of course, you were too young to understand."

"Well, I guess I wasn't such a great student in those regards."

"I learned pretty quickly that you could be a bit brattish. Still, you charmed me. I never married. I never had children of my own. Soon after, your mother died and I became your mother, at least in my mind."

Anna turned pensive. She watched Elizabeth put on her apron and start to wash the dishes. Anna helped tie the strings behind her nanny's back. "Elizabeth, I'm going to visit you more often. I'm going to take you to supper at a fine restaurant and then we'll see a show at Ford's. What do you think of that?"

"I think an imp is trying to make amends," Elizabeth said with smile. "And I accept. I want to see what these Floradora girls are all about."

CHAPTER 16

Two days later, Emmaline sent notes of appreciation to Anna and Elizabeth. Anna was taken by the simple act of saying "thank you" and how it could make the sender, as well as the receiver, feel as good as the promise of the season.

She regretted that she had not thought to send a note of gratitude to Emmaline's mother. She sent one anyway, thinking, *Better late than never.*

Anna had been greatly pleased with her Papa for allowing Emmaline into her life and his home. He was softening, she realized, especially compared to just a year prior, when he tried to control Anna's associations and courtships. He had been determined Anna must be just like her mother, Victoria (named for the great queen of his homeland), whom he lost to scarlet fever when Anna was two. Oh, how Anna had wanted to know her mother. She tried to get Papa to open up so many times. It would have made a lovely present on her eighteenth birthday. When the day arrived, there was no such gift wrapped in a ribbon of memories.

After enjoying a quiet dinner with Elizabeth, who gave her a hand-embroidered handkerchief to mark the occasion, Anna had retreated to her room with its canopied bed, Asian rug, and Georgian-style fireplace. She stretched out on the pillowed window seat, her favorite spot for dreaming, and conjured a different life, one filled with adventure and fun and, most of all, freedom.

She had never been to the Baltimore Zoo. She had never taken a boat ride on the lake at Patterson Park. She had never even eaten in a restaurant.

While Anna was daydreaming, she heard a knock on her bedroom door.

"It's Papa. May I come in?"

"Certainly," she said, standing at attention, as if ready for inspection.

"You are eighteen now. It's time you seriously started courting. It's time you became a wife. There is a highly suitable medical student I'm teaching. He shows promise in heart surgery, an emerging field of medicine. His work could prove quite lucrative and prestigious. I think he will make an agreeable husband for you. I've invited this young man to dine with us next Sunday. You will wear a simple frock, little adornment, and you will be on your most-guarded behavior. Do you understand? I don't want you to ruin this possibility, as you have with others I've provided. I think he is the one. Do I make myself clear?"

"I love you" would have been a more welcome gift.

Anna didn't protest; she knew it was useless. However, just like the few other arranged dinners with medical students Papa had brought home to meet her, she would sabotage this one, too, only without Papa being the wiser.

On Sunday, Anna donned her most conservative attire and arranged her hair in a tight chignon with Elizabeth's help.

"I know you don't like these encounters, but your father is only looking out for your future."

Elizabeth held Anna's gaze for about ten seconds after saying this before the two of them burst into laughter.

"Oh, Elizabeth, if only you were my mother."

"Don't say that. You had a mother, God rest her soul."

"You know what I mean. You could intercede for me."

"I am only hired help. I don't have the authority."

"I know. I'm sorry. Such a foolish thought."

"Promise me you'll behave. Promise me you'll not put a frog in his straw hat or spill Hollandaise sauce on his jacket. Really, how could you?"

Once again, the nanny and her charge stared at each other before a fit of giggles broke their composure over Anna's past transgressions.

Anna put her left hand to heart, lifted her right and pronounced, "I, Anna Bainbridge, will not put a frog in the *young man's hat. Nor will I spill Hollandaise sauce on his jacket."*

"Good, now I must get back to the kitchen or we will not have a meal to share with your guest."

Just as Elizabeth was leaving, Papa entered the room. "Let me look at you. Yes, that will do. We don't want to give the wrong impression."

"What was Mama like when you courted her? Did she wear dark colors? Was she unadorned? Or did she wear pink ruffles and blue bows and..."

"Enough of this. You know I don't like to speak of your mother."

"Why? Can't I even know what she looked like?"

"It's time to go downstairs. Your suitor will arrive soon."

His name was William and he was perfectly normal, polite, intelligent... and boring. He spoke only of something called aortic coarctation, a dangerous narrowing of an artery that could be fixed with a new surgical procedure. Talk of opening one's chest, talk of throbbing chambers, talk of clamping blood flow... while consuming saddle of lamb and Oysters Rockefeller!

After forcing down a lump of fried hominy with currant jelly, Anna could hold her tongue no longer. "Tell me, Doctor, what's it like to feel a person's heart beating in your hands? Do you picture yourself God?"

"Anna! You speak blasphemy! Apologize this instant," Papa said, his face turning as sanguine as the wine.

"It's perfectly all right, Dr. Bainbridge," the young man interjected, without a hint of outrage. "Your daughter asks a valid question. Miss Anna, I am not a full-fledged doctor yet and am only able to watch surgery from over the shoulder. I haven't actually held a beating heart in my hand. But I imagine the experience will humble me. I will not feel like God. I am just his servant. He will guide my hands."

"Well said, young man. Did you hear that, Anna? You could use a little humility yourself. You have much to learn from this fine fellow."

"I am more than happy to oblige in teaching Miss Anna anything she wants to learn about anatomy."

Anna's gaze met William's. She could have sworn there was a sparkle of lechery in his eyes.

"I am sorry," Anna said. "My apologies to you both."

Elizabeth cleared the dishes and brought out a simple pudding. The doctor and his student soon retreated to the den to continue their discourse on all matters of the heart.

Anna sat in the parlor, drinking tea with Elizabeth, waiting for William to take his leave so she could bid him farewell before retiring to her room. Hours passed with the two men remaining behind closed doors. Finally, Elizabeth woke Anna with a gentle touch. The poor girl had fallen asleep, slumped on the settee.

"Go to bed now," Elizabeth whispered. "I'm sure your father and the young man won't mind."

Elizabeth went to the kitchen to put things in order, leaving Anna alone in the parlor. She noticed William's hat and coat on the chair next to the door.

Papa's probably arranging the nuptials now. Time for sabotage, Anna thought. Maybe not a frog or Hollandaise sauce, but I didn't promise not to do anything else, did I?

At midnight, Dr. Bainbridge sent Anna's suitor off with an expensive cigar and a pat on the back. When William got home, he shook the outdoor mist from his coat and hat. A small piece of paper floated out of his hatband. He picked it up and observed a note written in feminine hand, punctuated with the scent of rose water. For a moment, his own heart skipped a beat. He read the brief missive. But the words were not those of an ardent lady.

William,

My beating heart will never be placed in your hands, no matter what my father commands me or promises you. I would rather it stop throbbing altogether. Let neither of us fool the other. I know your affection would always be tied to Papa's bankroll and his ability to advance your career, rather than to me.

Happy to be "Miss" Anna

If Papa wondered why the young medical student suddenly transferred to a teaching hospital out of state, he never uttered a word. In private, Elizabeth and Anna giggled into their handkerchiefs.

CHAPTER 17

In early 1906, the National American Woman Suffrage Convention was held in Baltimore at the Lyric Music Hall on Mt. Vernon Avenue, just north of downtown. Women from all over the United States converged from February 7-13. It was the 38th annual convention and a noteworthy one, for it would be the last for its most-important member, Susan B. Anthony, who was eighty-six years old.

Anna took an assignment to photograph the convention, a job she coveted. She received rare access to powerful people and felt privileged to find herself in the company of women who were rewriting history.

The event started on the first day with a prayer, followed by the singing of "America." Then Anna's friend and suffrage mentor, Emma Maddox Funck, welcomed everyone to her expanding city.

Over the next few days, women shared ideas on their roles in politics, the workplace, and as wage earners whose paychecks helped determine their futures.

On the final day, the esteemed Susan B. Anthony gave her speech to rousing applause. To close the event, the sister of Emma Maddox Funck, Miss Etta H. Maddox, sang a solo rendition of "Battle Hymn of the Republic."

Anna took pride in seeing her pictures in the *Baltimore Herald*, a permanent imprint of her contribution to the cause. Soon after, her newspaper would allow some of Anna's photographs to be used in books, such as *The History of Woman Suffrage*, written by several leaders, including Elizabeth Cady Stanton. Also, *Jus Suffragii*, written by the International Woman Suffrage Alliance. Anna's resumé lengthened impressively.

Not long after the convention, with Anna's mood soaring, she was summoned to H.L. Mencken's office. From the look on his face, Anna knew her good humor was about to crash back down to earth. She spoke first. "Mr. Mencken. You should have seen all the women at the convention. Young women, like me, joining the suffrage movement. People are saying this was the most impressive suffrage convention ever held. I'm sure you know what that means for Maryland. We are becoming the center of the..."

"Miss Bainbridge, I'll come directly to the point. The *Baltimore Herald* has been bought. Two newspaper publishers have purchased the paper's assets and will fold the operation into their own business. In short, the paper is about to print its last edition under its current masthead. I informed most of the staff while you were out of the building."

"What does that mean?"

"It means that, once the transaction is complete, you are all out of work."

"And you?"

"I have secured a position with *The Sun*."

"What about me?"

"What about you?"

"What will happen to me? Where will I go? Can't you take me with you?"

"I am your employer, not your guardian. You will have to find your own way."

"Aren't there any positions for photographers at *The Sun*?"

"Not at the moment."

"This is quite a shock. I'm actually frightened. My hands are shaking."

"This is no time for emotion. It is a time for evaluation and action. You are standing at a crossroads, young lady. You have any number of avenues you can walk to improve your livelihood. This could be a fortuitous opportunity for you. Or you can stand still and wallow in your own misfortune. Which do you choose? You align yourself with strong women, yet you oftentimes act as a ninny."

"I thought I would always be working here."

"There is a relatively new paper in Baltimore called *The Daily Record*. They publish news about business and legal matters."

"Yes, I've read it. My father sometimes has a copy at home."

"I doubt that you would like the assignments. They aren't as exciting as the ones you desire. But you are good at portraits and they sometimes need photographs of distinguished members of the bar and prominent businessmen."

"That doesn't interest me at all. Can't you help me?"

"I'm trying to help you. At this point, all I can do is write a letter of recommendation. I must say, I am a bit hesitant, given your selfish attitude and pushiness. You haven't been easy to work with."

"I get things done. Didn't I provide you photographs no one else had during the whooping cough epidemic this year? I went into hospitals. I risked my life taking pictures there. Didn't I also photograph the headmaster at Calvert School? What was his name?"

"Virgil Hillyer. Yes, you did."

"Didn't I go into his school before it temporarily closed because of whooping cough? I even wrote the story because David Jameson refused to enter a place where there might be disease. I stayed on that assignment, if you remember. I reported that, when the school shut down, Mr. Hillyer created lessons for students to complete at home until the sickness was gone. Other schools went on to copy that protocol. And that was, in part, due to my article about the Calvert School's great success. No other paper had such detail."

"You give yourself too much credit, Miss Bainbridge."

"And no one else had such engaging pictures of the suffrage convention. I put readers in the middle of thousands of women chanting and cheering at the Lyric."

"Yes, I know."

"And wasn't I there at the burials of firefighters who succumbed to lung damage so long after the fire?"

"Yes, you were."

"What more can I do?"

"You will do what all the other displaced workers at the *Herald* are doing. You will start over."

"Jubilee Week is coming up. The city has planned a great celebration to thank our firefighters for their bravery during the fire. I need to be there, representing my paper, taking pictures."

"This is not your paper. You are one of many employees who are about to be ousted, regardless of talent and contribution. You can still take pictures of Jubilee Week. Maybe you could sell them freelance."

"Ugh! And that will pay my rent at the boardinghouse? And what camera will take these pictures? The one I use now belongs to the *Herald*."

"I will intercede for you and see if the new owners will allow you to freelance for them. In that way, you could keep the camera. If they are not interested, perhaps you could purchase it from them."

Anna fidgeted with her gloves. "I appreciate that, Mr. Mencken. I'm, I'm, I'm at my wit's end. This is quite a shock."

H.L. Mencken stayed true to his word. But the new owners were not hiring. They did allow Anna and some of the other photographers to keep their cameras for a nominal fee. However, they would have to supply their own film, which proved costly. The risk was high. There was no guarantee the photographers would recoup their investments through freelance work, much less make a profit. And they would be competing against one another.

After a few days of sulking and a good "talking to" by Josefina, Anna regrouped and threw herself back into her work.

She did photograph Jubilee Week in Baltimore. Seven days of celebration and admiration for the firefighters who had bravely fought the Great Fire back in 1904. On September 9th, fourteen hundred firefighters filled the streets of downtown Baltimore, from Broadway to City Hall, some walking, some on their trucks, including Engine 15, which had been rescued from the rubble. Bands marched, flags fluttered and hundreds of onlookers cheered. No greater reception was given than to Goliath, the giant of a firehorse that had suffered burns in the early hours of the blaze but remained at his post.

Anna had difficulty focusing her lens. She fought back tears that blurred her vision. The memory of the fire and the two days she spent living at the core of it, taking pictures, overwhelmed her. That had been her first foray into adult life on her own. She wanted to do justice to this event to come full circle. She needed to compose herself. Taking a deep breath, she wiped her eyes on the sleeve of her suit and knuckled down.

The Sun purchased her pictures, even though one of its own photographers had been assigned. Anna's depictions were more involved, more at the center of the festivities. Projected more emotion. She had marched the entire length of the parade, stopping here and there to shoot pictures of joy and tearful admiration and scarred firetrucks and children dreaming of becoming heroes. And Goliath, now fully recovered, strutting as if he understood he was the main attraction.

Anna knew that H.L. Mencken must have had a hand in her good fortune. She sent him a heartfelt "thank you" note. She also internally thanked Frances Benjamin Johnston for teaching her to capture the feeling of the moment, whether written or photographed.

Despite the friction between them, Anna kept in touch with H.L. Mencken after his move to *The Sun*, hoping they might work together again.

She earned money shooting pictures for Ford's Theater. She also worked a few days a week at a portraiture studio in Baltimore. Her favorite freelance job turned out to be the least paying but most rewarding... documenting the reconstruction of the burnt district.

∂∘∘ᕠ

In March, Josefina tipped Anna off on a possible controversy at Ford's Theater. She knew the price could be heavy, her job, but felt compelled to speak up, nonetheless.

"Josefina, what is this play—what is it called?—*The Clansman* about?"

"It's about the Ku Klux Klan, those people who burn crosses on colored people's lawns and hang men and women just because they have brown skin."

"And Ford's is putting on a play about it?"

"Yes, two men—I think they call them 'advance men'—came to Baltimore yesterday to talk to the theater managers about it. Rumor has it that they went to the St. James Hotel, over there on Charles and Centre Streets, to check in or get a bite to eat, I'm not sure. Anyway, when the colored waiters found out what they were up to—I guess they overheard their conversation—they so much as kicked them out."

"What a bold and brave thing to do."

"Yes, the play is based on a novel written by Thomas Dixon, Jr., who used to study history and politics at Johns Hopkins. I hear none other than D.W. Griffith plans to make this story into a movie."

"What can be done about it?"

"Perhaps, a newspaper story?"

"I don't work for any one paper anymore. All I can do is try."

No newspaper that Anna knew of would touch the subject. There wasn't much to tell. So far, the theater hadn't booked the play. Anna wondered what might happen if they did.

CHAPTER 18

In 1906, Anna's future fell into a deep well of uncertainty. Her livelihood felt as tenuous as the buildings half-standing after the devasting San Francisco earthquake in April. So much destruction in yet another big city. She never knew when she would be assigned a freelance job, when she would make money and how much, so she penny-pinched and let her generosity in paying other people's way diminish. She stopped taking Elizabeth out. She traveled to see Emmaline less frequently. Papa offered to let her return home to live. Anna refused.

For months, she scrimped and saved, and took every job offered, especially documenting the rebirth of Baltimore. Baltimore City hired her to take pictures of the finished Chamber of Commerce Building. The fire had ruined a good portion of the four-story structure, leaving some of the façade standing. It stood at a prominent location in the financial district, on the corner of Commerce Street and Custom House Avenue. The newly-finished building was an architectural wonder, a Renaissance Revival design in terra cotta.

Anna proved herself particularly good at shooting architecture. Due to their tall, boxy nature, buildings posed problems for many photographers. Too many times, pictures looked as though the building leaned to one side or tilted backwards. Most photographers had yet to learn that they were standing too close when composing their shots. Angling up a tall building from street level caused distortion due to the distance from ground to roof. Anna changed the perspective by shooting the Chamber of Commerce Building from a farther distance and a higher vantage point, from inside another building, to correct the problem as much as possible. Then she composed closer shots of the intricacies in architectural relief and the building's rustication and quoining. From several stories up across the street, Anna could also photograph the fourth-story windows straight on with no distortion whatsoever. Soon Anna found herself shooting more often as, one by one, buildings were completed.

Such was the case with the Maryland Institute, a college of art that had been located downtown over the Centre Market, where many Baltimoreans purchased their seafood, fresh from the docks just steps away. The Great Baltimore Fire had made quick work of both establishments.

The Institute relocated to the Mount Royal area north of the city because of donations made by a banking and railroad magnet who worshiped at a church there.

As for the Centre Market, reconstruction continued into 1907 near its original location.

Capturing the re-emergence of Baltimore reminded Anna that she, too, would survive and come back stronger.

Wearing her jodhpurs and boots, she photographed workers installing underground gas lines, and electrical grids for the sections of street car lines destroyed by fire that would now be extended in all directions. She was there, camera in hand, as streets were widened and fireproof materials were used to erect new buildings. She was particularly proud to be on hand as fire hydrant hose couplings were standardized and adjusted.

When the Great Baltimore Fire had broken out in 1904, firefighting units from all over the Eastern seaboard had been called in to help. Most could not fit their hoses to Baltimore's hydrants. Firefighters had to wrap rags around the connections, resulting in lower water pressure that made it impossible for the precious liquid to reach beyond the second floor. Anna had seen the devastating results firsthand as fire leapfrogged, rooftop to rooftop.

From most tragedies, something good emerges. In this case, hose couplings were standardized throughout the country. Anna felt satisfied to come full circle as these improvements were made. It was a long, laborious task that would pay off should disaster strike again.

As 1906 came to a close, Anna's optimism grew. She took up whistling as she walked down the street, drawing more attention to her unusual attire. She didn't give a fig. She even offered to bake for tea at the boardinghouse without being asked. On the last Sunday of December, she looked forward to toasting the upcoming New Year with her fellow residents, especially Josefina.

"I'm sorry, Anna, but I won't be attending tea today."

"Why not? I baked your favorite, gingerbread cake made with molasses, just the way you like it. I know I'm not the best in the kitchen, but…"

"Why don't you save me a piece? I'll be happy to enjoy it with you when I get home."

"What's so important that you can't be here?"

"I have been seeing a gentleman. Just once, really, so far. He's coming here tonight. We're going out again."

"I'm so pleased. Don't tell me. I bet it's that stage-door Johnny."

"It is. I did as you said. It only took a little flirting before he introduced himself."

"Was he disappointed when he discovered you were not an actress or chorus girl?"

"Not at all. I think he was relieved."

"Tell me about him."

"Excuse me, ladies," Mrs. Pendleton interjected. "Your gentleman caller is at the door, Josefina. I'd like to be introduced, if you don't mind."

"Yes, of course."

"Where are you two going?" Anna said.

"We're going to share an early supper with his best friend's family," Josefina said, addressing Mrs. Pendleton more than Anna. "There will be several people there, including children and grandparents."

"Sounds quite proper to me," Mrs. Pendleton said.

"How do I look, Anna?"

"What?" Anna seemed distracted.

"How do I look? I borrowed this dress from Frances."

"Lovely, just lovely. I've never seen you in that color. You look good in yellow."

"Thank you. Would you like to meet him?"

"Not right now. I'm covered in flour and smell of cloves and cinnamon."

"Maybe next time. Goodnight, Anna."

"Goodnight," Anna said, barely above a whisper.

As Josefina and Mrs. Pendleton greeted the gentleman caller, Anna quickly cleaned herself, removed her apron, adjusted the stray hairs from her chignon and opened the swinging kitchen door just wide enough to sneak a peek.

She heard muffled voices, occasional laughter and, after a few minutes, Mrs. Pendleton sending the twosome off for the evening.

"It's been a pleasure," Mrs. Pendleton said. "And thank you for the Berger Cookies. The ladies and I will enjoy them greatly," Anna heard her say distinctly.

Anna stepped into the hallway. She hid under the stairs and peeped around ever so slightly to see Adrian offering his arm to Josefina.

In a split-second glance, Anna's and Adrian's eyes met. Adrian's face showed surprise and admiration, both quickly erased. He took Josefina's arm and escorted her out the door before she or Mrs. Pendleton, who was eyeing the cookies, noticed anything amiss.

CHAPTER 19

Anna couldn't eat a bite at tea or supper. She refused a Berger Cookie, one of her favorites.

Josefina and Adrian.

Well, Sam did say he had moved on. But, after the fire, when Anna was so confused about her future and whether she wanted a career or marriage, Adrian had said he would wait for her forever.

Adrian and Josefina? It didn't sound more palatable the other way around.

What were the odds that these two should meet? What did Adrian see in Josefina? A little bit of Anna?

The next morning, Anna couldn't wait to ask her friend a million questions. Josefina beat her to the punch. "Good morning! How are you this delightful day?"

"It's cold and gray outside. What's so delightful about it?"

"Everything."

"I assume that means you enjoyed the company of your gentleman caller last night."

"Oh yes, I certainly did. What a fine man, and so funny. You'd love him."

"Yes, I'm sure I would."

"We dined at the home of his friend Sam and wife Lillian. They have an adorable little girl named Lucy. And they're expecting another child in March. Such a lovely family life they have. So kind to one another and so welcoming to us."

The way Josefina said the word "us" bothered Anna. It sounded as if she and Adrian were already a couple.

"Josefina, how well do you know this man? What is his name?"

"Adrian, Adrian Crosby."

"It seems you've become enamored quickly."

"He's such an open person, I feel as if I've known him a long time. We've only been in each other's company twice. He works for a cookie company, as a salesman and sees that local merchants stock the product on their shelves. They don't last long, so he's quite busy."

"Let me guess... Berger's?"

"Yes, isn't that chocolate icing decadent?"

"Downright devilish."

"Anyway, I blush to admit this but I think Adrian is taken with me, too. Already he is talking of afternoons at the picture shows, and long walks in Patterson Park when the weather warms."

"How nice."

"Anna, I'm getting the sense that you're being sarcastic rather than genuine. Is there something wrong?"

"It's just that I worry for you. You are unschooled in the adult ways of the world. I have a little more experience in that department."

"Yes, I remember. You told me you were betrothed once. Tell me—was he open and funny and loving?"

"Another time. Right now, I'm more concerned about you."

"What seems to be the problem? I'm following proper etiquette. I introduced him to Mrs. Pendleton. Next week, I'm taking him to meet my parents."

"Already?"

"Yes, I need their approval to enter into a formal courtship."

"Do you think it will lead to marriage?"

"Who knows?"

"Are you forgetting you have a life in the theater? If he works all day, when would you see each other?"

"If we married, I would give up the theater."

"But you love it so. How could you?"

"After seeing the beautiful life Sam and Lillian have, I'm starting to rethink my own."

"I'm shocked. Have you taken time to ruminate? This is so sudden."

"Why, Anna, are you jealous?"

"No, no, I'm not. As a friend, I'm just looking out for your welfare. I haven't known you to act on a whim."

Josefina smiled and hugged her friend. "I'll take your advice." She tried to stifle a giggle, with no luck.

"What's so funny?"

"You are. You're the impulsive one. You're the one always saying it takes too much time for things to happen. Looks like the tables have turned."

"Yes, it certainly does."

❧

The next day, Anna sent Adrian a note stating that she wanted to meet with him discreetly. He suggested a late afternoon rendezvous in Patterson Park. Josefina would be at the theater by then.

"Anna, you are looking lovely as ever."

"I have no time for niceties. What are you doing in the company of Josefina? Of all the girls in Baltimore, why someone from my boardinghouse? Are you trying to make me jealous?"

"I had no idea you lived there. I go to the theater regularly. If you recall, I escorted you to Ford's often. Josefina and I met at the stage door."

"After the fire, you said that you would wait for me forever. What happened to your promise?"

"That was more than two years ago. What did you expect me to do? You never wrote to me. You never contacted me. I figured you had released your feelings. As you remember, I was working for the Post Office at the time, delivering mail in your neighborhood. To avoid any awkward meetings on Saratoga Street, I asked to have my route transferred. Then I changed jobs completely."

"Don't you even miss me? When I saw you at the boardinghouse, I sensed a glimmer of hope or love in your eyes. Was I mistaken?"

"I was merely surprised to see you. And looking so well."

"Then, you have no lingering feelings for me?"

"You will always occupy a tender spot in my heart."

"But now you're starting to have feelings for Josefina. Do you know that she's my best friend?"

"Yes, I learned that last night. She talked about you nonstop. Congratulations on your career. I understand you have become quite successful."

"You realize Josefina works at night. You sell cookies, or whatever you do, during the day. How is that going to work?"

"If we become serious, we'll figure it out. I imagine Josefina will give up her position. But we are getting ahead of ourselves. I haven't even met her parents yet to ask them if I may court their daughter. There is a long way to go after that."

"I see. Well, I wish you all the best in life." Anna started to walk away.

"Wait, please, come back." Anna turned slowly and took a few steps toward Adrian, who spoke. "Do you still have sincere feelings for me..." He paused a moment. "... or are you afraid of losing what we had once and for all?"

"I don't know what I think right now. I must go. I have an assignment to fulfill today. I have to shoot it before the sun goes down."

"I'll leave you with one last question. Which is more important? Taking time to address your personal desires, or using work as an escape from your emotions?"

"How dare you?" Anna said, her eyes stinging.

Adrian took Anna's hand and gently squeezed it. "Be realistic. Please don't hate me."

"I don't."

As Anna walked the next several blocks alone, she did hate Adrian. And Josefina. She knew she'd have to face both of them if their courtship endured. Once again, Anna felt a lesson in life coming on, like a headache or a fever. She wondered why she couldn't get through a single day without having her moral standards and decisions in life challenged.

CHAPTER 20

Throughout the next week, Anna avoided Josefina as if she had typhoid fever. Instead, she threw herself into her photography.

Securing assignments took on the aura of religious devotion. Anna introduced herself to potential clients, ranging from those in government to private companies and organizations. She left business cards as a lasting reminder of her availability. She felt especially happy when Franklin P. Cator recalled her photos of his millinery business not long after the fire. He hired her to preserve his newest merchandise on film for print advertising. Anna hoped the same would be true when she went to O'Neill's. They, too, asked Anna to take pictures of their new spring fashions, evening wear and chatelaines. Miss Hughes, the same woman Anna and David had met when they reported on the store after the fire, started to explain the intricacies of this unique jewelry.

"I know all about chatelaines. I have one," Anna said.

"You do? I'd love to see it."

"I'll wear it when I come back to photograph the items. Mine initially belonged to my nanny, who was also our housekeeper. My mother presented it to her as a gift before she died."

"Oh, I'm so sorry to hear of your mother's passing."

"Please don't be. It was a long time ago. I really don't remember her. My nanny treasured her chatelaine and wore it when she was doing housework. She pinned it to her blouse or skirt waistband. It contained small scissors, a needle and thread, a corkscrew, a letter opener and a few other utensils handy for mending or kitchen work. Yet, at first glance, it looks like a beautiful piece of decorative jewelry. It has real pearl inlay. She gave it to me when I left home."

"Sounds lovely. Our collection for spring is in the form of chatelaine purses, for eveningwear, galas and such. They don't contain work items."

"Oh, I see. How silly of me."

"We will provide a table with a velvet cloth you can use for background. We find midnight blue shows design and workmanship to their best advantage."

Miss Hughes looked around, then leaned in closer to Anna.

"I will let you in on a little secret. Mr. O'Neill is looking for a permanent photographer to take pictures of the store, our window displays and individual merchandise. If you do well, he might consider you. That is, if you are interested."

"Oh, Miss Hughes, that would be wonderful."

"We have a room upstairs that is well-lit. It was used by our staff photographer, who moved out of state suddenly to care for an ailing relative. We have been left quite empty-handed."

"I see. I'll do my best for you, Miss Hughes."

"I'm sure you will."

Anna returned a few days later. Miss Hughes admired Anna's chatelaine, which was pinned to the waistband of her best dress. The older woman left her alone in the "photo studio," as she called it. Anna hung dresses on mannequins and snapped pictures of them against a plain black background. One by one, she positioned the chatelaine purses on a velvet cloth and caught every glisten. It was slow, tedious work, trying to make sure the lights were shining "just so" to enhance unique qualities of the merchandise. The enthusiasm Anna had initially shown for the work faded as the hours passed. There was no movement to capture, no people, nothing newsworthy. Anna hoped she would not be offered the job permanently. She liked Miss Hughes and Mr. O'Neill and didn't want to offend them by turning down such a fraught opportunity.

Although they were pleased with her work, another photographer was awarded the job. Someone with more experience in merchandise photography. On one hand, Anna was relieved. On the other, she realized she had just lost steady income from a prestigious company.

She struggled for a couple of months, then was alerted to an available position by H.L. Mencken. Not at his newspaper, but at the *Baltimore American*, the newspaper born of the merger with the *Herald's* owners. She jumped at the chance and was hired, in part, due to Mencken's recommendation. Her new employer even accepted her unusual mode of dress. Now Anna and H.L. Mencken would be competitors. Anna forgot to send a "thank you" note to her mentor.

Soon after she started working for the *Baltimore American*, Anna received an invitation to lunch from Emmaline. They were to meet on the corner of Charles Street and North Avenue. Anna assumed Emmaline wanted to congratulate her on her new job. How, on earth, had she found out about it? Over the last couple of months, the two had fallen out of touch. And where could they eat together in that neighborhood?

"Anna, it's good to see you," Emmaline said. "You're looking well." The two young women almost entered into an embrace, caught themselves, and stood back.

"I'm happy to see you, too. Why here?"

"This is where I live now, in this building. We're going to have lunch together in my room." Emmaline led the way to a three-story building and, after climbing the stairs to the top, the two entered a small, lovely room.

"I'm speechless. You live on your own now, not in a boardinghouse. This is a real apartment."

"Well, it's only one room. The divan serves as my sitting area and bed. I have a small ice box over there next to it. I covered it with a cloth so I can also use it as an end table. I have no way of cooking here. Most of my meals I take in a café up the street. It's quite reasonable. And I share a bathroom with two others on this floor. I've prepared a simple meal of dried beef, beet pickles and biscuits I bought at the market. And Joe Froggers for dessert. I hope you enjoy it."

"I'm sure I shall. What are Joe Froggers?"

"They're spice cookies made with rum, an old recipe from the Revolutionary War era. You don't mind imbibing a little today, do you?"

"Why, you naughty girl. Not at all. This is something to celebrate. Where did the name come from?"

"As the story goes, a colored soldier named Joseph Brown was given his freedom from slavery because of his military service. He opened a tavern and served food his wife made. She came up with the recipe and name. The tavern was near a frog pond. She made the cookies in a cast iron skillet and, when she poured in the batter, it spread like frogs' legs until she filled the pan. At least, that's been the tale handed down."

"The cookies are as big as lily pads. I'm going to sneak a taste now, if you don't mind. Emmaline, how did all this come about? Did you stop sending money home?"

"No, I acquired a better job. I'm working in the newspaper business, just like you."

"What?"

"Well, not as a photographer. I'm the new accountant at the *Baltimore Afro-American* newspaper. It's nearby. I'm sure you've heard of it."

"Of course, it's been around a while. A very fine paper. This is wonderful. I must ask, what about Miss Cummings?"

"After your newspaper ran that article on her organization, she received a lot of money that needed to be managed. Over time, those funds slowed and she could handle the accounting herself. Oh, she's still doing just fine. Nothing to worry about. But we mutually agreed I was no longer needed. She introduced me to Mr. John H. Murphy, who started the *Baltimore Afro-American*. He offered me a position five days a week. Now I have enough money to send home and live on my own."

"Oh, I'm so proud of you. Mmm, this cookie is delicious."

"Anna, you gave me my start. Without your help, this would never have happened."

"No, that's not true. You did all the hard work. You acquired an education. You struck out on your own long before I came along. I just gave you a little friendly nudge. Your family must be over the moon. Are they well?"

"My father is having trouble with the gout in his left leg. He takes some relief from Bishop Gout Varalettes. The others are doing fine."

"I'll never forget that wonderful meal we had at your house with your whole family." Anna buttered her biscuit. "How is it that we can dine together here in your room? Won't your neighbors complain?"

"No, this area of Baltimore includes a white neighborhood on one side of North Avenue and a colored neighborhood on the other. We mix because we share the same market and other merchants. It's similar to Bare Hills in that regard. There's no trouble."

The two ate in silence for a few minutes.

"Oh, I almost forgot, I have news of my own to share with you."

Anna spoke of her freelance work and new position at the *Baltimore American*. "And, a while back, I traveled all the way to Connecticut by train to see a photography exhibit. My very first trip anywhere."

"By yourself?"

"No, my nanny went with me. Elizabeth, you met her. You see, there's a woman named Jessie Tarbox Beals. She's considered one of the first female news photographers in the whole country. She worked for the *Buffalo Inquirer* and another newspaper as far back as 1902. And she was invited to display her work at the Camera Club of Hartford. It was called 'Exhibition of Photographs – The Work of Women Photographers.'"

"Were any of your pictures shown?"

"Oh no, I'm not that important yet. Maybe someday. I couldn't afford to pay for the trip myself. Of all people, Papa offered to help me, as long as Elizabeth chaperoned. Can you believe it? He's finding it in his heart to understand my passion for photography. I had the grandest time."

Anna and Emmaline looked at each other with the realization that they had both come a long way since the night they met in the shadows. Over a plate of Joe Froggers, they clinked their glasses of Coca-Cola and smiled. As Anna spilled some of hers, Emmaline laughed and exclaimed, "Aren't we a couple of swells?"

CHAPTER 21

Just as Anna was getting ready to slip into bed, she heard a soft knock on her door. "Who is it?"

"Josefina. I need help unlacing my corset. It's awfully tight."

Anna opened the door to find Josefina dressed in a pale green gown with deep red rosettes embroidered around the neck. Her waist looked like it was about to snap. "That's quite a lovely frock. You've been wearing color lately."

"This is Jane Catherine's dress. She suggested I wear it tonight."

"It suits you, I guess. Have you been out on the town?"

"No, just a quiet dinner and stroll around Mt. Vernon Square."

"With Adrian?"

"Yes."

"I see. And did he like this dress?"

"Anna, please, my corset. The boning is cutting into me."

"Oh, certainly. Turn around. You know, fewer and fewer women are wearing these torture devices. This is so taut, it's a wonder you could eat a bite. Are you trying to flaunt your figure?"

"No, well, I guess I am. Jane Catherine pulled the lacings this tight. She said pain was part of becoming a woman."

"Well, for once, I agree with her," Anna said, through teeth clenched while trying to unhook the corset. "So, you're becoming friends with Jane Catherine?" Anna spun Josefina around to face her. "There. I have released your..." She paused a moment... "*flirtation.*"

"Something is wrong. It's obvious. Are you angry with me for spending more time with my gentleman friend than you?"

"No, that's not it."

"With Jane Catherine?"

"No."

"Then what is it? Ever since I started seeing Adrian, you've become distant. Have I offended you in any way?"

"No. I... it's just... well... I had a long day. I'm tired. I'll see you tomorrow."

"You and I were starting to enjoy each other's confidence. What's changed?"

"Goodnight, Josefina. I'll see you tomorrow," Anna said, practically pushing her friend into the hallway.

After Anna shut the door, the air in the room turned as stuffy as cotton. She opened a window and noticed the season was changing. It felt a little too humid, a little too close for her comfort.

≈∞≈

In the Summer of 1907, something happened that took Anna's mind off herself. She heard of an event coming to Baltimore so filled with potential for dramatic photographs, that Anna's spirit practically leaped from her soul and skipped down the street. An automobile race. It was called The Glidden Tour, named for Charles J. Glidden, a man who worked in finance and became an early fan of motor cars. Competitors, representing various manufacturers and automobile organizations, were to vie for a trophy and the right to advertise their success. Eighty-eight autos, ranging from Pierce-Arrow to Packard, carried up to four passengers each, people who wanted the thrill of traversing cities and towns over dirt roads, brick pavers, and dangerous gravel at high speeds. They could also help repair the cars, should they run into trouble on the road. Along the way, drivers had to stop at checkpoints, where officials waved checkered flags to authenticate passage.

"Please send me to take pictures," Anna pleaded with her editor, Mr. Jackson.

"Miss Bainbridge, I assume you know nothing of automobiles. Am I mistaken?"

"No."

"Can you decipher a Peerless from a Maxwell?"

"No."

"Do you understand engines? Do you know a crank case from a rear axle?"

"No, sir. But I'm more than adept at taking pictures that put people in the middle of activity."

"And how do you propose to do that?"

"I'm not sure yet. Give me time to think about it."

"No, Miss Bainbridge. I've already assigned one of our male photographers. He needs no training in mechanics."

The race originated in Cleveland, Ohio, and traveled through South Bend with a side trip to Chicago. From there, drivers returned to South Bend, and continued through Indianapolis, followed by Columbus and Canton, Ohio. From there, it was on to Pittsburgh and Bedford, Pennsylvania, before entering the state of Maryland. How would they reach downtown Baltimore? Perhaps via the Falls Turnpike?

An idea struck Anna like the urgency of a rubber-bulb horn. She sent a note to Emmaline, requesting a meeting.

"You want to what?"

"I want to ride in one of the race cars and photograph the vantage point of the passengers. I want to capture dust flying and people on the side of the road waving, and close pictures of the driver, wearing his muddy goggles, his hands trembling at the wheel."

"How on earth do you expect to accomplish that?"

"Well, cars break down. Cars have to stop at checkpoints. I want to be there by the side of the road to ask for a ride when they do."

"Do you know, for certain, that Falls Turnpike is part of their route?"

"How else will they arrive downtown? From Bedford, if they travel in a straight line south, they'll eventually pick up the turnpike. I'll be ready and waiting at one of their stops. The one nearest Bare Hills."

"Ohhhh, and that's where I come in. Is that right?"

"Well, yes, that's where your family comes in. Do you think they would let me stay overnight, so that I can be fully prepared for the race in the morning, no matter what time it comes through?"

"This is most unusual."

"Don't tell me your family would object. Why?"

"There really isn't a reason. It's just that it's not been done before."

"Good. I love being the first. Will you contact them?"

☙❧

Anna arrived at Bare Hills with a small overnight satchel, a bag of peaches and two packages of Berger cookies, which Emmaline's family greatly appreciated. She was given Emmaline's parents' bedroom against her protest. They said they preferred to sleep on the porch because of the heat.

Anna had to use an outhouse but adjusted quickly. No one made comment of Anna's manly suit and flat cap.

The next morning, she positioned herself at the nearest toll booth, a checkpoint for drivers. It was hot, even under the shade of a nearby tree. Anna waited for two hours before hearing the chug and tick of engines. Two cars arrived almost simultaneously. As they paid the toll and engaged with the checker, Anna invited herself for a ride. She received a curt "no" from the first driver.

The second competitor seemed to be having trouble with his car. Even though Anna knew little about mechanics, she could tell this one was overheating. "May I be of help?" she asked the driver.

"I don't think so."

"What's the problem? Your... ah, 'thingamajig' is smoking."

"Yes, I need to let the car cool down, maybe add a little water."

"I can direct you. I know where to get plenty of water."

"Good. Take me there."

"I will, if you let me ride downtown with you."

"Listen, sonny, this is not a cab."

"I know that. And I'm not a child. I'm a reporter and photographer with the *Baltimore American*. If you let me take pictures along the way, I'm sure they will get published in my paper and you'll receive plenty of free advertising for your automobile, win or lose. Wouldn't your sponsor love that? What do you say?"

The man seemed desperate. The car ahead of him had just been waved on. He turned around to see if anyone else was getting close. The road was clear.

"Agreed." He pulled the car off to the side near Old Court Road. Together, he and Anna scooped water from the nearby Jones Falls, a stream that snaked through Baltimore County and ended downtown. Anna couldn't help but take a drink herself. Her mouth was as dry as burnt biscuits and the day was still young.

As they stood up, the driver took in Anna's figure beneath the manly cut of her outfit.

"You're a woman!" he said. "You can't ride with me."

"A deal is a deal. I've kept my part of the bargain."

The driver blustered his way back to the car. He didn't even open the door for Anna. Once the car was drivable, off they went, along with the other passenger, a man, who remained silent.

As they got closer to downtown, the distance between race cars lessened. There was some sort of bottleneck. Cars jockeyed to get ahead. Anna was able to shoot pictures of vehicles close to collision. She captured crowds by the side of the road. They waved signs of welcome, American flags, and handkerchiefs. Fathers picked up sons so they could see. Some women cried. Vendors sold NECCO Sweets, the newest candy sensation everyone craved.

After a grueling fifteen-hundred-mile race, drivers reached the end of the road in downtown Baltimore. When they curved around Mt. Vernon Square, cheers rang out from the awaiting crowds.

Anna joined in, bringing not so much as a smile from her driver. He banged his fist on the steering wheel, knowing he would receive no prize. Anna stepped out of the vehicle and took a picture of him by his car. His face looked as stern and rigid as his engine. She asked him for his name and address, so she could send him a copy. He obliged, then ignored her as he spoke to his passenger about dinner.

Since Anna had not really been assigned by the *Baltimore American*, she had to pay for picture development herself. Most of the photos were somewhat blurred because of the car's jostling when she took them. She liked it. The images showed the excitement of the race, the movement, the bumpiness of the ride and what the drivers and their passengers experienced.

Anna made sure to seek out the winner of the race and take a picture of him just as he hoisted his trophy. She stepped in front of other photographers to get the shot.

When she showed her work to the editor of the *Baltimore American*, he dismissed it as useless, at first. Then he saw the images his assigned photographer had taken. They were too formal, lacked movement, fortitude and vigor. And his picture of the winner receiving the trophy was partially obscured by someone's head. Anna's pictures were powerful, dangerous, more masculine in style. Her photographs made the front page.

"Well, Miss Bainbridge, I misjudged you. You were quite capable in finding the unique angle of this story. I'll remember that next time," Mr. Jackson said.

Anna sent a "thank you" note to Emmaline and her parents, along with clippings from the story. Papa saw the pictures, too, and messengered a note to his daughter.

Anna:

I was quite perturbed to see the photographs you took of the Glidden car rally. It was obvious to me that you were risking your life, yet again, for your work. I will speak to your editor about assigning you such danger and give him a piece of my mind. Beyond your health, more is at stake, your reputation as a lady. You are to meet with me within the next few days. I want to have a word with you.

Papa

The moment Anna received the note, she raced home. Her father was not there and neither was Elizabeth. She took a handsome cab to the hospital where Papa served as a leading cardiologist and, after whisking past his secretary, found him in his office. This was the first time Anna had ever been to Papa's workplace.

"Anna, this is against protocol. I am in the midst of studying a patient's electrocardiogram."

"I must speak with you now. You haven't already talked to my editor, have you?"

"No, but I placed a telephone call and left a message with his secretary to contact me."

"No! You can't do this to me."

"I am responsible for every breath you take. I am your father."

"You don't understand. I wasn't assigned to shoot the race. I volunteered. Mr. Jackson declined my offer. I decided to do it anyway, all on my own. Once he saw my unusual perspective, he couldn't refuse to print the pictures."

"Am I to believe the fault rests solely on your delicate shoulders?"

"They are not delicate. I am a woman of great stamina and perseverance. I wasn't troubled at all by this experience. I enjoyed it immensely, even though I lost my cap somewhere along the way. And my riding suit got quite dirty."

"You wore men's clothing again? Even worse."

"No, more modest. I can get the oil out with a little Persil."

"Your sullied reputation is what I'm worried about."

"Papa, has it occurred to you that I might be admired for what I'm doing?"

"What is admirable about speeding through the streets of Baltimore with a coterie of greasy men, dressed as one of them? And how did you acquire a seat in one of these foul-smelling, rackety monstrosities in the first place?"

"I simply asked."

"What was the name of the driver? How were you introduced?"

"He didn't tell me his name, at first. I introduced myself."

Papa's face turned beet-red. He took out a handkerchief and blew his nose. Then, he poured himself a glass of water from a pitcher on his desk and barely took a sip.

"You are to return home immediately. Pack your things, resign your position, and tell your landlady I will pay any fines for your early departure. Do you hear me?"

"I hear you, Papa. But I will not comply. May I remind you that I can legally chart my own course in life?"

"You are heading full speed to Hell!"

"Papa!"

The office door opened a crack, slowly.

"Is everything all right, Doctor?" his secretary said.

Dr. Bainbridge sat up straight in his chair.

"Of course, Clarice. My daughter was given some unpleasant news and has chosen an emotional response. She will recover soon enough."

"Very well. Can I get either of you anything? Some coffee?"

"No, Clarice, that won't be necessary. Thank you. You may go."

Anna sat almost as tall as Papa in her chair.

"It is you who is getting emotional. You will not speak to Mr. Jackson. He had no hand in this. I will not move out of the boardinghouse, resign my position or return home."

"Then I will no longer support you financially."

"What do you mean, support me?"

"Since you moved to the boardinghouse, I have been paying Mrs. Pendleton a monthly stipend to oversee you and provide certain amenities, such as your favorite foods and the best linens in the house, among other things. I asked her to look out for your welfare. That seems to have culminated in failure. If you want to live on your own and make decisions, then pay your own way, in full. Do not come to me when you are starving on the streets."

"That will never happen. I won't allow it."

Anna got up and, without parting words, left the office. When she returned home, she sat down with Mrs. Pendleton and informed her of Papa's decision to dispense with extra money. Even after losing financial support, she reveled in the luxury of living on her own at the boardinghouse, no matter what.

"Pay my father no mind in the future. Do you understand?" Mrs. Pendleton nodded and sighed.

CHAPTER 22

The editor of the *Baltimore American* called a meeting of photographers. Anna, of course, was the only woman to attend. She sat near the front, as close to the boss as possible.

"I want to inform you of a new direction in photography the paper is taking," Mr. Jackson said. "Because of Miss Bainbridge's depictions of the Glidden race, we sold more copies of Sunday's edition than ever. Subscriptions have also risen since then. It appears our readers want more of these types of photographs, ones that show movement, putting the reader on the spot. Gentlemen, we should all congratulate Miss Bainbridge for this advance in newspaper reporting."

Inaudible murmurs were heard around the room, too low to tell if they supported Anna or berated her.

One man spoke up clearly through the din. He was the photographer who had been assigned to the rally, the one whose pictures were rejected. "What role does ethics play in acquiring special vantage points for taking such pictures?" he said.

"Why do you ask? Has something untoward happened?"

"Ask Miss Bainbridge how she came to ride in one of the race cars."

"I simply approached the driver and made my request," Anna replied.

"Did you make any promises about getting his picture in our paper?" Mr. Jackson said.

"Why, no. I said, well, I told him..."

"What *did* you say, Miss Bainbridge?"

"I can tell you," said the photographer. "After the race, I met the driver she rode with. He was none too pleased to have had her along. Said he only agreed because she 'promised' to get his picture in the *Baltimore American*. Isn't that quid pro quo? Isn't quid pro quo nothing more than bribery? Is that the new direction you want us to take?"

"Gentlemen, please return to your assigned duties. Miss Bainbridge, I'd like to speak with you in private."

As he exited the room, the photographer gave a knowing smile to his compeers then turned to make eye contact with Miss Bainbridge. His smile faded when he saw the fiery look she aimed at him in return. She turned to face her employer, whose tone of voice moved from pleasing to predatory.

"Miss Bainbridge, is this transgression true?"

After a slight pause, Anna replied softly. "Yes, Mr. Jackson."

"I was warned of your inexperience and lack of maturity. But I hired you for your photographic eye, your ability to step out of what is expected and deliver something new, fresh. It is one thing to break the rules of composition and lighting and clarity. It is another to part with journalistic integrity. The end does not justify the means at this newspaper."

Anna couldn't understand why her boss was so upset. She saw her actions as nothing more than moving a bookcase over to the courtroom door and taking pictures through the transom, as her idol, Jessie Tarbox Beals, had done. And that woman was revered in the newspaper world for her efforts.

"Had I discovered your violation before publication, I would have given you a good dressing-down and made sure those pictures never saw the light of day. But since the photographs were printed, the paper's high standards have been breached and I have no choice but to..."

"What are you saying?"

"... but to terminate your employment, Miss Bainbridge. The *Baltimore American* cannot uphold its probity when our reporters and photographers are making quid pro quo arrangements with subjects."

"You are letting me go?"

"Yes, I will see you are sent any renumerations still owed."

"No letter of recommendation?"

"I'm afraid not."

Anna stood up and left the office in a daze. Terminated. How would this look? Where would she find steady work after such a blot on her record? Why wasn't she honored for her efforts instead of berated? "What will Papa think?"

Anna returned to the boardinghouse and found it empty save for Mrs. Pendleton, who was bent down, peeking in the oven. She looked up in surprise.

"Anna, what are you doing home at this hour? Is something wrong? Are you ill?"

"Yes, I'm sick. I feel just awful." She pulled out a chair and sat.

"Shall I send for the doctor?"

"There is no medicine to cure my pain. I've been let go by the *Baltimore American*."

"Why? What rule did you break this time?"

Anna told her landlady what had happened. Mrs. Pendleton brewed some tea and filled a plate with anise drop cookies, hot and fragrant. Anna refused both.

"What are you going to do now?"

"I know what I'm not going to do. I'm not going to return home to Papa. I told him I would stand on my own two feet and that's what I intend to do."

"What will serve as money? Rent is due in three days."

"Mrs. Pendleton, would it be possible for me to move from the double room to Rosemary's old single? You haven't filled it since she got married. That would save me some money."

"I'm sorry. I just rented it to a lovely young lady, a milliner. She designs beautiful hats. I've seen some of them. Her name is Marjorie. Isn't that a melodic name?"

"What? Yes, it is."

"It's a shame I didn't know about this a few days ago. I turned away twins looking for a double room. I could have filled the entire boardinghouse in one swoop."

"Mrs. Pendleton, have you no concern for me?"

"I'm sorry. This boardinghouse is my work, my business. I must think of that first. You understand."

"What about the servant's quarters downstairs, where Emmaline slept that night? Can you give me a cheaper rate there? Can I do chores to work off some of my rent?"

"Oh, you don't mean to live in the basement. It's close to the boiler and the laundry basin. There are no windows, no fresh air. And I use that room for sewing."

Anna stood up and pushed her chair in. She started to leave the room. "I'll take it. I can move my things today, while everyone else is out. Find those twins, Mrs. Pendleton. If my finances cannot improve, at least yours will."

"Wait, have you thought about what Adelaide and Frances and the others might say?"

Anna stopped dead in her tracks. "Oh no, I didn't."

"You will be in for even more criticism, Anna. It will be vicious. And I will be unable to control it. This situation you find yourself in is most dreadful." Mrs. Pendleton took a sip of tea, then smiled. "But, maybe, you can use it for good."

"How?"

"Have you ever heard the phrase, *"Reculer pour mieux sauter"*?"

"Why, Mrs. Pendleton, you speak French. I didn't know that. What does it mean?"

"Loosely translated, it means that one must step back to make a leap forward. If you view your problem in that measure, it might help you plan your future and respond to any criticism."

Anna thought for a few minutes. She walked to the window over the sink and stared out into the backyard and beyond. A rare cardinal alighted on the washtub airing in the sun. It seemed to look straight into Anna's eyes, tweeting staccato encouragement, then spotted a grub on the grass. The bird abruptly ended its repetitive tune and attacked. It found opportunity in the most unpleasant of insects.

"Never mind Adelaide. I'll take care of her and the others will fall in line. I'll start moving my things to the basement right now."

Anna grabbed a cookie, kissed Mrs. Pendleton on the cheek, reached over her shoulder for one more confection, and raced upstairs to gather her belongings. Mrs. Pendleton shook her head, opened a drawer and searched for the phone number of the twins.

ॐ◌๛

At dinner that night, Mrs. Pendleton stayed close to Anna as she told the others of her move.

"So, all of your inflated talk of a world-changing career in the newspaper business has come to this, nothing more than an airless balloon," said Adelaide.

"Adelaide, this is a small setback, a mere case of '*Reculer pour mieux sauter*,'" Anna said, with a European flare.

She looked directly at Adelaide and found a confused look. Expressions of incredulity, fascination and reproach circled the table.

"Adelaide, don't you understand French? You spent time abroad, didn't you? You told me yourself that you were an enlightened woman."

Anna looked at Mrs. Pendleton, who was fidgeting with the doily on the sideboard. A slight smirk rose on her face, which she disguised with her hand.

"It means that in order to take a big step forward, sometimes one must first step back. It's a matter of physics. It's a matter of preparation and planning and aiming and momentum. Don't you see?"

No one answered. The meal was eaten mostly in silence, with an occasional request for the water pitcher. The other ladies finished before Anna, who helped herself to more potatoes.

After they left the room and retreated to the parlor, Mrs. Pendleton walked over to Anna and gave her a motherly hug from behind, whispering in her ear. "Anna Bainbridge, sometimes I want to throttle you. The other times, I think you a marvel."

CHAPTER 23

Anna possessed a talent for bouncing back from adversity while most people would still be mired in worry. She pursued freelance photography jobs and resumed silhouette portraiture. No assignment was too small. For a time, she worked for *The Democratic Telegram*, a newspaper that covered not only Baltimore but all of Maryland and beyond, even world news. Anna hoped to be sent out of town to photograph an event. She needed time away. She soon got her wish.

There was a chocolatier in Hershey, Pennsylvania, that was drawing attention throughout the eastern seaboard. Around since 1894, his business was now growing into much more than a candy company. It was sprouting into a town, a destination where people learned how chocolates were made and could enjoy the surrounding nature park. Rumor had it that amusement rides would be added in the coming years. The company hinted about a new product about to be introduced, a single chocolate, called a "Kiss," that would come hand-wrapped in silver paper. There was talk around the office that the *Telegram* was going to feature a story on the company's success and plans going forward. Anna asked for the assignment.

She had luck on her side when a staff reporter requested Anna to accompany him as photographer. His name, David Jameson.

"I wondered where you found work," she said, as they sat down to discuss their trip.

"After the *Herald* folded, I moved to New York, where my brother lives, and took a job with *The New York Tribune*. I went underground when the newest leg of the subway opened. It was remarkable, Miss Bainbridge. You would love riding it. It goes faster than anyone can imagine. But my biggest assignment was the murder of architect Stanford White."

"I remember reading a little bit about it."

"I'm surprised you weren't captivated. It's 'The Crime of the Century,' as my paper put it. Didn't you see photographs of the arrest? Hundreds of people gathered outside the prison where the killer was being held. And there was nothing to see. They just wanted to be there. I'll tell you the whole story when I drive us to Hershey."

"We're not taking transportation arranged by the paper?"

"No, didn't I tell you? I have an automobile now. You realize we will be spending the night, don't you? We can't possibly do it all in one day."

"Yes, I guess we have to."

"Don't worry. *The Telegram* has acquired separate lodging for us. We'll be in different boardinghouses. I'll stay at the YMCA, so everything will be above board. I advise that we eat separately, too, lest gossip finds its way back to the paper."

"Very well. I'm sure people will talk, just the same. What kind of car do you drive?"

"A curved-dash Oldsmobile, secondhand. It has no roof, so make sure you wear a scarf over your bonnet. You are wearing a dress, aren't you?"

"Yes, I suppose so. Maybe I should pack my suit, just in case."

"I hope it doesn't rain, or we'll have to stop and find shelter until it passes. There are few places to buy gasoline, so I have to carry my own. This is going to be a long drive."

"I'm looking forward to it."

As the twosome left Baltimore heading north, Anna asked David to tell him the story of the "Crime of the Century."

"Oh, Anna, wait until you hear. May I call you 'Anna' now?"

"Of course."

"You can call me David. Anyway, a very rich, most unstable man named Harry Kendall Thaw. He was an heir to a fortune, railroad money, you see. Well, he was in love with a young model and actress named Evelyn Nesbit, known for her risqué poses wearing little clothing. You know the kind. They appear on those little cards that men collect but don't show their wives." David sighed. "My, Miss Nesbit was a beauty! She had been a Floradora girl. It's no surprise that Thaw fell in love with her. While they were courting, she revealed a tragic story to him about her past.

A man named Stanford White had... that she had been... well... I can't say it in mixed company. But when she was sixteen, he took advantage of her youth, and he... well, he did the most vile thing a man can do to a woman. It happened while she was passed out, most likely from drink. Do you understand?"

"I think so. You mean, he deflowered her?"

"Yes. This man was an accomplished architect, widely known in New York and Baltimore. Stanford White designed the First Methodist Episcopal Church on St. Paul Street. You know the one I mean, don't you? He also designed Madison Square Garden II in New York. Well, Harry Thaw was no saint, either, as it turns out. He was known for throwing wild parties, where there was plenty of liquor, cocaine, even morphine. Who knows what went on? He planned to marry the girl, until she told him what Stanford White had done to her. Thaw became hotter than a locomotive fire box." David stopped talking and focused on the trouble he was having downshifting. The car jerked.

"What did he do?"

"He tracked down White and bang, bang, bang! He shoots the man, once in the shoulder and twice in the face, wiping his features right off his head, including that big bushy mustache of his."

"Please, David. Between your story and my churning stomach from all this rattling around..."

"Oh, I'm sorry. I didn't take you for one with a weak constitution."

"Can we stop for a while and rest? I need to find a place to ah... you know."

"Certainly."

David pulled off the road near a cornfield. They individually found places to relieve themselves, then sat under a big oak tree.

"Would you like some water or food? I brought a sandwich and canteen."

"So did I. Not right now. By all means, help yourself."

After a few minutes of silence, David said, "Not as stalwart as you thought you were, are you?"

Anna didn't respond. She was thinking of what Mrs. Pendleton had cautioned her about... being in the company of a man without a chaperone. And here she was, traveling to another state, overnight no less, with a man she barely knew. And she had gotten into an automobile with a stranger during that road rally. What could have happened to her? What could still happen?

Anna relented and took a few sips of water and ate a cracker.

"Do you want to hear more of the story?"

"Not right now."

"Well, I'll just say I was assigned to write the story. The trial's coming up in February. I can't wait. It's going to be one juicy event."

"You've changed."

"In what way?"

"You've become more caught up in the gruesome side of life. I honestly believe you're enjoying this tragedy. What happened to your journalistic integrity? I remember when you admonished me because you thought I was using my feminine wiles to get a story from Mr. Cator. You impressed upon me the importance of virtue at all times."

"Life in New York is different. The newspaper business there can be cutthroat, no matter the subject. There's a lot more competition."

"You were always polite and respectful. Now you seem desperate." She nibbled a cracker. "Why did you come home if there were so many opportunities for 'juicy' stories about 'deflowering' and 'shooting faces off,' as you put it, in New York?"

"I have a better chance of becoming a leading journalist here, someone to be revered. In New York, I was one of many."

"Then this assignment in Hershey must be boring to you."

"It pays the bills."

"I see." Anna turned her head to take in the scenery.

"Maybe I have gotten too caught up in the unsavory side of life. Being home might help me realize I'm talking about real people, however reprehensible."

"I certainly hope so."

"Anna, there was another reason why I admonished you at Armstrong, Cator & Co. I knew you were naïve and I didn't want you to leave the wrong impression, one that, if continued in another setting at another time, could lead to your ruin."

Anna was quiet for a while. Then she simply said, "Thank you."

David's gaze moved upwards. "By the looks of the sun, I'd say it's growing late. We should continue. Are you up to it?"

Anna smiled and said, "Let's carry on!"

They drove in silence for a time. Anna looked back at the many chances she had taken to get a story. She understood the warnings from Papa, Mrs. Pendleton, and her editors that she had not heeded. And how lucky she had been to this point. She started to see David in a new light. She once told him, *"I'll keep my eye on you."* That's just what she planned to do now. A more favorable eye because he was looking out for her.

CHAPTER 24

Anna allowed caution into her life after the trip to Hershey, Pennsylvania. Office gossip swirled through newspaper staff, which management quickly dispelled. Of course, Papa figured out that his daughter had traveled with a man, once he saw the byline. He planned to call his daughter on the carpet. Another story sidetracked his approbation, a story that would occupy everyone's mind for the months to come. It was called the Panic of 1907. And it would affect not only Papa's finances. It would affect his health.

The economic turmoil dated back a full year, with roots embedded in unstable soil clear across the country. Without warning, an earthquake had devasted San Francisco. Insurance claims piled as high as the rubble, some answered favorably, others refused. Approximately $250 million in insurance money flooded the area. Just as earthquakes have aftershocks, this one sent an economic ripple that was felt all the way to the shores of the Atlantic. It led to a recession. Most Americans had to pinch their pennies. To make matters worse, in October of 1907, two minor brokerage firms in New York City went bankrupt after a stock acquisition plan failed.

If the stock market represented a tall stone building, one would think it could withstand the shaking ground caused by a single deal gone wrong. But soon, scared investors feared other banks and trust companies would follow like tumbling dominos. They ran the banks, withdrawing their money. One by one, financial institutions tried to shore up their foundations for fear of total collapse. When all was said and done, the New York Stock Exchange dropped by almost fifty percent in a twelve-month period. The country fell deeper into the pit of recession, until rich men who ran financial institutions put up their own money and settled things down. They showed investors it was all right to come back. It would take more than a year before relief reached the average investor.

Much of Papa's money was tied up in these large investment firms. For the first time in his life, he suffered financial hardship. He cut Elizabeth's household allotment, asking her to serve simpler meals, to use less firewood and coal, and to walk to markets for groceries and other supplies, rather than paying for a trolley or handsome cab. Elizabeth, entering middle age, found the chilly house and long walks with heavy packages arduous. She needed someone to talk to.

"Anna, I'm so glad to see you," Elizabeth said. "Thank you for coming so soon after I sent you a note."

"What is it? Are you ill? Is Papa?"

"I'll get by. I always do. It's your father. He seems consumed by all this trouble with the banks. He has cut my household purse dramatically. You can feel how cold the house is."

"Is he getting proper rest? Are you giving him nourishing food?"

"He barely eats. And I know he paces the floor at night. Even in slippers, his footfalls above my head keep me awake."

"He must have lost a lot of money. Is he in danger of losing this house?"

"I don't know. I'm worried. Not just for his finances but his well-being. He looks sickish."

"Where is he now?"

"Where else? The hospital. He's working more hours than ever before. You know your father—he masks his inner soul. He chooses work over facing his feelings and problems."

"What can I do? How can I help?"

"I don't know. I just feel better having you here, talking to you. This has been a heavy burden these last few weeks. I'm tired. I'm getting older."

"Elizabeth, I can't lose you. I can't lose Papa."

"When we are both gone, you will get along just fine. You have already shown that you can live on your own, without our help."

"That's not what I'm talking about. You are the only family I have."

"Sometimes in life, we make our own families from the cloth of many. We become closer to people who don't share our blood, people who make up a new fabric that is woven tightly and cannot come unraveled. I found that when I came here. You must find it elsewhere."

"I never fathomed that either of you might die. I have never experienced the death of someone I loved. I never really knew Mama. I don't know how to feel. I'm completely befuddled."

"Death of a loved one is something we all have to face eventually. You are no exception."

"Is Papa so distressed that his health could be at stake?"

"Yes, it could be."

"Then I must see him right now."

"No, he's with patients at the hospital. Let him be. I just wanted to warn you. Should something happen, it won't come as a complete shock. I pray this crisis will pass and all will be restored to normal. Are your finances favorable?"

"Yes, I live within my means. I don't even have a charge account anywhere."

"Good for you. Now, we can at least share a cup of tea, can't we?"

Anna and Elizabeth talked of lighter subjects as they sipped Orange Pekoe and felt its warmth soothe the frayed fabric of their worries.

Later that night, Anna wrote a heartfelt note to her father, telling him that everything would be all right. She also offered to move back home, so she could donate part of her earnings to the household budget. In a curt return letter, Papa refused. It was obvious that his pride wrote the words. No doubt, he admonished Elizabeth for speaking out of turn.

༺ঙ৽ঙ༻

On a blustery evening, Anna received a phone call at the boardinghouse informing her that Papa was in the hospital, not as a doctor but as a patient. Anna raced out the door. When she arrived, she found Elizabeth sitting alone in a busy corridor.

"Anna, I'm so glad you're here."

"What is it? What happened?"

"It's his heart, I'm afraid. He was sitting in his den, reading the newspaper, probably the financial column, when I heard a thud. It sounded awful. By the time I got to him, he was unconscious on the floor, pale and clammy. I ran next door—you know your father never wanted a telephone in the house—and called for an ambulance. Then I called you. They've told me nothing since we arrived. It's been about an hour."

Anna stopped a nurse and demanded to speak to Papa's doctor.

"I'm sorry, he is still with the patient. I can't interrupt him."

"Where? What ward?"

"I'm sorry, I can't tell you."

"*I am Dr. Bainbridge's daughter!*"

"Please, miss, you must keep your voice down. Think of the other patients. Now just take a seat. The attending physician will be with you when he can deliver a diagnosis of your father's condition. Can I get you some water?"

Anna walked away without answering.

Elizabeth took Anna's hand and guided her to a chair. Together, they waited three more hours. Finally, a man in white approached them. "Ladies, I'm sorry to have kept you waiting. I'm Dr. Lane. I've been overseeing Dr. Bainbridge's care. Are you his daughter?" Anna nodded. "And you are?"

"His housekeeper," Elizabeth said. "I found him on the floor. How is he?"

"Dr. Bainbridge has suffered a heart attack."

"Dear God in heaven," Elizabeth cried out. Anna's head dropped to her chest as if insupportable.

"He's a strong man. It looks as if he will recover over time. He is awake and alert enough to talk about the need to hurry back to work. We will make sure that doesn't happen too soon. He must be patient and let his heart heal. I will need your cooperation with this when he returns home."

"Of course," Anna said, finding strength to lift her head.

"It's important he remain calm and unbothered."

"May we see him now?"

"Yes, he wants both of you."

Anna and Elizabeth walked up to Papa's bed tentatively. Seeing the figure of Dr. Bainbridge prone, weak, under blankets, being cared for by a nurse, shocked them. Anna had never seen Papa physically helpless. Elizabeth had, when Anna's mother died.

"Come closer, Anna," the doctor whispered, his voice too feeble to be heard across the room. "You, too, Elizabeth."

All Anna could say was, "Papa."

"Dear child, do not be put off by my appearance. I simply suffered a minor myocardial infarction. I have seen many patients through this myself. And now, I find that I am one of them. I will recover quickly."

"Not too quickly," Elizabeth said. "Dr. Lane told us to make sure you take this journey back to full vigor slowly."

"I will take it in my own time and at my own pace."

"No, you won't. You are outnumbered two to one. I will be helping with your care. And you know I can be one stubborn woman."

That brought a weak smile to Papa's face. "Yes, I know only too well."

"It's best not to argue," said the nurse. "I believe Dr. Bainbridge needs his rest now. You can come back tomorrow."

"Can't I stay with him tonight?" Anna asked.

"No, miss. We'll take good care."

Anna stayed with Elizabeth instead that night. Over breakfast they talked of Anna moving back home temporarily. She could help with Papa's care, and save rent money by living at home, money that could sustain the household.

Mrs. Pendleton understood Anna's quick departure and sent her off with a long, genuine hug. "Your room downstairs will be waiting for you whenever you want to return. I won't give it to another."

"Thank you, Mrs. Pendleton. You have become like family to me." Anna stopped for just a second and said, "I mean it. You really have."

Papa returned home after three weeks in the hospital, eager to get going mentally, with a body that refused to comply. Anna and Elizabeth had their hands full trying to keep him abed. They didn't want him thinking of work, so they wouldn't allow him any medical journals that came through the mail. Elizabeth also kept daily newspapers away from Dr. Bainbridge. It would be too dangerous for him to see the financial reports, which offered little promise. When Dr. Lane stopped by regularly to check up on him, Dr. Bainbridge demanded to know what was going on at the hospital.

Anna continued taking pictures during the day. At night, she slept on a daybed moved into Papa's room.

"There's no need for all this fuss," Papa said.

"Elizabeth and I are in charge, for the time being. You have no choice but to abide by our wishes."

"Tell me, how is the stock market?"

"I'm not supposed to discuss that with you." Anna decided to dress up the truth a little. "But I will say that things are looking up. J.P. Morgan has put some of his own money into his company to move things on the upswing. Other rich men are doing the same. They want to show people all over the country that it's safe to invest again."

"That makes me feel better. Thank you, dear child."

Anna had always hated when Papa addressed her as "dear child," as though it were a derogatory title, meant to demean rather than ingratiate. This time, she heard it in a completely different way. As an endearment. Anna smiled and held her father's hand until he fell asleep. For the first time since the heart attack, his countenance expressed peace of mind.

Papa eventually made a full recovery. He returned to the hospital on a limited schedule. Anna moved back to the boardinghouse. And slowly, the U.S. economy rebounded. Anna had been so busy caring for Papa, living at home, and only leaving to take pictures, that she forgot all about Josefina and Adrian. Upon her return to the boardinghouse, she was in for a big surprise.

CHAPTER 25

Anna arrived home to the clatter of excited women in the parlor. When she entered, Josefina ran to her with the biggest smile Anna had ever seen on her friend's face. It exuded pure joy.

"What's going on in here? You look as though you found a million dollars on the street."

"Even better. I have found love. Anna, I am betrothed."

"To whom?"

"To Adrian, of course. We have set a date and are making arrangements. It will be a simple affair."

"What? When?"

"On February 7th. Mrs. Pendleton has offered to host a party here after the ceremony at St. Alphonsus Church."

"St. Alphonsus? Why that was where we..."

"Where you what? Oh my, you've grown pale. Are you ill?"

"What date did you say?"

"February 7th. I know that's an important anniversary for you. That's the day the Great Fire started, the day you became a professional photographer."

It's the day Adrian and I were to be married at St. Alphonsus, Anna thought. *Why would he marry someone else then and there?*

"Why did you choose that date?"

"It's my parents' anniversary. I always planned to be married that day."

"This is all happening quickly. Have you thought it through?"

"I'm surprised to hear you say that. Adrian and I have been courting for some time. Don't you think we've waited long enough? Aren't you happy for me?"

Anna couldn't fight tears. To escape discovery, she quickly left the room and ran down the stairs to her quarters. Josefina started to follow but was stopped by Naomi.

"What's wrong with her?" asked Josefina.

"Most likely jealousy," replied Naomi.

"She knows marital bliss will never be hers," said Adelaide. "Pay her no mind. Come back and join the celebration. Look, Mrs. Pendleton is bringing us sherry."

Anna never made an appearance at supper, so Josefina went to her. She knocked on Anna's door. Silence greeted her. She knocked again.

"Anna, it's me, Josefina. I'm worried about you. Something is wrong. Have I offended you? Please open the door and speak to me."

Still, silence. Josefina wondered if Anna had left the boardinghouse by the basement door. She opened it and found her friend sitting alone in the yard.

"What are you doing out here? It's cold and dark. You'll catch your death."

"I'm fine."

"You cannot be. Come inside. We'll have some sherry and talk."

Anna reluctantly obeyed. Not because of Josefina's request, but because she didn't want to admit that the night air bore through her clothes and chilled her to the marrow.

Josefina was surprised to find Anna's room so bare and small. Anna read the expression on her face. "I've pared down my things to only essentials."

"I'm worried about you. Why have you chosen such a sparse life? There is no happiness in this room, not one personal item, nothing whimsical that shows you are a member of the human race. Nothing feminine. Nothing that connects you to another person."

"I have my chatelaine. Elizabeth, my nanny, gave it to me. It had been a gift to her from my mother. I'll show it to you."

"I've seen you wear it. I never knew its significance. It's even more lovely now that I know. What else do you have?"

"This is all I need to remind me of them."

"You're shivering. Put on your robe and come upstairs. I'll brew some tea. Mrs. Pendleton served butterscotch pudding tonight. I'm sure there is some left."

As the two women climbed the stairs, Josefina put her arm around Anna. Upstairs, the whistling kettle broke the silence. After the tea cooled a bit, Josefina resumed the conversation.

"Do you want to tell me what was troubling you earlier? Aren't you happy for me? Are you concerned that we will no longer be friends? Rest assured, that could never happen. I want you to still be a part of my life after I'm married. You'll love Adrian. He's so much fun. I want you near when he and I have children. I want you to be their auntie."

"Are you sure this is what you truly desire? You will be leaving the theater. All the excitement and fanfare. The lights, the applause. You'll be giving up your art, making costumes worthy of any museum for their craftsmanship. How can you relinquish your talents so easily?"

"I'm not giving up my talents. Adrian and I have formed a plan that will work for both of us. I will surrender my job at the theater. Instead, while staying at home and, we hope, raising a large family, I'll transfer my skills to creating clothing, which I will sell at the Woman's Industrial Exchange on Charles Street. Are you familiar with the place?"

"Yes, of course, they sell women's handiwork of all kinds. I've been there many times."

"It was Adrian who told me about it. He said he often enjoyed himself there."

Yes, with me, Anna thought.

"There's a tearoom, too, and sometimes they hold cooking classes. I intend to take them. Like you, I'm not the best of cooks. Anyway, I want to sell my sewn goods there, beautiful baby and children's clothes. Layette sets. Booties. Baptismal gowns. I have so many ideas."

"Can't people purchase those things at O'Neill's?"

"Yes, but my designs will become heirlooms, one of a kind. I'm sure there are people in Baltimore looking for something no one else has and are willing to pay the price."

"What about stage lights and fitting costumes to the theater's great names, like Maude Adams? Women are just gaining a foothold in the theater world, you know. Look at the playwright, Rachel Crothers. She's writing plays about independent women,

women who challenge men for equality in all things. She's even directing her own productions. Josefina, this is an exciting time in the theater. How can you throw it all away?"

"I'm not tossing anything away. I'm maturing, growing into the role of wife and mother. It's what young ladies of my age do. If you met Adrian, I'm sure you would approve. Would that make you feel better? I can arrange a little get together this weekend."

"No, oh no, you shouldn't do that."

"Why? What could you possibly have against it? I've asked you before and you've always had an excuse. Is there something I'm missing?"

"It's just that he doesn't seem to... doesn't have...?"

"Exactly what are you trying to say?"

Anna searched for any excuse. "He sells cookies. How could he possibly earn enough money to support a large family?"

"Come now. I've never known you to show concern for wealth or social standing. We will be like most young couples. We will find a way. And he doesn't sell cookies. He's a distributor. He delivers Berger Cookies to stores all over town. He's working toward becoming a manager."

"There she is, finally surfaced from the dungeon," said Jane Catherine, as she entered the kitchen. "Josefina, why do you bother yourself with this ridiculous 'woman' or whatever she is?"

"Jane Catherine, we are in the middle of a private conversation. What do you want?"

"I'm in search of butterscotch pudding. I didn't get enough at supper."

"You'll only have to pull your corset tighter," said Anna. "And you're getting a little thick around the waist, as it is."

"She's right," said Josefina. "Wasn't it you who said pain is part of being a woman?"

Jane Catherine stared at the ice box, then turned on her heels and retreated to her room empty-handed. Josefina and Anna laughed behind her back.

"Well, that's better. It's good to see you smile. Do you feel your old self once again?"

Anna lied and said she did.

"How about we finish the pudding before the house mice get it?" said Josefina.

The two ate in silence. Anna gave Josefina a cursory hug. They said goodnight to one another as Josefina climbed the stairs and Anna descended them.

⊱⊰

Days passed, with Anna making herself scarce at the boardinghouse. She didn't want to give Josefina the opportunity to arrange a meeting with Adrian.

It was Adrian who came to her, not in person, in the form of a letter. He disguised his handwriting on the envelope for fear Josefina would intercept it.

The missive was brief. He wanted to meet Anna in private, at a place where they would go undetected. Anna's spirits rose to the clouds at the thought he might have had a change of heart. In a return note, Anna suggested they meet at the grave of Mayor McLane in Green Mount Cemetery. If Adrian thought this bizarre, he didn't say so. On the appointed day and time, they arrived within five minutes of each other. A grey cloud loomed overhead.

"Anna, you are looking wan. Have you been ill?"

"Ill at ease, yes. I am quite disturbed by your upcoming nuptials."

"You cannot blame me for going on with my life. Did you think me a monk?"

"No, but why Josefina? You knew we were friends. Why did you continue to pursue her? Didn't you know how it would hurt me?"

"Love cannot be turned on and off like a light switch. I was already smitten when I learned of your association."

"That soon?"

"Yes, Josefina is easy to get to know. She's sweet and charming. I found her contagious."

"You found me that way once."

"No, I did not. In you, I found someone who needed freeing."

"So, you felt sorry for me. There was no real love."

144

"I cannot believe you are saying such a thing. You know I loved you wholeheartedly."

"That is difficult to believe, given your infatuation with Josefina now. You have cast off any feelings for me that remain and transferred them to her."

"It's been years."

"And how am I supposed to stay friends with Josefina and you? Should I just paint a perpetual smile on my face at the wedding and thereafter? Have you no regard for the position you two have put me in?"

"You haven't told her of our past courtship, have you?" Adrian said.

"No, I couldn't tell her."

"Then, you cannot blame her. You can hate me all you want but she is innocent."

"I do hate you. Why didn't you tell her yourself? Was I so unimportant?"

"I cannot damage our relationship. I cannot hurt her."

"Instead, you have hurt me."

"For that, I am deeply sorry. Once we are married and Josefina has moved out of the boardinghouse, your paths will not cross every day. Can you please be happy for us until then?"

"No."

"Have you become involved with anyone else yourself these past few years?"

"No."

"Then, I urge you to step outside the role of 'Anna Bainbridge, Photographer' and go back to the Anna I once knew. She was curious, eager and unabashed in her enjoyment. Do you remember her?"

"I remember rides at Electric Park, and the view from the top of the pagoda at Patterson Park, and dinner at the Carrollton when you proposed to me."

"We are no longer. I am betrothed now. You must accept that. If you recall, it was you who chose work over marriage."

Anna swished her shoe over the grass. Back and forth like a metronome. She knew their time alone was slowing to its end. A trickle of rain fell upon the former couple. "Goodbye, Adrian. I wish you all the best."

"Don't say 'goodbye.' I do hope you will support Josefina as she takes this big step in her life. She needs you now. After the wedding, do as you wish. Please, for me?"

"I'll think about it." Anna walked away. As she passed one grave marker after another, thoughts of how short life was, how complex, how cruel, and how painful, raced through her head. They haunted her like the spirits of the dead, like her mother, whom she wished to embrace, at this moment, with all her heart.

Little did she know, her mother was very near.

CHAPTER 26

Over the next two days, Anna couldn't focus on her work. It was the first time in her career she wasn't fully dedicated. She almost missed a deadline for an assignment, forgot a suffrage meeting and completely overlooked the due date for rent. She ate little, slept a lot, and found solace nowhere. One morning, near dawn, she awoke to the smell of rose water. It beckoned her. She got up, dressed and set out on a walk.

It had snowed overnight. A light dusting clung to sidewalks and trees, making the world twinkle like stardust and feel warm and cozy when it was cold as ice. The deception was not lost on Anna.

She wanted to share her troubles with Elizabeth, with Emmaline, with Mama. But her feelings were too personal. It would have been easier if she had suffered a broken arm. How could she possibly express the pain in her heart?

Anna walked until she no longer felt her fingers and toes. She stepped into a small café and ordered hot cocoa and warm cinnamon biscuits. She barely heard a voice call her name.

"Anna, come join me," David Jameson said. "You look like you could use some companionship. So could I."

Reluctantly, Anna sat across from the reporter. "I haven't much to offer. My papa has been very sick and my best friend, well... we're having problems in our relationship."

"Let me guess. Is there a man in the picture?"

Anna looked at him with surprise and wonder.

"I know a little about love and all its complications," he said.

"Are you courting someone, David?"

"Her name is Isabella. Our mothers arranged us. You might think we would resent an interference so personal but the ladies proved to be right. We fell in love."

"Seems like everyone is in love these days. Congratulations."

"This story doesn't have a happy ending. She met someone else and set me free."

"I'm sorry to hear that. How are you holding up?"

"I'm doing fine. My mother blames me. Her mother blames me. Said my work sent me hither and yon. I wasn't around enough to please Isabella. To take her places, to honey-talk her. 'Good riddance,' I say." David put more cream in his coffee. "Let's change the subject."

"What would you like to talk about?"

"Murder."

"You wouldn't."

"No, I'm not thinking of killing anybody. I'm talking about the Harry Thaw trial. It's set to start February 7th. *The Democratic Telegram* is sending me to New York to report the story, and I need a photographer. Are you interested?"

"Of course." Anna paused for a second. "Wait a minute. Will we have to stay overnight again?"

"Yes, I'm sure. A trial of this magnitude doesn't end in one day."

"I don't know. Papa won't be happy about my traveling with a man unchaperoned again. He's been recovering from a heart attack. I don't want to do anything that might upset him. I wouldn't want to be the cause of a relapse."

"If it makes you more comfortable, I'll assure him in person that you will be treated as a lady at all times. You have to be there, Anna. This could be a big break for you. You take pictures no one else can. They could make the national papers."

"When is this trial again?"

"It starts Thursday, February 7th. We should probably go to New York the night before. If the trial continues into the next week, we'll stay the weekend."

Anna thought, *What a perfect excuse to avoid Josefina's wedding, which was scheduled for the same day.*

"I'll do it."

"Excellent. I'm sure there will be no problems."

CHAPTER 27

The night before the trial, Anna and David stared out the window of *The Marylander*, a train that whisked passengers on the Royal Blue Line between Washington and New York, with a stop in Baltimore. During the long journey, David regaled Anna with stories of other news events and columns he had written. By the time they pulled into the station, Anna felt as though she had actually witnessed them.

"You're a good storyteller. No wonder you make a great writer."

"Thank you. I'm not used to hearing compliments coming from your lips."

At the word "lips," Anna blushed. She hoped David hadn't noticed.

"I'm hungry. Are you up for a late supper?" David said.

"I think I'd like to get a good night's rest. If you don't mind, I'll go to my hotel. I'm sure you can find a restaurant near the YMCA. Why aren't you staying with your brother?"

"He and Monica are touring Europe for a few weeks."

"Paris?"

"I'm sure."

"I envy them."

The next day in court, Anna wondered if photographers would be restricted. This was a big, sensational trial. Would she have to shoot the proceedings through the transom? Wearing her man-tailored suit, looking professional and prepared, Anna soon discovered that only designated photographers would be allowed in the courtroom. After a few anxious moments, she found her name on the approved list. There she was, Anna Bainbridge, covering the elite on trial in New York City. Despite the gravity of the crime, Anna smiled.

Before the swearing-in of witnesses began, the judge warned the press. No one could leave the courtroom once the trial began.

There would be no taking of photographs during testimony, only as witnesses came and went when called to the stand and during breaks. At no time could photographers take pictures of the jury. There would be no talking among the press or anyone in the gallery. And reporters were not allowed to interview the defendant, witnesses or members of the jury until the trial was over. David gave Anna a look that told her she must comply.

When the defendant, Harry Thaw, was brought into the courtroom, Anna's breath caught in her throat. He didn't look anything like a murderer. His countenance displayed a rather bland, simple man, adorned with a pair of round, clear-glass, wire-framed spectacles. His receding hairline had been slicked straight back. Harry Thaw was not a man one would notice in a crowd. Yet he was the center of attention at the trial. Until Evelyn Nesbit arrived.

She would have stood out in a mob of thousands. A raven-haired beauty, she sat down gently, her hair framing her face in a perfect bouffant. She possessed a comely expression that was attractive to men and women. Her figure, though tiny, curved in and out, her dress hugging all the right places. Even so, a demure innocence aroused pity.

What would be known, at the time, as "The Trial of the Century" began. The defense painted a picture of the murder victim as a man not innocent himself. In 1887, Stanford White had helped to open a gathering place for the "most depraved of society," as it was put, with an appropriate name to match. It was called The Sewer Club, nothing more than a place where men and women could engage in sex with one another randomly, without regard to gender or marital status or the slightest feelings of love.

When he was forty-six years old, White had met Evelyn Nesbit, a mere teenager. As the story goes, he plied her with drink until she lost consciousness. He raped her. To keep her for his own, he showered her with fine jewelry and furs. He installed a red velvet swing in their home, where she could while away the hours in childlike bliss.

Not long after, Evelyn met Harry Thaw, the alleged murderer. Their relationship was sexual in nature and incestual in spirit. White presented himself as a father figure to Evelyn, sending her to a boarding school for her "finishing."

On a trip to Europe, Evelyn told Thaw what White had done to her. He could not control his emotions, lashing out at her, in words and action. Under the influence of cocaine, he beat her with a riding crop and raped her himself. As if she were to blame for being violated by White.

Stanford White sued Harry Thaw for kidnapping his girlfriend and taking her out of the country, even though Evelyn's mother had accompanied them. Thaw put an end to the suit by marrying Evelyn in April of 1905. The union did not put an end to the hatred that consumed both men.

On the night of June 25, 1906, Harry and Evelyn attended a performance of the play, *Mam'zelle Champagne*, in the Roof Garden restaurant and theater at Madison Square Garden. It was there, Thaw saw White and shot him point blank, three times. White died instantly. Witnesses were aghast, screaming, running, fainting, rushing to help the helpless victim. Harry Thaw was arrested for murder on the spot.

Anna felt relieved to be seated when pictures of the dead body, with its blown-off face, were shown. Her stomach roiled. Her head spun.

It seemed to Anna and David that this would be a cut-and-dried case. But it wasn't. The testimony and jury deliberation spilled over into the next week.

Anna kept her distance from David as much as possible in the evenings. He had wanted to take in a show called *A Parisian Romance* but Anna feigned illness. When the proceedings resumed, David congratulated her on a remarkable recovery.

Just when everyone thought the trial would soon be over, the jury announced it was hung. Judge James Fitzgerald urged them to keep deliberating. When it became obvious it was going to take some time, Anna and David were called back to Baltimore, where they later learned the jury could go no further. Seven members had voted "guilty" and five "not guilty by reason of insanity." There would have to be another trial.

Anna could have stayed in New York forever. She feared what awaited her at the boardinghouse. Surely, minute-by-minute accounts of the wedding and reception.

After seeing where love and obsession could lead, she was in no mood for "happily ever after."

CHAPTER 28

Anna read all the articles about the trial from various newspapers. None of the pictures compared with hers. She had framed the subjects so tightly, they practically leaped from the page onto the readers' laps.

She also read stories written by some of the female reporters in New York. Shameful examples of yellow journalism, nothing but inuendo and gossip and hyperbole. These so-called reporters were labeled "Sob Sisters," not exactly a professional title. They wrote "sob stories," that bore little truth, anything to sell a newspaper. Often, they were accompanied by distorted photographs of all involved, including the judge. These pictures captured ugly expressions as if chewing food and blurred exaggerated gestures that looked like pulling taffy. Anna crumbled the Extra! edition of the newspaper printed that day and threw it in the gutter. Her reddened face declared the shame she felt for women who stooped so low to make a name for themselves.

When Anna arrived home from New York, she found a note from Josefina under her door. It was dated February 7, 1907.

My dearest Anna:

Today is the happiest day of my life and I regret that you are not here to share it with me. I know you will love Adrian as a brother, once you meet him. His sense of humor, love of music, and light-hearted outlook will draw you from your depression, I am certain.

The greatest wedding present you can give me is your time, your smile and your continued friendship. Will you visit with us on your return?

Your friend for life, Josefina

p.s. Please be happy for me.

Anna knew she would have to face the inevitable. She agreed to a dinner with the newlyweds and asked if she could bring an escort. Josefina was thrilled. Without telling David about her past with Adrian, she invited him to join her for dinner. He was more than happy to comply.

⁂

"Why, Anna, you are wearing color. You're always in brown or black. How lovely you look in violet," David said. "If I had known, I would have brought you a nosegay to match."

"There's no need. This is a borrowed dress. And we're just going to dinner at a friend's house."

On the way, Anna told David about her connection to Josefina, omitting everything about Adrian, other than he was her friend's new husband. Where she was concerned, the fewer people who knew the truth, the better.

Anna and David arrived at the couple's home in Canton, just east of downtown. Anna was already familiar with his apartment. She had been there before, planning her life with Adrian just a few years prior.

Josefina swung open the door and welcomed her friend. When Anna stepped into the parlor, she saw that Josefina had already added her feminine touches, with fresh curtains and chair covers, beautiful linen on the table and hand-embroidered napkins.

"What a lovely place you have," David remarked.

"Thank you, Mister...?"

"Oh, excuse me. This is David Jameson," Anna said. "David, this is Josefina."

"Josefina Crosby," her friend added.

Anna wanted to cry. Adrian sidled up to his wife.

"And this is her husband, Adrian."

"Nice to meet you both," David said.

There was an awkward moment of silence which Anna needed to fill, lest she burst into tears. "Josefina is a fine seamstress. She used to make theater costumes. No doubt, this is all her handiwork."

"You are quite talented," David said.

Anna wanted to scream.

"Please come in and make yourselves comfortable. May I offer you warm cider?"

"That would be fine," said Anna.

"Oh, I see you have purchased one of those new phonograph players," David said.

"It was a wedding present from Josefina's aunt," Adrian replied. "Would you like to see how it works?"

"Yes, I would. What recordings do you have?"

"I recently bought this one and haven't played it yet." He handed the record to David.

"'Anchors Aweigh.' Sounds like it could be a lively tune."

"It's performed by the Naval Academy Band."

"Let's hear it."

The rousing song put everyone but Anna in a jolly mood. Throughout dinner, most of the conversation focused on the newlyweds and their plans for the coming months.

Anna wanted to run.

Over dessert, Josefina took Anna aside and said, "David seems like a true gentleman. How long have you been courting?"

"We are just having dinner for the first time. We work together on the newspaper, nothing more. I brought him with me this evening to round out the table, that's all."

"I see something more in the way he looks at you."

"I assure you, I am not encouraging him."

"Time will tell."

"Yes, time will tell *all*."

∽∾

After Anna returned home, she lay on her bed and looked back over the evening. She wondered why Adrian deceived his wife. He hadn't been forthcoming about his one-time betrothal to Anna. How could he be this cold? So indifferent to Josefina's feelings... and Anna's? Or was he so nice that he didn't want to hurt anyone? That's what he had told Anna. Maybe he was nothing but a coward.

There was little time to think of such things. The re-trial of Harry Thaw was about to begin. David asked Anna if she would return to New York with him. She begged off, saying her father was still ill and she needed to remain close. Once she saw how the trial turned out, she realized she hadn't missed much. The jury found Thaw guilty by reason of insanity and he was remanded to an institution for the mentally ill.

Throughout the year, the country slowly pulled out of its financial morass, Oklahoma was admitted to the union of states, and a new publication came on the market. It was simply called *Baltimore Magazine*, printed by Baltimore's Chamber of Commerce.

Anna needed a challenge. And she wanted to avoid David. She had no romantic interest in him. She applied for a position at the magazine and they hired her for freelance work.

Over the next several months, she made the magazine her main priority, and newfound devotion to her father, second. She visited him and Elizabeth weekly, sharing meals and finding pathways into their good graces. Anna had little energy left for gentlemen callers.

On December 31st, for the first time, a shiny electric ball was dropped in New York's Times Square, like a beating heart in the center of the city. One hundred incandescent bursts of light marked the end of 1907 and the beginning of 1908. It was arranged by Adolph Ochs, owner of the *New York Times*, to call attention to the new location for his paper. Anna wondered what stories she would photograph in 1908. She needed some sparkle in her life.

CHAPTER 29

The early months brought changes to Baltimore and Anna's outlook. A new train line took passengers on a triangular route between Baltimore, Annapolis and Washington. The Baltimore station, located on Liberty Street, provided easy access for reporters and photographers to get to news stories at state and national seats of government. Anna had greater opportunity to become known by lawmakers and other officials. This was exactly what she wanted. It swept her away from her own triangle of Anna, Josefina and Adrian.

Quite often, David was given the same assignment as Anna, although they often worked for competing publications. She kept her demeanor businesslike at all times. That didn't stop him from trying to pursue her.

A new governor had taken office, a Democrat named Austin Lane Crothers. In March, Anna and David traveled on the same train to Annapolis, along with other journalists, to interview him about his first days in office. When they arrived, the politician seemed a bit nervous.

He pledged to improve state roads, and end corruption in political campaigns and inside the police department. He read a litany of intentions, which were all admirable but conspicuously left out a couple of key issues.

As Anna and David traveled home, they sat together and spoke of other things, like the new movie everyone was raving about, *Dr. Jekyll and Mr. Hyde,* starring Hobart Bosworth. Anna directed the conversation her way. "Do you think Governor Crothers was honest with us? Or is he, perhaps, a case of Jekyll and Hyde? Do you think he has two opposite sides?"

"He did seem a bit evasive when you asked him how he felt about woman's suffrage."

"Yes, I rephrased the question a couple of times, hoping to get a direct answer. He refused to snap at the bait."

"I might just mention that in the article I'm writing for my paper. What do you think?"

"You know where I stand. As a professional at a competing publication, I can't sway you one way or the other."

"It seems you've grown quite a bit. Can I sway you to have dinner with me tonight?"

"I plan to visit my father."

"I see."

Anna had no such plan. By the look on David's face, she knew that he knew it, too. Now who was being two-faced?

ॐ

Anna decided to look into the political background of the new governor, who hailed from Cecil County, Maryland.

After a year of running for office, Austin Lane Crothers won Maryland's gubernatorial election. He was relatively unknown because he had been largely unable to campaign. A bout with typhoid fever had sidetracked him. Once he was ensconced in the governor's mansion, Marylanders wondered what he would do.

Women wanted to know where he stood on suffrage but he wasn't forthcoming. He did, however, support a bill that would prohibit colored men from voting in Maryland by tying their right to vote to land ownership. This stance also spoke to women, telling them, inadvertently, that Crothers was against woman's suffrage just as much. Anna's intuition about the man proved true, despite the many good things he was doing in other areas.

After years in the newspaper business, Anna earned a more-than-comfortable income for her style of living. She surprised Elizabeth with a gift, a brand-new portable vacuum manufactured by the Hoover Company. This upright model allowed Elizabeth to clean carpets without having to bend her back or carry heavy rugs into the yard for a hefty beating.

In addition, Anna renewed her friendship with Emmaline. They had been corresponding but hadn't had much time to get together. In November, before winter beset Baltimore, Emmaline invited Anna to lunch at her apartment.

Emmaline rolled off the menu. "Tomato soup fortified with harvest vegetables, bakery bread and fried apples. And for dessert... Joe Froggers."

"You remembered how much I enjoyed them. Thank you, Emmaline."

"It's so good to see you again. What have you been doing?"

"Do you have all day?"

Over the next couple of hours, the two friends exchanged stories. Anna confessed her feelings for Adrian and the love triangle she had been unable to escape. Even though she hadn't seen much of Josefina and Adrian lately, she still felt tethered to their lives, which bound Anna to unhappiness. And, at the boardinghouse, talk of Josefina's new life still dominated more than one supper.

"Let's go for a digestive walk, Anna."

The two sauntered several blocks until they reached the offices of the *Baltimore Afro-American* newspaper, Emmaline's employer.

"Look at the beautiful doll in the window. What's it doing there?" Anna said.

"It's part of a contest the paper is running, a project that combines my previous position with my current one. Have you ever seen anything like this before?"

"No, I don't think so."

"Many people haven't. The history of colored baby dolls is marked with prejudice and suppression, not joy, like this one."

"What do you mean? How can a toy cause such controversy?"

"You obviously have never heard of a Topsy-Turvy Doll. Historically, it has two bodies and two heads, one is white and the other is colored. The white doll has a smiling face, framed by two red-haired pigtails. It's dressed in a nice frock with a folksy design. She is connected at the waist to the colored doll, who is upside down. That doll wears no smile. She's dressed in a cheap kerchief print, with a rag twisted on her head like a Mammie."

"What is the purpose of that kind of doll?"

"Well, slave children were often forced to play with the white offspring of their owners, to give them companionship. Each girl took a turn holding the doll. When the white child cuddled it, the black doll faced down in submissive juxtaposition. When the colored child cuddled the colored doll, she saw that her doll was sad and poor, while the other was happy and moneyed. The doll ultimately belonged to the white child, who learned, over time, that coloreds were beneath white. Here, in this window, we see an example of a colored doll, head to toe, dressed in a lovely outfit, meant to be played with and cuddled by a colored child only. And her face is pleasant. No white version attached. Do you see the difference?"

"Yes, I do. Even the name 'topsy-turvy' implies that things are not right; they're askew, confused. Emmaline, whenever we are together, I learn something so illuminating, I feel you are more than an accountant. You are a teacher. When we first met, you said you wanted to teach but it was impossible. Why? You are naturally gifted."

"There are very few colored teachers around. My kind aren't admitted to colleges very often. And it's expensive, so a teaching certificate is out of reach."

"I'm sorry."

There, in broad daylight, on one of the busiest streets of Baltimore, Anna embraced Emmaline. "I'm really sorry. Now, tell me why the *Baltimore Afro-American* newspaper is displaying this doll."

"The newspaper is running a contest to see who can guess the name already chosen out of these three printed on the sign. Chances cost only a penny. The winner gets to keep her as their prize."

"And where does the money go?"

"That's where my previous employer comes in. The money benefits the Colored Empty Stocking and Fresh Air Circle. They are trying to pay off the mortgage on that farm the colored kids go to in summer. It's called Emory Groves, near Reisterstown. They've acquired ten and a half acres there. My newspaper is displaying the doll and helping to publicize the contest."

"That's wonderful. And how is Miss Cummings?"

"She's doing just fine. Enjoying every minute of the organization's growth and success. She makes many a child happy and it delights her to no end."

"I couldn't be more pleased."

Anna, who always had a camera with her, offered to take a picture of the doll in the window, saying she'd try to get *Baltimore Magazine* to print it, along with a story.

Both women agreed to stay in touch more often and celebrate the new year together, if no other opportunities arose, of the male sort.

November proved to be an eventful month. Anna learned that H.L. Mencken was taking a secondary job, as literary editor and critic of an established national magazine called *The Smart Set*. The publication had been around since 1900 as a cultural alternative to the popular yellow journalism of the time, publications that pandered to readers' insatiable appetites for sob stories and gossip. On the pages of *The Smart Set*, Mencken delivered, to more sophisticated readers, the works of Theodore Dreiser and Sinclair Lewis, among many other notable authors. The position propelled H.L. Mencken into the national spotlight, elevating him to a pillar of literary journalism. Anna sent him a note of congratulations and was surprised to receive an invitation to meet at his office.

"Mr. Mencken, good to see you. You are becoming well-known not just in Baltimore but all over the United States."

"It is a burden, sometimes, Miss Bainbridge."

"Please call me Anna."

"Very well." He, in turn, did not invite Anna to address him as H.L., as his cronies did. "David has kept me apprised of your work with him. You've done well for yourself."

Anna resented that she had been discussed by these two men. And that David had felt compelled to assume they were some sort of team, with him as the leader.

"I do well on my own."

"He tells me you have been making prudent decisions and evaluations, that you are learning every day."

Anna should have been happy with such compliments coming from the great H.L. Mencken. She saw it more as condescension.

"I am twenty-three now. A grown woman. I have been working as a photojournalist for almost four years."

"I'd like you to think about the possibility of a change in your career."

"What do you mean?"

"What about becoming a writer as well as a photographer? You tried it once. And succeeded on your first endeavor."

"I did? You never told me that."

"I didn't want you to climb on a high horse too soon. Falling can be painful."

"I have written a few more articles since then. Why are you suggesting this more-permanent change?"

"Because you are ready for it. More women are entering this profession and succeeding. You must be prepared to not only compete with men but, even more so, with women. They will be twice as eager, twice as determined to find their place in journalism. You already have a head start. Why let them catch up? Think about it. You could have a career far beyond Baltimore, far beyond the state. I will offer you an updated letter of recommendation, if you so desire."

"Why are you doing this for me? You have never been a proponent of women working in men's jobs. You have never openly supported woman's suffrage. Most of your articles on the subject are relegated to the back page."

"I appreciate good journalism. The source no longer matters to me. Now, I have a meeting to lead with my staff. Good day, Anna."

"Good day, Mr. Mencken... and thank you."

No grass grew under Anna's feet. The next morning, she contacted Mencken's office, spoke to his secretary, and asked for that letter. The next time she saw David, she thanked him. He asked her if she would join him for a celebration over dinner. This time, she accepted, not out of gratitude but because she realized that a change in life could be a good thing.

The two dined at Lexington Market, where they enjoyed fried oyster sandwiches and bottles of Coca-Cola at a counter. David became quiet while they ate, then turned to face Anna. "I'd like to clear the air about our discourse on war heroes being memorialized, while women who do extraordinary things are not so honored. Remember when we reported on the unveiling of the John Eager Howard statue?"

"Yes, I do. It was quite upsetting. I must say, my respect for you diminished, which is partly why I have been reluctant to befriend you."

"I understand. My respect for you only increased that day. You made me think. I was spewing historical beliefs, not revealing my personal feelings. My intention was not to demean women."

"And how do you really feel about it?"

"I feel that people from all walks of life, men and women, of any race, should be honored when their work involves great risk, bravery and sacrifice."

"Good. I appreciate that you have revealed your innermost feelings. Men often have difficulty doing that. I know my papa does."

"Shall we go in search of something sweet? There's plenty to choose from here at any one of several dessert stalls. I have a favorite."

As they wandered around the market, looking for something to top off their dinners, David guided Anna toward the Berger Cookie stand. Anna spotted Adrian right away. He was smiling and laughing with coworkers as he unpacked supplies. When he took a break to wipe his brow, he spotted Anna, dressed in a black skirt, white ruffled blouse with a green bow at the neck, and a black tweed vest. Her hat, black with a hint of iridescent green feathers, was cocked slightly. She looked feminine but not prissy. When she saw Adrian looking her way, she gently put her hand through the crook of David's arm. It was an overt show of affection, meant to send a message to Adrian, also a means to pull David in a different direction.

"The Berger Cookies are this way," David said.

"I've had my fill from the oysters. Do you mind if we skip dessert?"

"If you wish. Would you like to take a walk outside?"

"Yes, the fresh air will be most welcome," she said, sending a backwards glance at Adrian.

As soon as they stepped out the door, Anna released her hold on David. He took notice that she had just dropped some sort of act, as if they were two performers who had stepped off the stage and into the wings.

"You look upset. Is something bothering you?" David asked.

"No. Not at all."

"Well then, would you like to take in a movie? I can tell you what's playing nearby. We could see *Pride of the Range*, with Tom Mix at 'The Auditorium' on Howard Street."

"That's a cowboy picture, isn't it?"

"Yes, but they have a vaudeville show right before it you might like."

"Umm..."

"Or we could see Mary Pickford's new movie, *Romana*. It's playing at Lubin's Theater on Baltimore Street."

"Oh, that's the one I prefer."

"Not the Tom Mix movie?"

"You can see that another time."

Anna's mood immediately brightened as they headed toward the theater. Anna insisted on paying her own way. During the film, David tried to hold Anna's hand, only to be refused. After the movie, they walked to Anna's boardinghouse. David took Anna's arm as they crossed Charles Street.

"I can manage myself. I do it every day."

"I'm confused. Back at Lexington Market, it seemed to me that you made a romantic overture. I am simply reciprocating. Did I misread your intentions?"

"It was just that it was difficult maneuvering the food stalls and there was spilled water I was trying to avoid."

"And how does that differ from crossing a busy, dirty street like Charles?"

"I was just feeling a little unsteady at the market. Maybe it was the oysters."

"Oh."

David acted as though he understood. Of course, he did not. It was becoming evident that Anna often had an ulterior motive in her actions, something that would result in her own benefit. It had happened on assignment, when she honey-talked Mr. Cator.

And when she invited David to dinner at her friends' home, then proceeded to ignore him.

They walked in silence for a time and, as they approached the boardinghouse, David spoke his mind directly. "Anna, are you interested in a formal courtship?"

"Why, I hardly know you."

"We've been together on many a news story. You should know something about my character by now."

"I'm a bit of a slow mover when it comes to romance. You must give me time."

"Is there someone else you are seeing?"

"There is someone else I am interested in."

"I see."

"Please give me time to learn my heart."

"Very well. Anna, I enjoyed this evening with you. If you find yourself wanting to see a show or take a walk in the park, I would be more than willing to escort you."

"Thank you for a pleasant evening. I see we have reached my home. Goodnight."

"Sleep well."

Chapter 30

After reading a letter written by President Roosevelt refusing to support suffrage, Anna's determination sparked anew. The letter stated that, even though he believed in woman's suffrage... as a politician, he found that no good could come of it. The letter was written to a man named Lyman Abbott, a theologian who believed in evolution, also a magazine editor and author.

The letter appeared in a magazine called *The Remonstrance*, which was published by The Massachusetts Association Opposed to the Further Extension of Suffrage to Women. It appeared in the November 10th issue.

Anna read the entire piece, underlining certain quotes by the President:

> Personally I believe in woman's suffrage, but I am not an enthusiastic advocate of it, because I do not regard it as a very important issue.

Later, he said:

> I do not think that giving the women suffrage will produce any marked improvement in the condition of women.

Still further:

> I believe that man and woman should stand on an equality of right, but I do not believe that equality of right means identity of functions; and I am more and more convinced that the great field,

the indispensable field, for the usefulness of woman is as the mother of the family.

It is in her work in the household, in the home, her work in bearing and rearing the children, which is more important than any man's work, and it is the work which should be that of the breadwinner, the supporter of the home, and, if necessary, the soldier who will fight for the home.

Hogwash! Anna thought. She looked for ways to fight this prejudice and remembered the famous quote by Edward Bulwer-Lytton in 1839:

"The pen is mightier than the sword."

Anna decided to adopt H.L. Mencken's advice. It wouldn't take long to put it in action.

The Baltimore campaign for a woman's right to vote took on heavier ballast in 1909, thanks largely to the efforts of a woman named Edith Houghton Hooker. She had been a member of the local suffrage organization but resigned to start her own movement. It was called the Just Government League and was affiliated with the National American Woman Suffrage Association. As more and more individual suffrage campaigns joined forces, women saw their ship stabilize with the wind blowing at their backs.

Born in Buffalo, New York, Edith Hooker was a product of Bryn Mawr College before becoming one of the first women admitted to the Johns Hopkins University School of Medicine. She married but had a soft spot in her heart for unmarried women who found themselves with child. She and her husband opened the Guild of St. George in Baltimore, a home for these women and their newborns, who faced scorn and snubs.

Without being assigned by any publication, Anna made an appointment with Mrs. Hooker. She wanted to prove to local papers that she could generate news stories on her own and could not only provide pictures, she could write the articles. She felt certain she would sell both.

Anna found her subject to be a woman of quiet strength, soft spoken but determined.

"How do unwed mothers fit into the suffrage movement, Mrs. Hooker?" Anna asked.

"Women do not lose their voices when they have children. In fact, they need to be all-the-more vocal. Unwed mothers must convince legislators that they need protections under the law, no less than married women. And that they have just as strong a need and right to vote as any other woman."

"Do they feel unwelcome in suffrage organizations?"

"Many do. There are women in our society who look down their noses at unwed mothers. They consider them immoral and unworthy of assistance because of their 'mistake.' They view illegitimate children with contempt instead of compassion. In my view, motherhood comes in many forms. The offspring of unwed mothers cry for food and comfort the same as any child whose parents have a marriage certificate."

"What are your goals for the Just Government League?"

"I want to work here in Baltimore for the same ideals as the National American Woman Suffrage Association. In other words, to see that passage of a national amendment takes place in the next few years."

"That is a mighty tall order to fill, wouldn't you agree?"

"Nothing is impossible if we women band together. Wouldn't *you* agree?"

The two women smiled at one another.

Then Mrs. Hooker continued. "I want to expand this organization beyond Baltimore and recruit women and men statewide. We mustn't forget the men who support the right of women to vote. Right now, my associate, Elizabeth King Ellicott, is meeting with state legislators in Annapolis. She did not go there alone. She is accompanied by a couple of women and my husband."

After the interview, Anna took pictures of Mrs. Hooker painting posters and signing on new recruits to the organization.

Anna pitched her article to several publications and found a home at *The Democratic Telegram* newspaper. She sent a clipping to H.L. Mencken and awaited a response. She never got one. Anna placidly moved on to her next assignment.

Just when Anna thought no one else in journalism would recognize her ability to provide pictures and words, *Baltimore Magazine* contacted her. They wanted an article on the opening of a new art gallery in Baltimore. Located at a prestigious address, Mt. Vernon Square at Washington Place, it was to be called "The Walters."

Anna attended the grand opening when Henry Walters, the gallery's founder, cut the ribbon. His father had bequeathed him a collection of art and artifacts amassed over a lifetime. Young Henry wanted to share these works and their histories with all of Baltimore.

At the opening, art lovers strolled through rooms filled with paintings and sculptures, antique crafts, gems, and many large-scale tapestries. Some of these treasures had come from the farthest reaches of the earth... China, Turkey, South America.

Baltimore Magazine asked Anna to expand her story to a full two pages. She had plenty of eye-catching photographs to enhance the spread.

The Walters drew fans immediately and became a place for Baltimoreans to learn about the world, while enjoying the beauty of someone else's creative expressions from far away and long ago.

It became a place she could share with her nanny and, she hoped, Emmaline. She craved the discussions a visit with others would bring.

Anna enjoyed the diversity of her freelance work. She wasn't pigeonholed in any one genre of story. Just as she was gaining momentum, insensitivity called her on the carpet.

ॐॐ

In April, a man from Charles County made headlines throughout the world. His name was Matthew Henson. His claim to fame? He, along with over twenty other men, accompanied Robert Peary, a Naval officer, to the North Pole.

Anna was asked to write a story for the *Telegram* about Henson's local connections and his rise in the ranks from cabin boy to navigator.

Matthew Henson was a colored man.

Anna called on Emmaline to see if she had ever heard of him. Of course, she had. Emmaline was always well-versed in stories of her race.

"He is a fearless man with a mustache to match," she told Anna. "I've seen a picture of him wearing a heavy fur coat all wrapped around his body and head. He's been with Peary on many an expedition. These two have tried more than once to reach the North Pole."

"What stopped them?"

"Poor planning, lack of food. One time, Peary broke his leg. His wife had to tend to him on the expedition until he healed."

"She went with him?"

"Yes indeed, her name is Josephine. She endured quite a lot, far more than expected."

"How do you know all this, Emmaline, and why don't I?"

"I know because the *Baltimore Afro-American* already printed a story on Matthew Henson. Didn't you read it, along with all the other local publications you devour on a regular basis?"

Anna was ashamed to admit she had not.

"I'm disappointed in you. Isn't news about my race just as important as news of yours?"

"I'm sorry, Emmaline. I am remiss. I've been told, on more than one occasion, that I'm a ninny. I guess I am in this instance, too. Tell me about Matthew Henson. It's important for all of Baltimore to know."

"I will share with you what I've read but you must interview his family in Charles County, the people who understand him best."

"Charles County is far away. There are no direct means of travel there."

"You can't dismiss the story on a flimsy excuse. Write them a letter. I'm sure I can get an address for you through my paper."

"Would you? I'd be so grateful."

"On second thought, it might pose a problem, being that my newspaper is a competitor of yours. I'll have to get permission."

"I'm a freelance journalist. I'm not tied to anyone's payroll. Of course, I wouldn't want to jeopardize your employment."

The conversation between the two women bordered on tension. Anna decided to cut the meeting short and make amends by subscribing to the *Baltimore Afro-American*. She knew it would ruffle the feathers of more than a few cackling hens at the boardinghouse.

Anna got the Charles County address on her own. She received an immediate reply from the family of Matthew Henson. They were proud to tell his story.

In 1887, Robert Peary was assigned by the Navy to survey areas for what they called the Nicaragua Canal. He needed a cabin boy and met one in the most unlikely of places... a clothing store. Matthew Henson worked there and struck up a conversation with Peary, who discovered Henson had a seafaring past. From that day forward, Henson accompanied Peary on all his expeditions, be they in tropical climates or frigid. Over the years, Henson became a trusted friend. Peary recognized his natural talent for exploration and reading maps and elevated him to navigator on the expedition to the North Pole that set out on the *Roosevelt* in July of 1908, after several previous failed attempts. The final leg of their historic journey began in February of 1909, with the group reaching their destination in April.

Henson's family in Charles County had not yet heard from him. Even so, they sang his praises to Anna, who meticulously wrote an article that made the front page of the *Telegram* and was picked up by papers in Washington, D.C., and Virginia.

Anna thanked Emmaline by inviting her to explore the many interesting artworks at The Walters. No one said a word about the two women coming in together and, if any heads turned, Anna and Emmaline ignored them.

Anna learned that prejudice can be fully intentional. It can also be inadvertent. It doesn't matter one way or the other. To the person on the receiving end, it is prejudice... it is painful, just the same.

❧

Sometimes, Anna wished she could fly above the problems and challenges of earth. Most everyone, these days, looked to the sky for escape and inspiration.

In 1903, the Wright Brothers had built the first successful airplane. From their humble bicycle shop, to dreams of building gliders, to crafts that crashed and the Kitty Hawk that flew, they raised the spirits of Americans.

Their first successful airplane got off the ground in 1908. Just one year later, the brothers arrived in Maryland to show off their work. Anna heard that a woman was going to fly with one of them. She begged the *Telegram* for the story.

She had already photographed the flight of the first Maryland pilot, Charles Elvers, on October 22nd of 1909. He had built his own plane, a Curtiss Pusher, in Owings Mills. The engine and propeller were located at the rear, allowing him to face the wind like a seagull, with any fuel smells trailing behind. Just weeks later, Maryland was at the center of aviation history once again.

On the given day, Anna arrived at College Park, Maryland, to interview the wife of an Army officer who intended to fly as a passenger with none other than Wilbur Wright himself. A few years older than Anna, Sarah Van Deman was married to Captain Ralph Henry Van Deman, an expert in military intelligence. Anna hoped to interview this pioneering woman after the flight.

At a little before 8:30 A.M., the captain's wife climbed into the tiny seat next to the pilot. He tied her skirt around her legs at the shins to keep her dress from ballooning in flight. After nodding his head to the ground crew, the propeller was turned and Wilbur Wright eased the plane forward. Just before takeoff, however, he stopped. Something displeased him.

Onlookers feared engine trouble. They heard a woman's mild cry. The inventor got out of the plane, fiddled with something, turned it around to its starting point, and tried again.

Once airborne, at sixty miles an hour, Wilbur flew as high as sixty feet, showing Sarah and spectators how he could direct the plane into turns this way and that. After four minutes aloft, he landed softly, prompting a smile from the first woman ever to fly.

When reporters and photographers descended on the plane, Sarah Van Deman simply cried, "Delicious!"

Once her skirt was freed and her shoes touched earth, she gave interviews and allowed pictures to be taken. Anna pushed her way closer, framed photographs, and was so excited, she yelled questions over all the others. She even elbowed Captain Van Deman, who was trying to get to his wife.

"How does it feel to be the first woman to ever fly?" Anna asked.

"It was exhilarating. I highly recommend it to anyone."

"Were you afraid?"

"Afraid? No, of course not. I was flying with the inventor himself."

"Why did he choose you to go up with him? Didn't he always turn down requests from women?"

"My husband and I met the Wright Brothers a little over a year ago and we became friends. I hinted that I would love to fly sometime. I think they saw that I was earnest and capable of controlling myself."

"What went wrong on the first attempt to take off?"

"I don't know. You'll have to ask Mr. Wright."

"Should women train to become pilots some day?"

"I don't see why not. They can do anything they put a mind to."

Pleased with her accomplishment, Anna wormed her way out of the group. Anna's pictures appeared on the front page, above the fold. She was praised for her work and looked back on her day at College Park fondly.

One of her most vivid memories was of Mrs. Van Deman's pearls glistening in the sunlight like a string of hummingbird eggs.

CHAPTER 31

Efforts to suppress the colored vote continued into 1910, when an amendment was introduced by two Democrats, Delegate Walter Digges and State Senator William J. Frere. Their goal, similar to previous attempts, was to tie the right to vote to land ownership. Called the Digges Amendment, it was backed by none other than Governor Austin Lane Crothers.

Anna needed to talk to Emmaline about it. The two met at the office of the *Baltimore Afro-American*.

"Did you hear about the Digges Amendment?"

"Yes, I did. It's terrible."

"Do I have my facts straight? White politicians are making sure every white man can vote but they tie the ability for a colored man to vote to what he owns."

"Yes, if he has had five hundred dollars' worth of land for more than two years and has paid all his taxes, he can vote."

"How many colored men can lay claim to that? How many white men, for that matter? Can your father? Oh, excuse me. I didn't mean to be so personal."

"That's all right. I admire your spirited disgust. No, my father owns land, certainly nowhere near that value."

"What can we do to stop this amendment from passing?"

"For now, all we can do is write Delegate Digges and Senator Frere to express our disapproval."

"I want to get something published in the paper."

"The *Baltimore Afro-American* has already voiced opposition."

"But white people don't read that paper. I want to get something published in the *Democratic Telegram* or the *Baltimore Sun*. I'm going to try to obtain an interview with one of those men."

"Why not go straight to the governor? He's supporting them. And I hear that the General Assembly is thinking about passing a measure that would make it so only white men can vote on whether or not the amendment passes."

"I'm going to do whatever I can. I'm going to try to enlist the suffrage movement, too."

"Don't be surprised if they turn you down. They have only one goal… to get *women* the legal right to vote. They're not going to muddy the waters one iota with anything else."

"We'll just see about that."

☘☙

Anna made an appointment to meet with Emma Funck.

"Well, Anna, I've heard you've been attending marches but our paths haven't crossed in a while. This is a pleasant surprise. What can I do for you?"

"I'll get right to the point. I suppose you've heard about the Digges Amendment."

"Yes, I have. Such a disgrace."

"That's what I was hoping you'd say. I'm here to ask you what Maryland Suffragists plan to do about it."

"What are you suggesting?"

"Will you organize a march against what Governor Crothers and his cohorts plan to do?"

Without hesitation, Mrs. Funck said, "Why no, Anna. I'm sorry. We must stay focused on getting women the right to vote. That does include colored women, you know."

"I've never seen a single one march in your ranks."

"They have their own agenda. They organize their own marches."

"I see."

"Anna, you are still green. You don't fully grasp…"

"I beg to differ. What if these politicians in Annapolis were to put the same voting restrictions on colored women as they have on colored men? Don't you support the voting rights of all people?"

"Yes, of course." Mrs. Funck was quiet for a moment. She walked to the other side of her office, putting distance between herself and Anna.

"You must understand. We are a women's organization. We have been working diligently, over many generations, for *woman's* suffrage. That has been our only mission. When interviewed, I often say, 'This one thing I do.' Day in and day out. If we add other goals to our platform, no matter how moral, no matter how necessary... we will dilute our primary message. And at a crucial time. Until recently, we had built steady momentum. Let me give you an example. Just last week, four hundred suffragists, not just from Maryland, but from all over the country, converged on Washington concerning a suffrage bill. They attended a House of Delegates hearing, only to be rejected. Quite a setback."

"Yes, I'm well aware."

"I'm sorry, I cannot help you. Your quest is praiseworthy. I wish you every success."

Anna left the office disillusioned. One of her heroines had just toppled from the dangerous height of adoration.

Now what? Anna thought. She couldn't return to Emmaline defeated.

Anna made an appointment to interview Delegate Walter Digges in Annapolis, indicating that she represented several local newspapers and one magazine. She took the train and, on the way, formulated her questions more succinctly than she had with Governor Crothers. She felt she had been too soft on him earlier; she hadn't pressed him hard enough. This interview, however, didn't go as planned.

"My, my, a lady journalist. I've never met one before," Delegate Digges said.

"I'm a photographer, too, sir."

"Well, this is quite a surprise. What can I do for you?"

"I have questions about the Digges Amendment."

"Now why would you worry yourself over something that men in high places are handling?"

"Delegate Digges, let's not waste your valuable time or mine. I'll come right to the point. Why are you trying to suppress the colored vote?"

"Miss, uh..."

"Bainbridge, Anna Bainbridge."

"Miss Bainbridge, what paper did you say you represent?"

"I am a freelance journalist," Anna said, as she started composing pictures.

"Who assigned you to interview me?"

Anna ignored him and continued to set up her camera shot.

"Will you please put that camera down and answer me?"

Delegate Digges's face turned as red and shiny as an apple.

"No one," Anna said, as she pressed the shutter.

"Then, why are you here?"

"I'm writing an article about the Digges Amendment on speculation that a Baltimore publication will decide to print it."

"I think you are here just to stir trouble, like those women marching in foul spillage in the gutter, thinking they will someday get to vote. As if writing names on a ballot were as easy as writing an invitation to tea."

"That is an insult to all women, sir. You are implying that we are too frivolous to understand issues and the voting process. Delegate Digges, I came here today all the way from Baltimore, fully prepared to ask questions on even the most minor language in your amendment. Now, let's get down to business."

"The only thing you are going to get is out of my office."

"Do you have something to hide, something you don't want the reading public to know?"

"I said put that camera down. Who sent you here? The *Baltimore Sun*? The *Baltimore American*? The *Democratic Telegram*? I know all their editors. I'll call every single one and complain about you, Miss Bainbridge. I'll see that you never get a byline again! Good day!"

"Rest assured, Delegate Digges. I will quote you on that."

Anna left the office in a flurry of black skirting. She wished she had worn her jodhpurs or man-tailored suit. She might have been taken more seriously.

On the train ride home, Anna wrote her story, not only about the amendment and its disgrace but, also, about Digges's dismissal of woman's suffrage and his refusal to take her seriously. She raised the question sure to sell newspapers: "Why does Delegate Digges only want white men to vote?" It would make a great headline on the front page. She knew this would enflame discourse on the subject, no matter which newspaper published it. Maybe Emma Funck would even take note.

But no one did. Not one local paper would touch the story. Too one-sided. Too incendiary. Too scattered. Too personal. H.L. Mencken summoned Anna to his office. She knew this would not be a pleasant exchange.

"What are you doing, Miss Bainbridge?"

"I asked you to call me Anna."

"I am speaking to you professionally, as your mentor. I cannot believe you practically burst into Delegate Digges's office and confronted him in such a bellicose manner."

"I did not. I was straightforward in asking questions. He didn't like that they were coming from a woman. He didn't like that I was getting to the crux of the matter."

"Maybe that's because you assaulted his authority."

"How? Would he have reacted the same way if the questions had come from you?"

"That remains to be seen. This is the problem with women..."

"Now, wait just a minute, Mr. Mencken. Before you start saying women have no business meddling in politics or journalism, let me remind you. I was the only photojournalist who provided you with pictures of the Great Fire. Or has your memory gone soft?"

Anna knew she had crossed the line. She did not cower, apologize or give Mencken time to rebuff. She stood her ground and pushed even further. "With or without your help, I have carved my niche among other female journalists around this country. I have fought for my place in newspaper history and I won't be chastised for doing my job. The questions I asked Delegate Digges were valid and pertinent to voters. The answers and their repercussions would have resounded in Maryland history for decades to come."

Mencken took two nervous puffs of his cigar.

"You think too highly of yourself. Your article was nothing more than a personal diatribe. It lacked impartiality and sound journalistic integrity. That's why *The Sun* rejected it. I read what you submitted myself."

"Delegate Digges knows he is doing the wrong thing and didn't like having to answer for it, regardless of the person confronting him."

"Be that as it may, a journalist, any journalist, must remain professional and impartial at all times. I understand you gave him 'what for' when he refused to engage with you."

"I was professional, until he became ridiculous."

"May I remind you that I am fully aware of your professional transgressions? You can be belligerent and rude."

"But I get the story, don't I? Are you always the pillar of professionalism?"

Mencken pounded his fist on the desk. "Yes! I think you are growing too big for your shoes. Not to mention your hats! I think you need a dressing down. Maybe a refusal by all local papers will be just the thing you need. You are walking a tightrope with no safety net. You are not only a woman trying to succeed in a man's occupation, you possess unfeminine traits that can be off-putting. You are aggressive, persistent, and too direct." Mencken softened his voice. "You need to gently persuade your subjects to trust you. You must build up some kind of rapport. Believe me, they will be more forthcoming in the long run. Perhaps, use your femininity to its best advantage."

"What are you suggesting, Mr. Mencken?"

"No, no, not what you are thinking. Not that at all. I mean you should relax your approach a little."

"Have you?"

"There you go again. Belligerent. I told you once before not to question my authority."

"I'm sorry."

"Are you?"

Mencken wandered over to the window and stared out over Baltimore, allowing silence to break the tension in the office.

He turned to Anna and spoke with a hint of compassion. "I understand your desire to report stories of magnitude. I understand your frustration when you are turned away. This business isn't easy, Anna. It's filled with rejection. If Delegate Digges turned you down, you should have found another way to get the story. Interview a member of his staff or an opponent in the House. Dig deeper to find the root cause of this bill. Talk to his secretary, his neighbor, his barber. Sometimes, the answers come from the most unlikely sources. And, please, for your own sake, leave your temper and personal opinions at home."

"That's probably the most difficult part of my work."

"It is for all of us. Just so you are aware, *The Sun* is going to publish a story on the Digges Amendment, not yours, one that will encompass various views on the subject."

"That's good to know."

"Remember, you cannot force your opinions on your readership. You present the whole story and let the readers decide where they stand."

❧

Anna returned home to find Frances standing at the wall of mail slots, engrossed in reading. Anna snuck up behind her.

"Boo!"

"Anna, good evening," Frances said, fumbling a bit. "I believe I picked up your mail by mistake. Here," she said, as she handed it to Anna. "I didn't know you subscribed to a newspaper for colored folks."

"I didn't know you had such difficulty reading. See, my name is over this mail slot. Yours is all the way on the other end."

"Silly me."

"Yes, you have hit the nail directly on the head," Anna said, as she descended the stairs. Even though she had been making a good wage, she remained in the tiny basement room. It suited her need to simplify. It served as nothing more than a base from which she could travel quickly to any news story.

As Anna sat on the bed, she thought over the last few days in her career and how complicated and difficult life had become. She thought of Mr. O'Neill and Miss Hughes and how they handled business with a strict but dignified hand. She thought of Emmaline's gentle fortitude and Elizabeth's quickness to forgive. And Emma Funck's diligent focus. And Mama's Victorian ways. At the same time, Jessie Tarbox Beals came to mind, climbing on that bookcase to shoot a trial through the transom. Forbidden, yet unrelenting. And Frances Benjamin Johnston, wearing men's clothes and riding a bicycle to get the job done.

How could all these people, with such admirable but diverse principles, roll into one tiny photojournalist from Baltimore? *I guess this is what it means to be a New Woman.*

CHAPTER 32

As time passed, marked by the gonging of the grandfather clock in the boardinghouse hallway, highs and lows filled Anna's life with confusion, despair and exhilaration.

She didn't know where her career was headed or if she had a future in the newspaper business at all. Feelings for David were starting to erase memories of Adrian, until she sat down to the breakfast table one Saturday morning. Anna was the last to arrive, as usual, and entered the dining room mid-conversation. Adelaide dominated the talk. "Her baby will be the best dressed in Baltimore."

"No wonder. Her work is impeccable," said Jane Catherine. "She's been selling quite a lot at the Women's Industrial Exchange."

"And now she's making the layette for her own little one," said Adelaide.

"Whose little one?" asked Anna.

"Josefina's, of course," said Adelaide. "I thought you two were such good friends. Didn't you know?"

"I've been busy."

"Well, the bundle of joy is coming along about September. Isn't it wonderful?"

"Excuse me," Anna said, as she got up from the table.

"Anna, you haven't eaten your breakfast yet," said Mrs. Pendleton.

"I just realized I have an engagement elsewhere."

Anna gathered her camera and purse and left the boardinghouse. Where she was going, she had no idea. There was no engagement elsewhere. After the Digges debacle, demand for her work had fizzled like flat ginger ale. The news of Josefina and Adrian's blessed event sent her emotions into a fireworks spiral, exploding in every direction. She couldn't be happy for the couple. She couldn't wish them the best of luck. She wondered why Josefina hadn't told her about her impending arrival. Why did she have to hear about it from Adelaide?

Anna walked the streets of Baltimore. Before she knew it, she stood on the steps of home. She took one look at Elizabeth when she opened the door, and burst into tears, shocking her nanny, who had never seen Anna cry since childhood.

"My dear, what has happened to you?"

"I am completely distraught. Nothing is going my way."

"Come in." Anna took off her hat, which Elizabeth put on the entry table. "Sit down and tell me, what has made you feel so downtrodden?"

"I made a big mistake when interviewing an important politician and now no one will hire me. The girls at the boardinghouse hate me. And, just this morning, I learned that Adrian's wife is with child. On top of all that, a young man has asked me to enter into a courtship with him and I'm confused. Yet again, I don't know my own feelings."

"You can't control the world, Anna. You can't force God's hand." Elizabeth smiled and cuddled Anna to her bosom. "You are still transitioning into womanhood. This is a time of learning who you are and where you want to go in life and with whom to walk that journey."

"How did you get through this time when you were my age?"

"I chose a much simpler life than yours. I chose a path familiar to young, single women back then."

"What am I to do?"

"Let me think about it. I'll put the kettle on."

After Elizabeth sliced a loaf of raisin bread and poured the tea, she offered her opinion. "If I were you, I would set my mind on regaining the trust of my employers. There is nothing you can do about Josefina and Adrian. You had your chance with Adrian and you let him go. Now, you must live with that decision. And you cannot make people like you. You have a unique, strong personality that can appear disagreeable to ladies still following Victorian ways and people who are jealous of your independence. You can always move back here, if you want a break. But I would advise that you try your best to build up your reputation as a photojournalist."

Anna stared out the window, letting Elizabeth's advice permeate her being and relax her like hot, steaming tea.

"Thank you. I always feel better after talking with you." Anna hesitated for a few seconds and then said, "Elizabeth, I love you."

"I love you, too, dear. You are always welcome here. It is your home."

"I know. For now, I need to stand up to my unhappiness and fear and start all over again."

"That's the way."

☙❦☙

As the months passed, Anna became reticent to confide in Emmaline. Her friend seemed to possess a serenity that could withstand a torrent of troubles, despite having far more stumbling blocks to navigate. Anna felt inferior in her childish, selfish ways. A mild, late-summer day cooled Anna's fiery responses to life, and the two met at Emmaline's favorite neighborhood café for breakfast.

Over boiled eggs and cornbread, they sipped molasses water and spoke of life. With a bit of perspective, Anna shared her problems.

"Anna, why did you not come to me when you couldn't find work? Why didn't you ask me if I would intercede for you at the *Baltimore Afro-American*? Why have you never tried to work for them?"

"I, well, I... I didn't think that..."

"Didn't think that they would hire a white woman?"

"Well, yes."

"Why would you assume that? After all the prejudices we have endured, how could you think we would project them on others?"

"It's not that... it's just that..."

"Go on."

"It's just that I'm a ninny, yet again. I'm so confused. How do you manage work, family, and daily abuses in society?"

"I know that I am but one person, with a finite number of hours in each day. I can do only so much. I can't control what happens to me. I can only control how I respond. I am a religious person. I was raised in the church and still go every Sunday morning and Wednesday night. I live by the principles my parents instilled in me from the day I was born. My mamma used to say, 'Emmaline, every dawn, in all its glory, is God's way of telling you He'll give you one more chance to get things right. Don't let Him down.' Every night, before I fall asleep, I lay in bed and ruminate on what I accomplished that day. I ask myself what I did wrong and what I did right. Then I vow to do better. I give myself what I call 'God's Homework'... assignments of what I need to work on the next day. Like being more kind to everyone I meet, or writing a thoughtful birthday greeting to a friend, or searching for ways to save the *Baltimore Afro-American* money. I find peace in small accomplishments."

"Emmaline, you are saintly. But don't you have personal desires? To make a name for yourself, or earn more money, or draw the attention of a gentleman?"

"If those things are meant to be, they will come in their own time and in their own manner."

"There's that word again... time."

"Yes. It is a powerful word."

Anna sipped her molasses water and dabbed her lips with a napkin. She met eyes with Emmaline. "Why do you put up with me?"

"Because we need each other. You came along at the right time. You were kind to me when I had no money. You showed me the beauty of living life to the fullest. I offer you balance, calm, and peace. That's important, too."

"How did I manage to find a sparkling diamond in the shadow of a building?"

The bill arrived at their table and Anna made a grab for it.

"It's my turn to pay," Emmaline said.

"No, you paid last time."

"I distinctly remember."

"No, you're wrong."

They went back and forth a few more times before realizing the very balance of their relationship had already hit a snag.

Laughter filled the café as they each reached into their reticules to pay separately.

෨෧

A few weeks later, Anna learned that famed French pilot, Hubert Latham, would participate in the "Baltimore Air Show." Anna wanted exclusive access to the pilot for a story. There was a problem. The event was sponsored by the publisher of *The Sun*, the newspaper H.L. Mencken edited. She hoped he had fully forgiven her and would give her one more chance.

Anna wasn't even allowed a meeting with her mentor. She sent a written request to represent *The Sun*, climbing all over herself with apologies for past mistakes, promising to be the perfect representative for his paper. She received a short reply, explaining that *The Sun* had many competent, professional photographers and writers on staff to handle the job.

All the local publications shut Anna out. No one would hire her to cover the story. Worry and anxiety overtook clarity.

David felt sorry for Anna and decided to help. They met for lunch at Lexington Market, where the potato and bacon soup was hot and filling.

"Anna, I hear that this event is more than an exhibition of the monoplane. There's going to be a test, a mock bombing..."

"A bombing?"

"Keep your voice down. Not a real one. Latham is going to drop a sack of flour on a specific target to show the military how airplanes might be used to fight future wars with greater accuracy. They've picked a certain ship's hull at the waterfront for the bullseye. I'll tell you where. If you position yourself correctly, you can be right there when the flour hits the ship and splatters everywhere. This could be dangerous for you. The government is involved, of course, so you'll have to perform magic to make it happen. Not many people know about this."

"Does *The Sun*?"

"Maybe. Maybe not."

"What about your own paper?"

"We're going to be focused on the hoopla in the air."

"Thank you for this tip. I owe you a dinner."

"I'll take you up on that. Promise me you'll be careful."

"I will."

On November 7th, Latham's plane, the "Antoinette," took off, looking like a giant mosquito, out for blood four hundred feet up, climbing to fifteen hundred. While most Baltimoreans stood on rooftops and looked skyward through opera glasses, Anna waited far below, on the wharf, near the ship David had told her was the target. She knew she'd face opposition. She didn't have to wait long to find it.

"Miss, this is not a promenade for strolling. This is a shipyard. What are you doing here?" said a naval officer with one stripe.

Anna had to make a quick decision... lie or tell the truth.

"Ensign, I am Anna Bainbridge, a freelance photojournalist. I do not represent any particular paper today. I am here, on my own, to preserve aviation, naval, and Baltimore history. There are no other photographers present, that I know of, to capture the flour sack when it hits its target and I have every confidence that it will. I want to record that moment, if you will allow me."

"Then you should have sought clearance through proper channels."

"My apologies."

Anna produced her business card and waited in full anticipation of denial.

"Don't go anywhere."

"Yes, sir."

A few minutes later, a man with two stripes hurried over to Anna. "Good morning, ma'am."

"Good morning, Lieutenant."

"Who gave you permission to be here?"

"No one, sir. I'm just a Baltimore photographer trying to report what's happening in my city. This is an historic day, wouldn't you say, sir?"

"How did you hear of this mission? What do you know about a flour sack?"

"Lieutenant, I am a journalist. It is my job to uncover and report. I cannot reveal my sources. It would be unethical. You understand proper protocol, I'm sure."

"Yes, ma'am." He thought for a few seconds. "How would you like to do something for your country?"

"What do you have in mind?"

"I will position you so that you can take the perfect picture of the drop... with one caveat. Agreed?"

"Sir, I need to know the stipulation."

"That you will turn over the photographs you take to me, to the government, that is, and will not withhold any to sell to anyone. You will receive no compensation. You cannot tell anyone you were here today, not even by implication. And you will never gain credit for your work. Your reward is service to your country."

"I understand, Lieutenant, and I agree."

Anna clicked the shutter at the perfect moment, she thought. She would never know because she didn't get to see the actual photograph or any others she took at the time. She fully complied with the Navy and handed over her film.

A few days later, Anna followed through with her promise to treat David to dinner, even though she had nothing to show for her end of the bargain. She was evasive, refusing to answer his questions, saying she was already thinking about what her next assignment might be.

"Why aren't your pictures in any of the newspapers?" David asked.

"I didn't exactly succeed in getting pictures to sell. Shall we order dessert?"

"I can't believe you missed the drop. That's unlike you."

"I think I'll order the chocolate ice box pie. How about you?"

"Apple," he said, knowing the discussion was over and wondering why.

When he walked Anna home, she was quiet until they reached the boardinghouse door.

"I have a lot of people with whom I must make amends, David. I really appreciate that you have tried to help me. If there is anything I can do for you, in return, please let me know."

"Just be my friend. Give me a chance. Goodnight."
"Goodnight."

CHAPTER 33

Anna knew she would have to acknowledge Josefina's impending motherhood. When the two met, a magnet's repulsion could be felt between them. They spoke in formal language and polite tones. It was as if they were meeting for the first time.

"Please sit down. Would you like some tea?"

"No, thank you. I can't stay long. I have pictures to take, lots of assignments."

"I understand. You must have little time for anything else."

"Where's Adrian?"

"He's working overtime. He's been doing that as often as possible to save money for the baby."

"How are you feeling these days? I'm sure you're weighed down... I mean, you need to take rests often and..."

"I know."

"Yes, of course. You are so far along and..."

"No, Anna, I mean 'I know.'"

"Know what?"

"About you and Adrian."

Anna's face turned pale and worried. "Neither of us meant to..."

"Adrian explained everything. At first, I felt betrayed by both of you. Then, I realized that Adrian wouldn't hurt a fly. He had been protecting me. I was so taken with him from the start that he couldn't risk hurting me. What I don't understand is why you didn't tell me."

"I... I was jealous. It's as simple as that."

"Adrian assured me that his feelings for me were sincere and that I had nothing to worry about."

"When did he tell you?"

"A few months ago. I think this secret was gnawing at his conscience. Naturally, I was upset. But, when I saw that the truth released Adrian from anxiety, I was happy he told me. Our relationship only deepened."

"I see. And how do you feel about me?"

"For a while, I just wanted to distance myself from you. I soon realized you were stuck in a difficult position. You were my best friend. You didn't want to spoil my happiness either. Silently, I released you from any complicity or guilt. I want you to be my friend again, if you think you can. I won't ask if you still have feelings for Adrian. I know that would be too personal. I won't press you. If being near us is too awkward, then..."

"I will be the best friend I can possibly be to you both." Anna evaded the question of residual feelings for Adrian. She wasn't sure, herself, what remained.

"That warms my heart. Now that we have things settled, I'm sure you have to get back to your picture taking."

Anna left feeling worse than before because of her dishonesty. She had no photos to take. And she would always hold dear some tenderness for Adrian that she kept unrevealed. And she had just committed her friendship, yet Josefina was the last person in the world she wanted to be with right now.

Anna rode the public jitney home. The population of Baltimore had grown to over half a million people and new forms of transportation were necessary. These little buses were nothing more than trucks with open beds jammed with as many passengers as possible. One person, always a man, stood on the back bumper to catch anyone who might be tossed from the truck bed should the jitney make an abrupt stop or sharp turn. It wasn't the safest mode of travel but it was the fastest. And Anna felt she needed to hightail it from Canton.

❧❧

Anna decided to take a much-needed respite. Even though her income had dwindled, she invited Elizabeth to accompany her on a three-day trip to Annapolis, where Anna wanted to sit by the water and mull things over, far from home.

Elizabeth didn't feel that she could leave Dr. Bainbridge alone that long. He was still working too hard and suffering minor setbacks in his health. Anna went on her own.

As the train departed Baltimore, Anna flattened her skirt on her lap, allowing all cares to be whisked away like biscuit crumbs. When she arrived in Annapolis, she checked into the Robert Johnson Inn on State Circle, just a few blocks from the dock area.

"There must be some mistake," the innkeeper said, as Anna signed the ledger.

"What do you mean?"

"The reservation is for 'Miss' Anna Bainbridge but I see none for your chaperone."

"I did not travel with one."

"What? This is most unusual. The Inn cannot be responsible for your..."

"Reputation? I can take care of myself, I assure you."

"Young lady, you are in a city unknown to you and..."

"Sir, I have been to Annapolis several times in the past. I am a photojournalist who has interviewed politicians in the statehouse just across the way. I have come for a weekend of rest. I will prepay you, if you like."

"That won't be necessary." The man collected himself. "Welcome to the Robert Johnson House, Miss Bainbridge."

"Thank you. I will carry my own satchel to my room."

"As you please."

Over the next two days, Anna sat on the docks, watching boats make strong ripples that went only so far, then melted into the greater expanse of water.

Anna went to Jonas Green Park, not far from the Naval Academy, and strolled its pathways, along the rocky shoreline of the Severn River. Oblivious to anyone around her, she listened to birdsong, stared at cloud formations and nodded to trees that seemed to bow as she passed. The park's beauty soothed Anna, as it had others dating back to its first owner, a humble printer.

Anna took some of her meals at the Maryland Inn, also on State Circle. It was one of those places where she could dine alone and remain in good standing. Annapolis was a military and boating town, so most of the eateries were taverns and pubs, no place for a lady. At first, the proprietor of the Maryland Inn, a reputable establishment, didn't want to seat a young woman alone. After insisting, a little on the clamorous side, she was given a table near a window. There, she enjoyed fresh oysters, and chicken pudding.

The next morning, she dined at her own inn, savoring apple fritters and oatmeal for breakfast. She was offered a newspaper to read as she ate. She declined.

The historic surroundings inspired Anna, recalibrating her will to succeed against all odds. She visited the Treaty of Paris Restaurant, where she took tea in the afternoon. It was here, on this very spot, where the Revolutionary War officially came to an end with the signing of the Treaty of Paris.

Anna could feel the power of men putting pen and ink to paper, the release of tension in the air, the news resounding from the room and reaching the farthest corners of the colonies and beyond.

Once refreshed and eager to regain her career, Anna returned home and made the rounds of publications, including the *Baltimore Afro-American*, which hired her on Emmaline's recommendation.

They asked her to photograph merchandise for businesses that wanted to advertise in the newspaper but had no means of creating ads. Anna provided pictures and the *Baltimore Afro-American's* layout staff created the type and sized the advertisements. It wasn't exciting but it was work Anna accepted with gratitude. Week after week, she produced the best pictures she could. The experience she had accumulated from shooting merchandise for O'Neill's had come in handy.

��•��

In late August, Josefina delivered a stillborn son. The hospital wanted to dispose of the tiny body but Josefina and Adrian insisted on a funeral and a grave marker that declared his name, William Adrian Crosby. His first name paid homage to Josefina's uncle, who had died in the Spanish-American War.

No solace found them during the early months of autumn. Josefina retreated into mourning and Anna felt uncomfortable trying to console Adrian on her own. She wrote several notes offering the couple assistance, all of which went unanswered. Anna decided to give them time, which she was learning to respect, and regenerate their friendship at the start of the new year.

❧

As the holidays approached, Anna received a phone call from the *Baltimore Afro-American*. They needed her to shoot a story discreetly. The newspaper asked her to take pictures of Eutaw Place, a white neighborhood on the western end of downtown Baltimore that was becoming the center of political controversy. The paper didn't want to send a colored photographer for fear of physical retaliation. A white lady seen taking pictures of townhouses there would not cause undue attention.

A local lawyer by the name of Milton Dashiell had been behind a proposed ordinance to keep colored folks from integrating residency in the Eutaw Place area. He had succeeded in getting approval by the City Council.

Despite the newspaper's story, no amount of ink conjured the outrage of private citizens. The ordinance was signed into law by Mayor J. Barry Mahool in December, closing the year laden with dissonance, not with a major chord but on depressing minor notes. It was a ground-breaking law against free residency, one that other cities soon adopted, especially those down South.

Anna felt compelled to speak with Emmaline. When they discussed the Eutaw Place story and the new law, Emmaline didn't seem surprised.

"Why aren't you outraged?" Anna asked.

"I am. What can be done about it at this point?"

"You could organize a march or get petitions signed."

"And what would be the result? More hatred, more segregation."

"I don't understand. You seem resigned to all these efforts to suppress your people."

"Anna, this has been going on for centuries. And every single day in our own time. You're just not aware of it unless you're assigned a news story."

"What does that mean? You act as though I don't care. I do. I'm not oblivious just because I'm white."

"Really? You are so quick to praise your beloved city's efforts to rebuild after the fire but you are blind to what's going on right under your nose."

"What are you talking about?"

"I'm talking about a concerted effort to further segregate Baltimore under the guise of rebuilding it."

"How?"

"You've often spoken about the streets being widened."

"Yes, now more coaches and cars can travel through the city."

"That's exactly my point. Widening the streets means the buildings that once lined those streets and were burned down in the fire are not being put back up."

"That's right. Newer, better, taller buildings are going up."

"What about the small churches? The ones for colored people who live downtown?"

"What about them?"

"They were not included in the plan. They are not getting rebuilt. Anna, you have to understand. The colored community centers around its churches. And, when they are moved, the congregation moves with it. As a result of the city's plan to rebuild, my people have been pushed farther west, where they must build new churches on street corners or worship in storefront churches. They create new communities that are only colored, which doesn't lend itself to integration."

"Is this true? I had no idea."

"Most Baltimoreans don't. They just see progress downtown."

"And to make sure coloreds moved away, landlords raised rents downtown, using the excuse that they had to cover fire costs. Few white people know about it because it rarely gets reported. You always complain about newspapers not doing enough stories on woman's suffrage. What about the plight of coloreds?"

"Emmaline, I'm ashamed."

CHAPTER 34

The first few months of 1911 put Anna on an even keel. Jobs were still few and far between, though coming a little more often. Papa enjoyed an upswing in his health, much to the relief of Anna and Elizabeth. Josefina and Adrian started to socialize a little more. And Emmaline was promoted to top accountant at the *Afro-American*. It seemed too good to be true and it was. Something was about to upset Anna's apple cart and, at the same time, bring her closer to David.

In the early evening of March 25, David called the boardinghouse. When Mrs. Pendleton answered, his breathless voice begged for Anna to come to the phone quickly. Luckily, she was just steps away, helping to pare potatoes for Shepherd's Pie.

"It's a Mr. Jameson, Anna. He seems to be in a tizzy."

Anna grabbed the phone. "David, what is it?"

"Anna, pack your overnight bag and meet me at the train station. Bring as little as possible. We can just about catch the 5:50 to New York."

"What's going on? What happened?"

"There's a massive fire raging at the Triangle Shirtwaist Factory. People are leaping from the building to their deaths. The *Baltimore American* is sending me. They gave me approval to take you for pictures if I accepted full responsibility for your behavior. Can you handle what you might see there?"

"It will take me no time at all to ready my satchel. David, won't the story be over by the time we get there?"

"I doubt it. This tragedy will dominate newspapers for days to come."

Anna could not even imagine what awaited her. What did a body that had fallen from several stories up look like on the ground? She couldn't dwell on it. She needed this opportunity, any opportunity to get back in the good graces of newspaper editors.

☙❧

Anna and David searched for each other through the crowd of passengers waiting at the station.

"Good, you've got on your jodhpurs and boots," David said, as they bought their tickets. "I meant to tell you to wear them."

"I figured it would be necessary to maneuver the scene. It would also make me blend in with the newspapermen. I wouldn't want to be mistaken for a passerby and chased away."

"Good thinking. Are you familiar with the recent history of this company?"

"I read a little about the troubles they had last month."

"Right. In February, they had union problems. Most of their employees are women, being that they hire a lot of patternmakers and seamstresses. These women were picketing for better conditions, nothing special, just humane treatment. They didn't get it. In fact, the supervisors started locking the doors so workers couldn't collect in hallways to organize further."

"If the doors were locked when the fire started... Oh, David, this could be really awful."

"And, in a clothing factory, the fire would spread quickly. I think we should agree to stick together. There are bound to be large crowds, many reporters, police, a lot of fire equipment and ambulances."

"I'm used to maneuvering around hoses and trucks, believe me."

"I know. Then I will follow your lead."

No amount of planning could prepare either one of them for the horror that awaited when they arrived at the Asch Building on the corner of Greene Street and Washington Place in Greenwich Village.

The fire itself had already been put out. David was told it took a mere eighteen minutes. Water-soaked bodies speckled the street, mangled and bloody. Body parts lay far from torsos. Skulls resembled smashed pumpkins. From the looks of it, the victims were mostly women. As she gazed upward, Anna's breath caught with the realization that these victims had not been carried down and placed on the ground. They had jumped to their deaths, rather than die by fire. Windows were punched out, indicating that workers decided leaping with the angels was better than consorting with the devil.

"Where are the fire escapes?" Anna asked.

She and David walked around the building behind the police cordon and saw only one, which had buckled under intense heat. Several bodies formed a mound beneath it.

"Oh, what a terrible way to die," Anna said.

David grabbed Anna by the shoulders. "We must stay focused on our assignment. Start shooting."

As Anna looked through her viewfinder, she relaxed, feeling separated from the disaster. The camera served as a barrier between atrocity and work. She composed each photograph as though it were a still life of fruit in a vase. Still, she stuck close to David.

He stopped firemen, witnesses and survivors alike to piece together the story. The blouse factory occupied the 8th, 9th and 10th stories of the building and the fire had started on the 8th floor. Doors to the workrooms had been locked to keep the employees at their cutting tables and sewing machines. He asked one of the survivors why the doors weren't unlocked when the fire started.

"I'll tell you why," a witness said. "See that man over there, the one talking to police. He's the foreman. He's the one who holds the keys. And look! He's safe and sound, probably one of the first to run out of the building, the coward, leaving all those people to..."

The witness crumpled in tears and couldn't finish her sentence.

Anna asked another passerby what she had seen.

"There were people jumping out of windows. Oh, they made an awful thud when they hit the street. I'll never forget the sound of death. Many had climbed to the roof. I guess all the stairwells and elevators were too smokey and they had no place to go but up. There was no way to rescue them. They jumped, too; many hugged or held hands just before leaping."

The woman put a handkerchief to her face and scurried away.

David stopped a fire captain and asked him what caused the fire.

"It's too soon to tell. But with big bolts of fabric and scraps lying about, it's no wonder that it spread so fast. When we arrived, smoke poured from the 8th floor, so that will be our first place to investigate."

"Do you know how many people lost their lives?"

"Not at this time. Could be well over a hundred. The factory employed five hundred people, mostly women. I don't know how many managed to escape. We're trying to contain them over there at Washington Square to get a count. Many have severe burns. They've been advised not to leave or talk to anyone from the newspapers."

Some of the bodies were covered, others were not. For Anna and David, it was difficult to look away. Faces and hair were gone on some of the victims, revealing that they must have been on fire when they jumped. How would they be identified?

"This is a clothing manufacturer, several stories up," Anna said to David. "Was there no alarm system for workers on each floor?"

"I don't think so. It looks as if it was every man for himself."

"Or woman," Anna said.

Anna continued to take pictures. Not so much for the newspaper but as a means of coping. Around her, women received treatment for their burns, grown men sobbed, others seemed to be running in all directions for no reason. Anna lost sight of David, then found him doubled over, vomiting into a trash can. She went to him.

"David," she said, softly.

He tried to recover his manhood. It was no use.

"This is horrible, the worst thing I've ever experienced," he whispered. "With Stanford White, I didn't care. He was a rapist. But these were innocent women. How could this happen to God-fearing people? Most of these workers were recent immigrants, coming to this country to find a better life. And what for? Seven dollars a week?" David stared at Anna with tears in his eyes. "And it all ends like this. What are we to learn? What am I to tell readers? How do I put this into any kind of perspective?"

"You cannot. No one can. It's too raw and emotional right now. We need time to stand back and assess and then act."

"Act? How?"

"Fight to pass laws that will protect the lowliest of workers. Something good must come of this. It has to. All of these deaths cannot have been in vain. Come, let's walk away from here for a few moments and breathe fresh air."

They found a bench on the edge of Washington Square, away from the area designated for survivors. They faintly heard the cries of workers being reunited in grief, the cries of women just starting to feel the intensity of their burns.

"Anna, what did you learn from the Great Fire of 1904?" David asked.

"It's hard to say. At first, I was too preoccupied with taking pictures. My camera became a shield between me and what I was shooting. It was almost as if I weren't experiencing it myself. I woke up one morning days later and took a walk through the rubble. I had my camera with me but, somehow, I didn't feel like taking any pictures. I was confused about a lot of things, why it happened, why I shamelessly took off for two days, documenting the fire, without telling anyone where I was going. I had never done anything so selfish or risky before.

"When I saw the aftermath of the fire, I started shivering and couldn't stop. I had to return home and take some tea. I went to my room and got under the covers. My nanny thought me ill. I knew it was a delayed reaction to the fire. My emotions had been suppressed and needed venting."

"That's the making of a fine journalist, pushing personal feelings aside in the moment to get the story."

"Yes. Eventually, they surface in some form or other. Some people drink alcohol in excess. Some become hardened and lash out at other people. Some become closer to God. After collecting myself, I returned to the charred mess near the wharf. There, I saw men pull a body from The Basin. I didn't get too close. He was badly burned. The *Baltimore American* later reported that he was a colored man. I don't think he was ever identified. So sad."

"I remember that story."

"Yes, it made me realize how close to danger I really was. Also, there was a man, a bad man, who accosted me on the street in the middle of the fire and tried to force me to go with him. Luckily, I outsmarted him and got away. He was later caught."

"Oh, Anna, how awful."

"You asked me what I learned from the Great Fire. I learned that something good came of it. Baltimore is being built up better than before, with improved electrical and sewage systems, bigger buildings, wider streets. Although, I'm told, they are not helping every citizen."

"Even so, it brings no solace to all those business owners who lost everything."

"It does say something for the greater good. Though the benefits seem to be aimed at white residents rather than colored." Anna told David about her conversation with Emmaline and coloreds being chased west of the city. "What made me wonder was this... why does something really bad have to happen for something good to follow? Why can't something good just happen all on its own?"

"If I could answer that question, I would be considered a great philosopher."

"New rules protecting workers will come from this fire, I'm sure. More safety precautions."

"Tell that to the mangled victims on the street right now."

"Yes, I know. It's all too much for us to understand. All we can do is photograph it and report it and let officials and the reading public decide what to make of it."

"Let's go home." David gently touched Anna's hand, not as a romantic gesture. He was acknowledging a bond that they had forged from this fire, one that would connect them as journalists who had been to hell and back together.

"No, we still have work to do. Let's see if we have the courage to keep going for a while."

"You are a walking inspiration. I'm proud to work with you."

When they returned to the scene of the fire, bodies were being put on trucks. David learned they were heading to Charities Pier near the East River, where family members would have to look at body after body, reliving their sorrow with each uncovering, in hopes of identifying their loved ones and being able to give them a proper funeral and burial.

At first, David and Anna planned to stay overnight, so they could get additional information the next day. They realized they'd most likely have to stay in a high-rise hotel and couldn't go through with it. David checked his timepiece. "No trains will be running this late. Are you amenable to staying with my brother tonight? I can assure you that you will be given utmost privacy."

"Yes, I think that's a good idea. Where does he live?"

"On the west side of town near Central Park, in a high-rise building called The Dakota."

"A high-rise? What floor?"

"Don't worry. He's on the first."

When they arrived, Anna noted that this ten-story structure had no fire escapes either. When she mentioned it to David, he said, "I'm so exhausted, I really don't care."

"You still look a bit green."

Anna noted the sibling resemblance to Robert Jameson, a lawyer. As the brothers hugged, Anna was made welcome by Robert's wife, Monica. Anna was shown to the guest room, where she put the satchel she had been carrying all night on the bed. Her arm felt stiff from holding it and her camera so tensely. Monica soon brought tea and a light supper of cheese, bread and vichyssoise. She then drew a warm bath for Anna.

"How is David?" Anna asked. "He was quite ill earlier."

"Robert is consoling him. He refused to eat. I think he needs a good night's sleep. What you both witnessed tonight will not easily be erased."

"There is no doubt it will remain with us forever."

No amount of bathing could cleanse the smell of smoke and death in Anna's nostrils. She crawled beneath the covers. Although she was not one to talk to God, she prayed for those factory workers and mourned the desperate decisions they were forced to make... burn or jump. She hoped her photographs would bring change.

In the morning, Anna and David thought about returning to the Asch Building but their hearts were not in it. Their hearts had already gone out to the victims and, more so, the survivors, who would have to live with the realization that they had made it out alive, while coworkers who had cut and sewed right beside them, moments before the fire, had not.

CHAPTER 35

The emotional pain of experiencing the Triangle fire tragedy lasted well into spring, which should have been a time of rebirth, fair weather and beautiful flowers.

In May, the Women's Civic League launched a new initiative to influence Baltimoreans to start their own decorative and bountiful gardens. It was simply called the Flower Mart. Held in Mt. Vernon Place, it offered blossoms and vegetable seedlings for purchase or perusing.

Neither Anna nor David had been assigned the story. They agreed it would be a pleasant getaway from their lingering sorrow over the fire. The tug of war that had started their working relationship had gone up in smoke in New York.

Anna wore a plain black skirt with suspender-style straps over a pale blue blouse. Atop her head sat a charming straw hat surrounded by a blue band with a small sprig of artificial lilies of the valley tucked into the side.

"You look lovely. I hope you are not offended by my saying so."

Anna laughed. "Have I really gone too far in my masculine attire?"

"Well, when you're working, I understand. It's not often I see you so relaxed and ladylike. I must say, I like it very much. You're pretty. Do you know that?"

"Look at these sweet violets. And what are those called?" Anna asked a vendor.

"These are hyacinths," the lady behind the table said. "Here, smell them. They're quite fragrant. I find that people either love them or hate them. If the white ones don't appeal to you, perhaps the pink or purple will."

"Would you like a planting? I'd be delighted to purchase a few for you."

"They're perennials," the vendor continued. "Once you put them in the ground, they'll bloom every year somewhere around Eastertide."

"I live in a boardinghouse. I have no place to grow them."

"Perhaps at your father's house?" David said.

"No, I'm not there very often. Thank you just the same. Although, I could plant them there to amuse Elizabeth, the housekeeper."

After David bought one in each color, the twosome continued walking by displays in pastel profusions and lacy designs. They stopped from time to time, interacting with vendors, learning about enriching earth, cultivating tubers, exposing certain plants to shade and others to full sunlight. They each knew the other was thinking about the delicate balance between light and dark, health and disease, life and death. When the sun started to set, ending a day offering hope and inviting reflection, they headed back to Anna's boardinghouse, where David kissed Anna's ungloved hand, smiled and walked away. Anna joined the ladies for dinner in the parlor but didn't hear what they were saying. The only thing she heard was the beating of her own heart. Springtime had obviously awakened something in her.

∾∾

Because Anna showed expertise in photographing architecture, she was hired by *Baltimore Magazine* to shoot the opening of the Emerson Bromo Seltzer Tower on Eutaw Street near The Basin. The late June day was clear and unseasonably cool.

Anna stood on the street and looked straight up the Renaissance Revival structure as it reached into the cloudless sky. It was the tallest building in Baltimore at two hundred and eighty-nine feet. A twenty-four-foot clockface adorned each of four sides. Before the grand opening, photographers had been allowed inside, where Anna took pictures of the inner workings of the spectacular clocks. But how could she get a good picture of the top of the tower from ground level outside? It was so tall. She walked several blocks west, turned around and composed a picture that showed the tower's perspective against the growing downtown skyline. She made sure to photograph it from every angle. Then, she took pictures of the ribbon-cutting and dignitaries giving speeches.

The tower was part of the Emerson Drug Company that included a drugstore and manufacturing plant. Isaac E. Emerson was the inventor of the bicarbonate digestive, Bromo Seltzer, made and sold on site.

Anna found the native North Carolinian to be a pleasant man. His walrus mustache made him seem non-threatening. Even though he was a wealthy man of high society, Baltimoreans felt comfortable calling him "Captain Ike," referring to his past service in the Maryland Naval Reserves.

That night, no matter where downtown residents lived, they gazed outside their windows, searching for the tower. It wasn't hard to find. A giant light, replicating the sapphire-hued bottle of Bromo Seltzer, revolved around the top of the tower, casting a blue beacon over Baltimore. It would surely sell a lot of the remedy.

When Anna's pictures were published in *Baltimore Magazine*, they proved to be the only ones with straight lines, no distortion. With these pictures, she righted her career. More jobs followed.

The rebuilding of Baltimore continued, with the completion of the underground sewage system, which became a model for other cities. From under the ground to the height of the clouds, progress became evident everywhere. The U.S. Army started a school for airplane pilots near Washington, D.C., in a town called College Park, where the University of Maryland had been founded in 1856. The Navy followed, with an airfield in Greenbury Point, Annapolis.

In September, Anna was hired to photograph another grand opening, this one near and dear to her heart, a brand-new railway station, replacing the Charles Street Union Station. This one took its name from its counterpart, Pennsylvania Station in New York, and would offer direct passage from Baltimore to New York City. Anna knew getting to news stories up north would be so much quicker, although she was in no hurry to return there. Too many bad memories.

The long, elaborate building, designed in a classical, ornate style called Beaux Arts, gave way to a grand entrance hall, lined with curved wooden benches, and a split-flap schedule board hovering over the heads of travelers. It clicked with excitement every time a train left the station. Green tile lined the walls. And, if passengers weren't in too much of a hurry, they could take in the massive stained-glass skylight, where sunbeams cast circles of light on passengers like halos on saints.

Just months later, the general election loomed. One of the pieces of legislation Maryland citizens would decide was the Digges Amendment, which attempted to suppress the black male vote. Anna and Emmaline crossed their fingers in anticipation. Luckily, Marylanders saw through the sham and voted the amendment down.

Anna contacted Emmaline to celebrate. There was no reply, causing worry. David agreed to go with her to Emmaline's apartment one evening, when Anna thought she would be home from work.

They knocked several times. Again, no answer.

"You won't find her there," an elderly man said. He jostled a bag of groceries as he attempted to put the key in the door to his room.

"I beg your pardon, sir." Anna said. "Do you know where Emmaline is?"

"Her father came down with some sickness, might die, she told me. She went back home to take care of him. I don't know where home is, though."

"I do," Anna replied. "Thank you, sir."

Anna turned to David and said, "Emmaline's parents live on Falls Turnpike, quite a distance north. It's too late to go now and I wouldn't want to barge in on them without notice. Tomorrow, I will send word and see if we can visit. Will you go with me?"

"Of course."

It was a week before Anna received a reply. It simply said that Emmaline's father was desperately ill and would likely not survive. It was his heart. She asked that, for now, Anna keep her distance, as Emmaline needed all attention to go to her family. Anna immediately talked to her own father. "Papa, I don't know specifically what's wrong with Emmaline's father, but I do know it's his heart. He probably doesn't have the proper medical care where he lives. Can you find a way to get him to your hospital? Can you personally take care of him? For me?"

"Well, I don't know."

"You had the finest care when it was your heart. Why can't he? Helping him would mean the world to me. Emmaline and her family have been so kind. Please?"

Papa agreed but only if he could examine the patient first to ensure that he could survive the trip to the hospital. Anna knew Emmaline would want to keep her father home, near his wife and children. So, Anna and her father showed up at Bare Hills unannounced.

"Anna, what are you doing here?" Emmaline asked.

"Don't say a word. Papa and I are here to help. Pack your mother's bag."

Papa determined that Emmaline's father had suffered some sort of heart attack. His pulse felt weak and his heart was beating erratically. Dr. Bainbridge ordered an ambulance, which transported him downtown, where the latest medical equipment could better diagnose his condition.

Over several weeks, just as 1911 came to a close, Emmaline's father was given a positive prognosis. He had to rest and wouldn't be able to build roads ever again. But he would be alive to love his wife and dote on his children.

There was no charge for his care. Dr. Bainbridge paid all expenses.

On New Year's Eve, in Emmaline's apartment, Anna introduced David to her friend and the three of them toasted better times ahead with hot apple cider and fruit cake.

CHAPTER 36

The Maryland legislative session, which convened in spring, brought changes for working women, much to the joy of suffragists. It was ruled that women in certain occupations, such as banking, industry and merchandising, could not work longer than a ten-hour day, whether forced or voluntary. Their weekly hours must not exceed sixty. While women wanted to work, this new law protected them from overbearing employers, who often assigned longer hours as a means of forcing women to quit. It also ensured that women would still have time to perform their duties at home.

In addition, child labor laws were tightened. Around this time, about eighteen percent of all children between the ages of ten and fifteen worked for pay in some capacity... newsies, errand runners, factory workers, stock boys, shoe shiners, miners, seafood processers and field hands. Young girls learned midwifery, sewing and cooking from their mothers. Sometimes, they worked in factories and fields, too.

The new laws limited work hours and the age range of child labor, allowing more children to attend school on a regular basis. These advances for women and children encouraged suffragists to step up their efforts for the vote.

৵৽৩

In early March, Anna was invited to a meeting with Edith Hooker, president of the Just Government League, which supported suffrage in Maryland.

"Thank you for coming. I've heard many good things about your talents, Miss Bainbridge."

"Please, call me Anna."

"I wanted to inform you of some exciting news that could involve you. As you have probably noticed, local papers barely touch the subject of woman's suffrage. It's been going on for some time."

"Yes, I've tried to convince H.L. Mencken to print more reports on marches and such. He's not one to budge."

"Well, he is of no matter anymore. You see, I invited you here today to tell you that on April 6th, newsstands will have one more publication to sell. I'm going to publish a weekly newspaper focused solely on the suffrage movement. It will be called *Maryland Suffrage News*. Isn't that exciting?"

"That's wonderful. Will you still run the Just Government League?"

"Oh yes, the newspaper will be supported by the league."

"What are your goals?"

"I'm going to unify and strengthen the suffrage movement in Maryland. There are so many factions, I want to make sure we are all speaking the same language. Also, I want to supply the general public with unbiased information about what we are trying to attain. We'll address women's issues head-to-head with lawmakers, subjects like education and working women, and more laws to protect them. We'll even speak out about corruption in government and crime in our streets. Those problems affect our cause, too. We can't march if our voices are stifled by unlawful politicians and lawlessness in our neighborhoods."

"And you need a photographer, perhaps? Is that where I come into it?"

"Not in the beginning. I have to see if we can make the newspaper viable. Until then, we will use artist renderings. But, once the paper catches on, and I really believe it will, I would want no one else but you to provide pictures of our meetings and marches. I know you have traveled often in your work. I might need to send you to other parts of our state for stories."

"Miss Hooker, this is the best news I've heard in a long time. I'd be honored. If you want, I'll give you pictures now at no charge."

"I wouldn't think of it. Photography is your profession. You have worked hard to provide something valuable to society. Don't undersell yourself. Women are often too concerned with 'pleasing' someone else. We have been raised that way. And it must stop. Learn to please yourself. Remember who you are, a photographer and a businesswoman. Fight for your position and the pay that goes with it."

"Yes, of course. Please let me know when you are ready for me."

"I will pay you the same rate that I would pay a man."

"I appreciate that. I must raise perhaps a sticky subject. Are you including stories on colored women marching?"

"Well, I hadn't really thought about it, but I suppose I could."

"You should. I'll take the pictures."

Miss Hooker was true to her word. Within a few months, after the paper proved its worth, Anna started shooting pictures on a weekly basis. She was thrilled to be earning money by supporting a cause important to her. She enjoyed the travel associated with her new position, too.

☜☞

On April 10th, the much-anticipated launching of the RMS Titanic made headlines throughout the world. The British passenger ship left Berth 44 at the port of Southampton, England. The sky provided a murky canopy, the temperature a cool forty-eight degrees. Passengers, bound for a new life in America, created the kind of hustle and bustle that proved both draining and energizing. The lines to board snaked long because each person had to undergo an eye test for trachoma, a highly contagious bacterial infection. Officials didn't want anything to go wrong during the ship's maiden voyage.

Once at sea, the Titanic made stops at Cherbourg, France, and Queenstown, Ireland, then headed west toward America. Only one-third of the passengers spoke English and they crossed just about every social stratum. Yet, they seemed to get along and enjoy the voyage.

The state-of-the-art ship provided every comfort, such as Art Nouveau cabins, a swimming pool, library, gymnasium and telegraph office for business and passenger use. Safety precautions, including watertight doors and compartments erased any fears of nervous passengers. They didn't know that there were not enough lifeboats, by far.

Hours after Anna went to bed on Monday, April 15th, the boardinghouse phone rang. And rang. And rang. Calls at this hour could only mean one thing... trouble. Mrs. Pendleton offered a tentative "Hello."

She heard shouting on the other end of the line. "You want to talk to whom?"

"Anna Bainbridge, it's urgent."

"Do you know what time it is, young man?"

"Yes, I'm well aware. Please hurry. It's life or death."

"Oh, my."

Mrs. Pendleton ran downstairs and shook Anna awake. "The telephone... it's for you. The man on the line said it's life or death."

"Papa!" Anna screamed.

She jumped out of bed and raced up the stairs. By now, some of the other residents stood on the main staircase, yawning and saying, "What's going on?"

Mrs. Pendleton shooed them back to bed. "It's none of your business. Go on, now."

Jane Catherine said, "Figures it would be Anna."

"Hello, hello!" Anna yelled.

"Anna, it's David. Something awful has happened."

"Is it Papa?"

"No... oh, I'm sorry if you got that impression. I'm really sorry, I should have stated my message to the lady who answered the phone right away."

"You just took ten years off my life. What is it?"

"There's been a terrible tragedy. The Titanic is sinking."

"What? That's impossible. She's as tight as a drum. No water could penetrate that ship."

"Early reports say it hit something. There's a hole in the side of the ship."

"Are they getting passengers into the lifeboats?"

"I'm sure they are."

"Where did this happen?"

"In the icy waters off Newfoundland."

"Why have you disrupted my household to tell me this? What could you and I possibly do about it? We can't go there and report on it. And how did you find out about it at this ungodly hour?"

"I was working late on another story and it came across the telegraph. I thought you'd want to know as soon as possible. It's so horrible, I felt like I needed to... to... be with you."

Anna lowered her voice. "I'm sorry, David. I didn't mean to scold you. Do you want me to join you at the paper? Are they holding the presses on the morning edition?"

"Yes, writers and editors are arriving by the minute. I'm sure there's something you can do to help."

"I'll get dressed right away."

By the time Anna arrived at the *Baltimore American*, it was almost fully staffed. Writers hammered their copy, which was updated every few minutes. There were reports of no casualties, reports that everything was okay, and reports that the ship was sinking with people on board. Nothing was making sense. The most promising reports mentioned a Coast Guard ship racing at full steam toward the Titanic.

Writers were yelling questions. Reporters monitoring the telegraph yelled answers. "Who is the Captain?" "Edward Smith." "How many passengers?" "Twenty-two hundred." "How many Americans on board?" "We don't know yet."

Anna's presence wasn't questioned. As a freelancer, she should not have been there. But she wasn't looking for pay. She just wanted to help in any way possible, tracking down information, running it from desk to desk to the writers. Making coffee. Taking phone calls. Emptying wastebaskets filled with scrapped stories already outdated. She saw no job beneath her. At one point, she noticed David looking frazzled. She offered to help write his copy. He was assigned to take the human angle and write a story about real people with real names, caught between life and death. He had been so good at it on other stories. She helped him comb the list of names, looking over David's shoulder. "Who is on the roster? Anyone famous?" Anna asked.

"Oh, yes. Some rich and powerful people. I'm trying to sort them all out now. Can you help?"

Anna sat down and got to work. "Why, there are members of high society on board. I can tell by their titles. Sir Cosmo Gordon and his wife, Lady Lucy Duff-Gordon. I know she's a fashion designer."

"And Ida and Isador Straus. He's a co-owner of Macy's," David said.

"He's also a Representative from New York," said Anna. "You'd better write about him."

"How about Benjamin Guggenheim? He's a prominent businessman here in America."

"Didn't he inherit a fortune from his father?"

"Yes, I think he earned his money in mining."

"Look here. John Jacob Aster IV."

"Good lord! He's one of the richest men on earth."

"All that money might not help him now. And I see his wife is with him."

"You know what the protocol for abandoning ship is, don't you?"

"No."

"Women and children first."

"You mean the men, whether married or not, have to stay back until every woman and child is on a lifeboat? How awful to be separated. Are there enough lifeboats?"

"I pray there are."

"Here's another person... Molly Brown."

"Her husband made his wealth in mining, too."

"I don't know about that. I do know she's a suffragist, not only working for the right of women to vote but advocating children's welfare and education."

"So many lives. So many lives could be lost senselessly. Anna, here we go again."

"That's what I was thinking. Let's put our minds to writing this story and hope everyone survives."

Near dawn, they got word that the ship had broken apart. A few hours later, they learned the great RMS Titanic had been swallowed by the ice-cold waters south of Newfoundland. Just 400 miles from land.

Over the next forty-eight hours, many newspapers printed incorrect information. *The Sun*, as reputable as it was, ran this headline:

All Titanic Passengers Are Safe;
Transferred in Lifeboats at Sea

Many other papers from around the country ran headlines that conflicted with the truth. Such as:

Titanic Lost. No Lives Lost.

Liner Titanic Goes Down. Passengers Are Safe.

Passengers Safely Moved
and Steamer Titanic Taken into Tow

None of these headlines resembled the truth. Faulty information crossed telegraph wires as chaos ruled the sea. Finally, after survivors revealed what they experienced, newspapers corrected their reports. Once the magnitude of the tragedy became clearer, the story consumed newspapers around the world.

After that horrible night, as dawn peeked above the horizon, the editor of the *Baltimore American* called Anna into the office. He thanked her for volunteering and said her generosity would be remembered and rewarded. She slipped out the door as the morning waned and returned to the boardinghouse, where she slept the better part of the afternoon.

A few days later, just after supper, David arrived at the boardinghouse with a bouquet of pink tulips and a nosegay of violets. Mrs. Pendleton answered the door.

"I assume you are the landlady Anna has told me so much about."

"I'm Mrs. Pendleton. And you are?"

"I'm David Jameson, ma'am, a business acquaintance, a reporter for the *Baltimore American*. I'm the person who woke you up the night the Titanic went under. I brought you these violets to make amends."

"They're lovely, Mr. Jameson. I'll put them in water right away. Won't you come in? I'll fetch Anna."

As David waited in the parlor, residents of the boarding-house wandered by the door, one by one, sneaking a look, reclaiming a lost item in the room, or flirting outright. David wasn't hard on the eyes, with his wavy brown hair and blue eyes magnified by round spectacles. Giggles in the hallway confirmed Anna's claims to David that her roommates were dunderheads.

He stood when Anna entered the room. "These are for you," he said. "I want to thank you for all you did the night of the sinking."

"It was nothing, David. What a sweet gesture. I love tulips. They're harbingers of spring."

"And better things to come, I hope. It seems that we've been thrown together by tragedy too often."

"Yes, it does."

"Would you like to take a walk?"

"I'm sorry. I didn't know you were coming. I'm going to a show at Ford's with my nanny in a little while."

"Of course, I should have called ahead. Another time, then."

"Yes, another time."

As David turned toward the door, he came back and asked, "Anna, when is your birthday?"

"October 16th. Why?"

"Do you know that new song called 'Happy Birthday To You?' It's a catchy tune. I was just wondering if you'd heard it yet."

"No, I haven't. When is your birthday?"

"December 1st."

"Oh, that's good to know."

"Why?"

"It's just good to know, I guess."

David made no effort to leave. He glanced around the room at knickknacks and vases and the chiming clock. He looked everywhere except at Anna.

He stared at the tulips and finally spoke. "Anna, I'd like to ask your father if we may enter into a proper courtship with the goal of marriage. Would that be all right with you?"

Now it was Anna's turn to be shy. She stared down at her shoes and up at the chandelier. She seemed to be stalling. David held his breath until he nearly turned blue. For two aggressive newspaper reporters, they surely were beating around the bush.

"I guess that would be all right."

"Thank you. Will you make the arrangements?"

"Of course."

※

Papa wanted to know all about David Jameson's education, his family lineage, his income and intentions. Would he want Anna to quit her job after marriage? Where would they live? Would they raise their children to be God-fearing?

"Papa, I can't answer those questions yet. We are just beginning our courtship."

"You've been around him often enough, all those times you reported on stories together."

"Yes, but we were working. Our relationship has been all-business, most of the time. All I can really tell you about him is that he likes oysters and tulips and cowboy movies." She thought for a moment, then added, "And he has a soft spot in his heart for people who suffer. I think he is a good man, Papa."

"Then we will have him over for dinner. Once I get to know him, I will decide."

"Thank you. I feel certain you will like him."

Anna looked at Elizabeth, who mouthed the words, "Don't worry."

※

Over dinner, Dr. Bainbridge did most of the talking about family responsibilities, parenting, religion, politics and the future of Baltimore. Neither Anna nor David could get a word in edgewise. She felt uncomfortable when the subject turned to motherhood and women who work. She had no intention of ever surrendering her career. And, for that matter, she had never given much thought to the possibility of having a baby. What was she getting into?

David and Anna grew vague when questioned about Anna's place taking care of home and hearth. They had never discussed the topic themselves.

Nonetheless, David must have made a good impression on Dr. Bainbridge.

A few days later, Papa blessed the courtship. Anna wondered if he was just happy Anna had attracted a suitor at all. Anna insisted, however, that she would not tolerate a chaperone on their outings. Papa had no choice but to comply. He had already endorsed the courtship.

Within days, Anna insisted that she and David slow things down. She wanted a long courtship, time to mull over where the "New Woman" in her was headed. All this talk of marriage and babies set her mind reeling.

It had happened once before.

CHAPTER 37

The *Baltimore American* hired Anna to photograph the upcoming Democratic National Convention, to be held in Baltimore, at the Fifth Regiment Armory, between June 25th and July 2nd. It was the first time the city hosted the event since 1860 and officials pulled out all the stops. David was assigned to write a column on it.

Red, white and blue bunting bedecked every building near the armory. Restaurants offered "Patriotic Specials" on their menus. Marching bands tuned their instruments. Speakers polished their presentations. Hotels filled rooms with bookings from all over the country. It was an exciting beginning to the summer of 1912.

Anna juggled assignments with the *Baltimore American* and the *Maryland Suffrage News*, which wanted stories and pictures on how suffragists could make headway. During this time, Anna and David saw little of each other.

The convention's official parade drew forty thousand spectators. Anna remained busy, photographing everything from first light to last. Once in a while, she'd run into David on the street. They would exchange a smile, a wave or the squeeze of an arm. Nothing more.

The convention proved to be electrically charged. The Republican incumbent, Teddy Roosevelt, was no shoo-in. Democrats would have to put their best candidate opposite him. Convention support for the Democratic candidates fluctuated daily. No one knew who would end up challenging the President.

One day the vote favored the governor of New Jersey, Woodrow Wilson. Many Baltimoreans supported him because he was a graduate of Johns Hopkins University. The next day, it was the Speaker of the House, Champ Clark, from Missouri. Their running mates came into question, with accusations of alcoholism and infighting during the campaign. Anna spotted

William Jennings Bryan in the crowd. She not only got a picture of him in his black suit and worn Panama hat, she also conducted a quick interview just before he took the stage to endorse Wilson. Jennings went on to accuse Champ Clark of being partisan to the moneyed crowd on Wall Street. Once again, the vote that had previously leaned toward Clark, swayed back to the Governor of New Jersey. Neither could obtain the necessary majority to claim victory.

When all was said and done, Woodrow Wilson secured the Democratic nomination to run against Teddy Roosevelt in the general election, just four months away.

By the end of the convention, Anna and David were exhausted. They took the train to Washington, D.C., one Saturday, just for a day of sightseeing and casual strolling.

"I can't imagine all that goes into running our government," Anna said, as they stopped to stare at the White House. "I wouldn't want that job for anything."

"No? I would think you'd like nothing more than to be in charge of, well, everything."

"Do you think me so vain?"

"I think you so ambitious and strong-willed."

"Will my ambitions get in the way of our courtship or marriage?"

"That's something we'll have to discuss."

"Why not right now? There's an inviting bench over there, under that tree. My feet are a bit sore anyway."

"If you like. Where shall we begin?"

"We'll start with the obvious. I love working. I love taking pictures. I want to continue to contribute to newspapers after we're ma..." Anna had a hard time getting the word out. "After we wed."

"I already know that. It's something we can arrange, I believe, at least for a while. If we partner on assignments. That way we're guaranteed to have time together."

"I don't cook very well. I tend to burn things. And I'm not the neatest person you'll ever meet."

"Neither am I. As for cooking, I can't even crack an egg. We'll have to dine out or live on food prepared at Lexington Market.

At some point, maybe we can afford help with cooking and cleaning."

"Where will we live?"

"Certainly not in your boardinghouse. Those women you live with are off-putting. From the brief encounter I had with them, they seem desperate and man-hungry." David realized his blunder and tried to recover. "I'm sorry for being so bold."

Anna laughed whole-heartedly. "I love that... 'man-hungry.' It's a perfect definition. The look on your face when you said that was so comical."

Anna placed her hand on David's arm in a sincere show of affection. There was no reading it any other way. David took the moment to take her hand and kiss it most earnestly.

"We couldn't live at the boardinghouse, anyway," Anna said. "It's for ladies only. You'd have to wear a dress." Anna laughed all the harder. David couldn't help but join her.

"We will work everything out. Don't worry. Let's just enjoy this beautiful weather and our day here in Washington, away from work, away from family and away from man-hungry women."

That sent them into another fit of giggles. When she collected herself, Anna said, "I could use a tall glass of lemonade."

"It shouldn't be hard to find. This town is filled with sourpusses. Shall we?"

Another round of laughter filled the air so near the President, at this moment making decisions about war and peace, prosperity and famine.

❧❦

One of O'Neill's competitors, Hochschild Kohn, held a new grand re-opening. They had recently expanded their store to encompass most of the block near Howard and Lexington streets, in the heart of the shopping district in downtown Baltimore. In doing so, they became Baltimore's largest department store.

Anna went there, not as a photographer seeking work, rather as a patron. It was time she bought more feminine clothes to wear when she wasn't working. She thought it was good to present herself as a lady for David. She felt bad about not shopping at O'Neill's. But Hochshild's was having a grand opening sale she couldn't resist.

Anna bought a couple of things to enhance her wardrobe, stopping short when she found herself in the Layette department. All those tiny baby things, items she had no idea what to do with. There was so much to learn about marriage, and children and how they should be raised. What if she were to birth a daughter? Would David allow her to raise the child to be independent, to speak her mind freely, to choose career over...

Here she was again. Wondering what to do. It had been different with Adrian. She knew he wanted a traditional wife and as many children as she could produce. Now, with David, expectations hung in the air. He seemed to understand Anna and her driven spirit. And her unwillingness to bend. What were his true desires?

Anna felt boxed in, confused.

"May I help you?" a saleswoman asked. "Are you shopping for yourself or someone else?"

"No, no, not for me. Not ever," Anna said, in tone a bit too forceful.

Anna escaped the Layette department and the store. By the time she reached East Baltimore, she was red-faced and out of breath. As she headed down to her basement sanctuary, Mrs. Pendleton followed her with a small white envelope in her hand.

"Anna, wait. I have something for you. A note... from that nice Adrian Crosby. He dropped it off himself. Said it was urgent. He looked a bit haggard."

Anna grabbed the message from Mrs. Pendleton's hand without acknowledging her. As Mrs. Pendleton climbed the stairs slowly, she said, to no one in particular, "Lord have mercy. What now?"

Anna ripped the seal open with her fingers and read the familiar handwriting.

Anna,

I must see you as soon as possible. Josefina has lost another child, just three months in. She is utterly distraught, as am I. We need you. We need your friendship. I wouldn't ask such a sacrifice from you if it weren't for our profound sorrow. Will we ever have a child?

Please come, Adrian

After Anna had returned from her respite in Annapolis, she had renewed her friendship with Josefina. It wasn't as deep and solid as before, but they were working on getting their relationship back on sure footing. Occasionally, Adrian joined their visits. It was obvious that he was creating a polite distance that only Anna could breach, if she chose to. He didn't want to do anything that could be misconstrued. Anna knew this encounter would define their future relationship.

She found the couple in their living room, Josefina prone on the settee, Adrian holding her hand, handkerchiefs wet with sorrow on their laps. "I am so sorry for both of you." She bent down and kissed Josefina on the cheek, then hugged Adrian without thinking. There was nothing but genuine condolence in the embrace.

Over the next months, Anna did her best to force Adrian and Josefina to participate in life. Aside from his work, Adrian stayed home with his wife, who showed little interest in going to the theater, taking in a movie, or dining out. She even refused restorative walks in the neighborhood, whether with Anna or Adrian.

"I am such a failure," Josefina told Anna one day.

"You are not. You are strong."

"That's what the doctor told me. I don't believe him or you. I have let Adrian down. He had his heart set on a large family. It doesn't look as if that will ever happen. I might never produce a single heir."

"These things are not in our hands. What we plan and what we end up with are often complete opposites. Adrian loves you with all his heart. His only desire is for you to remain healthy. You must recover not just your strength and energetic spirit, but your love of creating beautiful things, of going to the theater. You must try."

"You don't understand. You have never experienced such loss. I hope you never do. If you'll excuse me now, I'd like to rest."

"Yes, of course. Would it help if I sat with you quietly?"

"No, my mother will be coming soon. She's offered to stay while Adrian's working."

Anna settled Josefina in her bed, and refreshed a pitcher of water on her nightstand. She wondered if her friends' marriage could survive so much pain. She sincerely hoped for the best.

Looking around the apartment, Anna noticed it uncleaned. She opened the ice box and found rotting food. Unopened bills lay scattered on the kitchen table. Anna tidied and took the trash out. She put the mail in a neat pile and opened the curtains to let the sunshine in. She didn't want to burden Josefina's mother with such chores.

CHAPTER 38

Over multiple visits, Anna tried to encourage her friend, telling her that she was sure another child would come to them. But she didn't know what she was talking about. She really didn't have a clue what to say. For a burgeoning writer, words eluded her when it came to life's disappointments. Often, she just sat and poured tea and held Josefina's hand.

"How are you and David getting along?" Josefina asked.

"Oh, we are taking our courtship slow and easy. We both want to be sure we are doing the right thing."

"You could make quite the pair, one writing a news story and the other photographing it."

"That's our plan. It ensures togetherness. I really don't want to quit working after we're married."

"And David approves of that?"

"I don't really know. As I said, we have a lot to discuss."

"What about...?"

"Children?"

"I shouldn't ask."

"No, I don't mind. That's where I get confused. I'm not sure I ever want to have children."

"Oh."

"I'm sorry, Josefina. Here you just..."

"No, it's... well, I'm the one who brought up the subject."

This is how conversations went when Anna and Josefina got together. Would life ever return to normal?

෨෧෮

With a steady income, and assignments that sent her near and far, Anna decided it was time to start driving herself. She had saved enough money to purchase a used Model T from 1908. At least it had a top, which would protect her in bad weather. Papa actually approved, saying she would no longer be dependent on public transportation or riding a bicycle on roads getting more congested by the day. It took her no time at all to learn how to handle the vehicle and maintain it. When Anna asked her father if he wanted to take a ride, he declined the offer. Elizabeth grabbed her scarf and was out the door before Anna could pick up her camera. They drove north on Falls Turnpike, where Anna showed Elizabeth Bare Hills. All the way home, they entertained themselves with "In My Merry Oldsmobile," which Anna taught her nanny to sing.

"Anna, these lyrics are so naughty," she said, then laughed for all she was worth.

܀

Work often led Anna away from loved ones. In early March, she was hired by the *Maryland Suffrage News* to report and photograph a huge event for women up and down the east coast. It was the Army of the Hudson March, organized by the Suffrage Army. Women wanted to make a loud-and-clear statement to Woodrow Wilson on the night before his inauguration. Marches were to take place from New York to Washington, with several stops in Maryland, including Havre de Grace, Bel Air, Overlea, Baltimore, Laurel and Bladensburg. In all, two hundred thirty miles were covered, not just by women but, also, men. More and more men were showing their favor for suffrage, while others disapproved vehemently. And there were still many women staunchly holding on to the Victorian ways, opposing suffrage whole-heartedly.

The more-than-seventy-year fight for the vote edged toward an apex. Women from all over the country converged on New York. They marched in good weather and bad, on paved roads and untouched land. A woman named Rosalie Jones stood out as a leader. Over the long journey, newspapers called her "General Jones."

Along the way, these "suffrage pilgrims," as they were named, stopped for food and rest, delivered speeches, sang songs with encouraging lyrics, and most important of all, gave press interview after press interview. They knew that the more publicity they got, the better their chances of success. Anna drove alongside the marchers, offering rides to women with blisters and twisted ankles. She interviewed them with one hand on the wheel, the other jotting quotes.

As spectators lined the roads—some in support, others heckling—the marchers handed out leaflets they hoped women and men would keep and read.

Everyone wanted an interview with General Jones. Anna seized her opportunity just before the army reached Washington. Rosalie Jones looked bedraggled yet determined, more like one of the marchers than their leader.

"Miss Jones, do you like the title of 'General?'" Anna asked.

"If it will help get our message across to the right people, I'm all for it. But I'm just one more suffragist."

"I've heard the terms suffragist and suffragette. Which do you prefer?"

"I prefer 'suffragist.' It sounds more solid, more legitimate. And it welcomes men into our ranks. 'Suffragette' seems too feminine, as if we are an offshoot of a man's organization and shouldn't be taken seriously."

"What do you hope to accomplish in Washington?"

"We will start by participating in the National Woman Suffrage Parade. And give speeches to the masses. We'll try to convince the naysayers to join us. I'll do whatever it takes."

"You have a great deal of support already."

"Yes, but not from the people most important to me... my own family. My mother is an active member of the New York State Anti-Suffrage Association. She's a prominent woman in her community, a socialite. I don't feel she is putting her wealth and stature to good use."

"May I quote you on that?"

"Yes, you may. Excuse me." General Jones reached for a woman passing by. "Inez, do you have a moment? I have someone I'd like you to meet."

A striking young woman, probably in her late twenties, joined Anna and General Jones.

"Anna, this is Inez Milholland, a far more important figure in the suffrage movement than I could ever be."

"I beg to differ, General," the woman said.

"Inez came all the way from New York with me. She is a labor lawyer and an effective speaker, educated at Vassar and the New York University of Law. Yale, Harvard and Cambridge all denied her entry due to her gender."

"I'm happy to hear you succeeded anyway. I am Anna Bainbridge, representing the *Maryland Suffrage News*."

"I learned earlier that Miss Bainbridge is a self-taught photojournalist and writer," General Jones said.

"Quite admirable. Will you be joining us in the parade?" Inez remarked.

"I support you totally but will be driving on the sidelines reporting and taking pictures. My car is parked over there."

"Oh, you drove yourself. And I see you are wearing a man's suit. That's similar to... what is her name?"

"Frances Benjamin Johnston?"

"Yes, that's it."

"I had the pleasure of meeting her a while back," Anna said. "She taught me quite a lot about the business and how to navigate it as a woman. May I ask you some questions, Miss Milholland?"

"I have a few minutes to offer. Go ahead."

"How do you see a woman's right to vote in comparison to the right of coloreds to vote?"

"I'm very glad you asked me that question. I see the two as equal. I am a member of the NAACP, you know."

"You are? I didn't know white people could join."

"Yes, of course. The organization was founded by colored and white people to fight racism together. You should have known that."

"I guess I should. I have worked for the *Baltimore Afro-American* newspaper on occasion."

"A fine publication."

"Can I get a quote from you that I could use in that paper?"

"Certainly. When I march for suffrage, I march for the equal rights of all people, no matter their gender or race. I always say:

'Forward, out of error,

Leave behind the night,

Forward through the darkness,
Forward into Light!'"

With that, Inez Milholland was gone.

"Well, she is quite the whirlwind, isn't she?" Anna said to General Jones.

"Yes, she must be. Wherever she goes, people admire her looks over her intellect. Every day, she fights to be taken seriously as a political leader. She doesn't mind getting dirty in the fight for equality."

"How so?"

"As a labor leader, she has battled for the rights of prisoners, even getting arrested in work disputes. She entered Sing Sing to find out what life behind bars was all about. And went so far as to demand being handcuffed to understand the full experience. Wait until you see her in our march to the Capitol. She is what you might call 'A New Woman.'"

"I'm familiar with that term."

The day before the march to Pennsylvania Avenue, the *New York Times* headline foreshadowed trouble. It read:

WOMEN START INVASION

It was as though the suffragists were creatures from another planet, there to disrupt the American way of life. The parade itself proved to be well-planned and carefully carried out. It was some of the spectators who acted as alien creatures.

Estimates of suffragists in the streets ranged from five to eight thousand, while the people who lined the sidewalks numbered approximately ten thousand. Nine marching bands and twenty floats rounded out the parade.

And there was General Rosalie Jones, near the front, riding in a car draped in patriotic bunting. Most notable was Inez Milholland, sitting tall atop a pure white steed. A snowy-colored cape draped not only the rider, but the horse itself. Inez's hair had been set free from her chignon, pouring down her back in natural curls to her waist. A statement of unbridled womanhood.

Nearby, at the Treasury Department, a secondary march was in full swing, led by actress Hedwig Reich, dressed as Columbia, the American symbol of femininity. She, and other performers, put on a pageant.

Colored women joined this, the most important of all marches. They proudly held their own banners and walked in peaceful solidarity with white suffragists representing their same home states.

Women made their voices heard in Washington. So did detractors. It wasn't long before marchers were pelted with insults, spit, and objects ranging from their own balled-up leaflets to harder, more dangerous projectiles. The women marched on. Some were injured, as many as one hundred taken to area hospitals.

Inez looked like Joan of Arc astride her horse but refused to end up a martyr. She ignored the violence and held tight reins on her skittish mount. Anna was never so proud to be a supporter. She focused on her contribution, writing a story and taking pictures. She had a lot of competition.

The headline of the March 3rd edition of the *Women's Journal And Suffrage News* read:

PARADE STRUGGLES TO VICTORY DESPITE DISGRACEFUL SCENES

The subheading pronounced:

NATION AROUSED BY OPEN INSULTS TO WOMEN – CAUSE WINS POPULAR SYMPATHY – CONGRESS ORDERS INVESTIGATION – STRIKING OBJECT LESSON

Anna was surprised to see one photograph in a newspaper that inspired her more than any other. It showed a picture of the crowd from above, a shot taken from an airplane. She had never seen anything like it. The photograph didn't put newspaper readers in the middle of the action but expressed the magnitude of the event. Even though Anna was known for putting readers in the midst of a story, she would have given anything to shoot a birds-eye view of the parade, just to be the first one to think of it.

Meanwhile, blocks from the march, Woodrow Wilson arrived at Union Station to take his place in history. Few people were there to greet him. Hardly anyone even noticed.

CHAPTER 39

As soon as Anna returned home, a massive accident rocked Baltimore. On March 7, at 10:00 A.M., Anna headed to the offices of the *Maryland Suffrage News* in an aura of exhilaration over the Washington march. She thought nothing could shake her euphoria. Without warning, an explosion, followed by a rolling rumble, felled her and several others. At first, silence followed. Then, cries and screams could be heard. People were injured. An ominous plume of smoke rose above The Basin. Small bits of debris rained down all around Anna.

Oh no, not again, she thought.

Anna's body reflexively went into motion, much as it had on February 7th of 1904, when the Great Baltimore Fire destroyed most of downtown. Just as she had done then, she ran toward disaster. As always, Anna had camera in hand. There was only one difference between then and now. This time, Anna thought about someone else... David. Where was he? How could she get in touch with him? They needed to work in tandem.

She ran only a few blocks before hearing what was going on. She pieced together snippets of information and discovered that a ship had exploded near Fort Carroll. It was located on the outer area of The Basin, not near the city docks. Anna would need her car to get anywhere close.

She raced back home and steered her Model T toward Dundalk. Several times, she had to pull over to allow fire trucks and ambulances to race past her to the scene.

Fire raged, smoke plumed, the earth gave off aftershocks. No one could get to victims by land. Fort Carroll sat on a three-and-a-half-acre island in the middle of the Patapsco River southeast of The Basin. Only boats could reach the injured and dying. Tugboats were already on their way to the scene from The Basin and Fells Point.

Anna had to park a fair distance away to make room for officials and rescuers.

Why did I wear a dress today? Anna thought. *And where is David?*

Anna pulled a ballpoint pen and paper from her fan pocket and went from one witness to the next to discover what happened. Each person was eager to tell what they saw.

"The ship just exploded!"

"What ship? What is its name?"

"I don't know."

Another witness chimed in. "I do. It was the 'Alum Chine,' a steamer from Great Britain."

"What would cause such an explosion?"

"Who knows?"

"Did you see it?" Anna asked a third man.

"Yes, out of the corner of my eye. I was walking my dog on the edge of this pier when it happened. The loudest sound I ever heard. It blew out my eardrums. For a while, everything sounded fuzzy. My dog went crazy, barking and gyrating wildly. I had trouble controlling her. Pieces of the ship shot way up in the air and, when I realized they were going to come back down on me, I ran, pulling the leash hard. Finally, I had to pick up little Bessie here and move faster before getting hit. I'm sure many people are probably hurt, even dead."

Yet another witness butted in. "I heard a police officer say that dynamite was being loaded on the British ship from another boat that had pulled up to the island. The dynamite was bound for Panama, for building the canal."

"What triggered the explosion? Do you know?"

"Could have been anything, a cigarette or match or some kind of spontaneous combustion down below."

The first man spoke again. "Look! Here comes a tug full speed. That's the second one."

"Where's the first one? I don't see another."

"There was a tug nearby when the explosion occurred. It blew up, too. I think it was called 'The Atlantic.' And over there is a collier on fire. It's hard to see with all the smoke. Can you read the name on the side? I think it says 'The Jason.' That's a brand new ship. I spend a lot of time down here with my dog. I know."

The water, for as far as the eye could see, was littered with pieces of things that once made a ship, and pieces of flesh and bones that once made humans, and pieces of things still burning, whether man-made or human.

By now, Anna should have been used to morbid news scenes. She was not. Perhaps, being horrified proved she still retained her humanity and had not become hardened to the world. How was David sorting through this emotional upheaval? She worried for him. Anna kept looking through the crowds of people, only to come up empty. He should have been here by now. Maybe he was on the other side of the river.

Anna found a worker from the Port Authority and asked for his point of view. "Did you witness the explosion, sir?"

"I'll say. The crew of the ship was workin' with our stevedores when smoke came out of the hold. Everybody knew it was trouble, so they abandoned ship. Not in time, though."

"I heard they were loading dynamite."

"Three hundred and fifty tons of it."

"Then what happened?"

"The ship blew up. It lifted outta the water and up in the air. And it came down in pieces, some on fire. And the bodies... so many men. I don't wanna talk about it no more."

"Then I'll change the subject. How did the ship get its name?"

"'Alum Chine?' Well, she's from England. And, from what I heard tell, it was named for the Alum Bay in someplace called the Isle of Wight. She was only eight years old."

"What does 'chine' mean?"

"I have no idea."

"I do," said another man, standing nearby. It seemed everyone wanted to tell their stories. "It's the build of a boat, how the bottom intersects with the rest."

"This explosion will set back the building of the Panama Canal, won't it?"

"No doubt."

Anna asked the witnesses' their names and thanked them for the information. She stopped an ambulance driver as he waited for any survivors who needed to be taken to the hospital.

"Are there many injured?"

"Couldn't say. Too early to tell. Imagine so. Got a problem, though."

"What's that?"

"Just got word the Quarantine Hospital at Wagner's Point was rocked by the explosion. Some of the patients there were hurt. Have to find another place to take these here survivors... if there are any."

Anna pocketed her notes and set to taking pictures.

She would later learn that the impact of the explosion was felt all over the area, from Hawkins Point in the Patapsco River to City Hall above The Basin.

Windows were shattered, buildings wiggled like gelatin, leaving people to wonder if they were still safe to inhabit.

Families of dock workers arrived, only to be greeted with horror. Bodies and body parts lined the pier closest to the explosion. Mothers shielded their children, while failing to restrain their own emotions. Wails of grief cut through the mayhem. Authorities vowed to start an inquest immediately.

The evening newspapers ran chilling headlines:

DEATH TO SCORES IN FURIOUS BLAST
300 Tons of Dynamite on Ships
Drench Decks with Blood

HAIL OF DEATH FROM SKY
Tug Captain and Men Killed
in Heroic Attempt at Rescue

NAVAL COLLIER IS RIDDLED

Shockwaves had been felt in other states, including Delaware, where residents feared an earthquake, at first. Newspapers all over the country reported the tragedy.

Anna never did run into David. Where was he all this time?

The next day, Anna learned that, while she had been with the suffragists in Washington, David had been called to New York on a family matter. His brother had needed emergency surgery following an attack of appendicitis. David missed the story completely but read about it in New York newspapers.

Before he left Baltimore, he had dropped a note for Anna at the boardinghouse, telling her of his sudden call home. Anna had been too busy to check her mail slot or she would have known.

In the ensuing months, it was determined that a worker's bale hook had punctured a case of dynamite. Such a simple human error caused so much death and chaos and destruction of property. The number of those killed was never determined exactly, somewhere between forty and fifty, including the first tugboat captain to arrive in an act of mercy. As many as sixty were injured.

❧

Anna needed some good news. And she got it. Later in the year, Anna read a newspaper article about General Jones's newest plan to spread the suffrage message. She must have seen that aerial photograph from the march, too.

In May, she took off in a biplane in Staten Island, New York, carrying hundreds of suffrage leaflets. The pilot flew her over an airplane carnival, where hundreds of patrons looked to the sky. Yellow paper rained down on them like fluttering canaries, singing songs of equality for women. Upon landing, General Jones gave a speech, followed by the release of a hundred bright balloons, symbolic prayers to the heavens. General Rosalie Jones acquired a new moniker... "Pioneer Air Pilgrim."

More good news reached Anna. A Baltimore chapter of the NAACP had formed. Her friend, Ida Cummings of the Fresh Air Fund, had been elected Corresponding Secretary. After Anna heard that white people could join the organization, she did, too. She and Emmaline went to meetings together. They both congratulated Miss Cummings on her new position with Angel food cake and tea in Emmaline's room.

When she arrived, Miss Cummings introduced a guest she had brought. "I hope you don't mind, Emmaline. My brother dropped by just as I was leaving to come here."

"You are more than welcome, Councilman Cummings," Emmaline said. "Anna, this is Harry Cummings, the first colored man ever elected to Baltimore's City Council."

"Pleased to make your acquaintance," Anna said. "I never connected the names."

"Have we met before?"

"No, I'm well acquainted with your sister."

"Anna is a photojournalist," Miss Cummings said. "She reports for several papers, including the *Afro*. It was her article in the *Herald* that helped grow the Fresh Air Fund and call Emmaline's talents to my attention."

"Well, I must thank you."

"I'm somewhat aware of your accomplishments, sir," Anna said. "I remember reading about your speech at the Republican National Convention in 1904."

"It was one of the most rewarding days of my career."

"Didn't you also found a school?"

"Yes, the Colored Polytechnic Institute."

"You are doing more than many of your white counterparts. It should be reported in the newspaper."

"Councilman Cummings also helped a colored art student get a scholarship to The Maryland Institute of Art," said Miss Cummings. "Isn't he something special?"

"So are you," Anna said.

Together, the foursome enjoyed sweet treats and serious talk about the future of Baltimore, for everyone.

&⸺&

In November, Anna traveled to New York with David to meet his parents and see how his brother, Robert, was recuperating. While there, Anna suggested that she and David take in the latest play written by Rachel Crothers, a well-respected playwright and director in Broadway circles. Her newest work was simply called,

Ourselves. It premiered on November 13th to acclaim and controversy.

"Now, David, I must warn you. She is a feminist playwright who addresses many taboo subjects, such as women openly disagreeing with their spouses, refusing to obey, working outside the home after marriage, and the most taboo of subjects..." Anna lowered her voice and added, "... sex."

"I don't like your audacity in voicing that word, however discreetly. I think this isn't appropriate at all. We are not yet married. No, I won't go to see the play."

"Then I will go alone."

"No, you will not."

"Are you forbidding me?"

"Anna, think of what my parents might say. They will be outraged. You want them to like you, don't you?"

"I want to live my life on my terms and let the chips fall where they may, as a woodcutter would say."

"Anna, you have put me in an awkward position. I cannot go with you and I cannot justify you going by yourself."

"This is not some sordid presentation. Rachel Crothers is revered on Broadway. And the star is none other than Grace Elliston, widely respected. Let me explain the premise. Maybe that will convince you."

"I doubt it but go ahead. I know there is no stopping you."

"The play portrays life behind bars for women... actually, prostitutes who explore the stigma of their profession. When men stray from their wedding vows, they are often forgiven or their wives simply turn a blind eye. But the woman who participates in that encounter, perhaps a prostitute, is branded for life. Miss Crothers is merely pointing out how unfair that is. She also raises the topic of sexual practices within marriage. Usually, it is the husband who initiates sexual relations and they are, shall I say, 'performed' to his liking. She suggests that the wife should be the initiator and it is she who must communicate her desires to her husband."

"Enough! Please, Anna. I am shocked. This is a most unsuitable topic for us at this stage in our courtship."

"When would be an appropriate time? After we're married? We might discover that we have different expectations. It's obvious that, right now, we disagree on whether or not to see a play. How will we navigate more complex issues?"

"This isn't just any play, Anna. How can you be so cavalier? Can't we take in a musical?"

"Can't we discuss our marriage and what we both want to gain by it? Whenever I bring up the subject, you climb into a clam shell."

"Anna, what are you learning from these suffragists? First, they want to vote and now they are taking control of what goes on in the bedroom. What's next? These women are filling your head with methods for tearing down the very structure of marriage."

"And what is that structure?"

"That the man rules his castle."

"And the woman?"

"She is treated as a queen."

"And suppose she refuses to submit. Is it 'off with her head?'"

"I suggest we stay in tonight and return to Baltimore in the morning. I have some thinking to do and it must be conducted in solitude."

"I see."

"Will you abide by my wish and not go alone to the play? I cannot force you."

"Yes, David. I'm in no mood to go now, anyway."

The next day, they took the train home without a single word between them. The air, however, thickened with disappointment and failure.

∾

A week went by before Anna heard from her betrothed. The year painfully drew to a close. The holidays loomed rather than approached with anticipation. David made no mention of parties or dances or festivities of any kind. Once or twice, he and Anna shared a meal. Most times, they ate in silence.

239

One night, as David walked Anna home from dinner, without warning or explanation, he asked to be released from his commitment to her. He didn't need to offer an explanation. Anna complied.

Anna told Josefina about David and the conversation that led to their severing of ties. Her friend found Anna's sexual frankness appalling. Josefina's expression told Anna that Adrian would most certainly react the same way.

A few days later, after Anna relayed the same story, Emmaline nearly dropped her teacup, saying, "I thought you were a lady. Are you experienced in matters of marriage?"

"Of course not. It's just that those 'matters of marriage' are important and should be discussed before vowing to be true for a lifetime. Suppose a woman enters into marriage, only to find she and her husband are not compatible under the skirt."

"Anna! Must you?"

"I'm sorry. But haven't you ever thought of such things?"

"No, I would leave all that to my husband. I imagine he would already be experienced."

"Why?"

"It's just the way it is."

"Why can't a woman be experienced?"

"Because she would no longer be a lady."

"Would a man no longer be a gentleman?"

"You are upsetting me."

"David said that suffrage women were putting these ideas in my head. They are not. What they are teaching me is how to take my future into my own hands. And, for me, that includes every aspect."

"You wouldn't actually partake in intimacies before marriage, would you?"

"I might."

"What about self-respect?"

"Would you respect your husband if you found out he was experienced?"

"That's different."

"Is it?"

"Where have you gotten all these notions about... you know? Certainly, not from your nanny."

"Good heavens, no," she laughed. "From books. I've been reading a lot of novels lately, some of them dating back to the late 1800s, when women were told to tighten their lips when it came to politics but open their legs when it came to the desires of their husbands."

"Stop talking smut!"

"The women portrayed in these books were outspoken, straightforward, even aggressive."

"What books are you talking about?"

"Well, I read a novel called *The Story of a Modern Woman* by Ella Hepworth Dixon. It's about a lady who frankly addresses the sexual aspect of womanhood, including the unpleasantries of syphilis and how to avoid it. And, also, the work of George Egerton, a female writer. Her book of short stories is called *Keynotes*. Her female characters explore their lives in its many facets, including control of their finances, attaining higher education, and enjoying sexual freedom."

"And this is what you want? Anna, I'm worried about you."

"In some aspects, it is what I want. I would like to go to college, perhaps study writing. And I already have control over my budget and where I live and work."

"What about the other?"

"You mean...?"

"Don't say that word again."

"Come now. There's no need to be shy about it. At the moment, I have no man in my life. I'm just thinking out loud."

"Let's leave the discussion there, for now."

"You're not angry with me, are you?"

"No, just a bit shaken."

Anna wondered if her two best friends now thought less of her. Were they right and she wrong? At first, Anna decided it best to keep her opinions to herself. Then, she thought of all the suffragists changing the world, and the female writers challenging Victorian standards. She wanted to protect her friendships and the respect that formed their foundations. She also wanted to live the life of a modern woman. She decided, for the time being, to keep her opinion of sex a little closer to the vest. Perhaps, she didn't even know what she was really talking about.

✄✄

Anna enjoyed Christmas dinner with her father and Elizabeth. She told them of her broken engagement, stating that it was she who initiated it, blaming it on her own fickle attitude, so as not to go into the real reason.

Papa was both concerned and relieved. He knew of more medical students who might be suitable for Anna.

CHAPTER 40

The new year crept on tip toes. Not much worth reporting happened. The corner of Baltimore and Liberty streets was named McLane Place, in honor of the mayor who had weathered the Great Baltimore Fire and helped the city rebuild bigger and better. Even though it was rumored that he had died by suicide just three months after the fire, the city felt he deserved this honor at the intersection where the fire had started.

The corner showed no signs of fire damage. Multiple-story buildings had risen from the ashes. The Baltimore Bargain House took up one corner. A large billboard sat atop the building across the street. It lit up at night in big letters, "Pays to Advertise with Electric Signs. Get yours now." A smiling sun above it looked down on potential buyers. In the brick median near the intersection stood the statue of John Mifflin Hood, a Confederate Lieutenant, later to become president of the Western Maryland Railroad.

The understated ceremony unfolded slowly. The former mayor's wife, if there at all, went unnoticed by Anna.

In March, thoughts turned to baseball, as it did every year. Even people who were not fans of the sport looked forward to spring and being outdoors in moderate temperatures.

A new recruit on the Baltimore Orioles team was being talked up in the newspaper. His name was George Herman Ruth, Jr., a promising young pitcher with a questionable past.

He grew up in Pigtown, a neighborhood known for its many butcher shops and meat processing plants, just southwest of downtown. As a young boy, he often spent time in a bar run by his father. By the time he was seven, he'd found himself in St. Mary's Industrial School, a reformatory for incorrigibles, where he lived for twelve years. Authorities there were unable to contain George's spirit. His ticket to a better life was baseball.

On March 7, 1914, he signed with the Orioles, an International League team. His teammates didn't know what to make of this jovial, braggadocious, talented young man. Baseball fans started attending games just to see him pitch and hit. They claimed him for their own because he came from the streets of Baltimore.

By July, financial woes forced the team to trade the player, nicknamed "Babe," to the Boston Red Sox.

Anna admired his moxie and went to games before he left the team. She discovered that she liked baseball and found a companion in Adelaide, of all people. Over dinner one night, the two fell into a discussion about Babe Ruth and discovered they could discuss this one topic without argument. Together, they attended games at the Old American League Park on Greenmount Avenue and 29th Street in the Waverly section of Baltimore.

The city was expanding in all directions and Anna, with her Model T, could travel just about anywhere.

"I really have to hand it to you, Anna," said Adelaide, following an afternoon at the ballpark. "I don't think I could handle a car myself. I appreciate being able to attend baseball games in style."

"It's nothing, Adelaide. I could teach you how to drive in an afternoon."

"On my salary, it would take years to afford a car. Thanks just the same."

"You're still selling sheet music, aren't you? That's something fewer people are buying these days. Music lovers are going for those new vinyl records you play on a phonograph. Your job could become obsolete. Then, what will you do?"

"I'll worry about that when the time comes."

Anna was quiet for a moment. She wanted to have a serious conversation with Adelaide. She also didn't want to speak too frankly and damage what little rapport they had already built. She decided to tread lightly.

"Adelaide, haven't you ever sat in the window at night and stared at the stars and dreamed of doing something else, something great?"

"No. I was raised to marry well and have servants do for me. My destiny was women's clubs, and lunch with ladies just like me. Also, doing charitable work, you know, feeding the hungry and clothing the poor, and raising money to build monuments and planting memorial gardens. My parents' separation put an end to that. Our family fell from grace."

"Is that what you really want? To be the 'Lady of the Manor,' as they say?"

"Well, not really. It sounds nice on the surface. I imagine it would get boring after a while. And then there would be the necessary children to complete the picture of a perfect American woman."

"You sound as though you disagree with that."

"I'm starting to. Of course, I would like to marry a rich man. But I guess I'd like to do something special that would bring admiration."

"Like what?"

"Well, I have an idea I've been thinking about. It might sound implausible."

"Tell me. I won't criticize you for having an original thought."

"Well, I'd like to start an employment service just for women."

"You mean, you want to help them find permanent work?"

"No, temporary. It might be too far-fetched. Just a crazy proposition."

"Maybe not. It would be perfect for bored women who might want to work just a few days a week or whenever they are free."

"Or if their husbands are ill or recuperating from injury with no income, as a result. Or if their marriage breaks up and they're suddenly strapped for money."

"Adelaide, I think you are on to something. You could have typewriters and stenotype machines in your office, where women could learn office skills and such. They could practice phone manners and how to use an adding machine. Then you could place them wherever needed and take a percentage of their salaries as your income. I'm sure businesses need to fill temporary vacancies, like when an employee is recovering from surgery or someone catches a bad cold and can't work."

"You don't think it's a crazy idea?"

"Not at all. I think it's pure genius. In my spare time, I'd love to help you get started."

"That's very nice of you. Maybe you could help me advertise, that is, if I decide to go through with it. First, I'd have to learn the legal and financial aspects of starting a business. You know, taxes and so on."

"I'm at your service. I have a friend who works in accounting. She must know tax laws. I'll enlist her help. What do you say?"

"I say, 'Let's do it,' as long as it doesn't interfere with coming to Orioles' games."

"And eating Cracker Jack."

"It's a deal. Wait. How would I purchase office equipment and acquire a storefront to start this business? Women can't get loans from banks. I'd need a sponsor."

"Yes, that could be a problem. I'm friends with several important leaders in the suffrage campaign. I'm sure at least one could put us in touch with someone sympathetic to working women."

Adelaide stared at Anna as if seeing her for the first time. "This is wonderful of you. After all the times I hurled insults at you like a pitcher throwing a fast ball. I'm sorry. Perhaps, I was... jealous of your strength and independence. Now that I've gotten to know you, I feel some of it has rubbed off on me."

"You wear it well. Let bygones be bygones. And I will teach you how to drive a car."

Right there, in the ballpark, Anna and Adelaide became friends and business partners, of a sort. That very night, after dinner, they laid out plans on the dining table.

Mrs. Pendleton couldn't get over the change in these two women and neither could Frances and Jane Catherine, who continued to pick on Anna, only to be chastised by Adelaide.

Under her breath, Mrs. Pendleton said, "Will wonders never cease?"

⚮

In July, rumblings of war in Europe could be felt in Baltimore. Anna didn't think much of it. Such matters had nothing to do with her. Until it affected Papa and his purse. On July 31, the New York Stock Exchange closed, not to open its doors the next day. European investors had sold off their investments and redirected their funds toward the needs of the war. Immediately, financial institutions around the world shut down, too. Anna telephoned home after reading a dire newspaper account. It was good timing that Papa had finally relented and had a telephone installed in his home weeks before. He felt, after his bout with heart disease, that it would be a prudent move.

Anna called from the boardinghouse. "Elizabeth, how is Papa doing?"

"He's in his office. I couldn't get him to eat breakfast or even drink his tea."

"I hope this doesn't cause another heart attack. Shall I come home?"

"No, he said he wanted no interruptions. Having to entertain questions, even from you or me, would cause him more tension."

"I understand. Now that you have a phone, will you call me every day?"

"Certainly, not to worry."

Anna's thoughts were momentarily directed away from Papa, who remained tight-lipped about his finances, and toward her mother, whose name was rarely spoken.

President Woodrow Wilson officially designated the second Sunday in May as Mother's Day. It was a lovely gesture started by a daughter for her mother as a religious memorial. Now a national holiday, families all over the country celebrated motherhood in a variety of ways. Anna could play no part in the festivities. It pained Anna to see mothers and daughters, locking arms, enjoying long walks in the park, picking flowers, dining out. She invited herself to supper with Papa, instead. When she arrived, Elizabeth made excuses for why he wasn't there. "Emergency at the hospital. He asked me to convey his regrets."

"His apology is not accepted. He just doesn't want to face the questions he knows I have."

"Anna, he has much on his mind. Perhaps I can help you. Ask me what you like."

"Why was it acceptable for Mama to concern herself with fashion and hosting parties and playing the piano, but not me? I've always been dressed in drab colors with a rare piece of jewelry. I was not taught music or allowed to attend parties."

"That's a difficult question to answer. We tried to teach you piano. You just didn't take to it. You must understand... your mother was raised in the Victorian era, when decorum, genteel conversation, and moral femininity ruled a girl's upbringing. At that time, women were revered as figures of beauty, like a porcelain doll. They stayed in the background, smiling, pouring tea, playing the piano forte, only occasionally dancing a refined waltz with eyes averted from their partner. Papa wanted that for you. But you were different and social mores had changed. We knew, early on, you were headstrong, excitable, unreserved. In an effort to tame you, your father went too far in the opposite direction. He restrained your natural enthusiasm and curiosity. Perhaps, if your mother had lived, she could have tempered his strict enforcements. Do you see?"

"Yes, I think I do." Anna stared at her lap and noticed her hands had twisted into a knot. "Even though I never really knew Mama, I miss her."

"Of course, you do. I did my best to offer you affection and a safe place to nestle your fears and anxieties. But I was only a substitute."

"Oh, Elizabeth, I didn't mean to say... why, you have been wonderful to me."

"I understand, dear. Imagine if you were a mother of a rambunctious child living in polite society. What would you do? How would you raise her?"

"Yes, I'm beginning to see." Anna smoothed her skirt to give her hands something to do. "Where is Mama buried?"

"Would you like me to take you?"

"Would Papa object?"

"Maybe. Should I ask him?"

"No, just tell me where she is. This is something I must do on my own. That way, if Papa finds out, you are without blame. I can always say I found it while searching for someone else."

"I doubt he'd believe your lie. And you know you shouldn't fib to anyone, much less your father. Your mother is buried in the Green Mount Cemetery. It's a large graveyard. You might need help locating her resting place."

"I will find it. I'm quite familiar with the place."

"You are?"

"I've been there many times, to visit Mayor McLane. Thank you, Elizabeth."

ॐॐ

Anna had to ask the caretaker where to find her mother's grave. A simple headstone marked the birth and death and offered little else:

Elizabeth R. Bainbridge
Beloved Wife, Mother and Christian

Anna dropped rose petals on her mother's grave, already feeling closer to her, yet knowing their chosen paths in life could not be more disparate. She had nothing to say, even though she had so many questions. It would take time and maturity to get to know her.

ॐॐ

Baltimoreans found cause for celebration in September. Over a two-day observance, they commemorated the Centennial of the battles of Baltimore and North Point in the War of 1812, newsworthy all over the country. *Baltimore Magazine* hired Anna to document the events.

A parade from the Washington Monument, in the northern part of Baltimore, marched all the way to Fort McHenry in Locust Point, nearly four miles away, just beyond The Basin. Some 500,000 proud Baltimoreans crowded the streets and cheered marchers on.

The festivities were more than a commemoration of the past. The city was looking to the future. When the parade arrived at the fort, it was dedicated as a public park for all to enjoy and pay their respects. It became an historical reminder of the bravery of Maryland soldiers against British attack in 1812. Every visitor could look out over the fort and the waters beyond and imagine what Francis Scott Key saw, smoke and fire, death. And a piece of red, white and blue cloth refusing to curl its last wave.

It was Mary Young Pickersgill's handiwork that inspired Key to write the National Anthem. She had expertly sewn the flag that flew over Fort McHenry through the onslaught. Her great grandniece, Miss Esther Mabel Young, unveiled a commemorative tablet. Dressed in a simple high-collared white blouse with a sedate black hat to match her skirt, she expressed joy and reverence in her smile.

Schoolchildren formed a human flag. Little stars and teams of stripes moved the crowd to tears as they lined up. Anna climbed a parapet to get a good picture and was swiftly chastised by one of the many fort rangers.

The evening celebration included a "water carnival" with a decorated flotilla, navigating the waters like bobbing apples. A magnificent fireworks display illuminated the sky, mimicking the real bombardment, bringing oohs and aahs from onlookers.

The next morning, as people filed into churches, their remembrance became more somber, focusing on those who lost their lives over one hundred years before. Prayers for peace echoed through the naves.

ॐॐ

In late November, around Thanksgiving, a new theater opened on the west end of downtown. Located on Eutaw Street, near West Fayette and Redwood, "The Hippodrome" offered Burlesque shows and silent films. The stage performances ranged from comic to somewhat sexual, with men often portraying women to ward off any offense. But sometimes, scantily-clad women sang and danced and paraded their assets around the stage. Anna wondered what David would have thought of that.

She hadn't seen him in quite some time. She got a quick glance once at Ford's Theater, during a placid play, where he sat in the company of an attractive young lady.

In December, she heard through the grapevine that David was looking for a job, once again, in New York. The gossip was confirmed as true by David himself, who contacted Anna and made an appointment to meet with her.

"How have you been? You appear in full vigor."

"Yes, I'm doing fine. And you?"

"As well as can be expected."

"Why do you say that? Have you been ill?"

"No. I still think about you often, and the life we could have had together."

"We've been through this before."

"Is there any chance that you will change? We could decide that your foolish thoughts about independent women were nothing more than the naïve ramblings of an immature girl. Can you grow out of them?"

"Girl! You call me a 'girl?' I just celebrated my twenty-ninth birthday."

"I see I cannot get through to you. I should have known."

"I'm sorry you have not grown. You have not matured enough to accept that women's roles are changing. I wish you luck in finding the mousy mate you so desire. Good day!" Anna turned to walk away.

"Wait, please, just a moment. I am moving to New York to work for the *Tribune* again. I was hoping we could... well, it appears hopeless. I wish you all the best in life, good health and happiness. That's all."

After a few seconds, Anna turned and replied, "I'm sorry the stars were not aligned in our favor. Best wishes to you." Anna put out her hand in anticipation of a handshake. Instead, David raised her hand to his lips and offered a final, tender kiss.

After he left, Anna almost regretted losing him. David was, after all, a true gentleman.

CHAPTER 41

It seemed the House of Representatives wasn't understanding women any better than David. In early January of 1915, they rejected yet another proposal that would give women the right to vote. This time, the margin narrowed with 174 "for" and 204 "against," giving hope to the Just Government League.

Its leader, Edith Houghton Hooker, wanted to seize the momentum swing further in favor of suffrage. She contacted Anna for support. "Have you heard? We are getting closer by the day."

"Yes, I've been keeping track. Some states have already allowed women the vote, including Nevada and Montana."

"However, they have continued to exclude Native American women. There is still plenty of work to be done."

"What are your plans?"

"The league is growing by leaps and bounds. Through small meetings in home parlors and open-air gatherings in town squares, our numbers have swelled to 17,000 members. Our flyers and pamphlets can be found anywhere. And that's where you enter the picture. Oh, pardon the pun," she said, with an embarrassed giggle. "I mean, you can be a part of our plan."

"Me? How?"

"I want you to photograph our march this Saturday. Capture women pushing prams, dressed in their best, smiling as they parade. Too many times, suffragists are depicted as angry, defiant women, when they are ladies who love their families, practice their religions, teach children in school and have the support of their husbands. We will put those pictures in our advertising."

"I'd be happy to do it."

"I was hoping you would agree. I can't pay you much."

"That doesn't bother me."

"There is more at stake. Our next plan is to push for the right to serve on a jury."

"That could be a tall order to fill."

"I know. We've already reached out to government officials, only to be rebuffed. Told outright that women were just not smart enough. That we lack the ability to discern and deduce testimony. That we would rule with our hearts and not with our heads."

"Nonsense."

"And that women would be prone to fainting spells when presented with gruesome evidence."

"That's simply not true. I photographed the murder trial of Henry Kendall Thaw, who shot off the face of another man. I photographed burned victims of the Triangle Shirtwaist Factory fire and the explosion aftermath at Fort Carroll. It was shocking and bloody and heartbreaking, but I did it. The male reporter who was with me on one of those stories lost the contents of his stomach, while I continued working."

"Quite my point. Can you find a way to photograph a group of women sitting in a jury box, as if intently focused on testimony? We could use that picture on posters and flyers and such to show how women would behave."

"I'm sure we could gather women willing to pose. The problem is... how would I get permission to shoot in a courtroom?"

"I leave that to your own ingenuity."

ॐॐ

Anna met with Emmaline in a small neighborhood park to discuss the matter. Over a picnic of tea sandwiches and fruit, they wondered if any judge in Baltimore would allow Anna access to his courtroom, and for such a controversial reason. After a few minutes, Anna said, "It's no use. We'll never get permission. There's got to be another way."

"What do movie companies do when they want to shoot somewhere that might not be easy to access?"

"They build sets in movie studios. I've read about that in *Motion Picture Story Magazine*. Yes, they build sets. They fake the scene." Anna looked like a light bulb had exploded in her head. "Oh, what a great idea. Emmaline, you're a peach!"

"But we have no studio. How can we stage it?"

"We'll find a location that we can fix up to look like a jury box. Do you know of any such place?"

The two women ate slowly, savoring every conceivable idea.

"Would a chancel do?"

"A what?"

"A church choir area, where singers sit on benches during preaching. Usually, there's a railing in front of the seating. There's a church down the street from my apartment that closed. The congregation outgrew the location and they built a bigger house of worship a few blocks away. I think the old church is vacant. It might be worth a try. A church isn't that different looking than a courtroom."

Anna started packing up the picnic basket.

"What are you doing? We haven't had dessert yet," Emmaline protested.

"Let's go look at it right now."

The two women entered the church and found it empty. They looked for a choir loft near the organ. There was none. Anna vented her disappointment, while Emmaline walked around the church. "What about this?" she said.

When Anna found her friend, she was sitting in the elders' box to the right of the pulpit. "Emmaline, you're a genius. If I shoot this close enough, showing the railing that surrounds the chairs, it could work. The background is plain. No one would ever know it was shot in a church. And I could pose all the women looking toward a phantom witness stand that would be assumed. It wouldn't have to show in the frame. Just like in the movies."

"Do you think we can get permission?"

"Do you know the pastor?"

"I know some of the congregants."

"Then I'll leave it up to you. I'll even pay you part of my salary. Is it a deal?"

"We might have to pay a fee for use of the space."

"We'll do that, too. And I'll borrow lights from the portrait studio I sometimes work for, to make it look just right." Anna wasn't looking to become rich from this job. The creativity was satisfying enough. It opened her mind to more possibilities in the future.

Within a week, Anna presented Edith Houghton Hooker with photos for both projects. "This is great work, Anna. I knew you could do it."

"What's next?"

"Really? You want more of the same."

"I do, it's rewarding."

"Then I'll send you to a woman named Augusta Chissell. Do you know her?"

"No, I don't believe so."

"She helped start a new group called the Progressive Women's Suffrage Club, this one in a mostly colored neighborhood called Druid Hill."

"I'm familiar with that area."

ぶゃ⑤

Augusta T. Chissell projected bright eyes and a winning smile. A colored woman of prominence in her community, she worked toward the larger goal of getting all women the right to vote. In addition, she pushed for Prohibition, and comprehensive medical care and education for females. She worked closely with other local leaders in the suffrage movement, an anomaly in many cities, where suffrage campaigns were segregated. Without any particular headquarters for their organization, they held meetings in the homes of one another near Druid Hill Park. Churches, such as Grace Presbyterian, also provided places for women to gather unencumbered.

"What can I do for you, Miss Chissell?" Anna said.

"That's missus."

"Oh, excuse me."

"I'm a newlywed."

"Congratulations."

"You come highly recommended as a photographer. I'd like you to take some pictures for me. Right now, I'm focused on Prohibition. Women in our group often stand outside bars, trying to dissuade patrons from imbibing in alcohol. They are nonviolent women, merely singing hymns and quoting the Bible. I can give you a list of where they will be next week. Can you photograph them?"

"I'd be happy to."

"Young lady, every time we speak out in public, there is a threat of violence or arrest. I want you to be fully aware of that."

"Yes, ma'am. I'm not afraid. What will you use the photographs for?"

"They will line the walls of our meetings places to encourage women to persevere no matter what."

"I'll do my best for you."

Anna had no particular opinion about alcohol consumption. She chose not to drink because she didn't want the fuzziness that often followed. She got in enough trouble clearheaded. But it made her think about what she would do if offered work involving a cause or political candidate or business that she opposed. Would she still take the job? She asked Emmaline for advice over lunch in the park. When Anna opened the picnic basket, Emmaline reached for a square of spice cake and bit into it.

"What are you doing?"

"I remember what happened last time. That's why I'm eating dessert first."

"Emmaline, you're a gas."

"I beg your pardon."

Anna laughed. "It's a new way of saying 'you're funny.' I pick up a lot of street language when I'm working."

"Oh. Well, why don't you eat dessert first and you can be a gas, too."

The two women could barely eat. A fit of giggles overtook them. Every time they quieted, they'd take one look at each other and start laughing again.

Anna finally got serious. "I do have a question for you."

"I knew that was coming. Where are we off to now?"

"No, nothing like that. Would you ever work for an organization you didn't admire?"

"What brought that up?"

"I was just wondering if it would be morally wrong?"

"It would depend on how desperate you were for money. Many a man has had to take work they hated just to put food on the table. Maybe the best thing to do is always have a nest egg, so you never have to face that dilemma. Right now, I'm faced with a dilemma of my own."

"What's that?"

"This cake is sinfully good. Do I dare take another piece? Would it be morally wrong?"

"You're a gas."

Nearby, people taking strolls in the park must have wondered what was so funny.

A few days later, just as bars opened, Anna photographed several women standing outside a saloon in pouring rain. They never dissuaded a single man from entering the bar. They never stopped singing. Anna was glad she had taken the assignment.

ॐॐ

Through the boardinghouse grapevine, Anna got word that Josefina had returned to work at Ford's Theater. She couldn't wait to see her friend to offer encouragement and Fussell-Young ice cream. "How did this come about?"

"Well, I can't stay in this apartment all day. It's a small place, filled with memories of lost babies." Josefina pulled a handkerchief from her sleeve and dotted her eyes. "My mother had to go back home. She couldn't stay with us forever. She had my father to take care of and their home. My days became lonely while Adrian was at work. We talked things over and decided it might be good for me to return to the theater, just as a seamstress, not a tirewoman. I go there a few days a week to sew and mend costumes. I don't stay for the performances, so that I can be home and have supper ready when Adrian walks in the door. I've stopped making layette items for the Women's Exchange. I just couldn't do it anymore."

"Don't cry. I understand. This is what you need, I'm sure. Here, let me fix us each a bowl of ice cream. It's chocolate, your favorite."

As the women moved into the kitchen, Josefina said, "We're thinking of moving to a new place. This one holds too much sadness."

"I'm sure that will help lift your spirits. I'll keep my eyes focused on 'For Rent' signs."

They ate in silence for a few minutes. Anna wanted to give her friend all the time she needed to recover. Then, Josefina changed the subject. "I'm worried, though. You know, Ford's doesn't just put on plays. They run movies, too. There's a new film coming to the theater that could cause trouble. Real trouble."

"I can't imagine that. What could it be?"

"It's called *Birth of a Nation* and it's about..."

"I know what it's about. The Ku Klux Klan. There was talk at the newspaper about it. When is this film premiering? I want to be there to take pictures and write a story."

"Monday, March 6. Tickets are already sold out. Do you have Press credentials you can show?"

"Yes, of course."

Anna contacted the *Afro-American* and was given carte blanche to shoot and write the story. On premiere night, she sat in the Press box and noticed the audience consisted mostly of white men.

Despite public outcry from the newspaper, along with several civic leaders and some members of the public, the film broke all box office records over its seven-week run. The NAACP tried its best to keep the movie out of theaters around the country, but to no avail.

Audiences were split in their response. During the viewing Anna attended, some shouted racial epitaphs, while others pounded their fists on arm rests, denouncing what they were seeing. The usual theater decorum was dispensed with. Arguments spilled onto Fayette Street. Fear of violence permeated the city.

Anna's article and other reports expressed outrage. Weeks after its run, the movie continued to be the topic of conversation from the parlors of the elite to street corner cafés to colored churches.

Anna tried to discuss the movie with Emmaline, who refused to see it. She didn't even want to hear what Anna had to say, stating that such incendiary portrayals of hate and violence on celluloid must be destroyed. Moviegoers on both sides of the issue would only become more adamant in their views. There would be no meaningful discourse; there would be no reckoning.

తూత

In May, Anna was hired by the *Maryland Suffrage News* to photograph and report on the "Margaret Brent Pilgrimage," a single caravan of suffragists traveling from Baltimore to St. Mary's City, where the first-known suffragist in the United States had lived. Anna had learned about her when she first met Emma Maddox Funck back in 1904. An attorney, Margaret Brent had gone before the Maryland General Assembly in 1647 to request the right to vote, same as a man. She was denied. In her memory, these modern-day suffragists carried her mantle.

Anna accepted Mrs. Funck's offer to ride in the caravan, rather than follow in her car. With just four other women and one man riding in a horse-drawn covered wagon, it started at the Just Government League headquarters in Baltimore and headed south, making stops in various towns, such as Glen Burnie and Severna Park. The words *Just Government League* and *Votes for Women* blazoned the canvas covering, leaving no doubt who was sponsoring this tour and why.

Anna was told that the whole purpose of the pilgrimage was to make the front page of every newspaper in the state and beyond. And that's just what happened. At each small town and city, the caravan story garnered front page columns. The women spoke before mostly small crowds, resulting in some people joining the league.

Five days into their journey, unexpected stormy weather threatened the success of the pilgrimage. It brought pounding rain and unseasonably chilly temperatures. Wagon wheels became mired in mud, canvas tore in places, belongings got soaked. The group persevered, fighting for warmth, hoping for people to hear their message, regardless of their wet, bedraggled appearance. Sometimes, there was no one to greet them.

There were bright spots along the way and clear skies once they reached St. Mary's City, where a large crowd of women and men awaited. For the first time in their journey, they slept indoors at the behest of a local judge, who insisted they rest in his courtroom. Anna wondered if he would support women jurors but didn't want to wear out her welcome by asking.

In total, they covered 350 miles, stopping in close to 40 towns, some not even dotted on the Maryland map. Though the numbers weren't high, they agreed that 343 new members and a stack of newspaper stories were enough proof to declare success.

Anna was dismayed to discover that most newspapers identified the two married pilgrims as "Mrs. Frank Ramey" and "Mrs. Frank Snell" rather than by their given first names, even in the *Maryland Suffrage News*.

࿎

Anna and Adelaide forged a deeper friendship over hot dogs and lemonade at the ballpark. Between eating and cheering home runs, they talked through Adelaide's idea to start a temporary job placement service for women.

"Have you made any headway?" Anna asked.

"Not really. I'm afraid I don't know where to start."

"Neither did I when I became a photographer. Sometimes, you just have to throw yourself in the water and see if you can, at least, tread. You might surprise yourself to discover you can actually swim."

"I'm not as brave as you, or enterprising."

"What are you waiting for? I'm going to set up a meeting with my friend who works in accounting. I'm sure she can advise you on bookkeeping and acquiring funds to start your business."

"Sure, I'll do it, if you'll be there."

Anna arranged for Emmaline to join them at their favorite café on North Avenue in Emmaline's neighborhood. Adelaide's visceral reaction to seeing Anna's friend did not start the meeting on a positive note. The muscles in her face and neck tightened.

The rest of her body followed. Anna didn't notice because she was standing next to Adelaide, who sat down hesitantly and scooted her chair closer to Anna.

Anna had already informed Emmaline about Adelaide's idea. The three sat waiting for someone to talk. It was a waitress who broke the ice and took their orders. Adelaide declined even tea.

"Well, Adelaide, why don't you offer your questions to Emmaline? That's why we're here."

"Uhm, well, I'm not really sure I'm going to pursue this idea."

"Oh, don't turn shy now. Go ahead."

"Well, how do you keep a ledger? I mean, how do you break down the income versus the outlay? How much money do you put into a business before you can expect to show a profit? This is all new to me."

"First of all," said Emmaline. "I've never started a business. I suggest you find a mentor, someone who has already enjoyed success. Perhaps a clothing store owner, or a milliner. Anna, what was the name of that company you're always talking about, the one you photographed after the fire?"

"Armstrong, Cator & Company."

"Yes, they started small, I'm sure. Perhaps, you could speak to the owners or even get a job in their accounting department to learn all the requirements of good business practices."

"That's a wonderful idea," Anna said. "If not there, then maybe Hochschild's or O'Neill's. You could start in their office and work your way up to manager. Then you could branch out on your own."

"Well, I don't know."

"Adelaide, do you have any money saved, money you could live off of if things don't work out right away?" Anna asked.

"A little."

"Then give it a try. What do you think, Emmaline? Didn't you take a risk in the beginning? I did. And it paid off for both of us. The unknown can be invigorating, can't it?"

"Anna, I can't tell your friend what to do. I can only tell her my own experience. I doubt she wants to hear advice on how to live her life from the likes of me." Emmaline averted her eyes. So did Adelaide.

"What are you talking about? Is something amiss?"

Refreshments arrived before the conversation took an ugly turn. Adelaide, who hadn't ordered anything, offered thanks and took her leave, stating she had a great deal of thinking to do.

"Well, that was a hasty retreat," Anna said. "Did we scare her off?"

"I'm afraid I did," said Emmaline.

"What? How?"

"Once again, you are sweetly oblivious. Did you not see how Adelaide reacted when she saw who I was?"

"You mean, colored?"

"Yes!"

"No, I didn't. I never thought there would be a problem."

"Of course not."

"What does that mean?"

"You should have told her in advance who I was. It would have saved her from being stunned and me from being embarrassed. I don't think she wants my help. That's why I suggested other companies."

"I'm sorry, I guess I've become inured to our differences." Anna buttered her bread then put it back on the plate. "But Emmaline..."

"There's nothing else to be said."

When Anna returned home, she found a note from Adelaide under her door. It simply stated that, for now, she had abandoned the idea of starting a business. Anna knew the reason stemmed from more than her meeting with Emmaline. Adelaide had probably realized that she would mostly likely have colored women come to her, as clients, seeking jobs.

Anna didn't confront Adelaide. She knew some people were incapable of changing. She never invited her to a baseball game again.

ॐ

The spring calm shattered on May 7, when the British ocean liner, Lusitania, was sunk by a German U-boat. Built in 1906, the passenger ship's claim to fame had been its speed, winning an award for crossing the Atlantic at nearly twenty-four knots.

The ship was heading from New York to Liverpool when Captain William Thomas Turner got word that German U-boats were dangerously close. He was instructed to steer the ship in a random crisscross pattern to make it harder for a torpedo to strike its target. Captain Turner did not heed the warnings.

In the afternoon, one explosion rocked the ship, followed by another, perhaps due to the payload of rifle ammunition in the hold. It took a mere twenty minutes for the Lusitania to go under, taking with it the lives of nearly 1,200 people, over 125 of them Americans.

Word reached the streets of Baltimore that this attack would become the impetus to force the United States into war. Citizens waited to hear from President Woodrow Wilson. A few days later, he sent a letter of reprimand to Germany, softened by the writing of Secretary of State, Williams Jennings Bryan, who wanted no part of war. For now, the United States would refrain from military conflict.

Just the same, the sinking became the topic of heated discourse throughout the country, across dinner tables, amidst cigar smoke in dens, and over embroidery hoops in parlors. Anna feared for all the young men who could be drawn to foreign lands to fight. What might happen to Adrian and David? She worried for Papa, who would feel the consequences of war at the hospital and in his bank account.

"There is nothing we can do at this point, Anna," Elizabeth said, over the phone. "What will happen, will happen. We can only pray that we come through it all intact. I would love it if you joined me at Mass once in a while."

"You know me. I'm so fast on my feet, the devil would have a hard time catching up with me. That doesn't mean I don't pray or, at least, wish people well."

"Don't forget your rosary. You can always pray that in your room."

"I know."

Anna hadn't brought out her beads in a long time. They remained in a decorative box in Anna's bedside drawer. She was a person of action who held a strong belief in herself, not in an unseen power that gave breath to babies who would grow to commit war atrocities.

ॐ

The Ku Klux Klan made headlines once again. Whether due to the book, *The Clansman,* by Thomas Dixon, Jr., or D.W. Griffith's movie, *Birth of A Nation*, the organization celebrated a rebirth in its numbers down South, especially in Georgia. It seemed to be spinning its hateful and dangerous web north, with not only anti-black rhetoric but, also, anti-Catholic, anti-Jew and anti-just-about-every-immigrant who came to America's shores searching for a better life through promised freedoms. Anna feared for Emmaline and her family should the Klan infiltrate Maryland. She asked some of her newspaper colleagues what they thought and was told, the less mention in print, the better. One even said, "Let sleeping dogs lie."

Anna wondered. At some point, all dogs, whether gentle or rabid, wake up. They are hungry and search for red meat. Where would they find it? In cities and towns populated with colored and white, Jewish and Irish, Polish and Italian citizens? And, more importantly, when?

ॐ

In spring, baseball fans returned to the stadium like birds from winter migration. Aside from rooting for the Orioles, they watched the Baltimore Black Sox, a Negro League team, that had been in the Minors dating back to 1887, along with another team called the Lord Baltimores. Now they were playing in the Major Leagues. Anna went to one of the games. Coloreds and whites filled the stands, which were still segregated. Since she was no longer friends with Adelaide, Anna had wanted to invite Emmaline to join her but realized they'd have to sit in separate sections and wouldn't even be able to share a box of Cracker Jack.

Anna went alone.

She couldn't focus on the pitches and plays. She wondered if she should be there at all. Did her presence at the stadium cast approval of segregation?

Anna had some questions for Emmaline the next time they met. "Why don't you march with colored women for the right to vote? Why don't you write politicians about the need to desegregate schools and train travel and baseball stadiums and Ford's? Why aren't you fighting for your race's very survival?"

"Is this why you asked me to lunch? To berate me, Anna?"

"No, Emmaline. I'm sorry. I went to the stadium to watch the Negro League teams play last week, and the spectators were divided into colored and white. Many of the whites appreciated good baseball and cheered. Others specifically came to jeer and name-call. I wanted to take the microphone out of the announcer's hand and tell them to stop. And beg spectators to sit where they wanted."

"Anna, you have much to learn."

"Stop telling me that. You are too passive. You must get involved."

"I must live life the way I see fit. Don't you realize you're trying to take away my freedom right now? You want me to live life your way. This is what white people have been imposing on us coloreds for centuries. In the name of friendship, can we please change the subject?"

"I guess we better."

"I know you mean well. You always do. I ask that you think first, really think things through. Was there anything else you wanted to discuss? I've lost my appetite."

There was. Though now Anna was hesitant to bring it up.

She had read in the paper that the Maryland State Normal School was expanding, moving to a bigger campus far north of Baltimore in a town called Towson. It wasn't far from Bare Hills, where Emmaline's family lived. Anna couldn't wait to break the news to her friend. Until now. She broached the subject delicately.

"Oh, yes, I heard about that," Emmaline said.

"I knew I couldn't get one past you. Well, what do you think?"

"About what? This has nothing to do with me."

"The school will be bigger. They'll be able to accept more students. Maybe the tuition will go down as a result."

"So?"

"So, it's a teachers' college. You always wanted to be a teacher. And it will be located close to your home in Bare Hills. Now's the time to make your dream come true. And you know they already accept coloreds."

"I appreciate your eagerness. The fact is, college is still far out of my reach."

"I'm sure they offer scholarships."

"How can I take four years out of my life to pursue a teaching degree when I have my family to support right now? And, at the newspaper, I already make a decent wage, higher than I ever expected. I'm doing fine."

"But you want to be a teacher. You could teach mathematics and make accountants out of hundreds of students over your lifetime."

"I have my father and mother and brothers and sisters to take care of. I cannot abandon them."

"Don't you want to uplift yourself? Don't you want to fight for your rights as a woman and a colored?"

"I find this accusation most offensive. Don't you see? I am uplifting, as you say, in my own way. My mama never got much schooling. She married young and started having babies. But she saw that I got my education. Now I have a fine job, and good pay that I use to help my brothers and sisters."

"I..."

"Don't interrupt. Let me tell you a story. My brother, Toby, is an excellent guitar player. One of our neighbors, an old man, used to sit on his porch and strum in the evenings. Toby, as a little boy, sat on a stool next to him and watched how his fingers moved up and down the strings, bringing forth beautiful music from strands of steel. Old Homer taught Toby how to play and he took to it fast. When the old man died, his widow gave the guitar to Toby. He's no child now. He's over six feet tall. Toby's been performing regularly at the Arch Social Club on Pennsylvania Avenue."

"I've never heard of it."

"It's a men's organization that has entertainment but also looks out for the health and well-being of its members and the community. Toby's building his confidence, waiting until he turns eighteen, when he plans to move to New York, where artists of all kinds are living in a neighborhood called Harlem. Writers, painters, playwrights, musicians are there, expressing their humanity and equality through paint and poetry and song. My brother wants to be a part of it. I'm saving money in a 'Toby piggybank' just for him to reach his dream."

"Em..."

"My sister, Alice, will finish elementary school next year. I aim to see that she goes to the same Colored High and Training School I attended. She will move in with me to be closer, so I can help her with her studies. Alice loves nature and wants to pursue science. Now do you see? My parents lifted me up. I am lifting up my siblings and they will lift up all the people they affect with their work, as well as their own children. And I affect my broader community by ensuring the *Baltimore Afro-American* remains profitable. By living my life, I am advancing the greater good of my people."

"But..."

"I don't want to hear any more. I haven't seen your name bandied about among the great female pioneers of photography. The last you told me, you were shooting merchandise for print advertisements. And I don't see you drawing crowds who will hang onto your every word about woman's suffrage. Are you funding anything for the common good?"

Anna's crestfallen face felt weighty. "You're right. I guess I deserved that. I'm sorry."

"My dear friend, I didn't mean to hurt you."

"We can't be friends if we aren't honest with each other."

"I don't fault you. I can't, for long, Anna. You're only trying to help, as always. We have to realize we each have different lives, with different choices, even though we're equal human beings. And isn't that the point of it all, anyway?"

"I hope we will always choose to be friends."

"Me, too. Ready for some Joe Froggers and Coca-Cola?"

❧❧

Anna thought of David when she heard that Maryland had formed a State Board of Motion Picture Censors. A panel of three appointed reviewers watched every movie that was to play in the state before a single reel was wound in theaters. They determined if the storyline and portrayals were proper for moviegoers to see. Rooting out obscenities and sacrilegious acts, they deemed movies either moral or immoral. If objectionable, the movie was edited to suit the demands of the panel. If it was irredeemable, it was banned from Maryland theaters.

Anna wondered how the panel would have ruled on *Birth of a Nation*. And what would they have thought of Rachel Crothers's play, *Ourselves*, had it been made into a movie?

One of the first pictures they banned in the late months of 1916 was *War Brides*, based on a one-act play written by Marian Craig Wentworth. It was a picture that addressed war and pacifism from a mother's point of view.

As a play, it had been a sensation, selling out audiences, receiving standing ovations. As a picture, it built controversy over who would fight wars if everyone took a pacifist view. The plot revolved around a woman named Joan whose husband and brothers are called to fight. When word reaches home that her husband has been killed, she becomes so distraught she threatens suicide, until she realizes she is pregnant.

Joan uses her body as a form of protest against the government, saying that she will not bear any more children unless the government agrees never to go to war again. When that doesn't happen, she commits suicide.

The Maryland Board of Censors deemed this film immoral and unfit for viewing for two reasons. It might make men refuse to answer the call of duty. And there was fear that the suffrage movement might make pacifism part of their agenda. After all, as one New York newspaper said: "Women gave birth to soldiers. They could always withhold their contribution."

The movie met with accolades around the country. Marylanders had to travel out of state to see it and make up their own minds on where they stood.

With the spat Anna had engaged in with David over the feminist play she wanted to see in New York, she wondered what he might think of censorship of the arts, in general. She used it as an excuse to contact him.

Anna wrote a long letter to David and sent it to the address of his brother, Robert. In it, she questioned the value of censorship. She also expressed concern that, should tension throughout the world escalate, he might be called to war as a soldier or foreign correspondent.

David waited a few weeks before responding. He informed her briefly of his work with the *New York Tribune*, and said it was unlikely that he would turn into a war correspondent because he had become the newspaper's sportswriter. Reading between the lines, Anna surmised that David could no longer handle the blood and guts of tragic news stories.

He took no stand on censorship. Instead, David spoke of his brother's good health and his own. And offered best regards from the family, including his new wife, Melinda, "a fine lady from a good Connecticut family," as he put it.

Well, that was a definitive goodbye, Anna thought. *Another one has slipped through my fingers, once and for all.* Anna was a bit shaken by the news but sent the newlyweds a lovely set of embroidered linen napkins from O'Neill's.

CHAPTER 42

By 1916, Anna had stopped going to Ford's, for the most part, because of their policy of audience segregation. She was soon to find a substitute.

In November, a new theater, staging plays, opened inside the St. James Hotel on West Centre Street. It was called the Vagabond Players. A regional theater, it offered an alternative to the big productions at Ford's and large movie houses everywhere in downtown Baltimore.

Ensemble actors put on one-act plays, with smaller budgets, versatile set designs, and lower admission fees. Being such a tiny space, it was difficult to segregate the audience, who sat so close to the actors, they felt a part of the show.

The Vagabond Players held a spot on the ground floor of what was called the "Little Theater Movement" in the country, opening the theater experience to everyone. Anna loved smelling the greasepaint, reading every nuance on the actors' faces, and seeing beads of sweat glisten on foreheads when stage lights grew too hot or actors lost their lines.

She started shooting production pictures to put outside the theater and became friends with one of the actors, an older man named Richard. Perhaps forty, he could play parts as young as twenty, as old as sixty. He had the diction of an English aristocrat on stage and off. Whether real or feigned, Anna didn't know.

Off-stage, his thoughts flowed freely, his views mostly out of the norm. In Richard, Anna found someone to open up to and share her opinions on controversial subjects of the day. Or perhaps discuss art at The Walters. She didn't have romance on her mind.

Richard invited Anna to attend a concert of classical music. The Baltimore Symphony Orchestra had newly been formed, bringing a sophisticated air to the city. Anna wore a charcoal gray dress with a black herringbone waistcoat. A Tudor beret topped off her outfit, rather than a broad-brimmed hat. She opposed women wearing tall hairdos and mile-high millinery to the theater. How was someone seated behind supposed to see?

The orchestra played a diverse program of marches, waltzes, and a piano concerto, which enthralled Anna. She talked about it nonstop when they first left the theater. So completely engaged, Anna didn't notice where they were walking.

"I'm glad you enjoyed the show, Anna. We are lucky to have such a distinguished conductor leading our new orchestra. He was ma-a-a-avelous."

"Do you know much about him, Richard?"

"Oh, yes. I used to live in Boston. He had a great reputation when he conducted an orchestra there. His name is Gustav Strube. The maestro is a composer, too, said to have studied under the great Johann Strauss II. Strube was a child prodigy, playing in his father's symphony at the tender age of ten."

"How extraordinary."

"Strube also teaches at the Peabody Conservatory. Yes, we are most lucky to have him. By the way, he's a good friend of someone you must know."

"Oh, really?"

"H.L. Mencken."

"I used to work for him."

Richard took Anna's arm as they crossed the street, not breaking his grasp when they reached the other side.

"I guess one could say Mencken orchestrates Baltimore's newspaper world." Richard chuckled at the cleverness of his own analogy. Anna didn't join him.

"I found H.L. Mencken difficult to work with but inspiring at the same time. Is that possible?"

"In any creative endeavor, the two blend perrrr-fectly. Great things come from a little spontaneous combustion." Richard lifted one eyebrow as he said this. When he got no response, he continued, "Quite frankly, I find it hard to believe he hired you. H.L. Mencken strikes me as a 'man's man.' He doesn't have much use for women. Unlike me."

"Well, I really can't say anything bad about him. He took me under his wing and gave me my start in the newspaper business."

"He certainly seems to delight in hoisting a glass and savoring a cigar. He started a group called 'The Saturday Night Club' at the Rennert Hotel on West Saratoga. Did you know that?"

"Yes, that's not far from where I was raised."

"He and his cronies meet there for food and drink and intellectual conversations on just about every subject, as I hear through the grapevine. I've never been privy, myself." Richard released Anna's arm and pulled each of his gloves tighter with a quick jerk. "Gustav Strube is one of the members, however."

"I'm not surprised. Mr. Mencken knows everyone of importance. Oh, I don't mean to say you are not..."

"Perfectly all right. I've yet to receive my peerage in theatrical artistry. I must learn patience, like The Bard's Juliet. It will come. I know it."

"Mr. Mencken has never been much for small talk. He prefers stimulating conversation."

"Yes, as do I... stimulation, that is."

"I doubt, though, that he would ever attend the symphony. He doesn't seem to enjoy life much, outside of work and the bar."

"I know the type. All business. I, on the other hand, enjoy the finer things... music, art, international cuisine, and the company of lovely ladies, such as you, my dear Anna."

"I've never thought of myself as lovely."

"How do you see yourself?"

"I just see me as Anna. It's what other people say..."

"Do you mean they are unkind?"

"Oh, yes. Sometimes, they get under my skin. They often say I'm too indelicate, too forceful, independent and outspoken. I question everything. What's wrong with that?"

"I don't mind at all. There's a phrase for it. It escapes me at the moment. What is it?"

"'The New Woman.' It's attributed to women turning their backs on the traditional roles as demure, helpless, submissive wives and mothers."

"Yes, that's right. Shedding the Victorian norms. That must feel good... under one's skin."

"Oh, it does."

"Pray tell."

"It also gets me in trouble sometimes. I'm criticized for being naïve... for taking too many risks... for not being mature enough to make up my own mind."

"I see." Richard took Anna's hand, patted it softly and kept it in his possession.

"Where did you hear that phrase, 'The New Woman?'" Anna asked.

"Oh, I read a book, a novel about it. It was called *Anna Lombard,* written by an English author named Victoria Cross. I'm sure that's not her real name. How trite. One of the actresses gave it to me after she read it. It's what you'd call a 'laaaady's' book, but she thought I'd enjoy certain parts. It's quite shocking, really. And dare I say, steamy?"

"How so?"

"It tells the tale of a young woman who is betrothed. She covets another man and has an affair with him."

"Does her fiancé discover them?"

"Yes, and you won't believe how he reacts."

"He kills them?"

"No, he approves! Tells his fiancé to get it out of her system, once and for all, so that she will be true to him in marriage. Can you believe such debauchery?" Richard said with a smile. "The book also states that it must take a New Man to accept a New Woman."

"Are you a New Man, Richard?"

"Yes. Are you a New Woman, dear Anna?"

"I like to think I am."

Richard stopped walking. Anna looked around, not recognizing the street. "Where are we?"

"This is my apartment building. Would you like to continue this conversation upstairs? I have some fine French cognac."

"Ah, oh, uhm. Well, I don't imbibe, except when I'm eating a Joe Frogger. That's a cookie with rum. And I, uh, have an early assignment with the newspaper. Thank you for a lovely evening. I must go now."

"Perhaps we will clink our glasses together some other time."

"Perhaps."

"Ma-a-a-avelous. I look forward to it."

Richard kissed Anna's hand while staring her in the eyes. Then, he hailed a handsome cab as though he were delivering a soliloquy. He paid the driver to take Anna to her boardinghouse. Once home, under her own covers, alone, she wondered if she really was ready to become a "New Woman."

CHAPTER 43

In February of 1917, Anna received word that Josefina was with child yet again. Anna immediately visited her friend and found her abed, with her mother sitting on the edge. Adrian let Anna in and told her that his wife was only a few months along. A dangerous time in a pregnancy for someone like Josefina.

"She's so nervous that I fear for her and the baby. She's worrying herself to death."

"What does the doctor say?"

"She must remain calm, stay in bed most of the time, with short, easy walks. And she must eat. That's another problem. She barely takes a mouthful and loses most of it. The doctor wants her to take laudanum to help ease her nerves and sleep a little. But I know what it does to the body. If you remember, when I injured my leg during the Great Fire, I consumed quite a bit of it."

"Yes, I do remember. Your injury, on my account, still haunts me."

"I'm sorry I had to bring that up."

"Can she take just a little? It might do her good. If the doctor says so, it must. Just slip a drop or two in her tea."

"I'll have to think about it. For now, maybe you can take her mind off things. Tell her something fun, amusing. You're always full of stories about your adventures."

Anna replaced Josefina's mother bedside and held her friend's hand. She saw, right away, there was no consoling her friend. She tried anyway.

"You must calm yourself. Can you try, for me?"

"I can't help it. I am consumed with this child. It must live."

"Then you have to do whatever is necessary to ensure that happens. Have you eaten today?"

"Just a piece of bread with butter," Josefina's mother said.

"Have you taken a walk?"

"No," Josefina said.

"Not even around the apartment?"

"No."

Anna pulled the covers back and said, "Up. Get up. Where are your slippers?"

Josefina's mother looked aghast but helped her daughter into her robe, while Anna added the slippers.

"You are no invalid. You are a woman with child. If you want an energetic, happy baby, you must show some vigor and positive thinking yourself. You are to do this once every morning, and again in the afternoon and right after supper. Do you understand? You have Sergeant Anna Bainbridge in command."

When Adrian walked into the room, his eyes widened at the sight of his wife walking without assistance, gazing out the window, heading for the hallway and into the living room.

"What have we here? Look at you. There is a rose blooming on your cheeks," Adrian said.

Josefina smiled, the first in a long time. "Anna's quite the taskmaster," she said.

"Adrian, what were you planning for lunch?" Anna asked.

"I have some chicken broth and crackers. She seems to keep that down."

"Why don't you heat up the soup now? When it's ready, we will stop walking but not until."

Behind Josefina's back, Anna mimed a dropper being plunged, a signal for Adrian to add a little laudanum. He complied.

After lunch, Josefina fell into a peaceful sleep for three hours. When she awoke, Anna was still there.

"How do you feel?"

Josefina sat up. "I feel relaxed. That was a good rest."

"See, I told you walking would help. Want to try it again?"

Anna got Adrian and Josefina's mother into a daily routine of walking, napping and eating. And laudanum. Soon, Josefina stepped outside in the cold winter air and took longer walks around the block. Once her morning sickness subsided, she ate heartier meals, gained a little weight and graced her household with a perpetual smile. Anna visited whenever she could, often bringing food and flowers. One day, she brought a simple bouquet of snow drops, which touched Adrian.

While Anna devoted most of her time to Josefina's welfare and securing assignments to support herself, she became remiss in keeping up with news of the world. Foreign countries were engaged in what was called the Great War, distant places Anna felt could not affect her in any way. The United States had stayed out of it, so far. That was about to change.

After declaring neutrality, even after the sinking of the Lusitania, President Wilson asked Congress for a declaration of war against Germany. In the early months of 1917, Germany had forged an alliance with Mexico, promising that country they would be returned land once ceded to the United States. In addition, Germany violated an agreement with the U.S. government that they would not sink any more passenger ships. Something had to be done. Congress stood behind the President's request to engage in war. In May, all diplomatic ties with Germany were severed. It looked as though America was about to increase the magnitude of the war and draw young, hearty men, like David and Adrian, into combat. Anna counted on her fingers and figured that Adrian was now thirty-seven, perhaps too old. If the U.S. lost enough young men, however, older men would be called upon to serve their country.

A full declaration of war wouldn't happen until the end of the year. That didn't stop preparations from taking place. Nor did it stop fear from growing.

In May, the Selective Service Act was passed, giving the U.S. government the power to pull civilian men into armed service by conscription. They needed to grow Army ranks, which numbered around 120,000 men, relatively small for such a powerful country. President Wilson had not had much success in getting men to volunteer for service.

An unlikely boost came in the form of a newspaperman, George Creel, of Missouri. Usually, journalists stayed neutral, not even revealing political party affiliations to their colleagues. It helped with the checks and balances on presenting fair reporting. Creel, however, took a stand and a position in Woodrow Wilson's camp. He was named head of the United

States Committee on Public Information. It was incumbent upon him to stir interest in voluntary service in the U.S. Army. He sent out 75,000 speakers to cities and towns. They gave terse speeches urging men to step up. They did not. After three quarters of a million speeches spread across America, the campaign was deemed a lukewarm success.

One of those speakers came to Baltimore. The *Baltimore American* assigned Anna to report and photograph the event. Fliers were handed out on the streets of downtown, inviting all to hear an important speech by a representative of President Woodrow Wilson.

Anna went to a movie house on North Howard Street called "The Auditorium," one of several theaters in Baltimore that allowed speakers to give brief presentations before movies started. Most nights, every seat was taken. The speakers were called "4-Minute Men," because they had to limit their remarks, knowing patrons were eager to see the film. They also sold Liberty Loans in the lobby, telling every man and woman that they could do their part by purchasing these war bonds.

Anna took a picture of a Federal flatbed truck parked outside. In the back stood a six-foot poster of Lady Liberty holding a shield in her left hand while reaching for a sword with her right. Tall letters proclaimed **U.S. BONDS**. Committee men handed out information booklets and sold bonds to passersby.

Anna interviewed one of these government men.

"Are you having much success?"

"Well, folks seem more eager to open their purses and buy Liberty Loans than to sign up to fight."

"Why do you think that's so?"

"In town after town, we're being told that people don't want to get involved in war. We've been neutral so far. Why not continue? And they know the casualty rate is high. They read it every day in the newspapers."

"How is it that George Creel, a journalist, can run a political organization?"

"You'd have to ask him, ma'am. I just give out booklets and sell bonds."

"Are you concerned that you're recruiting men who might die?

"They might die if conscripted, just the same. Or they might die if we're attacked and do nothing to defend ourselves."

All over America, this scene was being repeated, speakers and Liberty Loan trucks, crisscrossing the country. By the time the campaign ran out of steam, it was clear Americans were reluctant to back the President of the United States when it came to war.

Anna wondered where it would all lead.

The Selective Service Act of 1917 was put into power, allowing the government to demand all men between the ages of 21 and 45 register for conscription. Anna knew this included Adrian, David and probably Richard, too. She couldn't bear the thought. How would this affect Josefina and her baby?

"She doesn't know," whispered Adrian, after letting Anna in the door and hearing her concern. "Her mother and I are keeping newspapers away from her. She seems to accept it without reservation."

"Good idea. I brought some pastries. I thought maybe she would enjoy a treat."

"That's thoughtful of you. She's sleeping now. Would you like to sit and take some tea?"

Anna joined Adrian in the kitchen as he heated water in the kettle. She helped set out the tea service and made small talk. For a moment, it felt as though they were a married couple, preparing a meal. Anna pushed the thought out of her mind.

"Adrian, how do you feel about possibly being forced to fight on foreign shores?"

"I am beside myself with anxiety, not for me, for my wife. How will Josefina get through her time? And what would she do if something happened to me? Her mother can help only so much. She has Josefina's father to take care of and her own home."

"I'm here, Adrian. I won't let either of you down. If you must go, I will help Josefina's mother any way I can. I offer you my time, money and friendship."

Adrian's chin started to quiver. He could barely speak the words, "Thank you, Anna."

When he recovered, his brow drew up in thick creases.

"What's the matter?"

"I worry for you. You might be called upon by a newspaper to become a war correspondent. Knowing you, I feel almost certain you would accept. Have you thought about that?"

"No, I really haven't. You've given me something to ponder, though. My father is still not fully recovered from his heart attack. And you and Josefina need me. I don't know what I would do, if asked."

"Is that all that's holding you back? Do you not fear the horrors you might experience? And what if you were to be taken prisoner, or worse? I can't tell you what to do, I can only ask you to think it through."

"I've seen the ravages of fire, dead bodies on the pavement. I've seen arms and legs floating in the Patapsco River. There can be nothing worse. I promise you I will give the subject reverent thought."

By the time Josefina awoke, Anna had gone. Her pastries and a warm cup of tea strengthened Josefina, who would need every bit of it.

As Anna walked home, she noticed how beautiful and peaceful the day appeared, despite rumblings of war. The air smelled clean of discord. Down the block, she saw a man with a janitor's broom, smoothing a poster into place on the side of a building. When she stopped to look, she recognized the picture of a bearded man dressed in red, white and blue stars and stripes, seemingly pointing directly at Anna. The poster read:

I WANT YOU FOR THE U.S. ARMY
Nearest Recruiting Station

She had seen this image before. It was an Army recruitment poster depicting Uncle Sam, the fictional father of the U.S. government. Chills rippled down Anna's spine. Even the midday sun couldn't warm her.

❧◦❧

In a continuing effort to support the government's ability to face war and support the economy, the Compulsory Work Law was enacted. It mandated that all able-bodied men between the ages of 18 and 50 be employed or face a fine. If unemployed, these men had to register with the newly-formed Compulsory Work Bureau, which would place them in jobs related to farming, canning or road construction, all important industries to the government.

Five-hundred-dollar fines or six-months' imprisonment awaited anyone who didn't comply. Some men preferred jail time. It would ensure food and shelter and no consignment to war.

Anna thought about Emmaline's father, who was still unable to work due to his heart disease. Would he be fined, anyway?

Anna's relationship with Emmaline had become tenuous since their spat over Emmaline's refusal to march for equality. In June, they attended a meeting of the NAACP and, what came of it, proved the perfect compromise.

The organization presented a plan to hold a Silent Protest Parade straight down New York City's famed Fifth Avenue.

The previous year, northeastern cities saw a rise in the colored population. Families and individuals of every age had been moving north to escape the Jim Crow laws down South. Most had come seeking higher education and good-paying work. What they discovered were jobs unavailable to them because they required a union card, something denied colored men and women. Some took jobs as strikebreakers so they could feed their families. Many northern residents didn't welcome this inter-ference. Racial tensions simmered like a summer mirage and reached a boiling point in St. Louis when whites attacked coloreds, killing dozens and burning down homes of thousands. Soon, beatings, riots, even lynchings cut a swatch through the United States, occurring across Texas, Tennessee and Illinois.

NAACP organizers urged members all over the country to participate in the silent protest. At the meeting, Anna looked at

Emmaline and whispered, "We'll go together on the train, sitting next to each other. I dare anyone to bother us. What do you say?"

Emmaline nodded with some reservation. But she nodded.

"I'll ask the *Afro-American* if I can photograph the event for them. I'm sure they will agree. And I'll wear a dress, I promise. I will do nothing to embarrass you, Emmaline."

Anna and Emmaline took the train from Penn Station in Baltimore to Penn Station in New York. They sat together and suffered no indignities, mainly because much of the train was filled with colored marchers.

The women didn't plan to stay the night. However, Anna kept David's brother's phone number handy, just in case. She wondered if he still lived at the Dakota and if he would welcome Anna and her friend.

The parade took place on Saturday, July 28th, with 10,000 strong, marching only to the beat of a drum. Women and children were dressed in white, a symbol of purity and harmony. Many walked arm-in-arm or hand-in-hand or hoisted signs pronouncing their goal.

Anna was asked by organizers not to march. Even though she was a member of the NAACP, the organization wanted their message to come solely from their own community. At first, Anna thought this was the same kind of prejudice marchers were fighting against. Then, she realized the importance of the moment and how strong a presence an all-colored parade would muster.

"I don't think I can march alone," Emmaline said. "I've never been to New York. It's so big. The buildings are so tall. How will I find you?"

"Don't worry. I will walk with you, on the sidewalk, every step of the way. The parade is going to turn at 57th street and finish at Madison Square Garden. Wait for me on the 7th Avenue side. I will find you. I promise."

Emmaline walked the length of the parade behind a man holding a sign that read:

**RACE PREJUDICE IS THE OFFSPRING
OF IGNORANCE AND THE MOTHER OF LYNCHINGS**

Anna ran a block ahead to position herself to take a picture. Many other signs proclaimed similar messages.

Spectators lined the sidewalks, while colored Boy Scouts disseminated fliers promoting equality of the races. Some bystanders took them, others refused.

There were no reports of retaliation at the march. That couldn't be said for the train ride home.

Anna and Emmaline were able to return to Baltimore the same day. They sat side by side and enjoyed an invigorating talk about the day's events. When the conductor came into the car to take tickets, he kept his eye on the twosome, who were sitting about halfway back. When he got to their row, he said, "You two ladies realize what you're doing? Breaking the law."

"We know it and we think that law is nothing but legal prejudice," Anna said.

"I can have you thrown off this train. And arrested."

"Then do it, if you must."

Emmaline leaned into Anna, saying, "Please, don't stir up anything."

"You think because you marched down Fifth Avenue you can do what you want on my train?"

"It's not your train. And we are paying passengers, same as everyone else."

Nearby riders heard what was going on. A couple of men stood and walked toward the conductor. One of them asked what the problem was. The conductor backed down, saying he had work to do. He moved on to collecting tickets.

"Anna, we must be careful," Emmaline said. "We're far from home."

"But we're not alone," Anna said, nodding to the two men who had stepped in. "Thank you, gentleman," Anna said with a smile.

They returned to their seats. One was white; the other, colored.

Anna and Emmaline made it home safely. Both knew that, without the intervention of those two men, and with their own refusal to separate, they very well might have been taken off the train, arrested and fined.

When they arrived in Baltimore, Emmaline said, "I admire your spirit and moral outrage. I couldn't ask for a better friend on this earth. But, please, don't invite me to do this again. In any colored person's life, there is always an undercurrent of fear that one day someone will insult or push or beat or kill. I feel it every single day. As much as I want to fight prejudice and injustice, I have a family to support. Please don't ask me to jeopardize that again."

"Do you have any idea how important today was? At that march, in your silence, your people spoke as loud as a megaphone could amplify words about equality, humanity and dignity. And then, on the train, we stood up to that conductor. And so did those men. With every step, whether 10,000 or two, we move closer to the day when we can do what we please, in the company of whomever we please, without repercussion."

"That day will not come in our lifetime. Maybe not ever."

"All the more reason to try."

"I am tired. It's been a day filled with emotion. When I walked with that group, for the first time in my life, I felt a part of something truly strong and powerful. I didn't feel alone. Then, on the train..."

"You're not alone. You have me."

"You don't understand. Every colored person feels alone, except when we're in church."

"Are you sorry you went to New York?"

"No. And seeing you walking on the sidewalk right next to me meant more than I could ever explain because I haven't fully appreciated it yet. No one has ever been so dedicated in friendship."

"Thank you. You've taken me into your family, shown me your world. I've learned so much from you. You've made me a better person and journalist."

"We're both tired. Let's get a good night's rest."

In a third floor walkup and a boardinghouse basement, two women climbed into their beds and sighed.

CHAPTER 44

Josefina went into labor a few weeks early. When Anna found out, she packed her satchel, canceled a photography job for the first time in her career, and raced to Josefina's side.

"Adrian, how is she?"

"She's fretting so. The doctor is with her now. He said her blood pressure is dangerously high. I know that's not good."

"How long has she been like this?"

"Since early this morning. She nudged me awake around 2:00 A.M. What is it now? Ten? Oh, it's been eight hours. Why doesn't the baby come? Maybe we should try to get her to a hospital."

"Sit down. These things take time. Can I get you anything?"

"Maybe just a glass of water."

Anna found Josefina's mother in the kitchen, bent over the sink, crying.

"This can't be happening again," she said. "I've prayed and prayed. There are no more words I can use to beg God to intercede."

Anna quietly started rubbing the woman's back. After a few minutes, she guided her to a chair and returned to Adrian in the living room. He wasn't there.

Anna heard the whimper of a cat outside. It wouldn't stop. She looked out the window, searching for it, wanting to throw Adrian's glass of water on its head to chase it away.

"What's that I hear?" Josefina's mother said, as she entered the room.

"Just a stray cat looking for food, I'm sure."

"No, it's coming from the bedroom. Could it be?"

Twenty minutes later, Adrian entered the living room carrying a tiny bundle. His smile reached his temples as tears streaked his face.

"I'd like you to meet Margaret Victoria Crosby." He handed the baby to her grandmother.

"Is she well?" Anna asked.

"The doctor said she's fine. You can tell she has healthy lungs."

"How is Josefina?"

"She's exhausted. The doctor is finishing up with her now. She'll probably sleep the rest of the day."

"I'm so happy for you both."

"Would you like to hold her?"

"What did you say her name was?"

"Margaret Victoria, named for Josefina's mother."

"I can't believe I never knew your name," Anna said, looking at the woman. "My own mother's name was Victoria."

"Most people call me Maggie. Now, it will be Grandma."

Anna took the baby and settled on the settee. She stared into her tiny eyes and saw Adrian. She wondered what life would be like if this were their baby. She pushed the thought away like an annoying stray cat on the stoop and handed the child to her grandmother, whose arms shook so badly, she had to sit down.

Anna slipped out and returned home. Life had certainly taken many cross streets since the Great Fire of 1904. Anna was now nearly thirty-two. What did she have to show for her years? A stack of pictures? She wondered where she really fit in. She didn't have much of a family, only a few friends. Where was true connection? Where was love?

☙◆❧

Around the time of Anna's birthday, the U.S. Army General Hospital established at Fort McHenry. So many soldiers were returning from Europe with serious wounds, missing limbs, and shell shock. The men were spread out all over the U.S. Maryland, being on the east coast, received the most serious cases. The facility soon became the largest military hospital in the country.

Anti-German sentiment spread like disease on the streets of Baltimore, particularly in South and East Baltimore, where many German immigrants had settled since the 1700s. Baltimoreans turned on each other. German-Americans were subjected to horrible name-calling and defacement of their homes and businesses, even by neighbors with whom they had, at one time, played cards, exchanged recipes, worshiped in church.

The German immigrants had been known for their hard work, building successful companies that bolstered the communities in which they lived. There was Eichenkranz Restaurant in East Baltimore, not far from Patterson Park. They served the best Schwinkoteletten Mit Apfeln, pork chops with apples. And, then, there was Berger Cookies, iced thick with rich, chocolate fudge. And Schmidt Bakery. The scent of their bread baking intoxicated Southeast Baltimore with a feeling of home. Now, they were the enemy to some. Most people hadn't known that Babe Ruth's heritage was German. Now a few former fans yelled pejoratives at him when he took the field. Even H.L. Mencken, also of German descent, was forced to respond to disparaging "Letters to the Editor" at *The Sun*. People destroyed copies of *Der Deutsche Correspondent* and *The Baltimore Wecker* at Baltimore newsstands before they could be sold.

German Jews were also targeted, especially in Eutaw Place, where many had moved, started businesses and built up their neighborhoods.

The German immigrant population in Baltimore was considerable, twenty percent of the total count, approximately 94,000 people.

"Aren't we all immigrants?" Anna asked Elizabeth over dinner. "Where did your parents come from?"

"Mine were Lithuanian. That's why I worship at St. Alphonsus. Most of its congregants are like me. And, yes, we are all immigrants, except for the Indians, some say. This war is making animals out of people who were once friendly neighbors."

"Why? What's causing it?"

"Fear, I suppose. People are afraid that their freedoms are about to be taken away. And since they can't direct their ire at the politicians causing all this trouble so far away, they turn on their neighbors."

"I wouldn't want to be a German in Baltimore right now."

"Vitriol is everywhere, Anna. Germans today, French tomorrow, English the next. Who knows?"

"We can't despair. We have to stand up for these immigrants, who came here to escape tyranny. They're not to blame."

"All we can do is frequent their businesses and be kind to one another. And pray."

"No, there is plenty more to be done. As a journalist, I can tell their stories."

"Be prepared for backlash. You must be careful."

Anna figured she could highlight German businesses the same way she featured companies rising from the ashes of the Great Fire. No local newspaper bought the idea. They felt any article aimed at bolstering Germans would enflame tempers rather than ease them. And would lose revenue for the publications.

Over the ensuing weeks, German names were quietly erased from the Baltimore landscape. German Street, near where the Great Fire began, was renamed Redwood. The German American Bank became just the American Bank.

Tensions continued to mount like a stack of insults, the top one compounding the one below it. How high would this monument to hate rise before toppling down on innocent people who had no hand in tyranny?

On December 7, 1917, the United States declared war, not on Germany, but on its ally, Austria-Hungary. The goal was to clear a path directly to Germany, who would then be seen naked, standing alone, without help from other countries.

The year ended with tentative hope that 1918 would be better. Everyone knew, deep inside, it would not. Anna shared a somber New Year's Eve lunch with Emmaline, and a simple tea with Elizabeth. She ate dinner with Josefina, Adrian and little "Vicki," as they had taken to calling her. It seemed as though nothing could damage their euphoria at becoming a family, not even concern that Adrian would be conscripted. Anna fed on their joy and optimism and returned to her tiny basement room at the boardinghouse, where she welcomed 1918, at midnight, alone.

Chapter 45

The new year brought anxiety and pain to Josefina and Adrian. Little Vicki was fine, growing from her tiny, premature frame to a robust, happy infant. It was Josefina, changing in a way most unexpected. Adrian called Anna to the apartment for help.

"It's been weeks since the birth and, despite Vicki's good health, Josefina cannot find energy or happiness in herself. This problem has come on her quite recently."

"She should be exhilarated that little Vicki is doing so well. What do you think is causing her malaise?"

"We don't know. The doctor has examined her almost daily and finds nothing wrong with her physically. She's recovering slowly but surely from giving birth. He thinks there's something mentally wrong."

"Like what?"

"We can't figure it out. One minute she admires the smile on Vicki's face, the next she hands her off to Maggie and runs to the bedroom crying. She pleads exhaustion, saying she's unable to take care of our daughter, accusing herself of being an incompetent mother. When you see her, Anna, you'll be shocked. She doesn't give a fig about how she looks anymore. Her hair is unbrushed, her face unwashed. She doesn't even clean her teeth."

"Oh, my goodness. I can't believe it. You don't think it's because of all the laudanum we gave her, do you?"

"No, I stopped that long before Vicki was born."

"May I see her?"

"Yes, of course. Don't be surprised if she treats you rudely."

Anna thought of knocking gently on the bedroom door. She changed her mind. Turning the knob with authority, she entered and found her friend on the bed, atop the covers, as if she had just fainted there.

"What's this I hear about you lolling around when you have a beautiful baby who needs her mother?"

"Please, leave me alone."

"I will not. Get up. I said, get up!"

Josefina didn't move.

"How long do you think Adrian is going to put up with you acting like a helpless child? That man has to go to work every day, all the while fretting for you. Then he comes home to find you haven't moved a muscle since he left you in the morning. Why, I wouldn't be surprised if little Vicki thinks Maggie is her momma. Do you want that?"

"I don't know why I'm feeling this way. Do you think I enjoy it? Do you think I don't want to be with my daughter? I'm constantly wrung out, physically and emotionally. I have nothing to give."

"Has the doctor prescribed anything for this? Has he put a name to your disinterest in life? Is it a disease?"

"No, he says the same thing you're saying. But I can't force myself to not feel this way."

"Well, I can. Get up."

Josefina slowly stood. Within seconds, she collapsed in tears, forcing Anna to put her back in bed. Anna stayed with her friend until she cried herself to sleep. Then she returned to the living room.

"Well?" said Adrian.

"It's as bad as you described. I fear she might do something drastic."

"So does the doctor. He wants to sedate her."

"Then let him. It might do some good."

"For how long? Vicki needs a mother now. And when she comes out of it, will she still be my Josefina?"

"After the losses she's suffered, I think time is what she needs. I'll be here for both of you whenever I can."

"I couldn't ask for anything more."

ॐ

Anna's funds started to run dry. The ebb and flow of freelance jobs worried her bank account. Perhaps if Anna were on a payroll permanently, she'd enjoy some form of stability. She decided to pay H.L. Mencken a visit.

"What is it you want now, Miss Bainbridge?"

Anna didn't like the formality. She knew he was already on to her.

"Why do I need to have a purpose for visiting one of my best mentors?"

"Now I know you're after something. Out with it. I don't have time for games."

"I need a job on staff. The freelance jobs are drying up."

"And you want me to give you yet another chance."

"I have matured, Mr. Mencken. I'm more professional, more responsible."

"Then why hasn't another newspaper snatched you up?"

"I want to work for *The Sun*. It's my first choice."

"I have nothing for you. Why don't you try some publication for ladies?"

"After all I've done to overcome the stigma of being a woman in a man's job, that's what you're suggesting?"

"Stigma?"

"Yes, stigma. That's exactly what it is, thanks to you and newspapermen just like you."

"Then you better hit the pavement. With your reputation, you'll be hard-pressed to find a permanent job in this business."

"What reputation?"

"You're known for breaking with proper journalistic protocol, being overbearing, pushing other photographers out of the way to get a picture, forcing yourself on subjects to get a quote."

"Isn't that what the men do?"

"It's different, coming from a man."

"And that's got to change. I'm a good newspaper 'woman' and you know I'm as good as any man, maybe better."

The two sat in silence for a few moments, while Mencken fiddled with papers on his desk. Anna made no effort to leave.

Anna's eyes wandered a bit and cast upon a book sitting on the desk. It was titled *In Defense of Women*. Anna picked it up. The author, she noted, was none other than H.L. Mencken.

"What is this?"

"It's a copy of a book I recently published."

"You just berated me as a woman and here you are praising women?"

"Not exactly. I'm highlighting the areas where womanly talent can be valuable and warning women of areas where they don't belong."

Anna flipped through the pages. She saw words such as: marriage, home, suffrage, adultery, intelligence, duty.

"May I buy a copy?"

"Take that one but don't tell me what you think. I really don't care."

"You're angry with me."

"There is a limit to my patience. Sometimes, you are as annoying as a gnat."

Anna read the book that night. It spoke of the push-and-pull of opposites Mencken found in women. Yes, they are often smarter than their spouses. No, they shouldn't object to waiting on their husbands, hand and foot. Yes, women should have some political rights. No, they should not vote. Yes, women are sometimes superior to men. No, they shouldn't poke their noses into manly subjects, such as politics and business.

Anna wanted to tell the author what she thought of his book in language that would make him blush but knew it would do no good. Her only consolation was that she hadn't spent a single penny for the drivel she read.

She discussed the book with a librarian at Enoch Pratt Free Library and discovered it was meant as satire. Mencken's sense of humor was lost on Anna, who saw nothing funny about women being dominated by men who refused to take them seriously.

CHAPTER 46

Spring flowers lost their allure as news of a dangerous disease became the talk of Baltimoreans. Doctors reported an unusual but similar symptom in some of their military patients... laryngitis so extreme, the patients' throats bled. It was not unusual for people to complain of sore throats at this time of year. Pollen and ragweed floating in the air could irritate the lining, even cause breathing problems but, certainly, bleeding was irregular.

The Memorial Day Parade took place, as usual. Crowds of people cheered as marchers made their way to City Hall, with little or no thought of contagion. For the first time, an all-colored military unit participated in the parade, the 808th Infantry. Pride swelled in Anna as she saw them head down Holliday Street.

Over the hot summer months, people went about their business, enjoying movies, plays, the zoo, and shopping in department stores. Authorities kept a watchful eye and were relieved to find the number of sick people decrease. They declared the spate of severe sore throats an anomaly.

By September, the disease yet to be named returned, often developing into pneumonia. Cases rose quickly, prompting local authorities to consider banning public gatherings. Frightened Baltimoreans feared going to work, movie houses, Lexington Market, or parties at one another's homes.

On September 28th, the Philadelphia Liberty Loans Parade went on, as planned, encouraging people to buy war bonds. Thousands lined the streets. Twelve thousand came down with what was now being called a new strain of influenza.

In Maryland, many public places shut down to avoid the spread... Ford's Theater, The Vagabond Players, movie venues, Enoch Pratt Library, public gymnasiums, houses of worship, department stores and schools. Lexington Market continued to serve the food needs of city residents, only because it was mostly an open-air market.

The number of deaths alarmed the city in October, approximately ten per day, mainly overtaking soldiers at Fort McHenry, just a few miles from downtown, and in outlying encampments, south of the city in Anne Arundel County and north in Edgewood.

People learned of some sort of virus having been reported in Fort Riley, Kansas, back in January. Was it connected? From that one case, many more were diagnosed. When the country entered the war, instances of the disease were noted in New York, from which many soldiers embarked to Europe. Soon, reports of sick soldiers came from Germany, Spain, France and England. The illness fast became a worldwide military disease.

Symptoms were similar to the yearly influenza that killed thousands but didn't frighten medical authorities too much because it always abated on its own. The federal government didn't want to cause panic among U.S. citizens. They downplayed the severity of this new strain and its pervasive nature, stating it was not much worse than the common cold. The military underestimated numbers, fearing men would refrain from enlisting. Private citizens were encouraged to live their lives as usual. How could that happen in Baltimore when public places were closed? People felt they were getting one message from the White House, another from medical authorities, and still another from the military.

Anna worried for Papa. His health wasn't as robust as it had once been. She wondered if he had to treat patients with symptoms that seemed to be quite contagious. Her concern extended to Josefina, slowly recovering from giving birth.

Anxiety over impending war casualties, influenza deaths, and a possible turnover of command in the United States, kept Baltimoreans staring at the ceiling from their beds at night. The Health Department issued guidelines, instructing citizens to clean their sinuses every morning and evening, keep their resistance up by taking brisk walks and eating nourishing food, avoid buses and subways, and sleep eight hours every night.

Businesses closed, leaving workers without paychecks. Not Anna. Newspapers churned out edition after edition, staying on the job to keep the public informed. Overjoyed for the work and money, Anna berated her selfishness when she saw pages had to be added each day to list the names of all who had succumbed.

Claims of discoveries to cure influenza filled peoples' minds with hope, though most turned out to be hoaxes perpetuated by money mongers.

Parents worried for their children and themselves. The disease affected people mostly from ages 20-45, while leaving no one completely immune. Anna had just turned 33.

In late October, all Halloween activities were canceled in Baltimore. As the month waned, the highest numbers of flu were revealed... 292,000 deaths in the United States alone. The holidays appeared bleak. No one dared to make gifts, invite guests for dinner parties, or gather for religious service, even in their own homes. When people had to leave their houses, they wore protective masks or scarves over their noses and mouths. Still, they feared bringing home the deadly disease. Many hoped the onslaught of cold weather would somehow freeze the germs, keeping them from spreading.

Staying well took precedence over all else. Posters, glued to buildings, warned the public:

**COUGHS AND SNEEZES SPREAD DISEASES,
AS DANGEROUS AS POISON GAS SHELLS**

In the midst of war and disease, another scourge struck Maryland... targeted brutality of colored men. Lynchings were still a threat, more so in the eastern and southern parts of the state. Hatred seeped into Baltimore.

Back in February, the beating of a colored soldier by a police officer had been reported to authorities. Judge Robert F. Stanton, who later heard the case, deemed the officer's actions unwarranted and condemned them. In June, it was alleged that police shot a man on Pennsylvania Avenue, one of the most heavily populated colored communities in Baltimore. These incidents did not reach the level of importance in newspapers as the pandemic and war overseas, leaving colored people to make sure these horrific events didn't go unnoticed on their own. They formed organizations, writing letters of protest to the Police Commissioner, newspaper editors, and government represent-atives. Not much came of it.

Authorities stepped up police presence in colored neighbor-hoods, keeping a watchful eye on them, not as possible victims, but as potential instigators and perpetrators. Coloreds were given heavier fines and sentences than whites for similar crimes. No white person championed the plight of the colored community.

Anna and Emmaline stayed apart, each fearing for the other's safety should they venture out together.

To Anna, the world changed, almost overnight, from a place of wonder and excitement, to frightening, unpredictable, unstable, and deadly. In November, that weight would be momentarily lifted.

❧

Much to the delight of all Americans, on the eleventh hour of the eleventh day of the eleventh month, governments came to an agreement to end the war. At last, something to celebrate. All over the country, all over the world, people flooded the streets, forgoing their masks. They stood shoulder to shoulder, cheering, waving flags, creating impromptu parades. They hugged strangers, kissed babies, and forgot there was a pandemic still waging its own world war.

The result of such close human contact was immediate and devastating.

A new wave of the disease swept over the globe. Thousands more became infected, so many needless deaths. One night, Anna found two urgent messages in her mail slot when she returned to the boardinghouse. One was from Adrian, imploring Anna to come quickly. The other was from Elizabeth, with the same message. Anna phoned home and Elizabeth answered as if she had been standing by the phone waiting. "Anna, Anna!"

"Elizabeth, are you all right?"

"Yes, it's your father. He's been diagnosed with influenza."

"Where is he, upstairs in bed?"

"No, he's in quarantine in the hospital."

"Do you mean to tell me I can't see him?"

"Yes, this disease is quite contagious. He must have caught it from one of his patients."

"He'll be all right, won't he? The doctors will show him extra care."

"The doctors have their hands full. He'll get the same treatment as all the others."

"That won't do. Give me a name, someone to call and complain."

"Anna, it will be for naught. There are hundreds of patients who need treatment. The medical staff must treat the most severe cases first. Your father is one of many."

"How bad is he? Tell me the truth."

"He became ill quickly. He passed out while tending to one of his patients."

"Oh, this doesn't sound good. What can we do?"

"Pray and wait. It's out of our hands now."

"What about you? When was the last time you were near Papa?"

"It's been days. He's been living, sleeping, eating at the hospital. I don't feel ill at all."

"Do you have food and other necessities?"

"For now, I'm fine. Are you protecting yourself? Are you still working?"

"Yes, I wear a mask while I take pictures. But I avoid close proximity to people. My pictures are not as dynamic as they should be but what can I do?"

"Please keep yourself safe from harm. Your father must have someone to live for."

"I will. Call me any time of day or night. I will be by your side in minutes."

"Thank you, dear."

Anna had no time to waste. Remembering her promise to always be a good friend, she needed to visit Adrian and Josefina.

They didn't have a phone, so she drove to their apartment and knocked on the door.

Maggie answered, her eyes bloodshot above her mask.

"Anna, I cannot let you in. This is a sick house. I'll come out and talk to you."

The two women stood far apart on the sidewalk but kept their voices down.

"Who is it?" Anna asked.

"My dear Josefina. She was not fully recovered from giving birth to Victoria. Her fragile body offered little resistance."

"She isn't..."

"No, she breathes still, though labored. Adrian won't leave her side. He bathes her with cold water to ease the fever and tries to get her to take some soup. She can't speak, her throat is so ravaged. Sometimes, blood comes up when she coughs. Sometimes it comes out of her ears and stains her pillows."

"How long has this been lingering?"

"Four days, so far."

"Why isn't she in the hospital?"

"We were told there are no more beds."

"I dare ask, is Adrian showing any symptoms? Are you?"

"No, not yet. We both keep our faces covered and we wash our clothes daily. We open the windows an inch for fresh air, even though it's cold."

"Where is little Vicki? Please tell me she's well."

"My sister, Flora, came and took her. Vicki is living with her family in Roland Park."

"Has Josefina shown no improvement?"

"None. She doesn't appear to be getting worse. That is our only hope."

"What can I do? Are you and Adrian eating? Can I bring you something?"

"Neighbors have been putting dishes on the stoop. We have plenty of food."

"What do you need?"

"Freedom from pain. Freedom from worry. Freedom from my poor Josefina's suffering. It's been too much to bear."

"I would hug you, if I could."

Anna returned to the boardinghouse, where she discovered that Adelaide had been taken to the hospital. Mrs. Pendleton and the other residents were scrubbing every inch of the three-story place they called home. Anna joined them.

"It came upon her so quickly," Mrs. Pendleton said. "Her skin changed colors. It appeared blotchy. She grew weak and disoriented, speaking nonsense."

"Have any of the other residents shown symptoms?"

"Not yet. Lord have mercy."

Anna spent a restless night. This pandemic possessed too much power, as strong as any fire but more destructive because it was taking lives, not buildings. The Great Baltimore Fire of 1904 ended in two days. This disaster's end might not come for years.

Word arrived through an early-morning phone call that Adelaide had died in the night. Anna was heartsick. Adelaide had never followed through on her dream to open a temporary job placement service. She had never tried to overcome her racial prejudice. Anna felt bad for wanting to berate her at this moment. It was unkind. She chose to dwell on their afternoons together at the ballpark.

Every time the boardinghouse phone rang, the women jumped. No one wanted to answer. Who would be next? Which one of them would lose a friend, family member or work associate?

They ate their meals in their own rooms, washed their own dishes and laundry, and stayed as far away from one another as possible. Few had jobs since many businesses had shut down.

Anna called Elizabeth daily. There was never a change. Papa wasn't worse or better. Josefina's mother placed a call through a neighbor, advising Anna to stay away, as Adrian had now also come down with influenza. He and Josefina had been removed to one of the newly-erected tent hospitals. At least, they would have nursing care.

Anna knew their chances of recovery were not good. Medical staff had been stretched to the limit. Newspapers were being asked to urge retired doctors, nurses, and orderlies to sacrifice their own health and volunteer their time and expertise.

By now, influenza had infected one in four Baltimoreans. Anna had already suffered a blow with Adelaide's death. She'd just seen her at the boardinghouse, looking fine, a few days before. What would happen to the others stricken?

How delicate life could be. Anna wondered what kind of monster this disease was and why God wouldn't do anything to stop it. Here she was, fourteen years after the Great Baltimore Fire, asking the same question. *Why doesn't God stop suffering?* This would prey on her mind as the New Year entered with a whimper and no one popped a balloon or drank a glass of champagne.

CHAPTER 47

Josefina died on New Year's Day, 1919. Adrian wasn't told for fear his condition would deteriorate. Funerals were banned, so he would've been prevented from saying goodbye with a proper burial anyway. His wife's body was sent to the morgue and later buried. Anna realized that little Vicki would never know her mother, just as Anna had not known her own. She cried for the child.

Adrian's recovery was as slow as a molasses tap. He relapsed twice, once when he nearly choked to death on his own sputum and, again, when he finally learned his beloved wife had passed. Later, doctors moved him to the same hospital where Anna's father still fought for his life.

When Adrian rebounded and was informed that he could go home, he refused. "I have no home without my Josefina," he told his doctor.

"You have a daughter who needs her father."

"I don't want to see her. In her delicate features, I will find, not my daughter, but my wife. I cannot bear it."

"Where is your daughter?"

"At her aunt's home in Roland Park. She is being well cared for, I hear. She will forget me."

"I don't think, for one minute, you really believe what you're saying. Here is my advice. Let your daughter stay with her aunt while you continue to recover. Don't go home. Find another place, the home of a friend. Have your own place sanitized. While that's being done, seek a new apartment, if you wish, a permanent home for you and your daughter. Move your belongings when you feel up to full vigor. You will need to find a nanny to care for your daughter when you return to work. Do you have any possibilities?"

"This is all too much for me to contemplate now."

"You must. Soon you will be released from the hospital. Where will you go?"

"I don't know. I can't do all this alone. My mother-in-law was living with us. All this time, she neglected her own husband. She can't stay indefinitely."

"Anyone else who could help you?"

Adrian didn't answer. He cried uncontrollably.

"Rest now, Mr. Crosby. Later, give your future some thought. Remember this. You have responsibility to your wife to raise her daughter to become the woman who made you fall in love with her."

Adrian moved in with his mother-in-law at the home she shared with her husband in Highlandtown. When Vicki was taken there, Adrian pulled her into his chest and cried until he lost all strength to hold the child. Over the next weeks, he settled into a daily routine, claiming a comfortable chair, reading the newspaper, gazing at an oak tree just outside a window, taking Vicki for walks in her pram, and becoming absorbed into a new family.

Anna was asked to stay away for the time being. She didn't understand why. Elizabeth explained that the road to recovery must be traveled in tiny, deliberate steps, so there would be no backtracking, no loss of balance.

"You mean, give him time."

"That's exactly what I mean. When he needs to call upon your strength and friendship, he will."

A whole new wave of influenza cases swept the entire country. Tens of thousands of Americans were diagnosed. It seemed a dirty trick. Just as people were feeling confident of its demise, it returned with vengeance. Somehow, life went on. Other news stories garnered headlines, some good, some bad.

On February 15, despite the pandemic, the National Woman's Party continued to push for suffrage in front of the White House. These declarations had been going on since 1917. Many women from Maryland joined others to picket, standing outside the gates, holding signs in non-violent protest. They were asked to leave. They refused. Officers stepped in and carried women away, as though they were store mannequins being moved from the dress department to millinery. The women gave no physical resistance, but their voices rang out, shouting disdain for tyranny. Many served time in jail, including Lucy Branham from Baltimore. When she got out, she joined other women who had been incarcerated. They proudly wore their prison records on their sleeves as they toured the country by train, telling their stories of persecution for the cause. The train, dubbed "The Prison Special," covered states coast to coast, their journey ending on March 10th.

Anna wanted to travel with them, taking pictures and reporting for any newspaper that would hire her. Instead, she stayed home, where she was needed.

Though miraculous, Papa's recovery was slow and arduous. In his heart and mind, he wanted to return to his work. His body wouldn't comply. Anna and Elizbeth argued with him every single day.

"Papa, you must rest," Anna said. "For a doctor, you are the worst patient. What would you say to someone in your care demanding to return to work so soon?"

Dr. Bainbridge offered a weak smile. He understood.

"Now, drink this broth before I dump it on your head."

Papa laughed, which turned into a violent cough. Anna and Elizabeth sat him up and patted his back. He took a sip of water and recovered.

"Anna, I would expect no less a response from you."

"Thank you. I accept that as a compliment. Would you like me to read to you from your medical journals? They've been piling up, you know."

"Not right now. I believe I'll take a nap. Maybe later." A serious expression overtook Papa's face.

"Is something wrong? Are you in pain?"

"I was thinking about your friend, Adrian. I want to express my condolences for the loss of his wife. To be so ill himself and receive such news..."

"Thank you, Papa. I appreciate your empathy and so will he. Sadly, you know of such things from experience. I'll relay your sentiments to him in a letter. For now, he wants to be alone with his family. I have not seen him."

"Be patient." Papa fell asleep just as the words slipped out of his mouth.

☙❧

First, Anna wrote a letter to Emmaline, inquiring about the health of her family. She received a swift reply, stating that she was fine, still working. Her family had escaped the pandemic so far because their community of Bare Hills was somewhat remote and most of the residents worked within a mile or two of home. It was agreed that no one would travel beyond their neighborhood without telling the others and staying somewhat sequestered upon their return, until they felt safe from symptoms.

By mid-spring, Dr. Bainbridge was able to return to work on a limited basis. He could not have one-on-one contact with contagious patients but could read charts and make recommendations for care.

Anna still hadn't heard from Adrian, even after sending him her father's condolence letter.

With April came the hope of warmer weather that would drop the number of influenza cases, as it had the past year. Everyone waited with bated breath.

Anna suffered a blow when she opened the newspaper one morning to read the obituary of Thomas J. O'Neill. Through tears, Anna read of his life in Ireland and his journey to Baltimore with little money in his pocket. He had secured work in a linen shop before opening his own store, building it into Baltimore's most coveted destination for shopping. He did not die of the virus. It was a stroke, suffered on Palm Sunday, after attending service. Anna remembered him as a man who possessed a big heart for his staff and customers. That generous nature extended into his last will and testament. He bequeathed large sums of money for the building of a new Catholic cathedral, a hospital, and the improvement of Loyola College in Maryland.

Anna felt certain O'Neill's would remain open. The staff knew what they were doing, with or without the store's owner. It would not be the same without Mr. O'Neill, dressed to the nines and greeting customers at the door by name. Anna felt sad but grateful that she had gotten the chance to meet him. She wrote a letter of condolence to Miss Hughes, who responded with a brief note, stating that she had retired from her position at the end of 1918, due to severe arthritis.

Later in the month, mail bombs arrived at the offices and homes of certain prominent citizens. One was placed on the townhouse stoop of United States Attorney General A. Mitchell Palmer in Washington, D.C. Windows were blown out, his office destroyed. He was unhurt. The blast could be felt throughout the neighborhood and alarmed Franklin and Eleanor Roosevelt, who lived just across the street. The ravaged body of the man who placed the bomb was found in the rubble.

The *Baltimore American* hired Anna to go to Washington, to photograph the damage and try to gain an audience with the politician.

She was rebuffed in both attempts. A. Mitchell Palmer's home was cordoned off and the Attorney General and his family were forbidden to give interviews. Neighbors, postal officials, even delivery boys, turned down Anna's request for statements. It seemed as if Washington, D.C., had stuffed a sock down its own throat. Anna was able to take pictures from across the street.

On the train home, Anna wondered how Adrian's friend, Sam, was carrying out his job as a mail deliverer. He and Adrian had met at the Main Post Office, where they both worked. Even though Adrian changed jobs, now working for Berger Cookies, they remained fast friends.

Anna returned to the newspaper pretty much empty-handed but was paid for her effort anyway. She felt a failure despite her editor's attempts to console her, saying that these things happen in the newspaper business. Sometimes, things just don't pan out.

A coordinated effort to shake the American status quo had begun. On the same day, bombs arrived at the homes or offices of people in government and law enforcement. Postal workers looked for suspicious packages and prevented sixteen more bombs from reaching their destinations, one targeting John D. Rockefeller. Mail bombs addressed to Judge Oliver Wendell Holmes, who was the Associate Justice of the Supreme Court, and also financial mogul J.P. Morgan were intercepted. Immigration officials, Catholic churches and industrialists found themselves in the bullseye. Who would be next?

Each package followed a pattern, wrapped in plain brown paper with similar labeling. Inside, a cardboard box contained the rigged dynamite. It was wrapped in green paper and stamped with a business logo meant to deceive. It read "Gimbel Brothers-Novelty Samples." Gimbels was a prominent, upstanding department store in New York. Certainly, it had nothing to do with the bombings. The store was used as part of the ruse. In all, thirty-six bombs went out to high-ranking government officials, clergy, businessmen and newspapers. As bomb experts carefully opened the intercepted packages, threatening notes stared back at them. Each read the same warning of war, bloodshed, death and destruction. Mailroom boys in government offices and at newspapers were put on alert to examine every package as though it were dangerous.

There were severe injuries. A senator from Georgia and his wife were maimed. The poor woman suffered severe burns and shrapnel wounds to her face. Her maid, who opened the package, lost both of her hands.

Anna masked her nervousness by going about her business. She wouldn't allow herself to feel too afraid to visit a newspaper office about a job.

Not thinking of the implications, she made a purchase at Hochschild's and asked the store to deliver it. She was on her way to meet with the editor of the *Afro-American* and didn't want a cumbersome package under her arm. When she arrived at the boardinghouse later that day, Mrs. Pendleton was all a tither.

"Anna, a package arrived for you earlier. It was heavy and frightened me, since you work in the newspaper field. And you know what's going on. It's wrapped in brown paper, like those bombs. I put it in the backyard, behind the bushes. I hope you don't mind."

"Mrs. Pendleton, I bought new galoshes for the spring rains, that's all. It's from Hochschild's."

"Just the same, I'd feel better if you opened the package outside."

"And, if it's a bomb, you don't mind that I get blown to bits?"

"Oh, I didn't mean that. It's just... I'm so on edge."

"Everyone is. The government will find out who's doing this. They'll take care of it."

At first, no one knew who was behind the terror attacks. Attorney General A. Mitchell Palmer needed to appease the public quickly. He put a lawyer named J. Edgar Hoover in charge of gathering information under the auspices of the Bureau of Investigations. Americans wondered if all the detonation cords would lead to valuable clues.

The influenza pandemic still raged. A whole new wave had swept Australia, Europe and the United States. People thought that if the virus didn't get them, a mail bomb would. They needed to release their tension and many vented their anxiety on each other. Papa ordered Anna to move back home. She refused.

The summer heat was rife for expressions of hate, frustration, fear, and impatience. If racial discord didn't make the headlines, bombings did. Headlines in newspapers shouted apprehension over who was behind the bomb attacks. Authorities leaned toward foreign anarchists, communists, socialists as they were called. Hospital reports of injured patients and now deaths gained attention. There was a name put to what was going on... "The Red Scare," with the color referring to communists.

At the same time, interracial fighting threatened to erupt into full scale rioting. Some papers called these months of violence "The Red Summer," with the color referring to bloodshed.

So much vitriol played out on the streets of Baltimore and elsewhere, undermining the Constitutional right to equality. Could things get any worse?

Anna met Emmaline for lunch at the *Afro-American*, rather than in public. They decided it was the safest place under the circumstances.

"Emmaline, I worry for you and your family. There seems to be no reason for all this. Victims are chosen without provocation. In asking questions, I've discovered that white people don't like that coloreds are moving north in record numbers. They're calling it the 'Great Migration.'"

"Yes, I know. We're seeing more coloreds from the South moving into Bare Hills. The neighborhood is expanding."

"Why did they come here?"

"To escape poverty and Jim Crow."

"We have Jim Crow laws here."

"Yes, but they're also looking for education and good jobs, two things often unavailable to Southern coloreds. They were prevented from going to school or finding meaningful employment as a means of suppression."

"Are they having better luck here?"

"From the people I've spoken to, no. There are a lot of jobs available because of all the factories and car assembly lines that have opened up, but the jobs are filled by union workers. Coloreds are not allowed union cards."

"That's unfair."

"I hate to say this, but it seems that white folks are looking for any excuse to start trouble—accusing colored men of violating white women when nothing untoward happened. There are beatings and gunfire now. What will be next, random lynchings?"

"Oh, no. That can't happen here in Maryland."

"Maybe it hasn't recently but it did in the past."

"You must be careful."

"I am. Usually, one of my coworkers walks me home. He lives in the same building. I don't go out after dark. My life is pretty much contained to one square mile, except when I visit home, which isn't often lately. You must be careful, too, in your job. Many people dislike newspapers right now. Will they ever discover who's behind those mail bombs?"

"I don't know. We're living in a disturbing time. Let's hope all this doesn't make the pandemic worse. Let's hope the second half of the year is better."

"How is your friend, Adrian?"

"I don't see him or hear from him anymore. He's built a new life around his daughter and his in-laws. I guess it's for the better."

"Don't you miss him?"

"I've been so busy, lately, I haven't had a moment to think of anything other than work, Papa and news headlines."

"Is your father well?"

"As well as can be expected. He pushes too hard."

"So, you come by it honestly."

Anna laughed. "Papa would never admit that. And what about this coworker walking you home? I assume he's a gentleman."

"Yes, there is nothing to the gesture. He's old enough to be my father. He's just being cautious."

"I see. I want you to know that you can always come to the boardinghouse to stay, if violence escalates. I don't care what the other residents think or say. I don't care about Mrs. Pendleton either. You have a safe haven with me."

"Thank you. I offer you the same."

"You are a true friend."

CHAPTER 48

The mail bombs were traced to a known anarchist, Carlo Valdinoci. His remains were found in the blast that rocked Attorney General A. Mitchell Palmer's townhouse.

Labor unrest boiled over during the summer. Strikers took to the streets. Alleged anarchists walked with them undetected, in hopes of indoctrinating their ideology and overthrowing the government.

Factories needed workers to stay in business. They hired colored men... strikebreakers, scabs to the white men walking the picket lines. Violence escalated. Colored men were pulled from buses and beaten just for being dark-skinned. Yanked from cars, they endured cracked skulls and smashed vehicles. It seemed that Anna's world had become a topsy-turvy doll, with white domination and colored subjugation stitched into its fabric. She documented it all, her film a testimony that couldn't be challenged. She hoped her pictures could help turn things around. She needed something good to happen.

On June 4, 1919, Congress finally passed the 19th Amendment, thanks to the state of Tennessee becoming the 36th state to ratify. The law was set to go into effect on August 18, 1920. Women all over the United States would become legally able to vote in the election just a few months later. Anna couldn't believe this day had finally come. She contacted Emmaline to celebrate over lunch.

"Here's to more successes for women!" Anna said, raising her cup of tea.

Emmaline didn't share her enthusiasm. She remained quiet.

"What's the matter? Aren't you happy about women getting the vote?"

"In theory, yes."

"What does that mean?"

"It means that you will easily get to vote in the next election. I might not. When slaves were emancipated, they didn't automatically get to share the same rights as white folks."

"They couldn't vote?"

"Not until the 15th Amendment was passed in 1870. It specifically granted the right for colored men to vote. Even so, especially down South, white men found ways to keep colored men from the polls. They gave 'understanding' tests, as they called them. Nothing more than literacy tests made too difficult to pass. They levied poll taxes that colored men couldn't afford. They said that a colored man could vote if his grandfather had voted. They called it being 'grandfathered in.'"

"No colored man's grandfather would have been allowed to vote. They would have lived before emancipation."

"That was the whole idea. And ridiculous 'jelly bean' tests were administered, forcing colored men to figure out how many candies were in the jar without emptying it."

"Who can make an accurate estimate?"

"My point exactly. Don't you think the same thing will happen to colored women in the next election?"

"We must prevent that."

"How do you propose doing that?"

"I don't know."

"We women are still at the mercy of men. A new law isn't going to change that. And the more rights we get, the more violence is likely to occur."

"Emmaline, I will go to the voting poll with you, arm in arm. You and I will place our very first ballots together."

"That I will toast... after it happens."

≈∘∾

To help celebrate the fortieth wedding anniversary of Emmaline's parents, Anna was invited to Sunday dinner at their Bare Hills home. Anna took several packages of Hostess Cupcakes, a new product on the market she thought they might not have had a chance to enjoy.

The dinner, at 3:00 P.M., was fine, the air pleasant, the family savoring a time of merriment and goodwill. Anna sincerely hoped it would last forever. Such a daring wish for so turbulent a time.

Anna had driven herself and looked forward to a pleasant trip home. Residual sunlight guided her as she left Bare Hills. It didn't take long for darkness unrelated to weather to engulf her, the kind she never expected to see.

As she drove through small villages and expanses of undeveloped land, she spotted firelight deep inside a clump of trees, where it was dark as night. Thinking it a brush fire, she pulled over and looked through the viewfinder of her camera for better inspection. It was no clearer. Just as she was about to get back in her car, she heard voices, male voices. She tried to discern what they were saying, without success. Careful not to make a sound, she edged closer. As she drew near, twigs snapped under her feet. The sound went unnoticed because of the crackle of fire in a tiny clearing... and angry voices of men.

There were only four of them, conducting some sort of meeting or ritual. Three wore white robes with pointed hoods that had owl-like holes where eyes should be. The fourth wore black. It is said that eyes are the windows to the soul. The hollowed sockets in the hoods on these men revealed the blackened sanctums within.

Anna hunched down behind an old, rusted oil drum. She wished she had worn pants and flat shoes. Taking off her hat, she dropped it on the ground. There would be only one opportunity to shoot a picture, if she wanted to get out alive.

Easing her way around the drum, she captured a shot without taking the time to fully compose it. Anything was better than nothing. And anything was better than getting caught.

Anna decided not to return to her car, at first. She waited to see if anyone had noticed her. The men seemed to be focused on their meeting. Slowly, Anna picked up her hat, and crept back out of the woods. Having parked at the top of a hill, she eased the brake and let the car drift until she felt far enough away to turn the ignition key.

Anna couldn't wait to have the picture developed. She planned to take her film to the *Afro-American,* first thing in the morning. She was stopped by thoughts of Emmaline's family, living just a mile or so away from a Ku Klux Klan ritual, however small. Would she be placing them in danger if the newspaper published the photograph? Would the good people of Bare Hills be accused of taking the picture and have to suffer retaliation that could be deadly? Anna wondered if she would better serve her friend by turning the film over to the police and letting them take the credit and wrath.

Anna didn't want to alarm Emmaline by asking her what to do. Yet, she had to tell her friend how close trouble might be.

Sleep did not find Anna a good portion of the night. She knew that, if any newspaper published this picture of a private Klan ritual, it would bolster her reputation as a photojournalist and bring her more jobs, a better income. It would also place her in danger, and Emmaline by association.

Early Monday morning, Anna stood outside *The Sun* building, waiting for H.L. Mencken to arrive.

"Well, this is just like old times. If you're expecting a little chitchat with me, you must make an appointment. I have a staff meeting and I'm already late."

"This can't wait, Mr. Mencken."

"Are you in trouble again?"

"No, sir. I have a picture, at least, I think I have a picture of a Ku Klux Klan meeting in a wooded area north of the city. I'm not sure what to do with it."

H.L. Mencken looked around. "Come inside."

Looking more serious than Anna had ever seen him, Mencken told his secretary to postpone the staff meeting. He instructed her to prevent any interruptions.

"Now, tell me everything."

Anna shared her story.

"Did you bring the film with you?"

"Yes."

"Will you entrust it to me?"

"Is *The Sun* going to publish it? If so, I need to warn my..."

"No, we are not going to publish it. It belongs in the hands of the authorities who can do something about it. Putting a picture this inflammatory in the paper will do more harm than good. I just want to see if you captured anything the authorities can use to track down these men."

Anna handed over the film and was told to come back late in the afternoon. When she arrived, Mencken was ready for her.

"Somehow, Anna, you managed to capture a clear photograph. I must commend you on your bravery and composure under the circumstances."

"Thank you, Mr. Mencken."

"These men were wearing hoods and are not recognizable. However, in the shadows, right over here... can you see?"

"Why, that looks like the picture of a fifth man. His hood is down. I can see his face. Why didn't I notice him before?"

"You caught a good profile. Thankfully, he wasn't looking your way. I think the police should see this picture."

"I agree with you."

"You won't receive credit for this photograph, even though I think it would win awards. Once you hand it over, it's no longer yours. And you should be happy about that. These men are dangerous. If they knew who you were, they'd think nothing of harming you. They are no gentlemen. Being a woman will not protect you. Do you understand?"

"Yes, sir." Anna thought back to the time she photographed the flour drop during the air show and handed over the film to the military. This was different. There was danger involved now. Anna hoped none of the Klansmen had seen her.

H.L. Mencken placed a phone call to county police headquarters and arranged a meeting right away. When they arrived, Anna explained what she had witnessed and handed over the photograph.

Police officers in plainclothes staked out the woods. Two weeks later, they rounded up seven men in a ramshackle house a mile outside of Bare Hills. After a thorough search, authorities found plans for a cross burning at a nearby synagogue. Grounds for arrest.

Newspapers did report that story, with no photograph.

Anna contacted Emmaline. She couldn't explain her brush with evil. She simply reiterated what had been in the newspaper. Emmaline's mother, Emma, already knew. She said the police had told her family and other residents of Bare Hills that these men had come south from Pennsylvania to recruit members to join the KKK and start trouble. They asked everyone to remain vigilant but hopeful that there would be no recurrence, including in the nearby Jewish community.

Anna quietly received a citation from the Baltimore County Police Department. She was asked not to display it.

స్తిం

While casually perusing the latest publications at the library, Anna came upon a new book written by H.L. Mencken. It was called *Prejudices*. Anna wondered why Mencken hadn't mentioned it to her, until she thumbed through the pages. She found a collection of essays on a variety of subjects, some approached with humor. Although it brought chortles, a bite to the levity could not be dismissed. Mencken's prejudices were as evident as the severe part down the center of his head. Some topics he criticized to death. It seemed that once Mencken disliked something, he tore it to pieces and stomped on it, then set it on fire. Anna concluded Mencken was best described as surly, except when in the company of like-minded men. In the book, Mencken pronounced his prejudices toward people and politics. Anna did not purchase a copy.

స్తిం

Anna rued the end of the baseball season. She had enjoyed many a game. Her greatest consolation? The Orioles won the International League Pennant. Her thoughts ran to Adelaide, who would have celebrated with her. For a moment, Anna missed taking Adelaide to the games and sharing Cracker Jack and Coca-Cola. She thought about her friend's wasted talents. Adelaide could have started a whole new career for herself and her clients, if only she had persevered with her business idea. Instead, she chose to let fear and faint-heartedness stand in her way. Anna couldn't understand why anyone would prefer to live in the safety of their own boredom.

In November, the *Baltimore American* hired Anna to write a story honoring the one-year anniversary of armistice. Her assignment? To tell the story of Private Henry Gunther, a native Baltimorean, who was the last soldier to die in World War I. Anna interviewed his family and friends and pieced together the story of a brave man, of German-American heritage, who served the 313th Regiment well, fighting the Germans, while battling distrust and prejudice in his own ranks.

Stationed on the Western Front in France for two months, he charged at the enemy and was shot by them in a hail of gunfire, just one minute before armistice on November 11, 1918.

Anna interviewed his fiancée in Highlandtown. "I'm sorry to stir up such unpleasant thoughts, but the reading public wants to know about your betrothed. Are you up to the task?"

"I think so."

"Tell me about Henry, not the soldier, the man."

"Well, before the war, he worked as a teller and bookkeeper at the National Bank of Baltimore. He had hopes of becoming a manager someday."

"Sounds like a good, solid job."

"Yes, he wanted to be able to provide for the family we hoped to have."

With that, the young lady started to cry softly. Anna told her to take her time. After a few minutes, Anna said, "He must have been a brave man to do what he did, I mean, at the end."

"Yes, his unit was mostly from Baltimore, you know. Some of his buddies told me what happened when they returned."

"Can you tell me?"

"Well, Henry didn't want to enlist in the first place—being that his name was Gunther."

"Oh, German. Yes, of course."

"He never wrote about it to me. His friends informed me. I guess he didn't want me to worry. Anyway, war makes people do funny things. Some members of his unit wondered whose side he was on. They didn't want to take orders from him, even though he was their sergeant."

"Sergeant? I thought he was a private."

"No, he was a sergeant. He got demoted after censors intercepted a letter home to one of his friends. He warned the young man not to enlist, saying that war was terrible."

"And, for that, he was demoted?"

"Yes, just for voicing his opinion. Losing his rank hurt Henry deeply. He wanted to prove himself to his unit and his commanders and regain his stature. On the last day of the war, they found themselves on the Western Front in a place called Lorraine, in France, of course."

"Go on."

"Well, his buddies said that they came upon two German guards blocking a street. Henry charged the guards alone. They shot him. Thankfully, Henry didn't suffer. He died instantly. One minute later, the armistice went into effect."

"Oh, how awful for you. I'm so sorry. Do you have a picture of Henry?"

"Yes, right there on the mantel, in his uniform."

Anna set up her camera and took a photograph of the framed picture above the fireplace. Henry Gunther had a square face, strong hairline and trim mustache. "He was handsome."

"Yes, just twenty-three years old."

"Where is he buried?"

"At the Most Holy Redeemer Cemetery on Belair Road."

"I'd like to visit his grave. Is there anything else you want to add to the article?"

"Yes, I won't rest until Henry's rank as a sergeant is reinstated. If you put that in the article, maybe it will happen."

"I hope that day comes soon and brings you comfort."

When Anna arrived at the cemetery, she found a small headstone, compared to the others around it. It depicted the three medals Gunther received, the Purple Heart, Distinguished Services Cross, and the World War I Victory Medal. Anna rubbed her fingers over each chisel.

She read the headstone aloud:

Highly Decorated For Exceptional Bravery
And Heroic Action That Resulted In His Death
One Minute Before Armistice

Though Anna was not one to pray, she found herself imploring God to award Henry Gunther an angel's bliss and a sergeant's stripes.

The story of Henry Gunther was the most emotional experience of Anna's career. Even more than the Triangle Shirtwaist Fire or the explosion at Fort Carroll. It focused on one man, who represented every soldier who had ever died for his country, regardless of citizenship, ethnic heritage, or loyalty. And it represented the people back home, who sacrificed for their country, too, and would forever feel the pain when loved ones weren't there to enjoy warm summer evenings, snowy holidays or their own wedding days.

In November, Attorney General A. Mitchell Palmer ordered raids at homes of suspected anarchists in the United States. After a lengthy investigation, thousands of men and women, immigrants from Italy, Russia, Ireland and Eastern Europe were descended upon and rounded up by the Bureau of Investigation and local police. Some of these people were anarchists. Many were taken into custody without cause. President Woodrow Wilson had ordered the raids in thirty cities, against the advice of his own Department of Labor.

Anna wondered what the definition of an anarchist was. People plotting to overthrow the U.S. government? Or people simply speaking out for equality? It seemed that many of those arrested fit the latter category. Some were deported. Others jailed and put on trial. It looked, to Anna, that the ensuing months would be rocky and the news, dangerous to report.

Anna happily said goodbye to 1919. Would the New Year be any better? The pandemic had started to abate but race riots had worsened. There were still threats of mail bombs. And the KKK continued to recruit men filled with a different kind of fear and hatred—the kind that would foul the air for decades.

CHAPTER 49

Anna had never dabbled in drinking alcohol. It didn't interest her. She'd seen how it could make a man brave and a woman weak. When Prohibition took effect on January 17, 1920, it meant nothing to her.

The law did not prohibit drinking. It was intended to curb liquor consumption by banning the manufacture, transport or sale of alcohol, including beer. Bars shut down. Restaurants served tea or coffee with their two-inch steaks. Privately, individuals hoarded spirits they had and reserved them for special occasions. Baltimore's elite had stocked their wine cellars in advance, knowing what was coming. Anna felt certain H.L. Mencken had done the same.

Maryland had been known as a "wet state," supporting the right to freely purchase and consume alcohol. Because most Baltimoreans had opposed Prohibition, they found ways to continue imbibing. Speakeasies sprang up across the city from Pennsylvania Avenue to Hollins Street to Harford Road. These private clubs were reserved for the "hep" crowd—elite drinkers, flappers, gangsters and their molls. Sometimes, local politicians and police officials turned a blind eye.

Steamed crabs were a coveted delicacy enjoyed by many Marylanders. The crustaceans paired perfectly with a tall glass of beer. Restaurants that wanted to please their loyal customers found ways to get around the law and elude detection. Owners hung "Seafood" signs with pictures of crabs on their doors, veiled communication that beer could be found inside to go with their crabs, usually in a back room.

One of the most vocal political opponents of Prohibition was Senator Cable Bruce, the same man who had befriended Mayor McLane and served as City Solicitor in his administration. He noted that the rise in crime, bootlegging and illegal sales could be worse than drinking itself.

It was no surprise that H.L. Mencken also opposed Prohibition, saying that it worked best on the poor, who were the real drunks, in his opinion. The rich always had ways of getting their hands on wine and liquor. He boldly stated that he made his own brew at home, "Bathtub Gin," as people were starting to call it.

Many others did, too. People simply fermented grape juice over several weeks. Others made liquor from humble dandelions. People also stole base alcohols from the government and private industry, who used them to produce ink and campfire fluid. Moonshiners distilled a potent potable that answered to no federal standards. Many drinkers were poisoned by the ingredients. In rural areas, moonshiners built stills to create liquor from corn mash, a safer base.

Anna didn't understand such a strong need for alcohol. She wrote articles for the *Baltimore American* about the pros and cons of Prohibition but couldn't gain access to speakeasies to take pictures. Women she interviewed said alcohol had been the root of marital problems, causing fussy, irritable spouses, who sometimes lashed out at home. She also learned that men deprived of alcohol could be just as vicious.

Doctors often prescribed whiskey or beer for their patients as an elixir for arthritis or headaches. Local drugstores could legally dispense the spirits. Patients found ways to steal prescription pads from their doctors, sharing "medicinal" alcohol with friends. It seemed that Prohibition only made the desire for alcohol desperate.

Rumrunners from the islands sailed the Chesapeake under darkness of night and slipped into channels up and down the coast of Maryland, where they found remote places to dock and offload. Police couldn't keep up with all the sneaky ways Marylanders found to acquire alcohol.

Anna got a tip that one of these rum-running boats would arrive in Essex overnight via Back River. With not much more than a few homes and a general store, this sleepy waterfront town proved the perfect spot to make land and deliver Caribbean-made liquor to be distributed throughout Baltimore at a handsome profit.

Anna hadn't come upon such an exciting assignment in quite a while and jumped at the chance, dismissing danger. The *Democratic Telegram* had folded in 1914, leaving Anna with one less source of income. No other paper had assigned her. No respectable paper would send a young woman out into the night on such a perilous mission. They might not even send a man. Anna assigned herself, knowing that if she succeeded and got a picture published, it would surely become the crown jewel of her distinctive career. She would earn the respect of fellow journalists, editors and local authorities.

Anna wore a man's black suit with a newsboy-style cap over her chignon. Driving herself, she parked about a quarter of a mile away from her destination. She walked through brush, past barking dogs, in the dark, until she heard men's voices, some speaking English, others a language Anna couldn't decipher.

The beach was mostly dark, except for a couple of torches the men had staked into the sand. Anna would have to get awfully close to capture a readable photograph. Could she run in, take a picture and make it back to her car before they overtook her? She counted the men, five in all. Their muscled shoulders warned her to remain cautious.

Anna didn't have time to fashion a strategy. Several men pushed through the brush behind her, rushing toward the boat, screaming indecipherable commands. Their guns drawn, they forced the rumrunners to stop unloading and put their hands up. Anna felt a tight grip on her arm, forcing her into the torchlight.

"Got another one here," a man said.

Anna's eyes befell a man wearing a badge that read, "Thompson."

"What? I'm not with them. I'm a newspaper photographer. See? Here's my camera. I was trying to get a picture of this crime taking place."

"Sure. And the earth is flat. The drop-off is out there beyond Back River."

"No, really. I have credentials."

"Listen, mister. You're talking to the wrong person. We just round 'em up and deliver 'em to jail. You can sell your story to the desk sergeant."

"I'm not a mister. I'm a woman. I'm a woman, Officer Thompson."

Anna took her cap off and showed the authorities her chignon.

"Well, I'll be. Look here, fellas, we have a female rumrunner."

"I'm not a rumrunner. I'm a journalist."

"For what newspaper? Who told you to come here?" another officer asked.

"No one. I'm a freelance photographer and reporter. I sell my work to the highest bidder."

"I'm sure you do," he said.

"What does *that* mean?"

"I never heard of a female rumrunner and I never heard of a female journalist. You should be home sewing a quilt or something."

"How dare you speak to me like that. I'll have you know I photographed the Triangle Shirtwaist Factory fire in New York and the boat explosion at Fort Carroll and several other stories. I've interviewed politicians and business owners."

"Let's see those credentials," Officer Thompson said.

"They're in the satchel I left in my car. I parked it about a quarter of a mile away."

"So that's your vehicle. We already searched it. Is this your bag?"

"Yes, give it to me. You had no right to take it."

"It's evidence now, lady."

With that, Officer Thompson pushed Anna into a police wagon along with the rumrunners. They were taken to headquarters in downtown Baltimore. After telling her story to the desk sergeant, Anna was fingerprinted and placed in a cell.

"You will go before the judge in the morning," the sergeant said.

"I'm not staying here overnight. I'm innocent. And what about my car? And my bag?"

"Save your sob story for the court."

No one missed Anna at the boardinghouse. It was not unusual for her to work strange hours. When she failed to join the others for breakfast, her absence wasn't even mentioned.

Anna had no pending appointments. Once again, there wasn't anyone to worry for her failure to show up. Anna had built an independent life. She had been a true friend to Emmaline, Josefina and Adrian. But she had never let them get too close to her. Now, she needed someone to care where she was and what she was doing.

In the morning, Anna went before the judge to explain why a tiny woman, dressed as a man, would venture to a remote neighborhood called Essex in the middle of the night. She thought it would be easy, that she'd be set free immediately.

After telling the judge who she was, even showing him her newspaper credentials, she was stunned by his response. "The men you were arrested with last night claim you are the ringleader of their operation. That you forced them, under threat of violence, to do your bidding. That you're selling this liquor to bars and private citizens for profit."

"Then where is my weapon? Did your men find one? No! If this had been a covert operation, Your Honor, why would I have a camera instead of a gun? Just call *The Sun, Baltimore American, Baltimore Magazine, The Daily Record*, or *The Baltimore Afro-American*. Any one of them will vouch for me."

"Which newspaper sent you to Essex last night? And how did they know there would be a rumrunning rendezvous there? Why didn't they alert the authorities? It would have been their duty."

"None of those publications hired me. I was working on my own. I got a tip."

"From whom?"

"A journalist doesn't reveal sources. There is sanctity in our work."

"Not when it involves something illegal."

"I beg to differ... with all due respect, of course."

"Miss Bainbridge, why would you risk your life when you didn't even know if you would make a single dollar for your work?"

"I'm trying to build my reputation for being just as good as any man in my profession."

"Well, Miss Bainbridge. I'd like to teach you a lesson by locking you up, but I have no legal grounds on which to base it.

I'm going to let you go. I find no credible connection between you and the rumrunners, other than you were all at the same place at the same time. Earlier this morning, I contacted H.L. Mencken, a friend of mine, and he told me all about you. Young lady, do I need to remind you that you flirted with danger last night? The men you had planned to photograph are rough characters. We confiscated guns and knives from them last night. They would have killed you if authorities hadn't stepped in."

"I realize that, Your Honor. I will try to be more careful in the future."

"See that you are."

"Will I have a police record as a result of my arrest?"

"No, the charges against you have been dropped. You are free to go. You can pick up your camera and satchel at the desk. By the way, did you take any pictures last night?"

"No, Your Honor. I didn't have time. Would you have confiscated them?"

"The prosecution could have used them against the defense."

"I see."

"Tread lightly from now on. Will you promise me that?"

"Sir, I cannot. I'm a journalist. I told you I'd try."

Anna planned to write H.L. Mencken a letter of thanks but decided to call on him instead. She was ushered into his office immediately. He didn't bother to greet her. "Exactly what were you trying to do last night, Miss Bainbridge? Get yourself killed?"

"No, sir. I was trying to do my job. Would you ask a male reporter the same question?"

"The circumstances are different for a man. He can defend himself. You cannot."

"I bet I could."

"Would you like to return to the scene from last night and test that statement? What would have happened had the police not arrived?"

Anna thought a minute then shook her head. "I don't know."

"Your bravado exceeds your ability, Anna. It always has. You must contain yourself. I've told you this before. When are you going to listen? And posing as a man makes you more vulnerable, not more powerful. Someday, I fully expect to receive a call to identify your bullet-riddled body at the morgue."

"Those are harsh words."

"You deserve them. Think about it. No publication worth its salt in Baltimore wants to print a headline about one of its reporters, a woman no less, being killed during an assignment. You are building the wrong kind of reputation."

"I understand."

"That's always your response. I don't think you do."

"Then give me a good assignment, something with meat on its bones."

"I will not reward your irresponsibility. Good day."

Anna returned to the boardinghouse and slept until suppertime, when she joined the other residents and ate in silence. No one asked her where she had been or why she slept through the light of day.

Anna reverted to shooting architectural photography. City government hired her to document the building of Citizens National Bank on Light Street. It would surpass the Bromo Seltzer Tower as the tallest building in Baltimore. Every week, Anna took updated photographs as the building slowly dwarfed everything around it. The job wouldn't earn Anna accolades but it kept her out of trouble and somewhat employed.

Anna hadn't seen Emmaline in a while. Just as she was about to invite her to lunch, Emmaline contacted her and did the same. At Emmaline's apartment, they enjoyed a simple meal of sliced meats and cheeses from the market, along with a fresh citrus salad.

"What have you been up to, Emmaline? I haven't seen you in ages, not even at the *Afro-American*."

"We've just been missing each other, I guess. I've been quite busy, lately, outside the newspaper."

"Have you taken up a hobby? Or are you seeing someone?"

"Neither, really. I've been studying."

"What? Have you gone back to school? That's my dream for you."

"No, no, wait a minute. It's not like that."

"Then, what?"

"It might take a while to tell you."

"Go ahead."

"When I was a child, my Aunt Chidimma, on my mother's side, took me under her wing and taught me all the stories of my ancestors going back many generations. She made me memorize their birth dates and death dates and who married whom and begot whom. This is a tradition with my ancestors, the Igbo people of Nigeria, who didn't have a way of writing down their history, so it became an oral preservation."

"What does 'Chidimma' mean?"

"It's West African for 'God is good.'"

"That's beautiful."

"My aunt is a beautiful lady. I mean on the inside as well as outside. She is called 'Griot,' which means 'storyteller.' Every family has one person who keeps track of their lineage and hands it down to a trusted member of the next generation, usually their own child. Aunt Chidimma had three, though none survived beyond the age of six. With my mother's permission, she chose me."

"I dare to ask... were your family..."

"Slaves? Yes, in the early 1800s, at a place in Baltimore County called the Hampton Mansion. They tended the gardens. Backbreaking work."

"I'm sorry. I really am. How long have you been studying with your aunt?"

"Since I was around ten. It takes years to impart all the information and make sure the student remembers accurately and always, so that she can pass it to her children. Aunt Chidimma assumed I would have them."

"What will happen if you don't have children?"

"I will choose one of my nieces or younger sisters, just as she chose me."

"That makes you an important member of your family. You should be revered."

"I accept my position with humility and grace. I see my work akin to a religious calling."

"What more is there to study at this point? Shouldn't you know everything by now?"

"Yes, but I am rehearsing for a presentation."

"To your family?"

"No. Now that more colored children are being schooled, teachers are discovering that there aren't many books in the library about colored people. Stories like *Anne's House of Dreams* and *The Secret Garden* don't mean much to us. Most of the books with colored characters portray them as simple-minded and unmannered, lowly. That's not an accurate portrayal and not the image we want to linger in little minds. Usually, griots tell their family histories only to their own next generation. These days, in lieu of books, griots are visiting schools to share real family stories of struggle and overcoming adversity. To inspire all children."

"And that's what you are working toward?"

"Yes."

"Why didn't you tell me before?"

"I wanted to surprise you. See that instrument up against the wall?"

"Yes, what is it?"

"It's called 'ngoni.'" Emmaline went over to the corner of the room and picked it up. "It's a traditional West African musical instrument, often used to accompany a griot's stories. I'll play a little for you."

Emmaline plucked and spoke of her ancestors. To Anna, it was poetic, friendly and enchanting.

"That was beautiful, Emmaline. Your instrument is similar to a guitar, isn't it?"

"Yes, a much smaller one with fewer strings. There are other instruments, like a 'kora,' which sounds like a lute, and the 'balafon,' which is akin to a xylophone, except it's made of wood. Most griots know how to play one of these. I took up the ngoni, this one handed down from my Aunt Chidimma. It's three generations old."

"Why have I not noticed it before? Has it been sitting in the corner all this time?"

"No, my aunt keeps it. She gave it to me for rehearsing."

"Do you realize that this means you are a teacher?"

"No, just a storyteller."

"I beg to differ. You're a genuine teacher, far more important than the book-learning kind. I'm so proud of you. When will you make your presentation and where?"

"At the Bethel African Methodist Episcopal Church on Druid Hill Avenue. My family is not Methodist but I was invited anyway. The church elders want the children in the congregation to learn about griots and what they have to impart. I'm getting nervous. The date is coming up, a week from Wednesday night at 7:00 P.M."

"I'll be there. You know, this should be reported, with a photograph in the *Afro-American*. Have you told the editors?"

Emmaline shook her head.

"You are too humble. This must appear in the paper and I'm going to see that it does."

The rest of the conversation that day centered on Emmaline. Anna didn't even tell her friend about her brush with danger and the law. For once, Anna saw someone besides herself worthy of the spotlight.

At the appointed day and hour, Anna sat with Emmaline's family down in front at the church. She could get photographs from this position without disturbing the reverence of the moment. Congregants filled every seat, including the balcony that wound around the nave. Anna looked everywhere but could not find Emmaline. She certainly wasn't sitting with the officiants on the altar. There was a woman there, wearing a loose, flowy dress in a beautiful geometric pattern in browns, blues and cream. A matching headscarf sat high on her head, tied to the side. *That must be Aunt Chidimma*, Anna thought.

After praise singing and a brief sermon, the congregation settled in their seats as Emmaline was introduced. Anna searched for her friend in the crowd.

The woman in the native costume stood and gracefully walked to the center of the altar. She carried the ngoni. Anna nearly jumped out of her seat. It was Emmaline! Such poise and nobility in her appearance.

Emmaline started by telling the congregants what a ngoni was, as she played it softly. Sound emanated, deliberate yet gentle. Emmaline eased into the history of her family, her voice and music rising from soft to strong. She mesmerized the more than one thousand people there.

Anna had never seen her friend so sure of herself, so perfectly aligned with what she was meant to be. A single tear streaked Anna's face. She made no effort to wipe it away. It blessed her friendship with the young woman Anna admired and had come to know as a natural teacher. That night, Emmaline taught Anna quite a lot, not about dates and events. She taught her about life and dignity and presenting your best attributes to the world. Anna hadn't always succeeded in those areas, especially in her fight for acceptance in a man's profession.

After the service, Anna met Aunt Chidimma, who had been sitting in the balcony with friends. She took no measure of the spotlight. Anna understood that Emmaline had learned humility from this kindly, tiny woman.

When the evening ended, Anna hugged Emmaline and whispered in her ear, "I've never in my life been more proud to know another person."

"Thank you, Anna. For a moment there, I did feel like a teacher."

"You *are* a teacher, through and through."

The *Afro-American* ran Anna's story and photograph on the front page. To Anna, it was her best work.

CHAPTER 50

Suffragists inched closer to the day they had been fighting for, when the U.S. Constitution would be amended to allow women to legally cast a ballot, thereby having a voice in their country's future. In February, it came time for the Maryland legislature to vote on the 19th Amendment. One senator, John Walter Smith, said "yea." Another, Joseph France, said "nay." The final vote leaned toward rejection, not over women's right to vote, rather *colored* women's right to vote.

Still suppressing the colored male vote, legislators were not about to allow colored women the opportunity. Anna wrote Joseph France a letter of complaint, receiving no reply.

❧◦❧

Much to her surprise, Anna heard from Adrian after the winter thaw. Snowdrops, the first flower of spring, popped up, seemingly overnight. Adrian said that when he saw some in bloom in his neighborhood, he thought of her. She wasn't sure why. He invited her for a walk in Patterson Park, close to where he lived with his in-laws. Anna accepted.

Adrian brought along little Vicki in a pram. The air felt cool. The sky offered a clear view. The lake in the park glistened with hope. Floating in the air were Alfred Lord Tennyson's words, "In Spring, a young man's fancy lightly turns to thoughts of love."

The pair walked in silence for a while, with Adrian cooing over his daughter. "Isn't she the most beautiful child you ever saw?"

"I'm sure she is. I'm not the best of judges. I haven't been around that many babies."

Adrian laughed. "I wasn't being literal. It's what every parent says."

"Yes, of course. She's..." Anna paused, searching for an appropriate description. "... darling."

"That's just the word."

They walked in silence for a time.

"How have you been, Anna?"

"Fine, for the most part. Papa's been ill lately. He had influenza, you know."

"Oh, I didn't know."

"He's slow to recover. Are your in-laws well?"

"Yes, they rarely leave the house, just to shop for food. Josefina's father is retired now. As for me, I didn't have much work after I recovered. Not many people bought cookies. They stuck to necessities."

"I'd consider cookies a necessity."

Adrian laughed again. "I've returned to the Post Office, not delivering mail, like I used to. I'm a supervisor now. I acquired managerial skills while working for Berger's."

"Congratulations. That's..." Again, Anna struggled for a word. "... wonderful."

"I make enough money to support us all."

"Is Sam still working there?"

"Yes, he and Lillian have three children now. Two girls and a boy. You wouldn't recognize Lucy. They've moved to a bigger apartment, not far from me."

"That's nice. You can raise your children together."

"Yes, they're more like cousins than friends. We share holidays and Sunday dinner, sometimes."

Anna thought that if this conversation got any more awkward and boring, she'd have to find a way to cut their meeting short. Just as she was about to say something, Adrian blurted, "Anna, I'm a lonely man."

"Why, you have Vicki and your in-laws and Sam and..."

"I'm not talking about that kind of loneliness. I need female companionship."

"Josefina has not been gone that long. Aren't you supposed to observe at least a year of mourning?"

"It has been a year. It's not so much that I want a mother for Vicki. I want a wife for me."

"What are you saying?"

"Would you consider courting again?"

"Well, I... I certainly didn't expect this. I must think about it. I'm sure you remember how things went the last time. I'm more dedicated to my work now than ever."

Anna quickened her pace as though trying to escape. Adrian had to catch up as Anna continued her excuse. "Surely, there must be a woman who would suit you better. Have you given this proper thought? Maybe, this is just an effort to erase the pain of losing Josefina."

Adrian stopped walking. "Maybe it is. I guess it was wrong of me to ask."

Anna turned around and faced him. "I'm not turning you down. I said I would think about it."

"Don't you ever yearn for male companionship? Don't you think about love?"

"I'm just starting to. Not at the expense of my career, mind you. I love that, too."

"You wouldn't want to give it up?"

"No."

They walked again in silence. Vicki fussed when the sun got in her eyes. "Looks like somebody needs to be put down for a nap," Adrian said to his daughter. He turned to address Anna. "Do you want to hold her before she gets too cranky?"

"No," Anna said rather quickly. "I mean, she's unfamiliar with me. It might upset her more."

"Oh, of course. I want to thank you for being so frank. I was just hoping, well, hoping that we could work something out between us."

"I promise you I will give your request the consideration it deserves. After all that I put you through during the fire, I'm surprised you even want to be near me."

"I saw another side of you when Josefina and I suffered the loss of... well, you know. We couldn't have survived without your care and support. You kept us going. There is a soft side to you. I would like to get to know her better."

Anna didn't respond. She nodded and they parted ways, Adrian heading to the rowhouse he shared with Josefina's parents a few blocks away, and Anna to her car that offered her total freedom to come and go as she pleased.

ॐ◌

"What do you think, Emmaline?"

"I can't advise you on matters of the heart. Only you can decide."

"It all goes back to when we were first together. We had such a grand time, going to the movies, picnicking, enjoying rides at Electric Park, which closed five years ago, I'm sorry to say." Anna thought a second. "Maybe that should tell me something."

"Anna, you cannot base such an important decision on the fate of an amusement park. You need to reach deep in your soul for the answer. You sound as if you're on some kind of schedule. You don't have to respond to Adrian today, do you? Give it appropriate time and sober thought."

"I guess you're right. It's just that I'm so used to the fast pace of my career, it spills over into my private life."

"Relax. This is an important decision. Take your…"

"*Time!*" they said in unison.

When their giggling waned, Anna said to her friend, "Have you ever been courted?"

"Not really. I've never met anyone who truly interested me. I guess I'm too particular."

"Not everyone is meant to marry. There's no shame in that. You're living a fulfilling life all by yourself."

"Yes, sometimes I think that my younger brothers and sisters are my children. I have enough responsibility on my shoulders, trying to see them to adulthood. I really don't want to complicate things further."

"I understand completely. We're a lot alike, do you know that? Except my assignments are my children."

ॐ◌

It took Anna a couple of months to respond to Adrian's request. She asked to meet him by the pagoda in Patterson Park.

"Remember this place?" she said.

333

"I'll never forget it. This is where we first decided to court years ago. Let's climb to the top again and enjoy the view. It looks promising."

At the top of the winding pagoda stairs, they leaned on the railing and stared toward Fells Point. Adrian didn't push Anna into conversation.

After a few minutes, she spoke. "Can we just start slowly? Maybe have dinner, as friends, first. I'll even pay my portion of the meal. I read an editorial in the *Baltimore American* that referred to this sort of arrangement as a 'Dutch Treat.'"

"Where did that phrase come from?"

"I think it was first used by the Pennsylvania Dutch, who refused to be beholden to anyone. An actor-friend of mine, named Richard, told me that bartenders use the phrase to keep patrons from 'sticking friends with their bill,' as he put it. I wouldn't know personally."

Adrian laughed heartily. "I certainly hope not. All right, if it will make you feel better, we will dine 'Dutch Treat.' I have a new restaurant in mind. It just opened near your father's house on Saratoga. It's called Marconi's."

"I haven't heard of it. Let's give it a whirl."

Adrian laughed again. "Okay, let's give it a whirl," he shouted out over Patterson Park.

Two nights later, Anna worried over what to wear. She didn't want to appear romantic, even eager in her attire. She chose a plain black dress in the newer style. Her skirt was shorter, just to her shins, and bubbled around her hips. The top sported a deep purple ruffle down the center. Her jacket wasn't form-fitting but had a purple belt that accentuated Anna's waist. The same Tudor beret she often wore to the theater topped off her outfit. Looking in the mirror, she thought she had reached her goal of being nothing more than appropriate.

"You look lovely tonight," Adrian said, with a smile.

"Thank you." She would never have admitted that the outfit was brand new, except for the hat.

They had met at Marconi's, to keep their evening together neutral and private. Anna didn't want the boardinghouse ladies who knew Adrian to see what was going on. It would have been the talk of the house for days.

They found the restaurant in a townhouse, not unlike the one in which Anna was raised. It stood only a few blocks away. Inside, the place retained its original layout, thereby creating small dining rooms where the parlor, den, library and dining room would have been if it were still a home. It offered guests a quiet, intimate atmosphere, embraced in soft green walls and romantic lighting, which made Anna a little uncomfortable. They were escorted to a table near a white marble fireplace, the embers giving off a soothing, intimate glow.

As soon as they were seated, a tuxedo-clad waiter greeted them with menus and a smile. "Would you care for a non-alcoholic cocktail? I recommend the Prohibition Sour for the gentleman and the Minnehaha Maid for the lady."

"What are they?"

"The Sour contains a simple sugary syrup made with lemon and orange, fizzed with carbonated soda water. The Maid offers the same syrup mixed with cranberry and grape juices."

Anna looked at Adrian. Adrian looked at Anna. Both seemed hesitant.

Finally, Adrian spoke. "I think we'll just have tea."

"Very well, sir."

Anna perused the menu and saw such items as Lobster Cardinale, Oysters Pauline, and Spaghetti with Chicken Livers.

"Have you ever heard of these dishes?" she whispered. "And do you see this?" She pointed to her menu. "They're charging extra for ice in drinks, and bread, even butter. Look at the prices! I'm glad we're going Dutch Treat. I wouldn't want to eat your whole paycheck."

Adrian stifled a laugh. This was too fancy a place for levity. "It might be cheaper if you did eat my paycheck but it would be less satisfying."

"Good thing we didn't order those cocktails. They were probably expensive."

Adrian took a deep breath, paused then said, "Let's just enjoy ourselves, anyway. We deserve it."

"Have you decided?" the waiter asked, appearing seemingly out of nowhere.

Anna and Adrian looked at each other and silently agreed to throw caution to the wind. They chose the chopped salad, Oysters Pauline for Anna and lamb chops with creamed spinach for Adrian. They even ordered bread and butter, an extra charge on their bill.

Whether it was the crystal chandeliers that made their eyes glisten or the realization that it had been a long time since they treated themselves to something truly sumptuous, Anna and Adrian enjoyed their meals. They talked of happy things, of good weather and movies they wanted to see and music they wanted to hear. Adrian spoke of phonographs and vinyl records. Anna told Adrian how much she enjoyed hearing the Baltimore Symphony play at the Lyric. Was she hinting for a second date?

They smiled throughout dinner, which was delicious. Anna's Oysters Pauline contained plump, salty oysters, topped with lumps of lobster meat finished in a cream sauce. She had never eaten lobster before and found it sweet and tender. Adrian's lamb chops were mild and juicy, cooked to perfection. Even though Anna and Adrian were sated, they followed their meal with vanilla ice cream topped with Marconi's special chocolate sauce, which the waiter called "ganache."

The two felt no guilt when the bill arrived. They were happy to pay it. The evening represented a "coming out" of sorts, like a debutante's ball or a spring flower blooming. These two people in their thirties celebrated their survival from the pain of loss and unpredictable twists and turns of life.

Adrian, who really needed to watch his money, felt generous after such a good experience. He proffered a large tip to the waiter, who bowed his thanks.

"Well, we might never be able to afford such a feast here again but it was worth every penny," he said, once outside.

"And every bite. Much better than eating your paycheck."

Adrian smiled and took Anna's arm. "Shall we take a digestive walk?"

"That's a good idea. I feel like a lobster about to burst out of its shell." She pretended her hands were pinching claws.

Adrian didn't hold back his laughter this time.

When they arrived at the end of the block, his face turned serious. They stopped and stared at the entrance to St. Alphonsus Church. This was where Anna had jilted Adrian at the altar. The Great Baltimore Fire of 1904 had just flared up blocks away. Anna fled the church and raced to document the blaze with her Brownie Box Camera. She had dreamed of becoming a newspaper photographer and snatched the chance at the expense of love. After two days of taking pictures, she resurfaced, much to the relief of Papa, Elizabeth and Adrian, who forgave her selfish, immature actions.

"I'm sorry for all the pain and embarrassment I caused you. It was thoughtless and careless and irreverent to the sanctity of marriage. And you hurt your leg trying to find me during the fire. I'm the one who should have gotten injured."

"My leg healed just fine. I will admit, my heart did not."

"Yet, you are trying once more. Aren't you the least bit skeptical?"

"Sixteen years have passed since that day. And we've each gone through many ups and downs. We survived. And I think we both know what we might be getting into now. I think we will take time to figure things out before we rush to the altar, if we make it there at all. For now, you bring me happiness, something I never thought would return after Josefina died. This evening has been such fun."

Anna held back tears. The two continued walking around the block, passing the Central Library and the oldest basilica in the United States. They found themselves, once again, in front of Marconi's, where Anna had parked her car.

"How did you get here tonight?"

"I took the trolley."

"Let me drive you home. Your in-laws won't be upset to see us, will they?"

"I only told them I was having dinner with a friend. Maybe you should drop me off a block or so away. I'm not sure they're ready for this yet."

As they ambled through light traffic, they fell into a silence that marked the end of their evening together. When they arrived in Highlandtown, Adrian said, "I must hand it to you. You're a real 'go getter,' as young people are starting to call each other."

"We're not that old. But, yes, I fit the description. This car gives me complete access to just about anywhere. You know, the government is starting to build what they're calling 'interstate highways.' Soon people will be able to drive from one state to another without worrying about getting stuck in mud or lost on back roads. The trip will go so much faster. Don't you think that's exciting?"

"Yes, it is. I'm afraid I haven't the funds to buy a car just yet. I did learn how to drive, though, when I worked for Berger's."

"This one is used, but worth the expense in gas and maintenance. I need it for my work. It takes me to assignments I never would have been able to accept. And it's saved me from..."

"From what?"

"Well, from danger, a few times."

"Oh, I can't bear the thought of you risking your life again for a picture."

"See, this is why I was hesitant about tonight. I cannot change who I am."

"Then I will have to learn that I'm in the presence of a woman who is the 'bee's knees.'"

"And just what does that mean?"

"Anna, if you want to keep up with me, you'll have to learn the new language of young people. I think they are called 'Flappers.'"

Now, it was Anna's turn to laugh heartily.

They parted amicably, with no touch of the hand or cheek. Adrian made a joke about needing another three months to save his money or, perhaps, going to the bank to take out a loan for their next encounter.

"Well, in that case, we can't go 'Dutch Treat,' because banks do not allow women to acquire loans."

"Then we'll be eating at the hot dog stand."

"I'll have mine with mustard and onions. On second thought, hold the onions."

Anna and Adrian decided to continue their journey down a slow, easy-going path in their courtship, the kind that meandered through a park with a pagoda, offering a promising view.

CHAPTER 51

Much to Anna's surprise and delight, the 19th Amendment finally made history, becoming ingrained in the U.S. Constitution in August. Anna rejoiced, knowing that American women would be able to vote for the first time in just a few months, though a dark cloud of legal wrangling threatened.

In September, Judge Oscar Leser of Baltimore contested the validity of the woman's vote. He sued the state, demanding that two specific Baltimore women be stricken from the list of registered voters, choosing them to represent all women. His grounds remained firmly stuck in the belief that only men should vote. And, since the state of Maryland had not ratified the 19th Amendment, its women should be denied suffrage. This was a court case that would not be heard prior to the election. For now, Maryland women were allowed to register and cast their ballots. This effort to suppress put fear in Maryland women that their journey had not yet reached the Promised Land.

Anna wouldn't be completely satisfied until she knew that all women, including colored, like Emmaline, would be right there with her.

It didn't look good.

All over the country, voting rights were left to individual states to enact. There was no effective, universal oversight of the process. Some state governments imposed poll taxes and literacy tests on colored women, just as they had colored men. In states inhabited by Indian tribes, there was blanket refusal of the vote, since Indians were not considered American citizens to begin with. Other ethnic people found nothing but rejection.

Anna and Emmaline defied the odds and registered together. Understanding the sanctity of the moment, they did not discuss candidates and affiliations. Being able to choose the fate of their nation in a private vote was too precious a commodity. The only commitment they made to each other was to cast their first vote at the same time.

On November 2nd, Anna and Emmaline met on the street at an appointed hour and walked to the polling place, carrying their voter registration cards. Both wore white. As they stood in line, Anna beheld her cardboard declaration of equality, reading a summary of her very being. Name, address, occupation, age, date of registration, party affiliation and official signatures.

"Are you excited, Emmaline? I'm overcome with just about every positive emotion you can name."

"I'm thinking about what a big step this is for colored people everywhere. I'm humbled by the thought that my vote will count for something."

"We're both lucky to be alive today, lucky to carry the mantel so many women fought for and passed to us. It's just you and me standing here, yet I feel there are hundreds... no, thousands of women surrounding us in spirit."

"Let's hope our votes help preserve democracy, not for a chosen few, but for all Americans."

"*Next!*"

Anna and Emmaline jumped to attention. They had moved to the front of the line, without realizing it.

"You go first, Emmaline. You deserve it."

Emmaline smiled demurely and stepped forward.

All over America, as women pulled levers on voting machines, they experienced a new freedom and responsibility. And what they did first was vote out politicians who had not supported suffrage.

The moment was joyous and somber. Anna and Emmaline knew that voter suppression kept many women and men from expressing their citizenship.

After they voted, Anna took pictures of all the women lined up outside, just as excited and eager as she was. Some cried into handkerchiefs, others explained to their young daughters the importance of the moment. Anna's momentous images would appear in *Maryland Suffrage News*.

Later in the morning, Anna picked up Elizabeth and Emmaline's mother in her car and saw that they voted, too.

"I never thought I'd live to see the day," said Emma. "I thank the Lord."

"Amen," said Elizabeth.

This was the first time the two women met. They fell into the comfort of each other's company with ease.

"Why don't the four of us have lunch?" Anna asked, after all was said and done.

"Oh, I'm not dressed for nothin' fancy," said Emma.

"You look fine, Mama," said Emmaline.

"I have your father's meal to make."

"He can manage, Mama. Come with us."

"Are you forgettin' that we can't share a table in restaurants?"

Elizabeth came up with a solution that pleased everyone. "I have a leftover roast in the ice box. I can make beef sandwiches and a simple harvest salad."

"That sounds perfect," Anna said.

The four women worked together to whip up a tasty lunch and sat at the small table by the kitchen window to eat. They became so giddy with the realization that they had just voted, Papa would have thought them tipsy if he'd been there.

"Your home is lovely," Emma said.

"It's not very welcoming," replied Anna. "Through no fault of Elizabeth," she corrected herself. "I mean, with all this fancy stuff no one can touch. I like your house, Miss Emma. Whenever I'm there, I relax."

"Thank you. I don't think we own nothing that can break. Otherwise, with my family, it woulda been swept in the ash can a long time ago."

The four women laughed. It must have been getting to vote that opened Emma up. She spoke freely of her growing-up years, and Aunt Chidimma, and her husband's health, and her children's successes, especially when it came to Emmaline. "My daughter has done me proud. Not only because she got her education and a good job. And not because she took up learnin' griot. It's because she walks with the Lord. She's a fine young lady, a lovin' soul, charitable to the core. She's good to her family. She even took me to get registered to vote. Without her, I wouldn't be here with y'all today."

Anna raised her teacup. "To Emmaline!"

Elizabeth made several sandwiches for Emma to take home to her family. The four women hugged one another and parted with the promise they would get together again soon. They didn't realize it would be under completely different circumstances.

That night, as Anna lay her head on the pillow, a sigh of relief turned to tears for all the women who sacrificed home and hearth and endured every abuse to bring about suffrage for women, going all the way back to Margaret Brent, who dared to stand before the Maryland Assembly, asking for the right to vote in 1647. And Susan B. Anthony, sounding the cry until the day she died at age 86, even after getting arrested. And Inez Milholland, her hair flowing, riding astride that white charger in the big New York parade. Anna cried for her mother, too, a woman who held fast to the reins of Victorian decorum. Would she have ever loosened her hold and embraced suffrage? Would she have shared the joy and pride and, yes, humility, surging through her daughter's veins at this moment? Would she have approved of her daughter's lifestyle at all?

Anna cried herself to sleep, just as a waft of rose water passed through the room and dissipated over her bed.

⁚⁚

Anna had never given much thought to football. It seemed a silly sport. A bunch of grown men running into each other, knocking heads and getting muddy. She preferred baseball. Less filthy, more fun. Adrian hinted that he wanted to go to a high school matchup on the gridiron, pitting Calvert Hall against Loyola High School. One was run by Christian Brothers, the other, Jesuits.

"They've built up quite the rivalry," said Adrian. "Many schools have. The games are fun to watch and so are the fans in the stands, waving banners, cheering their team on, yelling and jumping up and down, acting in ways they never would at home."

"Sounds like you've already been."

"Oh, yes. Sam and I went to the so-called 'City-Poly' game one year, that's Baltimore City College and Baltimore Polytechnic Institute. We had a grand time."

"Why don't you go with him again?"

"With three children now, he has to pinch his pennies. Aren't you interested? I thought you liked lots of activity."

"I do. I just never had an interest in football. I like going to the Orioles' games."

"Well, their season is over. Why don't you go with me? Even if you don't like the game, I bet you'll enjoy watching the cheering sections. This rivalry usually draws over a thousand people. I'll buy you a hot dog. Mustard and onions?"

Anna couldn't deny Adrian a good time. He needed it.

"All right. You buy the tickets and hot dogs. I'll drive."

"Sounds like a marriage made in heaven. Oh, excuse me. I didn't mean..."

"I know what you meant."

Anna had no idea what to expect at the game. She wore a simple dress with a light wool jacket and scarf. The sun felt warm, while the air had a snap to it, like a cracked horse whip.

After they sat in the stands, Adrian disappeared for a few minutes. He returned, juggling two hot dogs and two colas.

"As promised," he said.

"Thank you. Which side are you rooting for?"

"It doesn't matter to me. I just want to see a good, competitive game and watch your face light up."

"I don't really understand football. You'll have to explain the rules to me."

Over the next two hours, Adrian filled Anna in on the strategies, positions and point system. By the third quarter, long after her hot dog had been digested, Anna stood and cheered touchdowns and tackles alike. Her voice carried over the crowd. Most of the other ladies in attendance, although few, remained seated and fluttered banners as if waving to a friend. It was the men who went wild.

"That was a grand time," Anna said, when the game was over.

"I thought you'd enjoy it. Maybe next time we can go to a Baltimore Colts game. It's even rougher."

"That would be fun."

"I enjoyed watching you more than the game. You're so full of life."

"I don't get many opportunities like this."

"Neither do I. Well, we can remedy that. Let's enter into a formal courtship. I will ask your father."

"Adrian, I still think it's too soon. Can't we go on as we have been? Just seeing each other every now and again?"

"I can't force your hand. I'll try to be patient. When... *if* you are ready, I'll be waiting."

"It could be quite a while."

"Then it will be quite a while."

As they drove home, Anna brought up the subject of suffrage. "How do you feel about women voting in this past election?"

"I'm truly happy for them. My own Josefina... is it all right to speak of her?"

"Yes, of course. We both loved her."

"My own Josefina spoke of it often. She and her mother would get into tiffs about it. Her mother thought it too unladylike. She often said that women were stepping out of their bounds, upsetting the natural order. It went against their God-given nature to support their husbands' opinions and decisions. She thought voting women undermined their husbands' authority as head of the household."

"I'm glad you don't feel the same way. Getting the right to vote is important to me."

"I know how hard you worked for the cause. Now what?"

"What do you mean?"

"What will women do next? Is there some new plan?"

"I really don't know. I think for now we're still celebrating this milestone. I've heard that women who belonged to the various suffrage organizations are thinking of forming another, larger group. They want to make sure every eligible woman registers to vote. They'll help them fill out the forms, even drive them to the registration offices. And instill in each woman the importance of voting. It's paramount that these women understand that they don't have to tell their husbands who they're voting for. And..."

"Okay, okay. I see I've lit a fire. I've learned it doesn't take much."

"I'm sorry. I guess I got carried away."

"You are a passionate woman, Anna Bainbridge."

"Yes, I am." Anna got quiet for a few moments. She looked Adrian straight in the eyes with full intent. "I couldn't be more different from Josefina. I'm outspoken, always eager, sometimes unmannerly. Josefina was such a lady."

"Don't you think I know you? I admire your strength and determination. I'm not looking for a carbon copy of my wife. I'm looking for a new life, one that doesn't remind me of what I lost."

CHAPTER 52

Just as joy awakens the spirit, loss destroys it. Adrian had experienced it already. Now it was Anna's turn.

Elizabeth called. "Anna, your father is back in a hospital bed. It's his heart again. I think you better come quickly. I'm already here."

Anna hurried to her father's bedside. The nurse, adjusting his covers, nodded and offered a sympathetic smile.

"Papa, it's me. I'm here to make you feel better."

He opened his eyes and looked into Anna's, which were holding back tears. "Dear child, I don't think that is possible this time."

"Yes, it is. It must be."

"I'm a doctor. I know what's coming soon."

"No."

"There isn't much time left. I want to tell you about your mother. Will you listen?"

"Yes, I've been waiting so long."

Anna settled into a chair and held her father's hand. He spoke through labored breathing.

"She was the most beautiful woman I had ever seen, her features perfectly aligned. You will find a small, framed photograph of her in my desk drawer at home. She exuded grace and decorum just at a time when women were starting to break out of the Victorian mold. They went against just about everything a mother raised her daughter to be. They were opinionated, flirtatious, bold. Many wanted to work for pay, when it wasn't necessary to the family's welfare. Others begged for higher education. To what end?"

"Yes, I know about them. Didn't you want to see women become doctors and scientists and business leaders?"

"No, I always thought a woman's place was in the home. And, then there was the suffrage movement, women marching in the streets, holding signs, shouting, being arrested. Some of them rode bicycles to these protests."

"I rode a bicycle to my assignments."

"I found it unseemly and disgraceful, I must now admit. A woman straddling... I can't say it. They could become unable to bear children."

"I know what you're trying to say. Did their desire to vote also go against your way of thinking?"

"Yes. What kind of disruption could befall a family if the husband voted Republican and the wife Democrat?"

"I voted a few weeks ago."

"I assumed you did."

"There was nothing wrong with it."

"I know that now. Back then, when I was a young man, I wanted to marry the Victorian ideal. A woman who was more like a porcelain doll, a doctor's wife, who would host dinners and stand by my side and forgive my long hours at the hospital."

"How did you meet Mama?"

"It was an arranged courtship between my mother and her father. They knew each other from church. My mother used to wash and iron the altar linens at St. Alphonsus as a form of self-sacrifice. My future father-in-law served as an usher. They'd talk before Mass."

"Was Mama the ideal wife?"

"In every way."

"Then, when I came along, neither of you could control me."

"Yes, almost from the beginning. You were a fussy baby."

"Did Mama try to tame me?"

"She didn't know what to do with you. That's why we hired Elizabeth eventually. Your mother was quite delicate."

"Was she ill?"

"No, just raised to behave in a refined and elegant manner. She couldn't do that with you throwing temper tantrums."

"I'm afraid to ask this... did Mama not love me?"

"Oh, she adored you. Coddled you, stared at you as you slept. She and I simply didn't know how to raise a headstrong child."

"Did you argue over it?"

"We discussed it, not argued. We didn't always agree. I preferred a heavy hand. She thought patience and a soft touch would help."

"I guess I wasn't what either of you wanted in a daughter."

"I thought that for a long time, Anna. I was wrong."

"Wrong?"

"Yes. Times have changed for women, not always for the better, but sometimes."

"In what ways?"

"I've worked with a few female doctors in the last year or so and they have been quite good. In addition to their medical know-how, they exhibit a kind of compassion that men rarely show. Patients take to them and recover more quickly, it seems. It could be just my imagination."

"And what about me? Are you displeased with the way I've chosen to live?"

"At first, I was. More so out of embarrassment than worry. I thought too much about my own reputation. I also didn't want you to suffer prejudice, name-calling or suppression. People can be cruel when change threatens their status quo."

Papa paused and attempted to take a deep breath. It came out a mild sigh.

"Anna, my dear child, I am proud of you and everything you have accomplished."

"Papa..."

"Let me finish. I haven't much time. I admire your tenacity and courage, even when you were standing up to me. You are your own woman, not an unrealistic ideal. You are Anna Bainbridge, and I love you."

Anna threw herself at her father, careful not to weigh too heavily on him. "Papa, I love you, too."

"Let him sleep now," Elizabeth said.

"Have you been standing there all this time?"

"No, I just heard the last sentence."

Elizabeth guided Anna out of the room, so the nurse could administer medicine to Dr. Bainbridge.

"He does love me, Elizabeth. He said so himself."

"He knows you love him, too. Now, come along."

The nurse came out of the room. "He's growing weaker."

"Can I stay here with him? I'll be quiet."

"Why don't you get some tea? Let him rest."

Anna started to cry. Elizabeth helped her to a chair.

"I can't believe it. Papa's going to die. I'm not ready for this."

"No one ever is."

"You warned me. You warned me when Papa had his first heart attack. I didn't take heed. Now it seems so sudden. I feel lost already."

"I'm here for you. I won't leave your side."

Anna didn't have time to contact Emmaline or Adrian to lean on. Papa's condition deteriorated rapidly. A few hours later, the nurse called Anna and Elizabeth to his bed.

"Any time now," she said.

A hospital chaplain joined them, offering the Last Rites. Papa slipped away with Anna holding one of his hands and Elizabeth the other. All she said to Anna was, "I loved him, too."

Anna, Elizabeth, Emmaline, and Emma came together once again, at the funeral held at St. Alphonsus Church. Adrian offered a quick prayer, then left for work. He was not given a bereavement excuse from the Post Office. As large as the church was, every pew was filled, mostly with hospital staff and Papa's former patients. Many spoke to Anna and offered their condolences.

The four women stood in the vestibule as the casket was removed from the church. One of the doctors addressed Anna. "Isn't it nice that your help came to pay their respects?"

Anna realized this man was referring to Emmaline and her mother. He stared straight at them.

"They are not the help. They are my dear friends," Anna said.

"Oh, pardon me," the man said, with an inflection that lacked sincerity. He quickly walked away.

"I'm sorry for that," Anna said.

"We're used to it," Emma replied.

"You shouldn't be. You never should be."

⌘

A few days later, Elizabeth invited Anna to tea.

"Come in, my dear. I've made cream of chicken soup to warm your body."

"How are you feeling, Elizabeth?"

"It's odd. When your father was alive, he was rarely here, always at the hospital. Now that he's gone, I feel his presence constantly."

The two ate in silence, the trappings of privileged living having lost any ability to soothe.

"Elizabeth, may I ask you a personal question?"

"I guess so. What is it?"

"In the hospital, when you said you loved Papa, too, what did you mean?"

"I was with your father a long time, just about all of my adult life. I sacrificed my own desires to raise you and serve him. Your father could be a difficult man, but I came to understand him. He lived in a time of great transition for women and advances in medicine. He was dedicated to saving lives at the hospital and preserving the old ways at home. I didn't always agree with him. All I could offer was understanding. And isn't that what we all need and want, just as much as love? To be understood?"

"Did he bother to understand you?"

"Not really. Or, maybe in his own way. He always paid me fairly and provided me with a home to care for... and a feisty, handful-of-a-child to raise."

"I'm sorry for all the trouble I caused you. I know Papa often took out his displeasure with me on you."

"I've always admired your spirit, Anna."

"Thank you." Anna tasted her soup and dabbed her lips. "You know I've seen you as my mother all these years."

"It's been the greatest joy in my life."

"Did you really love Papa, I mean in a romantic way?"

"I guess I did. I always kept that to myself."

"I hope he felt it."

"I do, too. Finish your soup. I've made a sponge cake with chocolate sauce for dessert."

"Oh, let me tell you about the chocolate sauce at a restaurant I went to, right down the street."

The two women continued to talk of happier moments. Anna revealed that she was seeing Adrian sometimes, just as friends for now.

"Anna, what are your plans for this house?"

"I haven't given it a single thought."

"I need to know. I assume you'll sell it. I want to make other arrangements before it's too late."

"Elizabeth, this is your home."

"But I'm the only one living in it. This house, and all it holds, will bring you a pretty penny. You would be set for life and could take only the photography jobs you really want."

"Where would you go?"

"I'm getting on in years now. I'm in my fifties. The house is becoming too much for me. Any house might be too much for me. I guess I'll move into an old folks' home. There are a few of them around. I have a friend named Henrietta, who has invited me to stay with her. Perhaps I'll take her up on the offer. She lives several miles north, in Hampden."

"I can't imagine you anywhere but here. It's as if you are dying, too."

"Oh, don't say that. I still have some life left in me."

"Maybe you could live in my boardinghouse. There's a vacancy. Finally, after all these years, Jane Catherine is getting married. To a much older man with lots of money. He must be her father's age. She's the only resident left from when I first moved in."

"I don't know. I've saved a bit of money over the years. I've always wanted to take an ocean liner to Europe. Maybe I'll do that."

"Not without me!"

"We'll see. Think about what you want to do with the house, and I'll add it to my list of possibilities."

CHAPTER 53

Anna decided to keep the house but sell its contents. She wanted to shed all pretense and provide a comfortable place for her nanny to call home.

"Elizabeth, I'm going to live here with you. I've drawn up plans to extend your living quarters to include Papa's former office and library. This will be your home for as long as you wish. We'll furnish it in a more relaxed, welcoming style. And you won't have to lift a finger. I'll hire a new housekeeper and cook."

"You are sweet. I enjoy cooking. I would like to continue."

"If you really want to. Maybe you'll teach me a thing or two."

"I'd be delighted."

Whether it was the loss of Papa or colder weather, Anna sought comfort in Adrian's company. They attended a Baltimore Colts game, took in a show at Vagabond Players, and enjoyed walks in Patterson Park with Vicki in her pram.

Anna had a difficult time warming up to the child. Not because she was Josefina's daughter but because Anna didn't know how to communicate with someone who couldn't respond in a rational way. Baby talk confused her. Yet she felt an affinity for Vicki because they shared the early loss of their mothers.

Anna and Adrian packed up Papa's medical books and papers and donated them to the hospital. As the household furniture, art and gilded mirrors disappeared, they saw how large the house really was.

"This is an expansive place for just you and Elizabeth," Adrian said. "You could turn it into a boardinghouse."

"No, thank you. I've had enough of that. As soon as we refurnish this the way I would like, I'll be leaving Mrs. Pendleton and boardinghouse living. I think it's time I treated myself to something grander than a basement room near the boiler."

Anna and Elizabeth chose certain items of sentimental value to keep. While Elizabeth made refreshments in the kitchen, Anna and Adrian inspected the now-empty rooms.

"Have you seen the new style in furniture?" Anna asked.

"Do you mean Art Deco?"

"Yes, what do you think of it?"

"I like it just fine. It's functional and artistic, kind of fun. There's humor in some of the designs. I like that."

"I do, too."

"I can see a couple of fan-back chairs over there, with a small game table between them for playing checkers or dominoes."

"Or poker."

"What?"

"It's a card game, Adrian."

"Oh yes, played by saloon men who'd shoot each other over cheating. You know about that?"

"I learned it backstage at Ford's Theatre when I used to take production pictures there. Actors have a lot of time on their hands, so they often play cards."

"Anna, you are full of surprises."

"I'll teach you the game. And over here a sofa would go nicely with one of those new 'coffee tables' in front of it."

"And a phonograph would fit just right in that corner. And a cabinet for collecting records. I have a big stack."

"I think the chairs should be mint green with dark green drapes behind them."

"What color should we make the rug? I like..." Adrian stopped, looking embarrassed.

"Look at us," Anna said. "Playing house, pretending this will be ours."

"I wish this were real. I don't care where we live or what kind of furniture we have. I just want to be with you, permanently."

"But what about..."

"No what-abouts, Anna. If we truly commit to love each other, all of the wrinkles can be smoothed over time. I want you in my life every day. I need you. We can work around your career. My only question to you is... can you find it in your heart to love little Vicki as your own? I know you need time to decide such an important step as marriage and motherhood. That shows me you have matured. Last time, you were swept off your feet and didn't think things through."

"Adrian, I won't take long. I will give you my answer by Christmas."

ଶ∞ୡ

Anna spent the next few days thinking long and hard. She spoke with Elizabeth, the only living person who knew Anna's heart. She called on Emmaline's level-headedness and took long walks to clear her own mind. She even went to St. Alphonsus Church to pray for guidance. One day, she found herself at Mama's resting place, next to her father's grave. The sight of her parents, side by side, took Anna's breath away. She took a deep breath to recover.

There was that smell of roses again. It wafted around Anna like a mother's embrace and put her mind at ease. By the time she left Green Mount Cemetery, her decision felt firmly embedded in her heart.

Anna arranged a meeting with Adrian on Christmas Eve to give him her answer.

On the appointed day and time, Anna didn't show up.

Just as she was about to leave the boardinghouse, she spotted a note in her mail slot.

"Where did this come from?" she asked Mrs. Pendleton.

"It was in the regular mail delivery. Is something wrong?"

"No, it's just that I don't recognize the handwriting. I have a bad feeling about it, and I don't know why. How long has it been in my box?"

"A few days. You know how remiss you are to check it regularly."

Anna opened the envelope, which contained a cryptic note:

WATCH YOUR FOOTING.
PAY ATTENTION TO THE SHADOWS.

"Bad news, Anna? Are you stricken? You've turned pale."
"I'm quite frightened. Look."

355

"Oh, dear. This is a threatening note. You must turn it over to the police immediately. Have you made any enemies recently?"

"No. Unless, of course... well."

"Well, what?"

"Perhaps this is from someone who didn't like a story I wrote about them."

"Who would that be?"

"I don't know."

"You must take this note to the police station right now. I don't want you calling them here to the boardinghouse. It would be bad for business."

"I have an appointment I must honor first."

"If I were you, I wouldn't waste a single minute. Go now."

"I guess you're right, Mrs. Pendleton."

Once again, Anna would leave Adrian waiting and wondering.

She stepped out of the boardinghouse warily, with every intention of going to the police. Her car was parked a block away. She never got to put the key in the ignition because a man came up behind her, grabbed her by the arm and said, "Don't scream or try to get away from me, or your gentleman friend and his little daughter will pay." The man put his hand on Anna's camera. She released her grasp immediately.

"Dear God."

The man pushed Anna into another car, blindfolded her and signaled to the driver to go. When the car came to a stop, some forty-five minutes later, it was inside a building. Anna was taken to a room, where her blindfold remained. She heard the sound of someone tapping a table or desk in an agitated manner, followed by the noise of weight resting in a squeaky chair. A man cleared his throat.

Anna spoke first. "Who are you and what do you want with me? I demand to be released immediately."

"I was told you were a plucky little thing. Don't think for a minute you can out-fox me. I'm the wily one. I got you here, didn't I?"

"I am late for an appointment. People will report my disappearance."

"I won't keep you long."

"You won't keep me at all." Anna stood and started to take off her blindfold. She heard fingers snap. She froze. The door opened and Anna discerned the click of a gun being readied to fire.

The man behind the desk remained seated and said, "Care to rethink that decision, Miss Bainbridge?"

"How do you know me? I don't recognize your voice."

"Oh, I'm quite familiar with you, through my paid eyes and ears. They're everywhere. I know where you live and eat. I know about your gentleman caller and your colored friends and that other woman. What's her name? Oh, yes... Elizabeth. It would be a shame if something tragic happened to her."

"How dare you..."

"I wouldn't hurt them, unless, of course..."

"What are you saying? Get to the point."

"I like the way you think, Miss Bainbridge. Too bad you aren't on our side."

"What side? What are you talking about?"

"You cost me a lot of money, young lady, and I would like to be reimbursed. You see, I'm in the rumrunning business. A big shipment from the islands never made it to my clients and, therefore, I didn't make any money on its sale. That failure not only hurt my bank account, it damaged my reputation. A man is his reputation, wouldn't you agree?"

"What does that have to do with me?"

"You interrupted the most lucrative shipment of my career."

"Rumrunning is not a career. It's illegal."

"Nonetheless, you brought the police with you and even tried to take pictures of our little 'exchange' from boat to shore."

"I didn't bring the police. I was just as surprised as you. I was there to shoot pictures to sell to newspapers. If you know so much, then you know I was arrested, too, and spent the night in jail."

"That arrest was just for cover. You were released the next day, weren't you?"

"Yes, because they had no evidence against me. I was simply a photojournalist on the job."

"How did you know my associates were going to be there that night?"

"A journalist never reveals sources."

"Even with a gun pointed at her back?"

"I didn't reveal my source to the police and I will not reveal my source to you either."

"You are a brave little girl, though foolish, if you think I'll let you go without getting the information I want. At first, I thought it impossible that you were a newspaper photographer. Women don't work in that profession. But now, I see how tough you are. I believe your story, but I still want to know your source. Who tipped you off on our shipment?"

Anna stood rigid and remained silent.

"Miss Bainbridge, you are wasting my valuable time. Do you know what methods I can use to get you to talk?"

Anna stood rigid and remained silent.

"Right now, that child... what is her name? Oh yes, Vicki, is being pushed in a pram by her grandmother in Patterson Park. The child could easily be snatched in the crowd. The nearby lake is deep."

Anna took a step forward. "No! You can't! They're innocent."

"And you are not. There's a couch to your right. Find your way over to it and sit down. I will leave the room. In ten minutes' time, I will return. You will either reveal your source or my friend guarding the door will take care of you and later, that child. Do you understand?"

Anna nodded and did as she was told.

"Back to your post," the man said to the guard, as he closed the door behind them both.

When Anna heard the lock click, she took a risk that could have been life-threatening, not just for her but for Vicki. Anna removed her blindfold and looked around the room for an escape. There were no windows or doors other than the one guarded by the clodpoll.

There must be a secret passage. Her captor would never allow himself to be cornered by police or an enemy. She started pushing on wall panels, lifting the rug in search of a trap door. With minutes to spare, she found a door behind a full-length mirror, pushed on it and found herself in complete darkness. She closed it from behind to seal her escape, then fumbled, feeling her way with her hands on the walls and feet testing the floor. She came upon a flight of descending stairs, testing each step with her toe. Near the bottom a thin shaft of light underlined a door. Cold air raced up her legs. This door led outside! Anna could see the moving shadows of feet in that narrow strip of sunshine. Was another clodpoll guarding this exit?

Overhead, Anna heard a ruckus. Men scurrying, shouting obscenities, people being knocked against walls and finally, gunfire. The shadows under the door disappeared.

Anna froze and stayed put. She heard angry voices near the mirrored door. A bright light filled the darkness. The door had been opened.

"Police! You're surrounded. Nobody move."

Anna did as she was told. Within seconds, a flashlight found her face.

"Don't kill me, please," she said.

"Not you again," a man's voice said.

"I beg your pardon? Who are you? I can't see with the light in my eyes."

"Oh, we've met before. You look different in a dress but I'd know you anywhere. Remember? In the bushes, on the beach, in Essex. I arrested you then and I'm going to arrest you now. Keep those hands up. I knew you were part of their gang. You sweet-talked the judge into letting you go."

"No, you don't understand. I'm not with them, Officer, ah, Thompson, is that right?"

"Yes, then why were you trying to leave just now and how did you know there was an escape door?"

"I was brought here against my will. They sought revenge on what happened in Essex. I was trying to break free."

"I don't believe you and neither will the judge. I still don't understand why he let you go the first time. I caught you practically red-handed. But this, this could not be mere coincidence again."

"Listen to me. These rumrunners thought I was part of your plan. You thought I was part of their plan. When, all along, I was just trying to take pictures."

"Where is your camera now?"

"They wrenched it from my hands when they snatched me off the street. It must be upstairs somewhere. And so is a blindfold. I took if off myself and dropped it on the floor."

"Come with me, slowly, with your hands up. I don't trust you."

Anna emerged into the office where police and men in suits were rummaging through drawers and searching for secret hiding places.

"Well, it seems you came in the nick of time, once again," Anna said. "See, there's my blindfold by the couch."

"Don't play innocent with me again. We're taking you in as an accomplice."

"Please, let me find my camera first. It's my prized possession."

"It's ours, too. Crime evidence."

"You won't find any pictures. I just put a new roll of film in this morning. I was going to meet my... oh, dear God, I did it again! Look, I'll explain everything tomorrow. I'll come to the station and straighten all this out. But I'm late to meet my fiancé, well soon-to-be fiancé, if he'll have me."

"I can't imagine why he would," Officer Thompson said.

Anna ignored the slight. "You have to let me go."

"Not a chance, sister."

When they arrived at the police station, Anna had to go before the desk sergeant on the east side of Baltimore to tell her story.

"Would your fiancé be a man named, let me see here, it's somewhere on my desk, oh, here it is... Adrian Crosby?"

"Yes! How did you know?"

"Central Division put out a bulletin on a missing person by the name of Anna Bainbridge. It seems this man made a report after you failed to show up for a meeting with him."

"Yes, I was supposed to tell him my answer, that I would marry him. He'll be so happy."

"The guy must be crazy."

"Did you say something, Thompson?" the sergeant asked.

"No, sir."

"Then contact Central and tell them we have the girl here. I think we can straighten this out in short order. She doesn't appear to be part of a gang smuggling rum from the islands."

"Horsefeathers," said the officer under his breath.

"Did you say something, Thompson?" Anna asked.

"No, ma'am."

❧⚛︎

In mid-January, 1921, on a date that held no sentimental value, Anna and Adrian exchanged vows before a handful of people at St. Alphonsus, including Elizabeth, Emmaline, and Emma. Emmaline's father was too ill. Mrs. Pendleton was there, too. Adrian's in-laws did not attend.

"Adrian, I am sorry that Josefina's parents disapprove," Anna said.

"They think it's too soon, that it denigrates their daughter's memory. It does not."

"Adrian, you are the most sincere person I have ever met. I hope they come around, for Vicki's sake."

"I would never deny them their grandchild. Anna, if something should ever happen to me, promise that you will allow Vicki time with them."

"Don't speak of death on our wedding day. It's bad luck. Of course, I will grant them every opportunity."

When they arrived home on Saratoga Street, the dining table was centered with a beautiful bouquet of pure white snowdrops that Adrian had asked Elizabeth to place for him.

The newlyweds and their guests enjoyed a simple lunch in the dining room. It was the only room completely furnished. Elizabeth didn't make a fuss of the meal because her bags were packed and sitting by the door. In a matter of hours, she and her friend Henrietta planned to head to New York City, their first time there, to catch an ocean liner bound for England, where they would tour London and Stratford on Avon, and even Stonehenge and the north country. The timing was perfect,

361

leaving the house for the happy couple to explore their love. Josefina's parents had agreed to keep Vicki for a few days. It was the best wedding gift they could offer.

That evening, Anna and Adrian dined at Marconi's, this time enjoying Sole Veronique with Lyonnaise Potatoes and, of course, ice cream with chocolate sauce. They splurged on the Prohibition Sour and Minnehaha Maid and savored every sip.

Once at home, readying themselves for bed, Adrian took Anna into his arms. "I can't believe this is true, that you are finally mine."

Anna simply replied, "It's about time."

AUTHOR'S NOTES

Anna's Time is a work of historical fiction. While some events are true, others have been fictionalized. I aspired to portray accurate representations of real people and their places in history. For the sake of the narrative, some timelines were accordioned.

The book spans 1904-1921. I wrote it during the pandemic shutdown, months both peaceful and volatile. Being pretty much confined to home, I had all the time in the world to conduct research, ruminate, and write without interruption. At the same time, I witnessed the ravages of Covid, racial inequalities, political bickering, belligerence, and both peaceful and violent protest. I saw political turmoil following the November election tear the parchment of our country's Constitution.

As I sat at my keyboard, I was struck by the parallels between what I was witnessing to what happened during Anna's time. The Influenza Pandemic of 1918, with citizens disobeying orders to wear masks and refrain from celebrations... the Red Summer of 1919, when people of color were randomly attacked and killed without provocation... and constant fear of foreign and domestic anarchists attempting to overthrow our government, leading to more violence. And voter suppression, in its many forms continued to deny American adults full participation in American democracy.

To remain true to the vernacular of the era, I chose to refer to African Americans as "colored." This was the term used in everyday conversation by both blacks and whites in the early decades of the 20th Century. I mean no offense in using this language, only accuracy to the time.

I hope you savor this book, whether you are native to Baltimore or not, and see how everyday people helped build the city from the ashes of the Great Baltimore Fire of 1904. They influenced attitudes, political power, the changing roles of women, and the need for tolerance and equality in all things.

I want to send out heartfelt thanks to Demi Stevens, a thoughtful, supportive and expert book editor. Among her many talents, she has the rare ability to challenge a writer in the friendliest of ways. She possesses a keen eye for consistency, accuracy, pacing and storytelling. Just access Year of the Book (yotbpress.com) to see the many authors who have had the pleasure of working with her.

Hats off to the writing class at Renaissance Institute on the campus of Notre Dame of Maryland University. Their fair and frank critiques have always made me a better writer.

And, finally, many thanks to readers of my first novel, *Runaway Fire*. Words cannot describe the joy you have given me.

I used several historical resources in writing this novel:

BOOKS:

The Great Baltimore Fire – Peter B. Peterson

Baltimore Afire – Harold A. Williams

Goliath: Hero of the Great Baltimore Fire – Claudia Fridell

Baltimore's Historic Parks and Gardens – Eden Unger
Bowditch

The Skeptic: A Life of H.L. Mencken – Terry Teachout

Thirty-Five Years of Newspaper Work: A Memoir – H.L.
Mencken (Henry Louis)

Newspaper Days – H.L. Mencken

Prejudices – H.L. Mencken

In Defense of Women – H.L. Mencken

NEWSPAPERS & MAGAZINES:

The Baltimore Sun

The National Archives

The Spokesman Review

Black Quotidian

I also found many helpful websites:

WEBSITES:

welcometobaltimore.com

pattersonpark.com

history.com

spokanehistorical.org

catorfamilies.com

libraryofcongress.gov

aaregistry.org

newspapers.com

ghostsofbaltimore.org

famous-trials.com

federalreservehistory.org

earlyaviators.com

americanhistory.si.edu

msmagazine.com

gendisasters.com

mdhistoricaltrust.wordpress.com

time.com

Book Club Questions

Why can't Anna make friends with the boardinghouse ladies?

How did Anna's sheltered upbringing affect the decisions she made in adulthood?

Was H.L. Mencken a good mentor to Anna?

Was Anna's naiveté a help or hindrance to her career?

How did tragedies change Anna? Did they make her a better person?

What lessons did Anna learn from Emmaline and her family?

Does Anna go too far in her masculine appearance? Does it really help her compete with men?

Why did Anna's father wait until he was near death to tell his daughter he loved her?

About the Author

Donna Bertling holds a BA in English Literature from Loyola College (now Loyola University Maryland). She published her first novel, *Runaway Fire*, in October of 2017. She loves to inform and entertain through historical fiction, her favorite genre to read. Donna runs the Open Studio for Prose Writers at Renaissance Institute, Notre Dame of Maryland University. Several of her short stories have been published in *Reflections*, the institute's literary and art publication.

Author Photo by Norbert Bertling, Jr.

www.ingramcontent.com/pod-product-compliance
Lightning Source LLC
Chambersburg PA
CBHW030809260626
47169CB00001B/252